YOUR LAST FIRST KISS

AVERY MAXWELL

That's What She Said Publishing, Inc.

This book is for those of you who have tried to be everything to everyone while masking your own pain with a smile.

It's also for Tammy. Simmer down! You know why.

AUTHOR NOTE
YOUR LAST FIRST KISS

Dear Reader,

Penny's life is not easy, nor is it salacious. What it is though, is real, raw, and full of pining love. Penny's ex-husband is an alcoholic and this story shows how alcoholism and substance abuse, for some, can change the landscape of families. It's particularly true for Penny's oldest son, Kai, who experiences his father's choices the most.

Their world is full of chaos, but they soon learn that Dillon just wants to be a part of it, and he does so in spectacular fashion. He shows Penny and her children what being a family truly means with love, patience, and kindness. He's able to teach them that abuse, neglect, postpartum depression, and even death are not their fault, or their burden to carry. In short, he shows them how to live without the weight of other people's choices.

*While this is a complete work of fiction, I appreciate my sensitivity readers for all their help in making it realistic for the characters yet keeping the vibe you've come to expect from me. This story is the epitome of found family, hope, and as much love as I could fit on the page.

If you or anyone you know is struggling, please reach out for help.

https://www.aa.org/
https://www.samhsa.gov/find-help/national-helpline

PLAYLIST

YOUR LAST FIRST KISS

Music has always made me feel emotions in a big way. This
playlist is no different.

Each song tells a story of hope and longing—trust and
compassion. It's everything I wanted for Dillon and Penny.
Happy listening.

Luvs,
Avery

1. My Life, Andy Grammar and R3HAB
2. All That Really Matters, ILLENIUM and Teddy Swims
3. Give You Love, Forest Blakk
4. My Girl, Dylan Scott
5. How Honest Do You Want Me To Be?, Ingrid Andress
6. Next Thing You Know, Jordan Davis
7. Fade Into You, Mazzy Star
8. Wish You Were Here, Avril Lavigne
9. Fall Into Me, Forest Blakk

10. Come Home, OneRepublic
11. You're Beautiful, James Blunt
12. Enchanted, Taylor Swift
13. Head Over Feet, Alanis Morissette
14. My Best Friend, Tim McGraw
15. Accidentally in Love, Counting Crows
16. Labyrinth, Taylor Swift
17. Son of a Sinner, Jelly Roll
18. If You Love Her, Forest Blakk
19. Daisies, Katy Perry
20. Piece by Piece, Kelly Clarkson
21. Take My Name, Parmalee
22. Someone To You, BANNERS
23. Done, Chris Janson
24. Goodbye My Lover, James Blunt
25. Lonely If You Are, Chase Rice
26. Every Other Memory, Ryan Hurd
27. Home, Phillip Phillips
28. I Will Wait, Mumford & Sons
29. Little Bit More, Suriel Hess
30. COMPLETE MESS, 5 Seconds of Summer
31. TRUSTFALL, P!nk
32. Feel like This, Ingrid Andress
33. Good In Me, Andy Grammer
34. I Remember, Forest Blakk
35. imagine, Ben Platt
36. I'll Never Not Love You, Michael Bublé

Spotify: https://geni.us/YLFKPlaylist

CHAPTER 1

DILLON

SIX MONTHS AGO

"*Y*ou're fired."

Of course, that's not exactly what my childhood friend, Ashton Westbrook, said as he sat in my chair, smiling like this should all make sense to me. What he actually said was that he wants to diversify his investments. He wants to invest in my future since I won't, and when the time comes, he may have an opportunity for me that's a better fit than Envision.

What he meant was, I'm fired.

Or I will be.

Sort of. I don't think you can actually fire a partner. But if he walks from the company, he wants to take me with him. I just don't understand why.

That's not entirely true, though, is it?

Sometimes I wish I could put a muzzle on that voice in my head.

At thirty-nine years old, I live a comfortable—if boring—

life, and the company he wants to break into pieces is my cornerstone. Leaving it would mean starting over, and the asshole won't give me a single goddamned detail to make the decision myself.

I haven't really made many decisions for myself in years though. Why the fuck do I care now?

Grabbing the down comforter with more force than necessary, I drag it over my head to drown out that voice and to keep the frigid air away from my skin.

It's the middle of summer in Manhattan, but my air conditioning is run by a demon. It's so damned cold that my breath puffs like smoke in the air when I get out of bed in the morning. Then I step outside and sweat my balls off before I even get to the car.

I hate it here.

But I understand it here.

Everyone keeps to themselves and minds their own business. If you fall on the street, chances are three out of four people will step right over you.

Harsh but true.

New York is where you go to hide in plain sight.

Rolling over, I peel the covers back just enough to squint into the room right as the automatic timer pulls the blinds open to reveal another hazy day. Summer in Manhattan is like Satan's asshole. Hot, cramped, and full of too many people willing to sell their souls.

My alarm goes off next. I bury my head deeper into the pillow but hear the front door open, followed by the closest thing I have to a best friend calling for me from the entryway.

"Get up, asshole. I'm ready to play," Ryder says.

I kick back the covers with a groan. In the kitchen, metal clatters and drawers slam. I place my feet on the floor and immediately lift them again. The hardwood is like a block of ice. Gritting my teeth, I lower them again because I'm not a fucking toddler and stand to a serenade of crackling and popping. It's my body's way of saying it hates me as I enter my bathroom to brush my teeth.

Ryder calls my name, but I ignore him as I pull on the gym shorts I tossed over the side chair that no one ever sits in, then walk into the kitchen to find him filling two to-go mugs of coffee.

"You look like shit," he says without looking up.

"Great. Thanks for the commentary."

I follow him to the entryway and open the closet door to grab my basketball sneakers. I fucking hate Mondays.

"Why are you fighting this?" Ashton asks from across the court. He's dribbling the ball way too high, and I wave my hands, trying to get him to pass it to me before it gets stolen. Again.

Too late.

Ryder runs up beside him and takes the ball away easily.

"Damn. I suck at this." Ashton groans. "Tell me again why we play?"

"Exercise. We're getting old," I tell him.

"*You* are getting old. I'm younger than you." His reply is slightly breathless as he chases down Ryder.

"Back to Dillon," Ryder says, standing at the three-point line like he has all the time in the world. "You hate it in New York. And running a security firm doesn't seem like your dream job. What did you want to do when you were a kid?"

When I was a kid? My throat goes dry thinking about it because, in a lot of ways, that's when life was so much easier. My friendship with the Westbrooks kept me sane in those early years. Now that outlet comes in the form of being a partner at Envision, the security firm Ash is considering stepping away from.

"That was a lifetime ago," I mutter. "Things change. People change. Life has a habit of making choices for us that we never asked for, and those choices sent us all in different directions for a long time."

Kids are idiots. I was no different. I became a widower after a month-long marriage that changed the course of every other relationship in my life but felt necessary for those I cared about at the time.

My heart pinches, just to let me know it's still beating, whenever I think about Vanessa. She was one of my best friends, but I was never in love with her. We knew she was dying, but she couldn't let her disgusting excuse for a father get her trust fund. So we married. Then I walked away from basketball completely to piss off my alcoholic father.

At some point, I stopped living.

Jesus. Over the last twenty years, I've become someone I don't even recognize. I was wandering through life with no purpose until Ashton dragged me into Envision Securities. Now he wants to pull that out from under me all because he thinks he knows what's best.

Ryder takes a shot, then turns to me. "But you had dreams," he pushes—because he's a freaking nag sometimes.

"We all do," I say, shaking my head in frustration. "It doesn't mean that's what is supposed to happen. I mean, Ashton's brother Easton was my best friend growing up, and we had this idea. He would make furniture, and I'd run the business side of things, getting them into upscale hotels and homes."

Ashton opens his mouth like he's about to say something, but I throw my arms in the air, and he closes it.

"We were kids," I say. "And Easton is very talented, but it was just something kids dream about when they think they know how life will play out. It never works that way. There are responsibilities and other people who change your course without meaning to."

"If you're talking about Vanessa," Ashton says, and I know he's about to defend me because that's who he is. Easton would, too, if he were here. It irritates me even more.

Sometimes you don't need to be defended. You just need to be heard.

Damned Westbrooks.

Ashton pulls at the back of his neck. It's a family habit all his brothers have when they're upset. "We all cared about her, but you were the only one who could help her, so don't get that twisted in your head. She needed you, and everyone understands that now. We all made shitty choices as kids. Trust me, I know, but now? What are you choosing now that actually matters? Anything? I'm trying to offer you a chance at something different, something meaningful…"

As soon as the words are out of his mouth, he cringes.

"That's not what I meant," he grumbles, stuffing his hands into the pockets of his sweatpants.

"It's exactly what you meant," I argue. We've known each other our whole lives.

Something meaningful? My brain seizes on that. Once upon a time, all I wanted was something meaningful, to be someone who made a difference, but I lost that boyhood dream right along with my choices when I was a teenager.

"Time out," Ryder says. "Let's backtrack a minute, okay?" He stands with the ball tucked carelessly on his hip.

Ryder is one of my guys in the New York office of our security company. He's also the only one I spend any time with when I'm not working.

He's not looking at me, which makes the hairs rise on the back of my neck.

"Dillon, you do hate it here," he begins, and I bite my lip

so I don't say something I'll regret—something like *mind your own fucking business*. "The only time you're happy is on Wednesday."

"Don't," I interrupt.

"It's true," he says.

"Wednesdays with Penny," Ashton agrees, and I shake my head.

Walking away, I lift a water bottle to my mouth and squeeze.

"Your Wednesday girl makes you happy." Ryder bounces the ball at his side.

"And your volunteer time with the Boys & Girls Club makes you happy. And the money you donate to the YMCA kids programs makes you happy." Ashton lifts his head to find me shooting daggers at him with my eyes. "Oh, please," he says, rolling his. "You know I protect my family. The way I do that is with information. Is it really such a shock to you that I'd be watching you too? Regardless of how you feel about us, we still consider you part of the Westbrook family. That means when I dig around the dark web, I'm in your shit too. Deal with it."

"You know how fucked up that is, right?" Ryder asks, but he doesn't know Ashton well enough to push it too much.

"I'm so glad you both know what makes me happy," I grumble, but they don't pay any attention to me.

Ashton waves his hands for the ball. Ryder barely conceals a cringe before tossing it to him with an easy bounce pass even a child could catch.

Ash carelessly lifts his shoulders, like Ryder's assumption doesn't matter to him. "I was born a billionaire. My parents made sure we weren't entitled, but that also means we have to go about things differently sometimes. If keeping the people I love safe means watching their back, then I do it by any means necessary."

Ryder raises his eyebrows at me and shakes his head. He grew up like I did. Unlike me though, his best friends weren't part of one of the wealthiest families in the country.

"Listen," Ashton says, with his eyes on the ball he's dribbling. He tries—and fails— another layup attempt. Ryder puts us all out of our misery when he boxes out Ash to get the rebound.

How in the hell is he so bad at this?

"If I can work out the details, this opportunity would put you right on Penny's doorstep." Ashton bends over, wheezing, and braces his hands on his knees.

The stutter step my heart does thinking about Penny's home is completely natural. Really.

"Why are you this out of shape?" I ask, trying like hell to appear calm at the mention of her name.

But my mind immediately flips to images of Penny. There's nothing I want more than to spend as much time with her as I can, but I also understand her reasons for pushing me away. I've caught her lost in moments so full of mental to-do lists that the world faded away. It's not only her life she's protecting, and I feel that down to my very soul.

"I've been staying at home more since Hope was born," Ashton gasps.

"Haven't you been boxing lately?" Jesus. Is this what having kids does to you?

"No," he wheezes. Lifting his head but still doubled over, he holds my gaze for an uncomfortable second. I won't like whatever he says next. "This would allow you to help kids again like you did in high school before your father screwed you over."

He knows better than to bring up Dirk Henry. The fact that I even share his initials is too much for me.

Ryder nods. "Why not take this opportunity Ashton's

giving you and see what happens when your Wednesday girl turns into your everyday girl?"

Damn it, Ryder. So much for having my back. The guy just won't quit today.

"Plus," he continues, "I'll be primed for a promotion with you out of the way." He laughs, but I get the feeling he's only half joking. Envision Securities is what he was born to do. Not me. I'm still not sure where I belong.

"Penny is not a girl," I say. "She's a woman and has her own stuff to work through. Forcing my way into her life isn't going to suddenly make her have room for me. Besides, Ashton doesn't even have a plan in place. All I'm hearing about is an 'opportunity' with no details."

"Suddenly?" Ryder scoffs. "Suddenly? Dude, you've been having coffee with her every Wednesday for almost three years. Three years! It's time to shit or get off the pot. And for fuck's sake, tell her the truth about Marissa."

"Marissa?" Ashton raises his head in my direction. He pokes at the ball Ryder's holding, grabs it, and dribbles like a baby giraffe toward the basket. For all his billions, Ashton is a lot of things, but an athlete isn't one of them.

"First of all," I say, wiping the sweat off my forehead with my forearm. "The Bryer-Blaine is our biggest client, and Lochlan Blaine expects weekly reports."

Ryder pulls out his phone. "Yup. I put it on the calendar. It says every Wednesday at ten a.m., yet you still get to his office before nine. With coffee for his secretary." He smirks. He knows this is a hot button for me.

I grind my teeth, willing myself not to take the bait but lose the battle. "Penny is an executive assistant, and it would be rude to show up without getting her a coffee."

"Right, because you sit staring at each other for an hour every Wednesday," Ashton says from the basket. He's trying to make a lay-up for the third time.

Ryder takes pity on him, grabs the rebound, and quickly puts it in the hoop. Turning back to me, he asks, "What do you guys talk about?"

"Nothing." I grunt in frustration. Placing my hands on my lower back, I arch so I'm staring at the ceiling—anything to break eye contact with these two busybodies.

"Why don't you ask her out on a date already?" Ryder asks. At least it doesn't sound like he's trying to antagonize me this time.

Darting forward, I smack the ball out of his hands and take it to the hoop for an easy two-pointer that has Ashton rolling his eyes. I check my watch to note how much time I have. Thankfully it's not Wednesday, so it doesn't matter how I show up to work.

We won't discuss my need to dress up for a woman who has turned me down—multiple times.

"Wait," Ashton says seriously. "Did she turn you down?" He holds his hands out, and I reluctantly pass him the ball. The silence that stretches between us is deafening, and his eyes go wide. "How many times have you asked her out, Dill? Please don't tell me you've veered off into stalker territory. Hopefully, she doesn't call me to step in. Having a partner accused of stalking would not be a good look for Envision. You know, our *security* company?" His grin is mischievous.

Asshole.

Ashton and I may be equal partners now, but we tend to run Envision Securities like a souped-up frat house. No one is exempt from getting shit. The very nature of security companies has us on friendlier terms than say, a bank, because lives depend on our ability to trust one another implicitly.

"Shut up," I groan. Ashton dribbles the ball, and he's so awkward I can't help but scrunch up my nose as I watch him. "Didn't Easton and I ever teach you to play ball?"

He stands to his full height and dribbles while staring down at the ball. "I was too busy building computers, and these days I box, or did. I only play basketball with you because it's the only time you do anything outside the office. So when my mom calls, I can tell her how you're doing. And don't change the subject."

He throws up a brick, and it doesn't even come close to the rim. I cannot comprehend this level of incompetence.

"Back to your Wednesday girl," Ryder teases.

"Her name is Penny," I growl.

"So, you have asked her out?" Ashton asks like he doesn't know.

Of course he fucking knows. Why is everyone busting my balls today?

"Dude, your wife is best friends with her. You know I've asked her out."

"But not lately because…" Ryder wiggles his eyebrows, and we both turn toward him.

Fuck. Here it comes. Going out for drinks with him the other night was definitely a mistake.

"She still thinks you're seeing Marissa," Ryder finishes.

"Who's Marissa?" Ashton laughs, but I get the feeling he's goading me. He knows exactly who Marissa is—or isn't.

"Marissa is his imaginary girlfriend." Ryder moves toward the basket with a wide grin on his face.

"I never said she was a girlfriend. I said I was going on a date with her." I pass him the ball with more force than necessary. "Don't you have to get to work?"

They ignore me.

"You told Penny, the woman you can't stop thinking about, that you were going on a date with a made-up girl?" Ashton asks with wide eyes. His face has gone slightly pale. It doesn't bode well for me, and the sweat trickling down my spine has nothing to do with being an almost forty-year-old playing basketball.

"It seemed like the right thing to do at the time." It's a miracle they understand my words because my teeth are clenched so tightly, I can hear them grinding in my head.

"The right thing?" Ashton shakes his head.

"She kept asking why I wasn't seeing anyone. I didn't want her to feel weird around me."

"So, you lied to her?" he asks.

I'm not a fucking liar. That would make me as bad as my father, but Ash is also not technically wrong, and it makes my shoulders tense.

"No. There was a Marissa. From a dating app," I mutter. "I just never responded to her message."

"Because you like Penny. How long ago did this Marissa debacle happen?" Ashton stares at me warily.

"A few months ago." Guilt churns in my gut.

Penny and I have only talked about it twice. How far can one bend the truth before it's a full-on lie?

Jesus, now I'm trying to justify my actions to my own damned self.

"So she still thinks you're with someone else?"

Why the hell did I come to the gym today? I could have avoided all of this and met them at the office. "We haven't talked about it."

"You'd better, and quick. That's every Hallmark movie disaster ever made just waiting to happen," Ashton says with an expression of total disapproval.

He's right. Well, I don't know if he's right about Hallmark movies, but he's right about Penny.

"My boss needs to break up with his imaginary girlfriend so he can make a move on the girl who actually exists," Ryder deadpans.

"Shut the fuck up and pass me the ball."

"Don't think you can deflect the Penny issue forever," Ash calls to my back.

My stride breaks only momentarily. They have no idea how much headspace Miss Penny actually takes up in my mind. Late at night is the worst. But she's made her stance perfectly clear.

She doesn't have time for me.

CHAPTER 2

PENNY

"Your divorce has been final for years, Penny. It's okay to move on," Nova says gently from her spot at my kitchen table. Her one-year-old, Hope, sits on the floor below her, playing with pink and blue blocks.

"I know it is." And I do. But I have my boys to think about, and that takes all of my energy. I don't have time to do the laundry—how on Earth would I ever have time to date? The time not spent with my boys or cleaning something is dedicated to long train commutes and even longer work hours so I can give the boys the life they deserve, because if I don't, no one will.

Being both mom and dad is more challenging than I could have ever imagined. But my only goal as a mom, and maybe in life, is to make sure I raise good humans who don't turn out like their father.

"You look good." There's a smugness to her words, so I refuse to look at her. "But you always look good. Especially on Wednesdays."

"Nova," I groan.

"Tell me I'm wrong."

I don't because I can't.

The weekly time with Dillon is a sanctuary for me. He's a little slice of heaven who can steal my breath with a single look. But I'll never voice it, not to Nova, not to anyone. I can't. Putting it out in the universe will make my reality so much more painful because my life is messy and so freaking complicated. If I can barely handle our chaos, an outsider wouldn't last five minutes.

Personal wants and needs simply do not exist for a single mom…at least they don't for me.

But if they did? Each and every one would revolve around Dillon Henry.

"You've been playing this flirting game with him since my wedding, and you never did tell me what happened at the reception."

"Nothing happened. We danced. I'd never danced with anyone but Eddy. It was—it was nice," I whisper. "But nothing happened."

Her eyes soften as she looks at me. "Eddy's a douche. He doesn't care about anyone but himself." She lets out a shaky breath. "Not everyone will cheat on you, Pen."

I flinch.

"Sorry, that was harsh."

"Harsh but true," I mutter.

"Dillon's a good guy, you know."

"He is," I say quickly. Too quickly, and Nova picks up on it, so I keep talking before she can add anything else. "But the boys have been through so much already. Too much. I can't bring someone else into their lives right now."

No matter how desperately I want to. My only job is to protect them and give them as happy a childhood as I can.

Nova nods. "I get that. But they want you to be happy too."

Guilt mixes with dread like a lead weight in the pit of my stomach. "Did they say something to you?"

She leans down to draw Hope into her lap. "No, Pen. But they do."

I force my shoulders back and suck in a long breath. It does nothing to calm my heart.

"I know your reasons for not pursuing a relationship, but are you sure you're seeing them clearly?"

I open my mouth to speak, but she talks over me.

"Yes, your life is complicated. Yes, you need to protect your boys and keep anyone else from disappointing them. And yes, you have long days and little time. But your chaos is consistent, Penny. Your days are scheduled to the second and you've been settled into your new life for a long time."

Have I? Every day it feels like the rug will be pulled out from under me, but is it possible I'm not seeing the monotony of my life as she sees it? Isn't monotony exactly what I wanted after what Eddy put us through though?

"Tell me you don't dream about what it would be like to have Dillon at your side for the tough stuff. Or that you don't fantasize about having someone to confide in late at night."

I swallow hard but can't make my words come.

"He would be that man if you let him," she says gently. "You deserve the happiness you're fighting so hard to give your boys. Take it while you can. Embrace it with someone who has already proven they only want your time. Give Dillon a chance to be that someone."

My throat is thick with unshed tears.

If only she knew how badly I wanted to give Dillon a chance.

"Go, have fun tonight," she says, changing the subject when I'm quiet for too long. "My brother pulled out all the stops to celebrate his employees with this party."

I almost smile. Nova's brother is the best boss I've ever

had, but he's steadfast in his actions. This party is a direct result of the impact his amazing new wife has on his life.

"You and Lochlan couldn't be more different. You know this, right?" I aim for a light tone, but it's hard when my heart is so heavy.

"That's the best compliment anyone has ever given me." She laughs, and her little girl twists in her lap to touch her face.

"Lochlan throwing an out-of-season holiday party for his employees isn't something I ever would have expected from him, that's for sure."

I sit in the seat next to her with wild thoughts invading my mind. The thin band of my strappy sandals wraps around my ankle, and it takes some maneuvering to make sure my boobs don't pop out of this dress. The slit that runs up my left leg causes the shimmering gold silk to slip open, revealing freshly shaven legs.

I keep that part to myself too.

"Love changes even the grumpiest of grumps," she muses.

The air wooshes out of my lungs like a deflating balloon. I'm not sure I've ever had that kind of love, and the knowledge is a sledgehammer to my already fragile heart. Luckily Nova can't see me, and I have time to steel myself before sitting up.

"Well, thank you for staying with Gage and Landon tonight. Kai should be home from camp by eight, and then you can head home. He'll get the other two in bed. But if he isn't here by…"

Nova frowns as she tries hard to contain her expression—one of pity, probably. "If Eddy doesn't show up, Kai will call Ash or me, and we'll go get him. We have the kids covered. You go have fun. Lochlan will blame me if you're late, and then all hell will break loose."

A sad chuckle bubbles in my chest. Leaning in, I give my

friend a hug. She's quite a bit younger than me, but in the last few years, she's transformed and matured, so our relationship has gone from big sisterly to true, equal friendship. I'll miss her when they leave for California, but I'm so happy that her fashion line is really taking off.

I don't think she could ever fully understand how much her friendship means to me. Sometimes being a single mom is the loneliest job you could ever have.

I kiss Hope on the cheek, ignoring the ache that occasionally resides in my chest, knowing those days are over for me, and move to the kitchen window.

Ashton huddles behind a bush while Gage and Landon run around with water balloons in their hands.

I tap twice on the window, and three sets of eyes turn to me. Three happy sets of eyes that make my own mist. Seeing the impact Ashton has had on my children makes me hate their father a little more.

It should have been him out there playing, laughing, and loving.

But it's not. Eddy was my childhood sweetheart who grew up to be my biggest heartache, but I'll never regret him. Through unimaginable pain, he gave me three blessings. My boys.

Dillon wouldn't miss the chance to be out there. I know he wouldn't.

That thought stops me cold. By keeping Dillon at arm's length, am I also depriving my boys of a real relationship with a man who only knows how to love?

My hands shake, but I plaster on a smile for Nova's benefit and walk out my front door.

〜

THE DRIVE to the city is long, but at this time of day, it's not nearly as bad as when I take the train during rush hour. And it's a hundred times more comfortable. But it also gives me too much time to think. Too much time to make mental lists that never seem to get smaller.

Things like:

- Wash Kai's uniform.
- What would happen if I let Dillon in?
- Sign Gage's field trip permission slip.
- Landon needs new shoes.
- Dillon.
- Groceries! Always freaking groceries.
- Make a doctor's appointment.
- Would Dillon stick around if he knew how often I pretended to be okay?

The town car Lochlan insisted on pulls up outside his hotel, and my to-do list is immediately forgotten. Somehow, he's managed to make even the entrance look like a winter wonderland straight out of a fairytale. Silver and white trees sparkle on either side of the doors, and lights twinkle overhead like fireflies. It's truly impressive.

"Thank you," I say to the driver when he opens my door and offers his hand to help me out. I watch my very high heels so they don't get caught in the fabric of my very tight dress. Well, Nova's dress. I don't own anything this fancy.

I slip my hand into his, and electric static strong enough to make my dress cling to my legs tingles up my arm. With a nervous giggle, I try to remove my hand, but the driver holds tighter.

That's when I spot the driver off to my right, and my gaze snaps up to the man holding my hand.

Dillon Henry.

I've made a valiant effort over the years to never touch him. Being skin-to-skin with this man creates a chemical reaction stronger than any drug.

Not that I've ever taken drugs, but it's the best analogy I can come up with when the slightest touch from him fries every brain cell I own. Especially when he's this close. I swear he can break hearts with those hazel eyes, but you can see the sadness in them if you look close enough.

How many people look close enough?

"Penny," he rumbles. His voice is like dark wood. Rich and thick, it causes goosebumps to rise on my exposed skin. And then there's that grin.

His crooked grin reveals one dimple that always makes me melt. It's shy in a way that makes me think he doesn't quite believe he's entitled to happiness.

We have so much in common.

"D—Dillon." He's also been known to render me stupid with his handsomely chiseled face, and I have to really focus to make my words work. "Moonlighting as a valet tonight? Perhaps we should talk to Lochlan about a raise."

His resonant laugh vibrates through his body into mine where our hands are still connected, and I get a flash of a full smile. It's rare when it happens, but when it does, it blocks out the darkness in its blinding beauty.

My eyelashes flutter of their own accord as he brings our joined hands to his lips. The touch of his mouth causes a shiver to work its way down my spine.

"I was in the car behind yours."

I look over my shoulder to the line of town cars Lochlan sent for everyone, searching for a nameplate or something. Does it say *Penny Mulligan*, like at the airport? When I don't find any, I turn back to him. "How'd you know it was mine?"

His hazel eyes bore into mine with an intensity that sets my entire body on fire. "I'd recognize your profile anywhere,

Penny. When your car turned onto East 22nd, you were resting your chin in your palm, staring out the window."

My stomach flips. Then flips again.

"What were you thinking about?" he asks in a husky tone I crave like cold water on a broiling summer day. His thick brown hair is styled in an effortlessly careless way that makes him seem so much younger—even when his eyes always look sad.

What was I thinking about? Him. My boys. My life. The three things that run on a loop in my mind.

"My boys." It's the safest answer to give, but I can't quite keep the tremor from my voice, and his face falls. It's more concern than scowl.

Why does he have to be so…just so…aware?

"Are they okay? Is there anything I can do?"

My heart chooses that moment to dance a tango on my lungs. Is this what a heart attack feels like? I can tell from his expression he means what he says. If I needed help, he would be there, no questions asked.

He's going to make someone ridiculously happy someday. But the thought of him with anyone else causes my lip to tremble, so I look away. As much as I like Dillon, I can't be with him. Not when I fall into bed each night so exhausted my eyelids hurt. It wouldn't be fair to him. My boys will always come first.

But what if I did let him in? Nova's words ring in my head. Would it truly be the worst thing in the world?

Could we survive it?

I have no doubt he would cherish me and, by extension, my boys. Am I hurting my sons by not allowing this man into our lives?

My mind and heart are at war and I'm not sure which one I want to win.

Adjusting the small clutch Nova approved to go with this

dress, I tuck my phone under it to keep my hands busy. The bag isn't big enough to hold my phone, and I refused to leave it at home.

"Yeah," I say, shaking my head and focusing on the party going on beyond those double doors. "I'm sure everything's fine. Nova and Ash are with them. Kai's at a camp, and I'm waiting for a call to make sure his dad picked him up. That's all."

Dillon steps back and does a slow perusal of my body. His gaze is a caress that starts at my toes and lovingly smooths up my body, leaving a trail of flames in its wake. He's standing there like a modern-day Prince Charming, with shoulders broad enough to require a custom suit. What would it be like if he touched me? Really touched me.

"Where are you going to put your phone?" His voice cracks, and he snaps his eyes back to mine.

My throat is dry, and my mind is trying desperately to clear the daydream, so I wave my free hand and reluctantly slip my other one from his to give myself a moment.

Do not fan your face in front of him, Penny. Don't do it!

"Ah, I'm going to hold it until I know everyone's home safe."

He holds out his palm. "I have pockets. Put it on vibrate, and I'll make sure you don't miss the call. You'll need your hands free to dance."

"Oh, I don't plan on dancing tonight."

His gaze darkens as it scales my body like a mountain climber. "Penny?"

"Did you just growl?" I didn't mean to say that out loud. I bite my bottom lip to keep anything else from slipping past my defenses, but his eyes dance with mirth as he watches me.

Dillon slides my hand into the crook of his arm and pockets my phone in one smooth motion, then silently guides us forward. As soon as I fall into step beside him, he leans down and ghosts his lips across my ear.

"I got one dance with you at Ashton's wedding, and I've thought of nothing since." His growled whoosh of air has heat pooling in my belly. "If you think I can let this night go without at least attempting another, you don't know me very well."

Memories of our bodies pressed together on that dance floor as the band played Mazzy Star's "Fade Into You" has my throat going dry.

Is it sad that one of my most erotic memories happens to be on a dance floor, fully clothed, with this man beside me?

"But—Marissa." Her name tastes sour on my tongue, but I try really hard not to make a face.

"Marissa and I aren't seeing each other anymore." He flinches, and I take a guilty step back. Maybe I shouldn't have brought her up. Did she break his heart?

"Oh. Um, I'm sorry to hear that," I lie.

"No, I mean. Actually, we were never really together at all. I mean..." Dillon curses and runs a hand roughly over his face. It's hard not to smile. He's cute when he's uncomfortable. "There was this dating app, but I never... We never."

"Dillon?" My lips twitch because I'm trying hard to suppress a smile. Even though I have no right to be jealous, I can't help it. The thought of him with some faceless woman has been gnawing at me for weeks.

He stares down at me with eyes so honest and true I feel my walls crumble.

I don't know if it's Nova's encouragement or the loneliness that keeps me up at night, but suddenly, this moment feels like a sign. Like maybe I'm supposed to take this chance with him. I swallow twice before I'm sure I can control my voice. "I'm not a very good dancer. You'd probably have a better time with someone else."

He stops short, dragging me closer to his hulking body but still managing to keep all appearances of appropriateness.

"You, Penny Mulligan, are the only person who has my attention today, last year, and tomorrow. You. And I don't know if you're aware, but I don't dance, yet here I am. I've been counting down the days to this damn party because I knew you'd be here and there would be dancing. Do you know why that is?"

If I thought he was growling before, I was sadly mistaken. His words flick along my skin like flames. Everything about him causes an inferno.

I lick my parched lips. He follows the movement, and the muscles in his jaw tick.

"Why?" Jesus. My voice is breathy. Too breathy. Can everyone see the desire building in my core? I suppress the urge to look down at my belly.

He leans in. Less than a foot of space separates our lips when he speaks, and I smell the ever-present scent of root beer on his breath. Why does this man always smell like root beer, of all things?

"Because for the last year, the only thing I think about at night when I close my eyes is you. I know you don't want to hear this. And I know all your reasons why. They're valid reasons. But if I'm only going to get the chance for one dance a year with you, do you really think I'm going to miss that chance?"

"No?" I squeak.

He grins.

I melt.

"No, Penny. No, I'm really, really not."

CHAPTER 3

DILLON

I return her palm to the crook of my arm and propel us toward the party. Her hand lays heavy against my tuxedo jacket like a salve for a wound I didn't even know existed.

Why does it have to feel so right to have her with me like this? She's determined to keep me at arm's length, but I've never felt more at ease.

Every time I say I respect her boundaries, she shows up in my line of sight like a goddamned angel, beckoning me into her light.

And I did tell myself I would give her space tonight. I also swore to Lochlan that we were just friends, so I wouldn't be monopolizing all of her time at this party.

She has a way of making a liar out of me, though.

Then like all the stars had finally aligned for us, I looked up the moment her car turned the corner, and all bets were off.

I'm weak for her, and apparently, I can't control that weakness anymore.

We walk through the foyer and to the entrance of the

grand ballroom, only to be intercepted by Lochlan and his wife, Tilly. The dark, knowing smirk on his face has the muscles in my back tightening. He lifts his phone, and a small flash goes off.

"Dillon," he says at the same time Tilly squeals and rips Penny from my grasp in a giant hug.

"Oh my God, Penny! Look at you," Tilly says to my right.

Lochlan narrows his eyes on me. "You just cost me a thousand dollars."

I raise my eyebrows and wait for him to continue while keeping one ear open on Penny and Tilly's conversation.

When he doesn't respond, I take the bait. "How'd I do that?"

He leans to the side, drawing me a few feet away from Penny. "I bet Ashton you'd keep your distance from Penny, at least until the band started. He said you wouldn't make it in the building without her."

Lochlan is a tough read. He holds his cards close to his vest, so I shouldn't be surprised that he gives nothing away in his tone or facial expressions as he speaks.

I give a noncommittal shrug because I fear the truth—I may never be able to keep my distance. "Her car pulled up right in front of mine."

"Mm-hmm." He runs his thumb and forefinger along his jaw, then opens his mouth to speak when we're interrupted by Tilly's sister, Eli.

"Loch, you are so going to owe me for this," Eli hisses. "I'm not a party planner. I'm a fundraiser. I bring communities together. This is the exact opposite of what I'm trying to do."

Eli works for a nonprofit, bringing after-school programs to underprivileged youth in rural areas. I've admired the work she does for a long time, and Ashton's words of *something meaningful* use my brain as a snare drum.

Eli is making a difference in the world.

Lochlan leans in to give her a hug. "It's all taken care of, Li. You're simply the point person for everyone working tonight, so Tilly and Penny can enjoy the party too."

"You had better make this one hell of a donation to my After the Bell Foundation," she hisses before storming away. She's making a difference, all right, but she's a feisty little thing.

Lochlan chuckles, but Penny throws her head back and laughs, capturing my attention like always. What I wouldn't give for the privilege of being the one to make her this care-free all the time.

"Bloody fucket," Lochlan curses, clapping his hand on my shoulder. "You're done for, mate."

It's more difficult than it should be, but I finally tear my gaze away from Penny to find him staring at me with something close to understanding.

"You're playing the longest long game I've ever seen. I hope it works out. I do. But remember, it's not just *her* heart she's protecting." He keeps his voice low, but even Lochlan can't filter the emotion from those words.

He sighs heavily, like he's resigning himself to something, then points toward the dance floor. "Ladies, care to join us for a dance?"

Penny's breath hitches and it's like she sank a fishhook into my heart with it.

I can't decide if Lochlan's trying to help me with Penny or push me so hard I stumble right out of her way, but I've always been a patient man. And for Penny Mulligan, I could wait forever and never miss a thing.

Lochlan and Tilly lead the way, and Penny hesitantly takes my elbow.

"Did you put him up to that?" she whispers.

I grin. "No, but I will thank him later."

Her steps falter, and she looks up at me with wide, beautiful eyes. "Me too," she whispers. My chest expands as hope swirls dangerously beneath my ribs.

"Yeah?" I ask, then tilt my head to the side to watch her every reaction.

"Yeah." She smiles, and I know it's meant only for me. "It might be time to take some chances."

My heart stops beating. "What kind of chances are you talking about, Penny?"

She leans in, places her palm over my heart, and lifts onto her tiptoes so her lips nearly graze my chin. "The kind of chances that include you."

Penny doesn't allow me to respond, not that I could form words right now anyway, but she grabs my hand and leads me closer to the music.

We hit the dance floor just as a song ends, and I catch Tilly giving someone a thumbs-up.

A lone guitarist steps forward on the stage, playing a slow melody that's tied directly to my heart.

Penny gasps against my chest as I pull her in. "Did you do this?"

I can't speak as "Fade Into You" begins, so I shake my head slowly instead.

Even with her heels, she has to tilt her head back to look at me. Her heart beats rapidly against my lower ribs, so I sweep my hand across her back in a soothing motion.

Fuck me. My palm hits bare skin, and my eyes nearly roll out of my head.

The back of her dress is completely open. I follow the column of her spine, fighting to keep my hand from trembling, as her breaths become as shallow as mine.

"This isn't a holiday song," she rasps.

This woman has always kept me at bay, but now I feel how her body betrays her. All I can do is thank my lucky stars that I'm not alone in this desperation that overtakes me when I touch her.

I lift my head to stare at the ceiling.

Get your shit together, man.

My throat is dry and scratchy as I say, "Do you ever get the feeling that everyone in your life is a meddling nuisance?" Penny peels her head away from my shoulder, and I count to three before I make eye contact. "I think Tilly's been meddling."

She turns her head to the right, and I follow. Tilly and Lochlan snap their gazes away from us like a yo-yo that hit the end of its string.

"My kids," she whispers.

"Are your whole world. I know, Pen."

"I haven't been able to date, Dillon. Not after what their father put us through."

I wrap my hands tighter around her middle. In the past, she's always turned me down because of how that bastard treated her boys. It's the first time she's acknowledged she's been hurt, too. A rush of protective feelings I've never experienced before make my head want to explode.

"I like you, Penny. I can be patient." My words are a whispered promise. With my chin resting on the top of her head, I close my eyes for the inevitable letdown. The "just friends" speech.

But it doesn't come. Instead, I'm floored by her confession.

"You make me want to try though. With you, I want to try for more."

I swallow hard, taking those seconds to steady my voice. "I promise, if you give me a chance, you'll never regret it."

We search each other's eyes as our faces drift closer. Her sweet scent of peonies fills my nostrils, and her warm breath sears my body through my clothes. I inch closer. The desire to kiss her consumes me with a kinetic need. We're a breath apart when I realize it isn't my body vibrating but her phone.

I pull it from my pants pocket with a shaky hand and see Ashton's name. Her eyes widen, and my gut tells me our night is over before it's begun.

Penny places one hand in the center of my chest and takes her phone with the other. She taps her fingers against my lapel, tattooing her beat to my heart.

"I— This— Ashton wouldn't be the one to call unless something was wrong." Her face contorts with pain only a loving mother could ever know. It's a concerned expression I've seen in Ashton's mother many times over the years.

"I know. Come with me," I demand, taking her hand and leading her away from the dance floor. "I'll get you somewhere quiet."

She may not hear me because she pulls her hand from mine to plug her free ear. "Ash? What's wrong?"

I usher her ahead of me and then guide her through the crowd with a hand on her bare lower back.

Penny moves gracefully, but there's tension in the knotted muscles around her spine. Her head is down as she tries to hear our friend on the other end of the phone. She allows me to maneuver us out of the party and into a smaller conference room down the hall.

We slip inside, and I close the door, carefully giving her space as she paces beside a conference table.

"Is he okay? Did Eddy leave? What did Coach Remy say?"

A tear slips from the corner of her eye. I move to wipe it away, but she turns her back on me.

It's worse than rejection. She's shut me out. I have no right to feel slighted, but it cracks open old wounds I thought I'd put to bed years ago. The ones that say no one will ever want you, and you'll never be enough.

"No, it's okay. I'll come home," she whispers. Ashton must

protest because Penny shakes her head in the silence. "No, Ash. Thank you, but this is my mess. I need to talk with Kai."

I hate how her voice breaks. I hate that she won't allow me to comfort her, and I really fucking hate that her ex can still cause this much pain.

"I'm leaving now. Thanks, Ash."

Penny stands with her back to me. Her calf muscles tighten against the silky fabric of her dress, then her beautiful ass clenches before she straightens her back. She's fortifying her resolve. It's like she's wrapping herself in protective armor from the tips of her toes to the top of her head.

I have no goddamned clue what she lives with every day. I have no right to demand answers when I haven't proved that I can fit in her world, but fuck me if it isn't what I want to do.

"I should have known better than to ask for more," she whispers. Her voice cracks like old sandpaper and my heartbeat rages in my ears. But she's so quiet that I doubt she meant those words for me.

She turns, and her expression fillets me.

"I'm sorry, Dillon. I—I'll never have the time you deserve. It was unfair of me to even think I could try..." Her chin drops to her chest and her shoulders tremble. A lock of golden brown hair falls from her ear to cover her face.

"I know. I'm sorry too."

Her gaze snaps to mine. "Why are you sorry?"

She gets a tiny wrinkle between her eyebrows when she's confused, and my focus stays there as I speak. Even sad she's fucking adorable.

"I like you, Penny. So much that I fear I'm making things hard for you that really should be quite simple. You've told me what you're capable of, and I still show up here wanting to be your prince."

"No, I told you I wanted to try, but it was selfish of me. I can't— My life, it's—"

I hold up a hand to stop her. "I'm a patient man, sweetheart."

Her phone buzzes in her hand, and she jumps. "It—it's Kai. His dad showed up at the gym and started a fight with another parent. Kai got in the middle of it and—and…"

That acid that materializes anytime her ex is mentioned sits raw in my throat. "Is Kai okay?" The words don't sound like my own. My voice is low, with a dangerous edge to it.

Penny shifts from foot to foot. "Yeah. Yes. But I…"

"I'll walk you to your car." Turning, I open the door and wait for her to pass before following her out. We're silent on the short walk through the lobby and out onto the street, where I flag one of the waiting town cars with a Bryer-Blaine card on the dashboard.

"I'm sorry," she says as I open her door.

"Don't be. Never apologize for things that are out of your control. I got my dance. My holiday wish was fulfilled."

She slips into the back seat with a sad smile. I wait for her to get situated, and then I gently close the door.

It isn't until the taillights of the car are long gone that I turn to find Lochlan standing a few feet away, hands in his pockets.

"Nova called," he says. "Her ex is a twuntytit determined to ruin every new beginning she tries to make."

Unable to find the right words, I nod.

"You coming back in?" he asks.

Shaking my head, I clear my throat. "Nah. I got my wish. There's nothing left for me here."

I don't mean to say it, but as I hear the words, I know I'm talking about more than just the party. "I'll see you next week. Great party, Lochlan." I infuse as much enthusiasm as I can into the statement, but it still falls flat.

"Dillon?" His tone sends alarms ringing in my ears.

"I'm good."

"You're good to her."

"She makes it easy," I say. "But she has her priorities straight. She's a good mom."

Lochlan frowns, and I almost laugh when he tugs harshly on his tuxedo vest. It's an odd habit I've grown accustomed to when he's upset about something.

"She is a good mom. She gives everything she has to those kids," he says quietly.

I nod because I already know this about Penny.

"But do you ever wonder who's taking care of her?"

Every damned day.

CHAPTER 4

PENNY

"*P*enny!" Lochlan bellows from behind his closed office door. Every stinking time he does that, I jump like someone threw a bunch of spiders at me.

The precious caffeine I was cradling in both hands sloshes out of the cup because I can't help but fill it to the tippy top.

"Geez," I hiss through clenched teeth as the hot, muddy-colored liquid drenches the front of my blouse for the second time today. Now I'll be riding the train home with the delicious scent of coffee mocking me the entire way. Again.

It would also help my frazzled nerves if I could stop daydreaming about that dance with Dillon. Or how it felt to be held by him. No matter how many weeks pass, the memory won't fade. It hurts.

Lochlan wrenches his door open, then stops short when he sees me.

"Bloody hell. I did it again, didn't I?" The British lilt he got from his father is strong today despite the fact that he spent most of his life in the US.

"It's a good thing you pay so well," I mutter.

"Sorry, Penny. I'll have some new tops sent up next week."

I open my mouth to argue, but after three years, I know it's pointless. Lochlan is a demanding boss, but he's a good man. This is his way of making amends.

"Tilly's pregnancy is turning me into a raging lunatic," he grumbles.

He is one hundred percent right. He tugs on the bottom of his suit vest, and I fight a smile because I know he wouldn't thank me for noticing.

"It's okay, Lochlan. I'd be worried if you weren't nervous about becoming a dad. But between you and me, I think you're going to be an excellent father."

His features soften, but he can't hide the fear lurking in his eyes.

"Thanks, Penny. I was coming to say that you don't have to stay late tonight. I'm going to head out soon to meet Tilly anyway. But…" He glances down at a folder in his hands, and his frown returns. "How do you feel about Dillon Henry? I know you're friends, and my sister says he's great. He's technically my friend, but you've spent the most time with him. What do you think?"

My hands tremble, and I turn away to set my mug down. It gives me a chance to get myself under control. Blushing in front of my boss isn't something I'm too keen on.

"Ah, Dillon's great," I say with my back to Lochlan. "We've become sort of friends, I think." A nervous giggle escapes my throat, and I want to smack my palm to my forehead. Instead, I ball up a handful of tissues and squeeze them against my wet shirt.

"Good," Lochlan says, but his tone doesn't sound happy. "Would you be okay working closely with him, ah, more often?"

Okay. I'm pretty sure my heart just stopped. Or skipped.

Or perhaps did a little jig? Whatever it did has me desperately wanting to gasp for a breath I can't seem to take.

"What do you mean? Work with him how?"

"Ashton and I have been—brainstorming." He says it like the words taste bitter on his tongue.

"You don't sound too excited about that." I grin because I still don't think he's happy about having a Westbrook as his brother-in-law, but truthfully, he couldn't have asked for a more devoted husband for his sister than Ash.

"I didn't get a say in whom my sister married. But I have to admit, Ashton's vision is—interesting. And in the long run, I think it might be the best thing for my hotels and for you."

"Me?" I squeak. "What do I have to do with anything?"

"Jesus, Penny. I hope that someday you'll be able to see your potential like the rest of us do."

Compliments make me sweaty. And panicky. And so uncomfortable that I start searching for an escape from this conversation.

Lochlan hands it to me in the form of the folder he's clutching tightly in his fist.

"Nothing is set in stone yet, but we have big plans for your future within this company. As long as you don't mind working with Dillon and we can sort out the details, I think we've come up with something that will be better for your family. I know that's not a lot of information, but I'll fill you in once we've nailed down a few more things."

"Nothing like dangling a really stressful carrot in front of a starved rabbit," I mumble.

He laughs. "I'm not being intentionally vague. There are a lot of details I need to finalize before I get anyone's hopes up. And before I agreed to anything, I wanted to make sure you were okay with seeing more of Dillon. I know he hangs around here because of you."

God, I actually feel my face flush a hundred shades of red. "Like I said, we're friendly."

"Good." He stares at me for a beat too long, then nods like he's made a decision. "That," he says, pointing to the sealed folder in my hands. "Can you drop that off to Dillon? The address is on the front. Then you can head home early, for a change."

The pile of folders on my desk belies that statement. I give Lochlan a horrified look.

"Leave them for tomorrow. There's nothing in there that won't keep overnight," he says.

With a shrug that reaches my ears, I finally give in. "Okay. I'll take them home with me to work through tomorrow. So, just drop this off with D—Dillon?"

He smiles down at me. "That's it. As soon as I know more, I'll let you know."

Shit. I wasn't planning to see Dillon today. It's not Wednesday, for crying out loud! My shirt is ruined. I'm a mess. It's the story of my life. I guess it's time Dillon saw me for who I really am—a messy, uncoordinated disaster of a human.

Using another handful of tissues, I do my best to dry the stain down my front, then shrug into my thick raincoat. At least I have this. I feel marginally better when I zip it up all the way to my chin. Perhaps he won't have to see my ruined shirt after all.

CONFIRMING the address on the envelope, I look up at the building before me. It's nothing like I was expecting. This looks more like condos in an old factory than somewhere a massive security firm would be.

I check my outfit one more time and sigh. At least my

boring black jacket covers the spill. Seriously, I might need to start investing in adult bibs. Is that a thing? Or at the very least, Scotchgarding my clothes.

I square my shoulders and march into the building. An older gentleman sits at the information desk with a kind smile. His nametag reads "Tony."

"Hi. My name's Penny Mulligan. I'm here to see Dillon Henry from Envision."

"Ah, Penny. Yes. He said he was expecting a visitor," the older man says with a smile.

He did? Huh. I guess Lochlan called him.

The man stands and points to a bank of elevators around the corner. "Take the last one on the right. I'll access his floor for you from here."

After so many years of being ignored, I've made it my mission to acknowledge everyone, especially people like Tony, who see hundreds of people every day who will never remember him. It's a basic human decency that most people ignore these days, but I know what that can do to a person after a while.

"Thank you, Tony. I'll only be a minute. I have to drop something off."

"Not my business, Miss Penny, but I'll see ya when you're done. I'm here all night."

"Right. Okay. Thanks again."

I hurry past him to the elevators and try to relax my hands. The death grip I've got on this folder has crinkled the corners. I haven't felt this nervous since prom night. And prom was a very long time ago.

Gah! Grow up, Penny. Honestly, I'm not a teenager anymore. I shouldn't get this worked up over seeing a friend.

A friend.

My stomach revolts. Why does calling Dillon a friend cause such a visceral reaction?

The elevator is smaller than I expected it to be, so it takes less than a second to scan the entire space. Where the hell are all the buttons?

Unease climbs up my spine, but before I can form a plan, the car moves quickly, and the next thing I know, the doors slide open without a sound to a small hallway.

It does nothing to calm my racing heart.

There's only one door, and it's straight ahead, so I take a deep breath, and walk forward. No signage gives any information about the company, but this has to be his office. Right?

Opening the door, I expect to find a reception desk. What I actually find is an open-floor-plan apartment. Wide open. Like a loft.

Surprise freezes me two steps into the definitely-not-an-office. The door clicks shut behind me.

"I'll be out in a minute," Dillon calls from somewhere to my left.

"Dillon?" I don't mean to speak, but as soon as I do, I spin toward the door. Can I get out of here before he consumes me?

"Penny?" His voice is off, but I'm too nervous to turn around. "You're not who I was expecting." A smile lightens his tone.

"Oh, God. This isn't your office, is it?"

"Turn around."

A shiver runs through my entire body. His words are rough and commanding, setting off fireworks low in my belly. He makes me want to obey, and I stopped taking orders when I divorced Eddy. But God help me, I want to drop to my knees for this man, and all he said was *turn around.*

"Penny?" He sounds closer. He sounds sexy.

Now I'm just making things weird. *Turn around, you idiot!*

Slowly, I release a deep breath, turn around, and instantly wish I hadn't.

I slap a hand over my eyes and tilt my head toward the ceiling. "You're naked!" I screech.

"I'm wearing a towel." He chuckles, making me imagine how his chest moves.

I peek through my fingers, and my mouth goes dry. He's only wearing a towel, and there's water running down his naked man-chest. His hard, muscled man-chest. Eddy never, ever looked like that. And yup, his pecs dance like Magic Mike's, but I can't stop my eyes from drifting lower.

Holy shit. I might pass out. Do not pass out. That would be mortifying.

Dillon's laugh rubs like rich velvet against my skin. "If you keep staring at me like that, this towel won't cover what should probably remain covered."

Oh, geez. He can tell I'm staring through a crack in my fingers like a lovestruck teenager. I tighten my fingers over my eyes.

"Lochlan gave me your address. I thought it was your work address. I'm supposed to give you this," I say, thrusting the folder out blindly.

He takes it, and then strong, thick fingers close over mine and pull my hand away from my face.

My body is inches away from a naked Dillon Henry. I gulp. Loudly. The mental gymnastics it takes not to say something stupid, something like *you're so freaking hot,* is putting me through a workout.

"This is where I live." He's gentled his voice, but he's so close that his words ghost across my heated cheeks, and I almost swoon. Like for real, I nearly black out. "I like having you in my space."

Oh, God.

He drags his long finger down my cheek, and my eyes

close involuntarily as I lean into the touch like a stray cat starved for attention.

"Oh, Penny. I like having you here a lot."

His words worm into the cracks of my heart, and I swear to all things holy, I can feel them stitching up my broken pieces. If only my life were mine to give.

That thought has me taking half a step back and breaking our connection. I drop my head to stare at my toes and blink furiously to keep the stupid tears at bay. My life is not my own. It belongs wholly and completely to three little boys who need me to be their entire world.

CHAPTER 5

DILLON

*H*ow many times have I dreamed of Penny standing in my apartment? Hundreds? Thousands? But in all my dreams, she was never staring at her shoes, trying not to cry.

"Penny," I say gently. "Look at me."

I can't tell if she's shaking her head or trembling from the effort of not crying, but it guts me.

"Please look at me," I say again.

I watch her chest rise and fall heavily like each breath is painful.

The door behind her crashes open, and time stands still as Ryder barrels inside, balancing a large pizza in one hand and a six-pack of beer in the other.

"Ah, hey," he says as his eyes dance between Penny and me.

She's like a statue. Frozen. Well, everything but her eyes. Those are wide and confused and boring a hole into my soul.

I move past her with determined strides, tuck the folder she handed me under my arm, then take the pizza and beer from Ryder.

"Thanks for dropping this off," I say with a jerky nod toward the door.

"Dang, man," he drawls, leaning into my personal space. "Is this your Wednesday girl? No wonder you're so wound up."

"Out. Now," I say through gritted teeth.

His grin is mischievous as he saunters out the door, but not before calling over his shoulder, "Nice to finally meet you, Wednesday."

Penny gasps behind me, and I drop my head with a groan. "Sorry about him." I turn toward her. "That was Ryder. He's normally a friend."

"Wednesday?" Her voice is timid, but laced with a hint of humor.

"Come on. Let me put this down and throw on some pants."

"Oh, I should…"

"Penny, come in and sit down."

I don't know what comes over me. I'm not an asshole, but every domineering gene I possess comes screaming to the forefront when she's around. And something tells me that if I don't get her to stay, even for a little bit, I'll never get this chance again.

She wrings her fingers together, and I want nothing more than to place my hand over hers before she rubs the skin raw. But my hands are full, so I head toward the kitchen island, dropping the folder on the coffee table on the way and silently begging her to follow.

By the time the pizza and beer are on the island, she still hasn't moved. I grasp the edge of the granite and release a heavy sigh. She's not coming to me, and that rejection weighs on my heart.

Turning, I find her hovering at the entryway. She's the poster child for nervousness as she plucks at a damned elastic around her wrist, and I curse the fireflies trying to light up my chest.

"Should I take off my shoes?" she asks, staring down at her feet.

Her tall boots reach all the way to her knees. Yes, I do want her to take them off so I can ogle her legs, but instead, I say, "Whatever you're more comfortable with. I want you to make yourself at home."

She opens and closes her mouth like she's going to say something, and I hold my breath. I don't release it until she cautiously walks forward and sits on the sofa with her back to me.

I round the kitchen island slowly, giving myself a minute to calm down, but as soon as I see her, I nearly swallow my tongue.

Penny is sitting on my sofa with her delicate legs crossed primly at her ankles. I have the ridiculous urge to dirty her up in the best way, but I control it. Barely.

My deepest, darkest desire to own her body plays in the background of my mind.

"You didn't take off your jacket," I say.

"Oh, ah, it's okay. I shouldn't stay long anyway."

She's looking for an escape, but I won't make it easy, not if this is my only chance.

"When are the kids expecting you home?"

Her gaze jumps from my eyes to my chest and an obscene amount of pride makes me smile, but I do grasp the knot holding my towel up just in case.

"Well, they're with my cousin tonight because I usually work late."

The clock by the TV says it's quarter of five.

"So, you have some time?" I ask hopefully.

"No," she says with a wild shake of her head that has her hair falling from its pretty bun. "I should get home."

"Have some pizza with me. I never get to see you outside of Lochlan's office."

I will happily beg for whatever this woman can give me. With sudden clarity, I see my future: years and years of living with blue balls. And I'd happily endure it for decades if it meant moments like this with her.

"But, I—the train. It's scheduled."

I cross the room in three long strides. Careful not to crowd her, I lean down just shy of her personal space. "Today's your lucky day, Penny. I'll drive you home."

"Oh my God. No. Dillon." She looks anywhere but at my chest, making my heart beat erratically. "Seriously, with traffic, it'll take you hours to get there and back."

I pick up the folder she'd given me from the coffee table. "It's not a problem. I have to talk to Ashton about this anyway. It's pure luck that he lives in the same town." I grin so hard my cheeks hurt. She can't argue with me now.

She swallows, and I follow the graceful movements of her neck—a neck I want to mark as my own with my teeth, my hands, and my cock.

How far would she let me push her?

Her expression holds a look I've never seen from her before. She wants me as much as I want her. There's no doubt about that. But she holds herself apart for her boys. Fucking hell, if that doesn't make me like her even more.

"Um…" She bites her bottom lip, clearly searching for a way out of this, but I won't allow it. Reaching out, I grab her chin between my thumb and forefinger and pull just enough that she's forced to release her lip.

I memorize the slight indents left there by her teeth and can so vividly picture what her lips would look like after my mouth takes hers.

"Dillon?" she whispers, and I take a step back.

"Take off your jacket, then I'll get dressed and get us some pizza."

"I can't," she says too quickly.

I pause to study her, then nod as something akin to glee fills my body.

"Did you spill something on yourself again?" I ask with a grin. She's probably regretting telling me how often she spills stuff right about now.

I never smile as much as I do when I'm with her. It's another reason I'm always so desperate to be in her presence —she chases away the sadness that follows me like the worst kind of shadow.

She lifts her eyes to the ceiling. "It was Lochlan's fault this time."

A deep chuckle rumbles in my chest. "Let's see the damage. Take it off." My dick twitches at the demand, but I discreetly adjust my towel and tell him to stand down.

With a roll of her eyes, she stands, then lowers the zipper of her coat to reveal a dark brown stain down the front of her cream-colored blouse.

That won't do. Leaving her on the sofa, I head to my bedroom and dig through a dresser drawer, searching for blue fabric. A t-shirt I got freshman year of college. It's old and soft from years of washing, and I'm a perv for wanting to see her in it.

Standing in the doorway, I hold it in the air and gesture behind me. "Go change. I'm going to get some sweatpants from the laundry room, and I'll meet you back here."

"Oh, no, that's—"

"Penny, change. Now."

She narrows her eyes at my tone, but her cheeks flame, and she can't hide the smile trying to break free. She glides toward me and grabs the shirt from my hands.

I take off in the opposite direction because if I watch her

walk into my bedroom, I'll follow until I have her naked body pressed against the door.

～

I FORCE myself to stay in my small laundry room next to the kitchen for a few extra seconds to make sure I can control myself. I only have sweatpants on, and if I walk out with a raging hard-on, she'll flee as fast as her little feet can carry her.

She has me so twisted up that I forgot my cleaning service came today, and they always put away my laundry. I'd live out of hampers and laundry baskets otherwise.

When I'm finally mostly sure I can face Penny, I hurry to the bathroom, where I left the T-shirt from my shower.

I open the door and my jaw falls open.

Penny spins toward me with my UNC shirt held tightly against her stomach and like the man-child I am, I can't drag my gaze away from her perfectly round tits. She's better than any wet dream I've ever had.

She's a goddamned vision, and this image of her holding onto my T-shirt will be imprinted on my brain forever.

"You're beautiful," I say. There's a gruffness to my voice that gives away my desire.

She taps her fingers against her stomach. Compliments have always made her a little twitchy.

I don't know who moved, but we're now standing mere inches apart. Her breath heaves, causing her breasts to rise and fall rapidly. The softness of her flesh bounces with each harsh exhale.

She licks her lips and watches intently as I lift a single finger to the strap of her beige bra.

"Dillon," she whispers as I trace the strap on her right shoulder with my finger. A delicate moan slips from her lips and my cock roars to life. There's no hiding an erection in gray sweatpants, and she stares at it with hungry eyes.

"Jesus, Penny."

Using only the tip of my fingernail, I trace the edge of her bra down one breast, then up her sternum to her throat, watching with barely controlled lust as I leave a light line on her skin in my wake.

We stand, suspended in time, where only she and I exist. A blip in the grand scheme of our lives, but it's a moment I'll remember forever.

"You're so fucking sexy." I groan. I've never meant anything more.

She shakes her head and glances down. A flush erupts on her fair skin. "Dillon, I'm not even… I mean, this bra is probably ten years old, and trust me, nothing on my body falls where it used to." She gasps and drops her head while trying to cover herself more. "Why did I say that out loud?"

"Don't do that with me," I order quietly.

Her head snaps up with a surprised expression. "Do what?"

She brings out a dominant side of me that I've never once explored. It's terrifying and exhilarating and so fucking painful trying to keep it in check.

"However you see yourself, I can promise you, it's not how I see you." Slowly, possessively, I run my gaze up her body. "It's not the bra that consumes me, sweetheart. It's you. All of you."

My finger slips beneath the silk covering her right tit, and that delicious moan of hers goes straight to my dick when her palm lands on my bare chest.

"Dillon," she says on an exhale, and the heat from her mouth brands my skin.

I'm slow and deliberate with my movements, praying she doesn't stop me. I inch my index finger along her skin until I find her hard nipple. Then I flick it, just twice, but it's enough to make her knees buckle.

"I know why you put your children first, and I admire that," I say. Lowering my head, I run my nose along her collarbone and inhale her scent until my lungs feel as if they could explode. Her entire body trembles, and I fucking love that I can do this to her. "But what you haven't considered is how flexible I can be—how much I'm willing to bend to fit into your world. I don't need all of you, Penny. I just need the pieces no one else has earned."

She swallows, then tips her head back, and I take that opportunity to lick a line up her neck. The pads of her fingers flex against my skin, and it's all I can do to keep my lower half from thrusting forward to reach her.

"You don't need another person to take care of, sweetheart. What you need is someone willing to take care of you. I want—no—I *need* to be that man for you. And I desperately want you to see yourself as I see you."

My hand falls to her hip, and I pull her flush against me. As expected, she gasps, and her eyes flash with longing.

"How do you see me?" The insecurity in that whispered plea sets my teeth on edge.

I'm on her in an instant, lightly grasping her face with both hands so she can't look anywhere but straight into my eyes as I seal our bodies together.

"I see perfection. I see a mom giving everything she has to her boys. I see a woman so deprived of love that she's forgotten how to love herself."

She reaches up and cups my face, then gently slides her thumbs along my skin.

She reached—for me.

Knowing she needs to hear my words, I continue with a shaky voice that conveys my emotions. "I see a woman I can't stop thinking about. I see a woman I vowed to keep in the friend zone, and yet I dream of her every damn night. I see a queen who hasn't yet learned that she holds all the power, and I can't wait to see you when you finally fix your crown."

I expected her to pull away or even close her eyes, but she's locked onto me beautifully.

"That is who I see, Penny Mulligan. Perfect in your perceived imperfections. Gorgeous in your self-doubt. Vibrant in a way that makes angels sing. Perfection. That's who you are to me."

With agonizing slowness, she inches closer to my face. Our lips are a breath apart, but I'm afraid to move and disrupt the magic of this moment. The moment she finally chose me.

Tears well in her eyes, and I want nothing more than to kiss away her sadness, but when I lean in a fraction of an inch, she turns her face toward the door. It's like someone took an ax to my balls.

She tilts her head in an odd way, and that's when I realize her attention isn't on me but on a strange ringtone coming from my family room.

It happens in an instant. She turns away from me, tugging my shirt over her head, then slips out of the room and away from me.

"Hi," she says, sounding breathless.

I lean against the doorframe and watch her. She's flustered and desperately trying to pull herself together for whatever conversation is happening on the other end of her call.

"Did she say how long she would be gone?"

Silence.

"Did she even ask if I was home?"

The way her words turn shrill at the end has me standing taller even as guilt and fear invade my body.

"Jesus, Remy. I'm so sorry. I..." Her gaze flicks to me, and

I watch her walls rebuild like the last round of Tetris. "I'll get home as soon as I can. There's formula in the pantry, and Kai should be able to help Lia with whatever she needs. I'm sorry," she says again before nodding and lowering her phone.

"Dillon," her voice is shaky and fragile, and each word feels like it's slicing me in two. "My life doesn't belong to me. I can't start something when I need to give everything I am to my boys. Their father—he, he's really hurt them."

She looks away and lifts her jacket from my sofa. "I have to be their everything because otherwise, they have nothing. I'm mother, father, rule enforcer, Uber driver, maid, boo-boo kisser. My ex-husband's girlfriend just dropped her two baby girls off with Kai without asking and without an explanation. I wish I could say that's a first, but it's not, and I have nothing left to give by the time my day ends."

She takes a deep, shuddering breath before facing me again. "I—I'm sorry. You have no idea how much I wish things were different for me. How badly I wish my circumstances weren't what they are. Or how often I think about what life would be like if I could…"

"If you could what?" The words sting as I say them. It's like I've taken on all her pain, and it's sliced me open from my heart to my throat. It burns.

Her guileless blue eyes find mine, and she stares with an open mouth. I want to know what she's feeling. I ache for her to understand that being guarded with me is unnecessary.

"If you could what?" I ask again with more urgency as I involuntarily drift closer.

"If I could be normal and accept a date. With you. If I could be yours." Her voice is quiet but filled with a heartache that churns my stomach.

"Sweetheart, you never, ever apologize for being the mother those boys need. You never apologize for doing what's right for your family. I'm sorry. I'm so sorry I keep pushing."

Shaking my head, I take a small step back, putting some distance between us. "I don't know what it is about you, but having you in my life, in any way I can have you, feels as necessary as the air I breathe. I—fuck."

I scrub my hand roughly through my hair and down over my face. "I know I crossed the line just now, but I won't apologize for what I said, only for making you uncomfortable, because I meant every single word. But I will do a better job of respecting your personal space."

Jesus. The sadness on her face stabs me in the gut. I'm bleeding out, and there's not a damned thing I can do about it.

"I need you in my life too, Dillon." Those words are a balm I never expected. "Life for me doesn't contain many rainbows. But when Wednesday rolls around, I swear everything looks a little brighter. A little happier. You're the rainbow in my rainstorm of a life. Is that weird?" She huffs out a tiny laugh, breaking the tension. "That's weird, isn't it? I'm such a dork." She reaches for her purse, and I feel our time evaporating like smoke.

"It's not weird, Penny. But it does make me feel a hell of a lot better about all the shit I told you." Finally, she looks at me, really looks at me, and I allow a smile to spread wide across my face as fast as lightning.

So.

Damn.

Cute.

I walk with her to my front door. Each step feels like a slow, painful death.

This is what heartbreak feels like.

"Wednesday girl?" she asks. For some reason, the hope in her voice brings me back from the edge of sadness.

I shrug and stare at my feet. "I like you, Penny. So I might talk about you a lot. Ryder's an ass, but he…" I look up and hold her gaze. "He likes how I am on Wednesdays. He rightfully attributes that to you."

Even her sad smile shines brightly. "My cousin calls you Mr. Wednesday," she admits with a pretty flush to her cheeks.

"Oh yeah? I kinda like that you talk about me, Penny. I like it a lot."

"Why?"

I flash my most wicked smile.

"Because it means while you may not have time for me in your life, you have space for me in your mind, and I'll take any piece of you I can get."

"Dillon," she chastises, but her blush deepens and edges beneath the collar of my shirt.

"I'm a patient man, Penny. I always will be."

She nods and reaches for my front door. My mouth is saying patience, and I know that's what she needs from me, so I'll respect it. But my body and heart scream that she's the one.

And I'm fairly certain that I'll wait a lifetime for her.

CHAPTER 6

DILLON

*A*shton fiddles with his daughter's shoes as he talks. They're tiny, pink glittery things on the right side of the video call and not something I ever would have imagined in his world a few years ago. He's come so far from the kid I grew up with, the man I worried would never find his way out of the dark. Now he has a wife and a little girl and a life that's hard for me to conceive and even tougher not to be envious of.

How can fucking shoes make me feel so damned lonely?

My skin prickles. It has all morning. I blame Lochlan for pushing back our weekly meeting by a few hours. Seeing Penny at nine a.m. every Wednesday has become like a drug for me, and now I've been jonesing for a hit of her for over two hours.

"Will you do me a favor?" he asks, dragging my attention back to him. "Before I hand off my shares of Envision, will you do something for me?"

"Yes." The favor doesn't matter. Ashton has always given

all of himself for everyone in his life, including me, and the least I can do is help him out in return.

He smirks, and it makes him look so much younger. "You don't even want to know what the favor is?"

"You wouldn't have asked if it wasn't important to you."

"True, but this favor has more to do with you than it does me."

That seems odd, but whatever. I shrug at him.

"Our tenant is moving out soon," he says. The glint in his eyes is suspicious.

"Okay?"

"Chance Lake is where I learned to live again. I think it could do the same for you, but you have to be willing to stay there for a while and..." He looks at something beyond his computer.

"Stay there and what?" I wish he'd get to the damn point.

"And I need you to keep an open mind. Nova is gearing up for awards season, so I have to be in LA with her to take care of Hope, but this is something that could have a profound effect on the entire town."

"What does that have to do with me? My skill set is limited at this point, Ash. I don't even know what you're asking of me." His large wooden desk takes up half my screen and illustrates the differences between a home where life happens and my far-too-modern condo in the middle of Manhattan that's always cold and lifeless. I didn't even decorate this place.

Do I even know what I like anymore?

"It's going to take you back to your roots. Back to who you were before you took on Vanessa's last wish and life made all the choices for you. You'll have the opportunity to help hundreds of kids."

"With what? What do you want me to do?" Frustration has my leg bouncing. Why is he being so cagey?

"Sports. Life. Community. It all centers around one thing, but I can't do it myself because I'm not there, and the owner, well, let's say he's old school, and this isn't a business to him. It's a way of life."

"I don't know the first thing about kids or community," I grumble. The truth is, I'm barely living myself. "And 'one thing' doesn't tell me a damn thing."

"You don't have to know everything now. But you do know sports, and you know more than you think about community. I need someone willing to be there as the face of the company. The owner won't sell to just anyone. It has to be to someone with good intentions, someone with a love for the town. I think this could be a fresh start for a lot of people, including you, and all you have to do is be there for six months or so."

He looks beyond the camera again. "Sorry, man. I have to run. I'll send you the details."

The video shuts off abruptly and the time pops up on my screen.

Shit. I'm late. And being late for Penny is unacceptable, so I grab my keys and rush out the door.

After her visit to my home last summer, I vowed to be grateful for her friendship. I promised myself I wouldn't push or leer like a pervy old man. I even swore that I'd make a wholehearted attempt at dating.

Well, three out of four ain't bad, right?

I tried to date.

I am trying to date.

Sort of.

I can't help it if they never make it past the app.

And it's not because I'm holding everyone else to Penny's impeccably high standards.

I'm not.

Mostly.

I roll to a stop outside of Penny's favorite coffee shop and send a quick text letting them know I'm here. A disgruntled-looking teen hurries outside with my order a minute later. I hand him a large tip, then ease back into traffic.

PULLING up to the valet at the Bryer-Blaine, I toss him the keys and show him my badge allowing me access to the entire hotel.

After three years, everyone knows my face, but I'm setting a precedent for high safety standards. Safety is my job, at least for now. Plus, my badge ensures my car won't leave the property.

My mind is flooded with questions. What the hell could Ashton have up his sleeve that has to do with kids and sports? I hate that the familiar itch of competition makes my fingertips twitch. I haven't had that sensation since I was nineteen, and I gave up the only goal I'd ever worked toward.

My basketball scholarship.

And I did it to piss off my dad.

Stupid fucking kid.

Inside the Bryer-Blaine hotel, employees offer a hello as I pass. The friendly greetings shake me from memories I have no desire to delve into, and I head straight for the private elevator around the corner from the front desk.

I scan my palm to enter the elevator and try to dismiss the sense of dread that's growing more uncomfortable, like a blanket of ice weighing me down. Something's wrong, and somehow I know a shit storm is about to rain down on me. Ashton fucked up my morning by dredging up old memories I buried a long time ago.

Finding Penny's desk empty and Lochlan pacing behind it when I reach their floor doesn't make me feel any better.

Lochlan Blaine is a creature of habit. He likes what he likes when he likes it, and he rarely deviates. That goes for everything in his life except his firecracker of a wife who constantly throws him curveballs.

The fact that he's wearing jeans and a sweater stops me in my tracks. I've never seen him in anything but a three-piece suit that's been pressed within an inch of its life.

"Lochlan?" Alarm bells ring in my head as I stare at him, a tray with two coffees still in my hand. "Everything okay?"

He stops mid-stride and turns to me with an aggravated expression. Then he throws his hands in the air and shakes his head before marching closer. "Is this for Penny?"

"It was," I say as he takes it from me. "Is she okay? She's usually—"

"She's usually here waiting for you. I know." The aggravation clears and he allows a small smile to pull at his lips. "She had to take her son to the doctor this morning."

Breathing becomes difficult. "Is he okay? Which son?" I manage to rasp.

Lochlan stops and looks at me. Really looks at me. "You *still* like her."

I nod. There's no use in hiding it. It's not like I can do anything about it. "She's not interested, though, so I'm fine just being her friend."

He raises his eyebrows like he's going to cross-examine me, so I throw him my own curveball. "What's with the jeans?"

Lochlan's entire posture goes rigid, and I swear a curse slips out under his breath. "Tilly's very pregnant."

"I'm aware." I start to grin. "What does that have to do with you wearing jeans?"

"She wants me to be comfortable and casual. And for Christ's sake, man. She's hormonal. Yesterday she burst into tears because she had a hole in her sock. I can't stand to see her cry even one more time."

"So, you're wearing jeans. For her."

"Yes."

A low chuckle bubbles up in my chest. "The things you do for love."

"All the things. I do all the things. Tilly gave me life. I'll wear whatever the fuck makes her happy."

"You're a good man, Lochlan."

The elevator dings and we both turn. The doors slide open to reveal a young man I know mostly from pictures, and those alarm bells ratchet up to nuclear levels.

Penny's oldest son, Kaiser, stands in the entryway, wearing an expression that screams both pissed off and terrified. I start toward him, then realize he may not even remember me. I've only met him in passing a couple of times at Ashton's since I've been avoiding his house like the plague, and it's been over a year since the kid saw me last.

"We added her boys' fingerprints to the system the last time they were here," Lochlan mutters under his breath and steps forward, so I move with him. "The littlest one has a habit of running off."

I stare at him from the corner of my eye but turn back to Kaiser when Lochlan speaks again.

"Kai? What are you doing here?" Lochlan approaches the kid like you would a wounded animal. Clearly, it's not only me with weirdness looming in my chest.

"Mr. Blaine, I—I'm sorry. I didn't think. I just thought… I mean, I didn't know you'd be in a meeting." His eyes are wide, scanning every inch of the space we're in.

Stepping forward, I hold up a hand. "Hi, Kaiser, do you remember me? I'm Dillon. Your mom has told me a lot about you. Enough that I know you're a long way from home on a school day. Are you okay?"

Lochlan elbows me in the side. An overprotective stranger is not what Kaiser needs right now. But my neck prickles with the awareness that he's probably here with news that would upset his mother.

"You're friends with my mom? You're Mr. Wednesday?" His brows pinch together, and my lips twitch.

"Well, I have coffee with your mom every Wednesday while I wait for this guy to show up." I hook my thumb toward Lochlan. "So, yeah, I guess I'm Mr. Wednesday."

"She likes you," he blurts. Then he starts wringing his hands and shifting his weight from one foot to another.

How old is he? Fifteen? Sixteen? Definitely not old enough that Penny would be okay with him coming into Manhattan all by himself.

"I like your mom too. But you must know she isn't here. Is everything okay? What can I do? What can we do?" I amend, looking over at Lochlan.

Kaiser turns to Lochlan then and juts out his jaw. He's trying to keep it from trembling, and my heart aches for this kid.

He's tall, growing into a man, but lanky and timid in a way that makes him still a boy.

"Mr. Blaine?" Kaiser looks nervously at me, then back to Lochlan. "Please don't fire my mom. She needs this job and—and..."

"Hey, Kai." Lochlan's voice is a gentle tone I've never heard from him. It's authoritative but fatherly. "Why would you think I'm going to fire your mom? She's very good at her job, and I'd be lost without her."

The elevator doors open again, and Michael, the security team leader, enters with a grave expression.

"Mr. Blaine?" Glancing around, he takes in each of us but lingers on Kai. With a grim expression, he shakes his head. "There's an Edward Damon downstairs demanding to speak to you. He's—" He pauses, like he knows what he's about to say should be handled sensitively. "He's belligerent. Normally we'd call the police, but he says he's Miss Damon's husband."

"Ex-husband," Kaiser and I growl at the same time. Our eyes meet, and the general dread I felt earlier becomes very distinct.

Kaiser is living my childhood.

Fuck me.

"I understand her ID says Damon, but we call her Miss Mulligan, so I assumed this was a—sticky situation," Michael says gently.

"Yes, she uses her maiden name at work," Lochlan says while pinching the bridge of his nose.

"We'll handle it," I tell Michael. "Put him in a conference room." He nods and walks back to the waiting elevator.

"Him. He's the reason," Kaiser says. His voice spikes with panic, even as his shoulders slump forward in defeat. "He's always the reason." He blinks rapidly, and I look away.

He deserves to keep his pride intact. I have a feeling it's stripped from him regularly.

DILLON

Lochlan and I share a look with a million words we don't speak out loud when Kaiser steps away from us with his head in his hands.

"Please, Mr. Blaine. He—he..." The panic in his crackling voice pulls at every string connected to my heart. Ones I thought had been severed years ago.

"Kai," Lochlan says carefully. "I know your dad is sick."

"He's not sick," Kaiser yells. "He's an alcoholic who's ruining our lives." The color drains from his face when his brain catches up with his mouth, and I watch, nauseous, as shame washes over him.

I know that shame. I lived it for too long.

"I'm not going to fire your mom," Lochlan promises. "There isn't anything he can say or do that will make me fire her. Okay? How did you get here?"

Lochlan peers at me over the top of the boy's bowed head. It shows how defeated he feels. On a good day, he must be pushing six feet already, but standing here between Lochlan and me, he's still a little boy trying to be the man of the house.

"I took the train. I know I'll be grounded for it, but it was important. My dad came to the house this morning, and I wouldn't let him drive Gage to school. He—we... There was an issue, and I knew he was coming here next. He wants mom's paycheck or something."

I search Lochlan's eyes as he processes this information. He's a good guy, but I don't know if he's had any experience with this type of thing.

He places both hands on Kaiser's shoulders. "We don't even issue paper checks anymore, Kai." He keeps his tone gentle as he speaks. "You know my wife, Tilly?"

Kaiser's shoulders shudder as he nods.

"Her father was also an alcoholic. I've heard her stories, but I've never lived them. I can only sympathize through her experience, but I will promise you, man to man, your mother's job is safe."

I can almost feel Kaiser's eyes roll. When you spend your life being let down by the one man who is supposed to be your safety net, it's hard to believe in a good one when they stand before you, making promises.

"Thanks," Kaiser finally mutters. "I'm sorry about whatever he's going to say down there, but I should go. If he finds me here, well, it won't be good for anyone, and I need to get home. Gage isn't old enough to be home alone yet, and I don't know how long Landon's appointment will go, so I need to get back before school gets out."

"You didn't have school?" Lochlan asks.

Kai looks away. "It's exams week. My grades are high enough that I'm exempt from most of them, so I didn't have to go in today."

"Smart kid." Lochlan gives him a warm smile.

I open my mouth to speak a word of praise, then promptly close it. Kids like Kaiser don't take compliments from strangers to heart. It would fall on deaf ears. I need to earn his trust before inserting myself into his business.

Lochlan gives me a questioning look, and I incline my head. Whatever he's asking, I'll do it.

"You know that Nova is my sister, right?" he asks Kaiser.

Kaiser nods, but his brows pinch together. Lochlan appears to understand and takes a step back, giving the boy some space.

"Well, Dillon is business partners with her husband. You might have seen him at their house a couple of times?"

"Ashton?" Kaiser's eyes light up, and a pang of jealousy stabs at my heart.

"Yeah. I guess you got pretty close to them before they left for LA, huh?"

"He's crazy smart."

"He is," Lochlan agrees. "So, both Ashton and I can vouch for Dillon. Would it be okay if he drives you home while I talk with your dad? My wife would kill me if I let you get back on the train by yourself."

Kaiser looks between Lochlan and me, but his eyes are a tiny bit less haunted. That counts as a win.

Holding up my hands, I smile. "I'm an excellent driver."

The boy shrugs. "Sure. I'm already going to be in trouble. Getting in a car with an almost stranger can't make things any worse."

I chuckle. This kid probably has a great sense of humor when he's not stressed out.

Holding up my hand in a small wave, I say, "I'm Dillon Henry. I'm thirty-nine years old. I'm a partner at Envision Securities, and I have coffee with your mom on Wednesdays. That, unfortunately, is the extent of my life. I'm kind of boring, but I'm not a stranger anymore, either. Loch and I will both put in a good word for leniency if you promise to never take off to the city like this without your mom's permission again."

Kaiser snorts. "Mister? You don't know my mom as well as you think you do if you think anything will make her go easy on me after this."

That causes a bark of laughter from both Lochlan and me. "Fair enough. I was raised by a mostly single mom too. She was tough because she had to be, but it made me a better man. Just remember, she does it all because she loves you."

He lets out a heavy sigh. "I know. Sometimes I just wish she could take care of herself like she takes care of us." Kaiser tenses, and his eyes squeeze shut.

His face falls, and I'd be willing to bet he didn't mean to say that out loud.

Placing a hand on his shoulder, I offer a gentle squeeze of support. "I get it, Kaiser. More than you could ever know. That secret is safe with us."

Together with Lochlan, the three of us enter the small elevator car. Silence hangs heavy as we descend to the first floor. But when the doors open, we're hit with the sounds of violent shouting. Kaiser steps behind us, but he's not quick enough.

"What the hell are you doin' here, boy? Jesus, she really has you brainwashed, doesn't she? Such a little bitch," the balding, middle-aged slimeball slurs, then takes a menacing step forward.

Thankfully the security team holds him back while Lochlan and I close ranks. Standing shoulder to shoulder, we block Kaiser.

"Get out of my way," he seethes while attempting to push through two of my guards. "Let me see my little asshole son."

Lochlan moves faster than I've ever seen him. Skirting the men holding back Kaiser's father, he grabs the greasy loser by the scruff of the filthy white tank top hanging out of his unbuttoned shirt. "If you talk about my employee or *her* son like that again, it will be the last thing you do. You do not get to come into my hotel, stinking like cheap whiskey, and call my employees or their children names. Do you understand me?"

My respect for Lochlan just tripled. And it's time to get out of here because fear as thick as fog is rolling off the boy behind me.

"Let me go. I'm gonna have a word with my snitch of a son."

Lochlan twists his arm and drags Edward toward the opposing wall but not quite out of earshot. I take that as my cue to gently guide Kaiser out of the lobby. I spot the valet immediately, and he runs forward to hand me my keys.

Thank Christ for small miracles.

I usher Kaiser to the right, where they keep my car during my weekly appointments.

"Kai, you little traitor. Get back here," his father yells, but Kaiser keeps step with me.

I know exactly how many years of disappointments and embarrassments it takes to get a son to turn his back on his own father. It guts me that Kaiser has reached that limit already. It took me a few more years to get there, and it tells me all I need to know about the kind of life Edward Damon is creating for this family.

I'm reasonably certain Kaiser doesn't breathe until we're outside and the hotel doors slide closed.

"Thirty-two Reina Lane," he says quietly.

I drove Penny home once. And memorized the address.

Thinking about her turns my blood to lava, and I unzip my jacket. She's going to be pissed and probably terrified.

I've only been to Chance Lake once since Ashton and Nova moved to Los Angeles so she could work with some high-profile clients. Apparently, she'll dress them for awards season, and Ashton has decided to become a full-time stay-at-home dad.

The thought sends a chill down my spine that has nothing to do with the 30-degree temperature outside.

I don't know what to do with kids.

Do I?

Glancing at Kaiser, I can't help the feeling that, once again, I'm lying to myself.

When he doesn't look back at me, I add his address to the GPS to avoid questions I don't know how to answer and turn on the heat. "Are you okay?"

"Yeah. Fine. Thanks," Kaiser says in wobbly staccato. He turns and looks out the window. It's my signal to get moving, so I put the car into drive and pull out onto the city street.

"GPS says it's going to take at least a couple of hours to get there," I tell him. "There must be an accident or two."

"It took one and a half on the train," he tells the window and passing cityscape. "You have an accent."

Taking my eyes off the road for a second, I study the boy, not yet a man, hunched over in my passenger seat. "I grew up with Ashton in North Carolina, but I lived in the 'country side' of town."

This has his attention, and he turns toward me. "What does that mean?"

"You've heard of the haves and have-nots?"

"You mean like the rich and the poor?" He scans my expensive clothing with suspicion.

"Yeah, like that. I was on the poor end of the poor. My mom grew up country. Real country," I say with a smile, infusing as much twang into my words as I can. "Ashton's parents grew up a little more refined, so his accent isn't as thick. But one of his brothers, Preston? When he gets mad, the country boy shines stronger than even mine."

He smiles, and the anxiety in my chest eases a little.

"I want to be like Ashton when I grow up," he says quietly.

I ignore the pinch that it causes in my heart. "Oh yeah?"

"He's honest. And smart. And loyal."

"He is. All good qualities in a man. It takes more work to always be a good person than it does to be a jerk. But karma is a real thing. Good things usually find their way to good people."

"I'll believe it when I see it," he grumbles.

I can't make him believe me. But hopefully someday I can show him.

It doesn't take long before the specks of snow begin to accumulate, slowing traffic to a near-crawl, but we're both lost in thought, and the drive north is relatively quiet.

Eventually, I pull off the exit that leads to the sleepy town of Chance Lake at a snail's pace. The snow is coming in heavy sheets now, causing the streetlights to turn on hours before their scheduled time.

I don't have a ton of experience driving in this shit, and I have precious cargo onboard, so I make no effort to rush.

GPS directs me through the quiet town until I pull into Penny's driveway.

"You ready?" I ask quietly, killing the engine.

Kaiser started wrestling with his hands about a mile back. The kid is nervous, but when I open my door and get out, he follows. Happy shouts greet us from across the street. I turn toward the noise and see a handful of teenage boys throwing snowballs at each other.

They're too far away, and the snow is too thick to recognize features, but there's no mistaking the sounds of joy coming from the kids.

How often is Kaiser able to be carefree and happy like that?

"That's Take A Chance, the sporting complex for a bunch of surrounding towns," he explains. "Thanks for the ride."

He stalks past me, eyeing my car, and stops right in front of it. "Are you driving back to the city tonight?"

"I was planning on it." A large snowflake sticks to my eyelashes, and I blink it away.

"In this?" He looks down at my Tesla again, and I nod. "Come on in. I'll get you the tow truck number just in case." He shakes his head, and I laugh.

"It does better in the snow than you would think."

Kaiser looks up to the sky, then back at me. "Not with this kind of storm coming. Honestly, you'll probably want to think about staying here tonight."

Logically, I know by here he means in town. But his front door has an undeniable allure, and that flutter in my chest makes it hard to breathe. Jesus, my lungs might actually explode before this day is over.

"I'll see how it is after I check on Ashton's house."

The kid stops with his key to the door and turns to look me up and down. "You are going to check on his house? No offense, but do you know what to do if the heat is out or the roof gets a leak?"

"I promised him I would keep an eye on it. Plus, I grew up with a mostly single mom, Kaiser. I started fixing things around the house before I finished grade school."

He furrows his brow and faces the door again. "Sorry," he mumbles. "I just assumed because you grew up with…"

"The Westbrooks have never cared about money. They care about people. It didn't matter that I was poor. Or that I couldn't afford the same shoes everyone else was wearing. They've only ever cared about me."

A lump forms in my throat. Like recalling the good things about the family that both kept me sane and showed me what I was missing in my childhood smooths the ragged edges of my memories.

"Yeah." He nods and opens the door. "Ashton and Nova

have always been good to us. They've been good to my mom."

The warmth of their home engulfs me like an embrace. It's so different from the constant cold that seeps into my bones at my apartment, and my body heats instantly. The starchy scent of pasta cooking makes my mouth water. I'm not sure where to look first, but Kaiser drops his bag on a bench to the left and slips out of his shoes, so I do the same.

He bends down, tucks a smaller pair of shoes onto a shoe rack, and picks up the crumpled sweatshirt on the floor beside it. "My brother Gage can't quite reach the hooks yet," he explains.

I place my snowy dress shoes neatly on the welcome mat and inhale sharply. Seeing my shoes next to Penny's and three mini versions of mine makes my chest feel like the blades of a helicopter about to take off.

Kaiser walks farther into the house while I'm mesmerized by the little shoes next to mine. A pair of worn duck boots. A pair of tiny red Converse sneakers. And her high heels. Penny's high heels. The ones I've seen carrying shapely legs around the office, and once again, it's shoes that threaten the walls I've carefully constructed around my heart.

CHAPTER 8

PENNY

*E*xhaustion is a funny thing. I never feel it until I stop moving, so on days like this, I make it my mission to never stop moving.

I stir the cheese sauce and check the clock one more time. I really do try not to be a helicopter mom, but it's harder than you'd think, especially after all my boys have been through. It's also tough to acknowledge that Kai is growing up and deserves a *little* freedom. Twenty more minutes. Then I start blowing up his cell phone.

And there will be a conversation about turning his location setting off. That won't fly. Not with the ticking time bomb that is my ex. Goddamn Eddy—

A voice behind me makes me jump a foot high.

Holding a hand to my heart, I turn to face Kai and smile. He's so handsome and kind. It's moments like these that I want to pat myself on the back. It's hard work raising good humans, but my oldest proves I'm doing my job right.

"Sorry, Kai. What did you say?"

"Mr. Dillon is here for—for..." he mumbles and looks down at the floor.

My brain is foggier than I thought because those words are English, but they make no sense.

"Mr. Dillon, Mom?" Kai finally repeats with a nod of his head toward the front door.

"What?" I whisper-yell and race to the edge of the doorway, where I poke my head through just enough to see my front door.

Nope. I didn't hear him wrong. Dillon Freaking Henry offers a shy little smile, and a strange "eep" escapes my lips as I duck back out of view.

"Kai! I'm not even dressed. I don't have a bra on, and I'm in…I'm in. Oh, crap." Staring down at my chest, the letters UNC smile up at me, mocking me, and my entire body goes up in flames.

Dillon's footsteps echo in my head, and I spin in a circle, desperately trying to find something to put on, but it's too late.

"Penny." His throaty voice with that gravelly tone makes my core spasm. I drop my chin to my chest in resignation. He's going to find me in his t-shirt and my dancing bear pajama pants, and there's not a damned thing I can do about it.

Slowly I turn to him. His sharp intake of air is like jumping into the deep end of a pool. It engulfs me. He engulfs me, and he hasn't even moved.

His gaze is intense and heated in a way I've only ever read about as he does a slow sweep of my body.

A full-body tremor works its way from my head down to my toes. I fight it, trying not to let it show, but then he goes and licks his lips, and my breath seizes in my lungs like the first blast of sub-zero air. It singes down my throat and into my chest.

Dillon wipes his palms on the thighs of his pants before lifting one arm and scratching at the back of his head. He mutters something under his breath that I can't make out, but I feel it everywhere.

I watch him intently as he takes in my world around him. Landon sits at the corner table, working on a history project while my mac and cheese sauce bubbles on the stove. I move quickly to turn it off before it burns, ridiculously thankful for the distraction.

Finally, I turn back to him and force my words to come. "D—Dillon. Sorry. I, ah, I wasn't expecting company." His eyes darken when they land on his shirt. Damn it, no bra. I quickly cross my arms over my chest. He has a way of making me forget myself.

He looks down at the floor with flushed cheeks.

"I'm sorry to interrupt. I—uh…" He scans the room again, but I have no idea what he's searching for.

"Mr. Dillon," Kai says.

"Just Dillon," he says, and my gaze ping-pongs between them.

"You can call me Kai," my son says without making eye contact. Then he turns to me, and the fear in his expression causes my stomach to twist painfully. "Dillon gave me a ride home, Mom."

I blink away my worry and address Dillon. "Were you checking on Ashton's place?"

"We were just there," Landon says flatly without looking up. "No one was home."

My throat tightens at Landon's monotone voice. He wasn't always this serious, this melancholy, and it makes my mom guilt reach up into my throat, threatening to suffocate me.

"We checked on it after Landon's appointment," I explain. "A single woman is renting Ashton's place, so I wanted to make sure she was all set for the storm."

"No, Mom. I—I..." Kai twists his hands together roughly. "I went to see Mr. Blaine."

"In the city?" My voice is two octaves too high, and I place a fist to my chest like I can hold my heart steady. "Kaiser Edward Damon," I say through clenched teeth.

"Don't call me that," my son bellows, and Dillon shifts his weight from foot to foot beside me. "Dad showed up here this morning. I knew he was going to Mr. Blaine's next."

"Kai. You should have called me. How many times do I have to tell you that you're not the parent here? What if something had happened to you? I wouldn't have even known where you were."

My hands shake, and my eyes grow hot. I've never felt fear so intense as I do as a mother. If something happens to one of my boys, it will literally kill a piece of my soul.

"You can't do everything, Mom, and he was..." Kai looks ready to cry too and faces Dillon.

"Kai, go to your room and wait for me."

"Mom..."

"Now, Kai." The command is stern, but my body is trembling.

He glances at me again, and my throat constricts like someone is squeezing the life out of me. Then he spins on his heel and stomps toward the stairs.

A timer goes off on the stove, and I turn away from them while keeping my arms crossed over my chest.

But really, I'm simply holding myself together. If I release my arms, I know I'll break.

"I'm sorry. I—Lochlan and I thought... I wanted to make sure he was safe." Dillon's voice is low and melodic. His words feather over me, wringing out my tension muscle by muscle.

It's both comforting and maddening that he can do such things to me with simple words.

Landon grunts, and Dillon moves closer to see what he's working on. It gives me a second to tame the chaos swirling around my overcrowded mind.

Without looking at him, I finally say, "I appreciate that, Dillon, I do. Just—what was he thinking?" I drift closer to the window where the snow is coming down thick and fast. "Wait, did you even check the weather before you came out here?"

I find an old Damon's Details sweatshirt on the floor behind the chair and pull it over my head, but I don't miss the way Dillon's eyes narrow on the logo. I don't like wearing my ex-husband's name like a branding any more than he apparently does, but I need the extra protection right now. One more layer to keep me safe.

"I told him I'd get him the number for Tanks so when he needs a tow, he'll know who to call," Kai yells from the top of the stairs.

"Kai. Room. Now," I holler, then turn to Dillon while worrying my lip raw. He's going to be so pissed. "We're getting a Nor'easter, Dillon. They've already canceled school for tomorrow and will probably end up canceling the rest of the week too. Do you know what that means?"

He reaches into his pocket and pulls out a piece of candy. I watch in fascination as his jaw crunches away on it before he shrugs. "I guess it means my week is about to get a lot more interesting." His smile is arresting, and I forget to breathe.

Damn him.

My head is spinning with lists that never end. One piles on top of the next until I'm sure I'll drown.

One thing I do know is that I'm going to kill Eddy, then Kai. Then Eddy again for—for everything.

Dillon takes a step forward. His giant frame dwarfs me in

my tiny kitchen. God! Does anyone else hear how shallow my breathing is?

"How much snow are we talking?"

I probably shouldn't be staring at his lips. Lips that are so full they'd make any woman jealous. And let's not discuss the first hints of scruff covering his jaw. Or the way his messy brown hair makes me want to run my fingers through it and pull him to me.

It's cruel and unusual punishment to constantly be reminded that something you want so desperately is the same thing you can never have.

"Two feet," Landon says quietly, jolting me back into reality. He's spoken more in the last five minutes than he has all day, and I narrow my eyes on him.

"Two feet today. There's another storm following right behind this one, though. It's going to take a while to clear it out, and your car doesn't even have snow tires on it," Kai calls from the upstairs hallway.

I count to ten before I yell at my stubborn firstborn.

Dillon turns toward the stairs, and I follow him into the hallway. "They're all-season tires."

"All-season is for North Carolina. You're in New England. You need snow tires," Kai shouts down the stairs.

"Kai," I warn. He's not wrong, but his tone is dangerously close to being disrespectful.

"Noted," Dillon says kindly. I appreciate that he didn't snap at my kid.

"I should have said something at Mr. Blaine's, but I—I wasn't thinking," Kai says quietly. If it weren't completely silent, we would have missed it.

When I peek up at the staircase, I find his head poking out over the banister he's resting his chin on. He appears so much younger like this. God. Why can't he always look like a carefree child and not like he's carrying the weight of adult decisions he's not fully equipped to handle yet?

It's a stupid question. I know why. Eddy Damon.

There's something in Kai's shaky tone that has my mom-senses spiraling. But before I can question him, a car door slams outside, followed by a herd of elephants stampeding up my front steps.

"Gage is home," I say. I'm not sure where to look and end up volleying between Dillon standing next to me and Kai on the stairs.

What the hell happened today?

Dillon must see something in my expression because he steps closer and lowers his voice. "He's okay, but it was a rough day for him."

A lump cements itself in my throat as my eight-year-old barrels through the front door like a bull in a china shop. The kid is wholly incapable of doing anything at half-speed.

A gust of frozen air sweeps into the house as Gage and my cousin's daughter, Izzy, tumble inside. Miller follows a moment later with his arms full of supplies. The tension in the air rises when Dillon makes eye contact with him.

Miller, being Miller, merely smiles in the easy way he has with those amber eyes that are always ready to stir stuff up. On his way by, he waggles his eyebrows at my outfit with a wild grin.

"I salted your steps, but you'll need to do it again in a few hours," he says, placing the bags on the small island that's already overflowing with dinner ingredients. I was hoping to have dinner done in case we lose power, but I can't think with Dillon here, let alone cook meals.

I follow Miller back into the kitchen with Dillon's heat at my back.

We're not two steps into the kitchen when Miller turns to

Dillon with a Cheshire-like smile and holds out his hand. "I'm Miller. It's nice to meet you."

CHAPTER 9

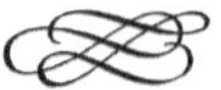

PENNY

illon grips Miller's proffered hand and shakes. "Dillon Henry," he grunts.

My house is too small on a good day. With both Miller and Dillon standing like peacocks, I swear the walls are closing in. They're both wearing smiles, but each blink that passes causes anxiety to bounce in my stomach like it's flying over speed bumps.

Miller turns to me and wraps an arm around my shoulders, and we both watch Dillon's reaction like a dark storm cloud rolling in. It's instantaneous, and I elbow Miller in the side.

Now he's just being a jerk.

"Dillon, this is my cousin, Miller."

"Her ex-husband's younger, more handsome cousin," Miller smirks with a careless shrug. "But close enough."

Dillon's shoulders are so tense he might crack.

"You have any ex-wives we need to know about?" Miller's tone is jovial, but my stomach plummets. Dillon has told me about Vanessa. I'm about to intervene, but Dillon beats me to it.

"I'm a widower," Dillon says with an eerie calm that does not fit his posture right now.

"Oh. I—I'm sorry. I didn't mean…" Miller's expression drops, and I know he genuinely feels bad, so I step forward.

"Miller," I say, but Dillon cuts me off with a single nod of his head.

"It was a short marriage of convenience for a very dear childhood friend," Dillon explains.

Thank goodness Gage waves his hands in Dillon's direction and eases some of this tension.

"Hey, Mr. Dillon. 'Member me?" My youngest plants himself directly in front of Dillon. When he drops his gaze to my little boy, his features relax, and now it's Miller's turn to elbow me.

"Hi. Gage, right?" Dillon squats so they're face to face. That one small gesture makes my heart rate spike and my mouth go dry.

"A little different than Eddy, huh?" Miller whispers to my left.

My ex-husband has only ever talked down to us all.

I can't breathe.

"Yup." Gage nods like an overused bobblehead. "You staying for dinner? Mom said she's making mac and cheese tonight. With *ham!*"

The corner of Dillon's mouth ticks up into a smile and flashes that sexy dimple. "That's my favorite. But I actually promised Ashton I'd check on his house and tenant. And since I'm in town, I should probably do that before I get stuck here."

"Great." Miller groans, then makes a point of looking out the window. "You're planning to head back to the city tonight?"

"Gage? Izzy?" I say. "Why don't you go put on a movie?"

The words aren't even out before they run toward the TV. Then Gage stops and turns back to Dillon.

"Hey, Mr. Dillon. Anyone call you Dill Pickle?" My little boy's entire body shakes with laughter that you can feel down to your bones.

"Not since I was little," Dillon says. There's an odd expression on his face. Like he's confused but happy.

Gage runs off, and Dillon must remember that Miller asked him a question because he says, "It was an unexpected trip." I know he's speaking to Miller, but he stares at me.

"Hmm," Miller hums while nodding his head.

Dillon glances at Landon, and my heart melts a little. He may not understand the situation he's walked in on, but he's protectively cautious around my boys.

"Kai went into the city. By himself. Something to do with Eddy," I say under my breath. "Dillon drove him home."

"Shit." Miller curses under his breath. When he lifts his head, he's wearing a smile, though. "Nova and Ash have been trying to throw you two together for years, and it ends up being Sweaty Eddy to get it done."

"Miller," I hiss.

"Dillon, how do you feel about small towns?" Miller asks, ignoring me.

Dillon crosses his arms over his chest. His expression is amused even if his body is a ball of wound-up muscle. "I grew up in one. They're okay."

"Glad you don't have an aversion. You're going to be here for a while."

My gaze snaps to Miller's, then back to Dillon, who barely flinches.

"Can Izzy stay with you for a bit?" Miller asks. "I'll run Dillon over to the Westbrook place. Paisley's probably fine, but we can pull out the generator for her."

"Paisley?" Dillon asks. He frowns like he's trying to place

her name. Surely he doesn't remember every detail that comes out of my mouth.

Miller raises his eyebrows with a smile to match, but suddenly extra tension is visible in his shoulders. He's had a thing for Paisley since she moved into town. "She's renting the Westbrook house."

"Of course Izzy can stay. I got you," I say.

"Got you too," Miller replies.

It's always been our thing. We've got each other even when it feels like we're all alone.

"The yoga instructor," Dillon says. "You took a class with her that made your legs shake for two days." Miller and I both turn to him, but his eyes never leave mine. It's like he's cataloging my every reaction, and I'm not sure what to do with that. No one has ever paid this much attention to my feelings. He's the only one who has even tried to look beneath my walls, and by the way he's staring, I'd bet money he sees me to my core.

"Yeah, we better get moving. The storm isn't going to let up anytime soon," Miller says, forcing me to break the connection with Dillon.

"But where is he going to stay?" Landon asks from the table.

We all turn to look at my son, then follow his gaze out the window. The blanket of white makes it impossible to see very far.

"He can stay with us," Miller says with a sigh.

"I'm sure I'll be fine," Dillon grumbles. "I'll find a hotel or something."

"There aren't any hotels, motels, or Airbnbs anywhere you can get to in this storm," I say. "Miller has a truck with four-wheel drive and a plow. It's probably safer to let him drive you. By the time you get back from checking on Ashton's place, the highways will be closed anyway." To

Miller, I say, "Izzy will be fine, and I'll finish making dinner."

Miller nods but glances between Dillon and me before speaking. "I was going to stop by Eddy's to make sure they were all set, but I can do it after we make sure Paisley's okay."

I keep my face neutral. It's an effort, to say the least. My ex-husband has turned my life into a nightmare, but Miller's right to check on his new family. Eddy certainly doesn't do it.

The frown on Dillon's face has a nervous energy working its way up both my legs.

"Come on, Dill. I'm not that bad. And Tanks probably already has a waitlist for tow trucks. I'll run you over and give you a tour on the way. You can pay for room and board by helping me make sure everyone's settled for the storm."

Freaking Miller. He has something planned. I can tell by his tone.

Dillon looks from Miller to me and back again before nodding.

"Miller is the unofficial mayor of Chance Lake," I say, knowing he'll put Dillon to work.

"We're a tight-knit community. We care about our neighbors," Miller explains.

"Especially Paisley," Landon deadpans. Miller's face turns red, but he ignores the comment.

"Izzy? You're going to stay here for a bit, okay? I'll be back after I check on a few things."

His eight-year-old daughter gives a halfhearted wave from the couch where she's watching Disney+ with Gage.

"I'll talk to her," I say gently. I know Miller is disappointed Izzy's mother didn't show up yesterday after a month-long plan with their little girl.

"Thanks, Pen." He leans in for a hug, and that light rumbly sound comes from Dillon's direction again. Miller's shoulders bounce against me as he chuckles. "I got you," he whispers.

"Got you, too," I say.

Turning to Dillon, Miller pastes a pleasant smile in place.

These two will either love or hate each other.

"I think we should put your car in the TAC garage before it gets buried in snow and you block Penny's driveway," Miller says. "Then I'll take you to Ashton's. Guess we'll have to stop by my place to get you some clothes too."

"What?" Dillon and I say in unison.

"Well, he's bigger than Ashton. Even if Ashton left any clothes at his house, he wouldn't fit into them, so unless he plans to shovel snow in whatever designer made that suit, he'll need some jeans at a minimum." Turning to Dillon, he laughs. "You're going to be here a while."

"How long is a while?" Dillon's gone a little pale.

Miller pats him on the back. "We're in New England. There's really no way to know. Come on. You can tell me all about what my idiot cousin did on the drive over. The TAC — Take A Chance—is across the street. I'll plow a path for your Batmobile."

"It's a Tesla," Dillon grumbles. He glances over his shoulder, and I cover my mouth with both hands when a giggle tries to break free at his horrified expression.

Just before he reaches the front door, he speaks over his shoulder in a hushed tone, "Kai is a good kid, Penny. But he was scared."

Dillon holds my gaze for a moment, then glances around my home. Heat rushes to my cheeks as he takes in the mess that comes with having three boys and never enough time. He focuses on the pile of shoes for a beat too long and I pull at the hair elastic on my wrist. But when he turns his attention back to me, it isn't judgment I find there. It's something much more dangerous to my heart—understanding.

"I guess I'll see you soon?" The hope in his tone makes me more than a little melty.

I nod and watch him walk out the door. The second it closes, air rushes out of my lungs like a popped balloon.

What the hell just happened?

"Mom?"

I turn to find Kai sitting at the bottom of the stairs. He has almost six inches on me now, but with his shoulders slumped and fear in his eyes, all I see is my little boy.

"What happened, Kai?" I sit next to him on the steps, and he rests his head on my shoulder.

A little boy so close to manhood but with so much left to learn.

"Dad," he chokes out. "He went to talk to Mr. Blaine. I…I wasn't thinking. I didn't want him to ruin the one good thing you have for yourself."

I wrap my arms around my not-so-little boy. "Kai, you're not the parent, buddy. I am. And I can handle your father. But most importantly, my job isn't the one good thing. I have you and your brothers. You're the only ones who matter."

He nods, and his shoulders shake against mine.

"I'm sorry your dad scared you, but you have to trust that I can take care of us, okay? You should have called me and let me handle it."

Please trust me, baby boy. I'm working as hard as I can to provide for us. I just need a little more time to get all the kinks worked out.

"I—I know," he whispers. "I knew as soon as the train took me into the city. But then I checked our family tracking app and saw he was in the train car behind mine. Mr. Blaine said he wouldn't fire you. He said you're good at your job."

Once again, Eddy's carelessness put my son in danger, and I guarantee he doesn't even remember that app is on his phone.

"Mr. Blaine is a good boss," I say into Kai's hair.

"Dad was—" He chokes on his words, and I squeeze him a little tighter. "He was drinking. And he was really mad at the hotel. But I got so scared, Mom. He wanted to drive Gage to school, but I could smell the sour stink on him. I knew he'd been drinking, and it wasn't safe. We—we had a big fight, and he—he…"

I close my eyes and pull Kai in closer. How can I be drowning with no water in sight? It takes a full minute before I'm strong enough to speak. "Did he hurt you, Kai?"

"He just shook me a little. I kept Gage in the house, so he didn't see anything."

I can't hold the tears back. They fall from my eyes no matter how hard I try to force them away, but I refuse to make a sound. I hate Eddy with everything I have, but he gave me my whole world.

"I'm sorry you had to handle these adult things, Kai," I say, wiping the tears away with my free hand before he can see them. "I'm trying to be everything you need, and I'll do better, but no one, not even your father, has the right to put their hands on you. Not ever, do you understand?"

He nods against my shoulder, and I release a shaky breath. "I will always protect you. I promise, but I need you to trust that I can handle everything. And I'll talk to Mr. Blaine in the morning. Then I'll deal with your dad."

"I…" His voice breaks with his first tears. "I know you can take care of us. And you're the best. But who takes care of you?" He hiccups, and I hug him so hard my knuckles crack. "I'm sorry."

Oh, sweet boy.

"Me too, sweetie. I'm sorry too. But I'm a big girl, Kai. I am strong enough to take care of us all. You have to believe that. I need you to believe that." He nods again and his tears soak the cotton of my sweatshirt.

We sit listening to Gage and Izzy laughing. Landon mumbles at the table, and I count. I count to ten. I count my blessings. I count my mistakes.

"I still have to ground you. You know that, right?"

"Yeah, I know."

"Two weeks. School, home, and practice. And when you're home, no phone."

He silently hands over his phone like he knew it was coming. "Mr. Dillon is nice."

That catches me off guard, and air stills in my lungs. "He is."

"He likes you."

I don't move. We're in unchartered territory here. "You and your brothers are my top priority. You always will be."

"I know."

"Do you?" Pulling back, I wait for him to lift his face to look at me.

My baby looks exhausted, scared, and more than a little sad.

"Talk to me, Kai. What are you thinking?"

"I wish things didn't have to be so hard for you."

"Oh, Kai. I'm stronger than I look. You don't have to worry about me." I give him a smile, and pray that my chin doesn't wobble.

He looks like he wants to say something but can't find the words. Finally, he says, "If I don't, who will?" Without giving me a chance to answer, he stands quickly and roughly dries his tears with the back of his hand. "I'm going to clear the first path before the snow gets too heavy to do it with a shovel."

I press my lips together to stop the tears from trying to escape. Then I pull him into a hug and hold on for dear life. "Let me get the kids settled, and then I'll get dressed and come help."

He nods once but doesn't say anything as he pulls away and reaches for his snow gear.

It wasn't supposed to be like this. He was supposed to be a kid worrying about girls and basketball. Not his alcoholic father or the disasters he leaves in his wake.

Silently, I issue another apology. *I'm so sorry for failing you, Kai.* Then I trudge to the kitchen.

Life is a series of kicks to the heart, and if it misses you the first time, it'll always get you on the backswing.

CHAPTER 10

DILLON

I pull my Tesla into the garage across the street from Penny's house and look around. Miller parked outside and guided me into a stall on foot.

Turning off the engine, I step out and find Miller adjusting something on the wall. "What's that?"

"Alarm," he says with a shrug. "We don't normally set it on this side of the building because there's nothing here."

"High crime in Chance Lake?"

His chuckle echoes in the mostly empty garage. "Nah, but better safe than sorry."

I follow him through a door and into an unfinished space.

"What is this place?" I look up at the rafters and try to make sense of what I'm seeing. It's open like a barn, but the structure is wrong. Like someone started building and quit halfway through.

"It was going to be a hotel," Miller says, walking across the room and turning on the overhead lights. "This would have been the lobby. My grandfather had a plan for this place. An entirely self-contained sporting complex to host a variety of tournaments."

Ashton's words echo in the back of my head. I search the space with a clinical eye and choose my words carefully. "What happened to it?"

"Politics. For as long as I can remember, this town has been mostly funded by the Brandts, from the shitty jobs they offer to the donations they make. They own a chain of car dealerships. Remy, my grandfather, said they wanted naming rights, and when he refused, the permits started getting rejected or pulled altogether. Before you knew it, years passed, and my grandfather was losing his shirt financially, so he had to scale back on his dream."

"So it just sits empty? Kai said he plays here."

"The gym is open. And the kicker? The next generation of Brandts now have a son who plays here because it's the only facility in the area."

"Why doesn't your grandfather try to build it now?"

Miller laughs darkly. "We're talking about a feud passed down over generations. Remy's seventy years old now. He's still the best-damned coach any of these kids have ever had, but the second he finds a buyer, he'll be sipping Bud Lights out on the lake."

"He's selling?" Ashton's vague plans sit heavily on my shoulders.

"This place has been for sale since I was a kid. The Brandts are the only ones with the money to keep it running, and Remy will burn it to the ground before he lets them have it. So it sits in a stalemate."

The only ones who can afford to run it unless you happen to have a trust fund that sits untouched. Fucking Ashton.

"You don't want to take over?" I ask.

"I'm a physical education teacher, Dillon. And a single dad. My bank account gets maxed at Christmas time. I can't afford it, and Remy can't afford it much longer either."

"How many kids play here?" I walk around the dusty

space. My hands itch with familiarity and, even more concerning, longing.

"We have twenty-seven teams, ranging in ages from five to eighteen."

"Wow."

"Yeah." Miller pulls off his winter beanie and runs his hands through his mop of hair as he watches me. "Want to see the gym?"

"Yes." There's no hesitation, and he laughs.

"Were you an athlete?"

I give him the side eye. "I think I should be insulted that you asked that in the past tense."

He laughs but holds open a door to a wide hallway that reminds me of the tunnels leading from locker rooms out onto football fields.

"We were all something at some point," he says. "But if I'm being honest, Ashton actually told me you were pretty good."

I snort. "Why does it always feel like that guy is silently guiding my life?"

"I wouldn't put anything past him." He nods toward a set of double doors. "That was the indoor pool. We had to shut it down because the insurance to run it was too high. Down that hallway are the indoor turf fields."

"You have more than basketball here?"

His grin grows to just shy of maniacal. "We have everything here. Or had, anyway."

We reach the end of the tunnel, and I get my first glimpse of the courts surrounded by stadium seating. Miller steps to the side, and I hear the nostalgic whoosh and jolt when he lifts the breakers. Whoosh, whoosh, whoosh sounds in my ears as the overhead lights turn on one by one.

Memories from my youth assault me when I look around, and the banner along the wall catches my attention. "The Demons?"

"Welcome to the messy parts of life, Dillon. Eddy is my cousin by marriage, so Remy let him sponsor the teams a few years ago before things got real messy. But he was drunk when he placed the order for uniforms and spelled his name wrong. So now the uniforms say Demon's instead of Damon Detailing, and he doesn't have the money to fix it. I may have run with it," he says, pointing at the posters with a smirk.

"That must be embarrassing for Kai," I mumble.

He stops short and curses. One hand drags roughly through his hair with his eyes cast to the floor, and the other hand falls to his hip. "I hadn't thought of that. He never said anything."

"He wouldn't." I walk onto the court and find the rack of balls. Taking two, I bounce them until I'm on the three-point line and shoot one-handed. The first one falls short of the rim. The second hits nothing but net.

"Catch," Miller shouts, passing me two more balls.

I make them both.

"Damn. Ashton was right. When's the last time you played?"

I stare at him, and my arms tense with adrenaline I haven't felt in years. "I sort of played with Ash for a while, but that was more coaching than playing."

"Day-um," he says when I sink four more balls.

Why didn't I get this jolt when I played with Ash and Ryder? I rub a fist over my heart—it's beating faster than a jet engine.

I could do something here. I could make a difference here and be closer to Penny. My mind spirals. There are a lot of changes that need to be made.

"You're better than good," Miller says. He shakes his head but passes me another ball.

"Muscle memory," I mutter, trying to shake away the surge coursing through my veins.

"Right. Well, you're welcome to come back and test that theory anytime, but I should get you to Ashton's so I can check on Eddy's house."

The stagnant air suddenly attacks my senses like a bad memory. "Why are you checking on his house?"

"Well." He looks me up and down. "Screw it. Come with me. I'll give you a glimpse behind the curtain of your Wednesday girl."

"Wednesday girl?" Ashton wouldn't rat me out like that. Would he?

"I'm sure you call it something else, but dang. You've been courting Penny for three damn years."

"Courting." I snort. "We're not living in the fifties."

"What would you call it?" He pulls the heavy breakers, turning off the lights one by one. The system is so outdated. It must cost them a fortune to keep it running.

"Friends. I'd call us friends."

"All right, friend. Come on. My apartment is on the other side of the complex. Let's get you some clothes, and then we'll get this shit show on the road."

MILLER'S CLOTHES make me feel like a different person. When I put them on, I recognized the brand from high school. It's been a long time since I've worn something from Kohls, but I admitted defeat when I saw the snow that accumulated on the truck in the short time we were in the gym.

I've never experienced snow so thick and heavy.

We checked the town square to ensure no one was out or stranded in their businesses, then headed toward Ashton's. The change in Miller happened the second he stepped onto the porch.

I'd bet money that he's got sweaty palms aside from the fact that it's twenty degrees outside.

Paisley is a tiny little thing with dark hair and bright green eyes. What she lacks in size, she makes up for in personality.

"That's quite the outfit, Pais."

She turns those green eyes on Miller. "What's that supposed to mean, Matty?"

Matty?

"Jesus. Nothing. I'm just here to help," he grumbles.

"Is your name Matty?" I whisper.

"Matt Miller. Everyone calls me Miller."

"Not me," Paisley taunts.

"No. Not you," he says with a fondness that has me watching these two with new eyes.

Miller stares at her like she could harness the sun in her rainbow one-piece snowsuit that looks like it was made for a middle schooler.

When we showed up, she was using every ounce of her body weight to drag the generator out of the garage.

Miller was out of the truck before we'd even stopped rolling. I watched from the side as they circled each other. I swear his posture changed when she finally relented and allowed him to do the heavy lifting.

"I've got it from here, Dillon. Can you make sure the extension cord is connected to these posts, so we don't lose it in the snow?"

I nod and follow the bright orange cord. When I'm sure they're all connected, I walk back to find Miller and Paisley standing close enough to be considered inappropriate, but with so much tension between them that sparks should start shooting out soon.

"I'll meet you in the truck?" I hook my thumb toward his vehicle, but he nods and turns to follow me.

After shutting the door, he cranks the heat up higher. The noise of the fan drowns out an uncomfortable silence, but eventually, it becomes unbearably hot, and he turns it down.

"So, what's going on with you and Paisley?"

Miller's head snaps to mine, then, just as quickly, he returns his gaze to the road. At least, I think it's the road. I can't see a damned thing.

"Nothing. She owns Karma, it's on the green. It's a yoga studio and kickboxing gym."

"Yoga and kickboxing? Sounds like a contradiction."

"That's Paisley." His voice is ragged, and I can't tell if his white knuckles on the steering wheel are from the dangerous driving conditions or our conversation. Since he holds my life in his hands, I let it go.

"This is Eddy's place," he says a little while later. We pull into what I assume is a driveway, but I can't even see a house through the snow. "We're on the other side of the field from Penny's. They own the houses, and they lease the land from Remy. It used to be more common years ago when everyone was a farmer, but, well, anyway. Eddy's always around."

Everywhere I look is white, so I can't get my bearings, but the fact that this tool is always within reach makes my head ache.

The overhead light turns on when Miller opens his door. "Should I come?"

He stares at me, his eyes shifting back and forth between mine for an uncomfortable minute. "It won't be pretty," he finally says, "but it might give you a little insight into why Penny has twenty layers of Kevlar wrapped around her heart."

"Would she want me to see this?" My voice is thick with emotion.

"Probably not. But you've been dancing around her for

years, and you're still here. I want you to understand why you have to be all in or get the fuck out. Got it?"

I nod, and he slams his door. Am I betraying Penny if I go in, knowing she wouldn't want me to see this? Is there any way I can't see it?

Nervous energy works through my body until I'm vibrating with it.

Blowing out a breath that has my cheeks expanding, I follow him a second later with my heart in my throat and memories of my past clawing their way to the surface.

CHAPTER 11

PENNY

My eyelashes have turned into tiny little icicles that make my eyes burn. The snow is coming down too fast for Kai and me to keep up, but he's determined to get the first path cleared, so I follow him with a second shovel. My biceps ache with each heavy load and my back feels like it'll snap in two, but I've always done what was necessary, and right now, I think Kai needs this outlet.

"Mom!" Landon shouts from…somewhere. The heavy snow distorts everything, and I've already thought I heard him three other times. But this time, when I lift my head, his little body is peeking out of the hood of his coat, so I hurry to the porch.

"Aster called." His chin quivers. "Mari was crying. I could hear her."

I sink to my knees in front of him, letting the padding of my snow pants cushion the fall, as he speaks.

"She forgot to get the baby milk again, and I could hear Lia singing to her in the background."

I bite my tongue so hard I taste blood. Dahlia is four years old, and Marigold isn't even a year yet.

Forcing my feelings down deep into the pit of my stomach, I force a smile I've perfected over the years. It's the one that says everything is fine, even when everything's really going to shit.

"Okay, buddy. It's okay. I bought some at the grocery store last time, just in case. I'll run it over."

"Why do you do that?" Kai says at my side. I hadn't realized he was listening.

"Because they're babies, Kai. And they're your sisters."

He turns, but I catch his arm. "We aren't making any progress out here. We have to wait for it to slow down, and I need you to go inside with your brothers. I'll have to walk the formula over to your dad's before the snow is too high to get there. The road won't get plowed until Miller gets to it, so it'll take me a little while to get there and back."

Kai grabs my shovel and stalks to the front door without a word. I grip Landon's hand and follow them inside. After removing my boots, I hurry to the kitchen, put some dinner into Tupperware for Dahlia, and grab the cans of formula I bought on sale last week.

"I'll be back as soon as I can. I'll call the house phone when I'm walking back from your dad's."

Kai is standing at the window with his back to me but nods.

"They're babies, Kai."

"I know. But their parents aren't."

I can't argue with him. Aster is twenty-two but acts like she's fourteen. I head for the front door with a heavy ache in my heart.

"I love the girls, Mom. I just wish they had someone."

His words cut like razor blades. "They have us, Kai. We'll do the best we can."

He turns and walks away, and I let myself out into the

storm that feels an awful lot like my life—never-ending blankets of shit.

~

A WALK that should take only a few minutes takes me nearly twenty with the snow up to my shins and a thick layer of ice under it. I'm almost to Eddy's when Miller's parked truck comes into view. He came from the opposite direction, plowing as he went, so the snow abruptly goes from six inches down to one where his truck cleared a path.

The snow is melting on the hood of his truck, so I know he hasn't been here long. I move quickly up the steps of the small two-bedroom, ranch-style home. Miller and Eddy may be cousins, but Miller's patience has been running thin lately. The last thing these girls need right now is to witness them fighting.

I knock, then open the door. Knowing what I do about Eddy, they wouldn't hear the knock anyway.

This house is even smaller than mine, and it's made smaller by all the people inside.

Miller is moving about the room that serves as both the family room and the kitchen with a garbage bag, tossing empties into it. He's cursing at the passed-out form of my ex-husband on the sofa while Aster sits at the table on her phone.

Dillon's sitting in the corner, holding my ex-husband's four-year-old on one leg while they feed the baby nestled into the crook of his other arm together.

I can't drag my eyes away from the scene before me. "Miller?" I croak.

He stands like he just realized I'm there. Everyone stops and looks at me. Miller's gaze drifts to Dillon on the floor.

"He was with me, Penny. He offered to help out, and I

keep a few packets of powdered formula in the truck, so…" He blows out a harsh breath that makes his nostrils flare.

"I know," I whisper. It's all a mess. I know. "It's okay." Better Dillon sees it now anyway.

Eddy groans on the sofa and rolls over. The movement sends two more beer cans rolling to the floor.

"Jesus Christ," Miller grunts.

Shaking myself into motion, I cross the room to Aster, ignoring the way my feet stick to the floor like this is the basement of a frat house and not a home with two baby girls. The stale scent of cigarette smoke makes my already woozy stomach revolt, but no one else seems to notice.

Aster was only eighteen when Eddy got her pregnant, but she made her choices. It's something I have to constantly remind myself of.

Circumstances change us, but they don't define us.

"Aster."

She lifts glassy eyes to mine, and I wonder, not for the first time, if the baby blues have her in their clutches, or if there's something more going on here. The one time I tried to talk to her about it, she not-so-nicely told me to leave, and when I ask the county to do a well-check, they always leave having found nothing wrong.

She smiles like she just noticed I'm here. Then she frowns. "Penelope," she says, popping the p's to annoy me.

My name is not Penelope, but I bite back the snark. "How did you forget the formula?"

She shrugs and lifts her feet to the edge of the chair. Resting her chin on her knees, she scans the small room. When her gaze lands on her girls, she blinks rapidly. Does she just forget about them?

"I didn't," she says quietly. "Eddy took the SNAP card."

"SNAP card?" I hear Dillon snarl.

"It's like digital food stamps," Miller whispers.

I ignore them. "Aster? You need to hold on to that card. No matter what he says, you cannot give it to him. Hide it if necessary."

She nods, and a tear slips out of the corner of her eye. "I'm not a good mom," she mutters. "I never even wanted this."

"Well, guess what? It's too late for that. You have to grow up and be here for those girls." My voice is much stronger than I feel.

Aster and I don't have any kind of relationship, but she goes from resentful to grateful and back again in nearly every encounter we have. Before she can change gears again, I put the food on the table and turn to Dahlia.

"Lia? Honey? Are you hungry?"

She looks from Dillon to me and nods.

"Come on. We'll get you set up."

"Burps, Dewey. Burps."

Dillon lifts a panic-filled expression at me. "Marigold needs to be burped," I explain. "Dahlia has a hard time with some letter combinations."

Miller walks over, lifts Marigold to Dillon's shoulder, and shows him how to do it.

Time stands still as I watch him gently pat the little girl's back.

Lia smiles at him, then scrambles over to me. Her little belly rumbles, and I turn to Aster.

"She had a peanut butter sandwich for lunch," Aster says defensively.

I focus on the task before me and try to block out the embarrassment I feel at Dillon seeing my life for what it really is. A mess I have no control over.

Miller cleans Eddy's trash, Aster finally takes a sleeping Marigold to her room, and Dillon slips outside. I don't blame him.

Lia sits in the middle of it all without saying a word but gobbling up the macaroni and cheese like it'll be her last meal.

"You were a big girl singing to Mari," I say gently.

The little girl keeps her eyes on the table.

"I'm proud of you, honey. You know how to use the phone, right? Kai showed you. Do you remember?"

She nods and brushes her hair away from her face with the back of her hand.

At least she's clean today.

I glance at the house phone and confirm the note Kai duct-taped to the wall with our numbers on it is still there. He worked for a week straight, teaching her all the numbers and how to call us.

"You can call us anytime, okay? If you need anything, you call just like Kai taught you, okay?"

Lia nods with a sadness no four-year-old should ever know, then slides out of her booster seat. With a small wave, she walks down the hallway toward the room she shares with Marigold. My gut twists at the thought of leaving them just like it does every single time I come here, but I'm not their mother. I have no rights here. All I can do is check on them.

Another list starts in my head.

- Get on a schedule with Miller to make sure someone stops by every day.
- Make sure Kai feels like he can be a kid.
- Try to talk Aster into seeing a counselor.
- Tell Eddy to stay the hell out of his car if he's drinking.

The enormity of the last one holds all my biggest fears because he's always drinking.

"It's as good as it's going to get tonight," Miller says behind me. "Come on, we'll drive you home."

"They don't deserve this." My throat is thick, and the words sound like they're muffled by quicksand.

"Neither do you, Pen. Come on. He's out for the night. Aster should be able to manage without him barking orders."

He places an arm around my shoulders and guides me to the door. "I'm sorry I let Dillon in like this. I wanted him to know what you're dealing with, but not like this."

"We're friends, Mill. Well, we were. You stick around this shit show because you're family. No one would willingly sign up for this. Not even a friend." I bump my shoulder with his. "I learned that years ago after Eddy drove away everyone I cared about."

He stops short on the porch. "He drove away the ones who didn't deserve you, Penny. But maybe he can't drive everyone away."

I squint up at him with snow pelting my face, but he isn't looking at me. He's staring at something in front of the truck. Or someone. A silhouette I've memorized.

Dillon.

He stands facing us with his hands on his hips, and his chest heaves like he's fighting for breath and control both. Each violent exhale sends a puff of steam from his mouth and nostrils like a fire-breathing dragon.

Tears freeze to the corners of my eyes, making it difficult to blink them away, and my body deflates. "This is too much for anyone, Mill."

I walk through the snow until I'm face to face with Dillon, mentally preparing myself for a gentle let-down.

A brush-off.

A goodbye.

"Is this what your life is like every day?" he asks. The muscle in his jaw pulses while he waits for my response.

I look back at my ex-husband's home, but Dillon's frozen hands cup my face on either side, and he drags my attention back to him.

"Cleaning up messes one ex at a time and trying to raise my sons to be better. Is that what you mean?"

"Yes," he says through clenched teeth.

I answer with a shrug but can't quite bring my eyes to meet his.

His lips land on mine.

They're warm against the frigid air. Soft against the harshness of my life. Prodding my lips open with his tongue, he savors and demands but gives so much in return that I'm dizzy. All I can do is feel, and experience, and fall head-first into this man who tastes like root beer.

I clench my fists in Dillon's shirt and hear Miller chuckle. He sounds far away, but his boots crunch in the snow beside us, and a few seconds later we're illuminated by his truck's headlights when it roars to life.

Dillon pulls back just enough to rest his forehead against mine. My fingers race to my now-warm lips, and he smiles. He's so close his lips brush against the backs of my fingers.

"W—What was that?"

His eyes sparkle. "That, I hope, was your last first kiss."

I'm shaking my head as his grin grows. It spreads across his face, and like a magical masseuse, the knots in my shoulders slowly relax.

"But…" But what? What the hell do I say to that?

"No buts, Penny. Just give me a chance. I like you. I like you a lot."

"But Eddy. And the boys. I've got…"

"You've got a lot on your plate, but I only have me. I have plenty of room for your mess. I just need a chance to earn it."

My mind goes blank.

"You want to earn my mess?"

Okay, maybe I didn't hear him correctly.

"Your mess. Your heart. You, Penny. I want to earn you."

"I—I." Holy crap. I guess I did hear him.

"You don't have to do anything but give me a chance. We'll take it slow."

My fingers still cover my lips like they can hold the heat from his kiss there for eternity. "This was slow?"

"No." He chuckles. "That was me showing you that you deserve to be taken care of." There's heat in his eyes when he licks his lips. "But I'll go slow from now on."

Miller honks his horn, and I stumble, but Dillon is there to catch me before I land on my ass. "As much fun as this is, we need to get moving," Miller yells from his window.

Dillon holds my hand like I'm precious and tugs me behind him to the truck. He opens the door and sticks his head inside before I can climb in. "Asshole," he mutters, and Miller laughs.

He leans out of the way but keeps a hand pressed to my lower back as I climb into the cab. I have to slide along the bench seat toward Miller so Dillon can climb in behind me.

"Friends," Miller starts with a chuckle.

I glare at him, daring him to say anything else.

"Chance Lake is about to get interesting."

CHAPTER 12

DILLON

I hated leaving Penny home alone with her boys, but short of demanding a sleepover, there wasn't much I could do when Miller announced it was time to head home after the best mac and cheese I'd ever had. I can still taste the rosemary in her cheese sauce on my lips.

Miller's apartment on the backside of the TAC complex is small but surprisingly homey for a single guy. The refrigerator is decorated in colorful artwork, and the counters are full of papers, crayons, glue, and so many other crafting supplies I couldn't name if I wanted to. There are two bedrooms and a bathroom that all three of us took turns using while changing out of our wet clothes from the still-falling snow.

I've just finished taking a piss when Izzy comes barreling into the small room.

Fuck.

I was already tucking but turn to face the toilet so she doesn't get an inappropriate show. In my rush, I almost catch my dick in the zipper and bite back a curse.

"Izzy?"

She turns on the faucet and sticks her little face into the spray with an open mouth. What the hell am I supposed to do here?

Miller arrives in the doorway a second later. "Iz, you have to knock." He looks at me and laughs when I shoot him a dirty look.

She looks between the two of us while swishing water around her mouth, then spits a mouthful of light pink water into the sink.

"But I lost a tooth!" She holds up a tiny white tooth with bright red roots that make me want to gag.

"What if Mr. Dillon had been taking a dump?"

She looks from her dad to me and laughs. "Misters don't poop, Dad."

"They don't?" he asks, crossing his arms over his chest.

"No. Remy said misters are full of shit."

My mouth drops open. I don't know if I should laugh or hold it in. It results in a weird choking sound.

"Izzy. Shit is an adult word. You can't say it."

She shrugs and pushes the tooth closer to me. "See?"

"I see," I say.

"So were ya?" she asks with the tooth still held high in the air. Her mass of unruly hair covers half her face. Why doesn't she pull it back? Wouldn't it be annoying to have it all in your eyes like that? "Well, were ya?" she asks with a tap of her foot, finally brushing back a lock of golden hair.

"Was I what?"

"Pooping?"

"Not this time."

"But you do?" she asks with a frown.

Is this kid serious?

"Poop?" I ask. Confused doesn't begin to describe this interaction.

"Yeah. Do ya?"

Miller laughs but does nothing to intervene.

"Yeah, kid. I poop. We all poop. Everyone poops," I say, throwing my hands in the air.

"Huh." She shrugs and pushes past Miller. "I need a bag, Dad. Think the tooth fairy can get through the storm?"

"I'm sure she'll manage," he says easily. Turning to me, he shrugs. "Want a beer?"

I hold up my hands. "I was taking a piss. After I wash my hands, I'd love one." But even as I say it, I know that's not the truth.

"Piss is a bad word, too, Mr. Dillon," Izzy calls from somewhere in the apartment.

"Izzy! Stop swearing, or I'll wash your mouth out with soap," Miller demands, and I have a newfound respect for him.

"Do you do that?" I ask in a hushed tone.

He pauses and looks at me over his shoulder. "Wash her mouth out with soap?"

"Yeah." I stick my hands into the water and scrub.

"I haven't had to, but I'm a single dad. I'll do whatever it takes to make sure she doesn't end up with the vocabulary of a trucker or like…"

He doesn't finish that sentence, but I'd bet money it ends in *like Eddy.*

I'M SITTING on Miller's sofa that will double as my bed for at least tonight when he comes out of Izzy's room, looking a little haggard.

I heard him sing at least five songs before her incessant questions finally faded to silence. He walks straight to the fridge and removes two more beers. He hands one to me and plops down heavily into the recliner across from me.

I hold it in my hands, but looking at it makes bile rise high in my throat. I didn't tell him that I dumped the first one he gave me.

"Where's her mom?" I ask as a distraction.

He pops the top of his can and raises his eyebrows at me simultaneously. "Cutting right to the tough stuff, huh?"

Now it's my turn to shrug. "You kind of threw me into the deep end with those little girls. I figure it'll make us even."

Miller holds up his beer in silent cheers. "Fair enough. But I didn't know it would be quite like that. It's been a while since I've seen Eddy that bad. And for all her faults, Aster usually does a better job of at least meeting the girl's needs."

"Meeting a need is not the way to parent," I growl.

He nods in agreement. "Bella is chasing her dreams. She was never going to stay in Chance Lake. Not for me, not for anyone. She loves Izzy in her own way, but we knew she'd never give up her dream, and the life of a traveling musician isn't family-friendly. Do you have family?" Miller keeps his tone light, but he's watching me closely.

"Not like you and Izzy."

"What's that mean?"

"It means the Westbrooks include me so I'm not alone, but it's not the same as having a family of your own."

He takes a long pull of his beer. "Is that something you want? A family of your own?"

Is it?

I frown.

The heat that creeps up my neck fires warnings behind my eyelids. "It's not something I've ever aspired to have. I didn't have a great example for a father, so it's not something I ever spent much energy on."

"It sounds like there's a but in there," he says.

"I don't think it's a but. I just can't stop thinking about Dahlia. I never wanted to be a father, but holding her and her sister today? I know if it happened, I wouldn't repeat my father's mistakes."

Miller nods thoughtfully. "There are a lot of kids in Penny's life."

"Yup." I rub my newly sweaty palm on my thighs and lean forward to set the beer down on the coffee table.

"Did you ever picture raising someone else's kids?"

The question has me sitting up straighter. "I've never pictured kids, period. My own or anyone else's."

"Well, you'd better think long and hard about it before you go kissing Penny again because if you hurt her or those kids, they'll never find your body. They've been through enough. Understood?"

I swallow hard past the sadness his statement stirs in my throat. "Yeah," I finally manage.

He leans back in his chair and stares at the ceiling. "You know, Ashton and Nova offered to invest in the TAC."

My head snaps up, but Miller keeps his smiling face pointed at the ceiling. Probably better that way so he can't see the nervous twitch happening in my left eye.

"Why didn't they?"

"Remy declined the offer because they were moving to California. But they did come to an agreement."

"What kind of agreement?"

He sits up and takes a gulp of his beer. "I don't know. They wouldn't tell me, but my gut says it has everything to do with you."

"Me? What makes you say that?" But even as I say it, Ashton's words are unfurling in my mind like a runaway train. I shift uncomfortably and my knee bounces at a rapid pace.

Miller leans forward and hands me a folder I hadn't seen tucked away on an end table. I open it to a prospectus for what appears to be updates to the TAC. Turning to the last page, I find that it's signed by Ashton and Remick Miller. But it's the last line that has my jaw clenching: *Dependent on D.O.H.*

"What is this?" I grip the folder so tightly that my knuckles turn white.

D.O.H. could be purely coincidence.

Or it could be Dillon Owen Henry.

"I found it in Remy's office last week. It appears to be a contingency offer."

"I see that," I grind out. "But what's the original offer?"

He turns a grin my way that has sweat rolling down my spine. "I think that's dependent on you, D.O.H."

Finally, Ashton's words begin to make some fucking sense, but can I do it?

CHAPTER 13

DILLON

The sun finally begins to rise, so I give up all pretense of sleeping. My feet hang off the end of the sofa, but that's not what kept me up all night.

It was the plans for the TAC Miller had handed me. This wouldn't be a six-month gig for me. This is a lifetime commitment, and I'm shocked by how much I think I want it.

All night my mind raced with possibilities. The sports we could offer, the investment it would take. That the trust fund Vanessa left me would finally have a purpose. At some point, I started scribbling plans all over the inside of the folder—things like refinishing the courts and updating the lighting, heating, and cooling systems.

The only other time I've felt this alive in the last twenty years was when I was dancing with Penny and then again when I kissed her.

After Miller went to bed, I spent an hour trying to call Ashton so I could demand answers before I got too ahead of myself, but there was no cell reception.

Tossing the blanket to the side, I stand, work out the

kinks in my lower back, and then reach for my phone. I'm walking around the apartment with it held high in the air when Miller comes out of his room.

"Cell tower's down. You won't get reception for at least a few days." His voice is rough with sleep, and he scratches the side of his jaw.

"What if there's an emergency?" I look out the window. Can I see Penny's house from here?

"Your reaction is pretty telling," Miller says mildly.

"What reaction?"

"Look at yourself. Standing there all grizzly bear, trying to burn a hole through my window to get a look at your lady's house. It's over there, by the way," he says with a smirk and points in the opposite direction of where I'm staring. The wall with absolutely no windows.

"That's not what this is. She's made it very clear what she can and can't have in her life right now."

"Has she? Is that why you kissed her like your life depended on it last night? Is that what she said she could handle?" he asks sarcastically.

He dumps spoon after spoon of coffee grounds into the high-tech coffee machine.

"Are you having company?" I ask, nodding toward the coffee in his hand.

"Nah. It's going to be a long-ass day. Just prepping. I hope you're not too soft 'cause I'm putting you to work today. I wasn't kidding about you being here for a while. Our town is just far enough off the grid that we're usually the last ones to get help from the state. That means all the roads leading to the highway will be unpassable in your Batmobile."

I should be worried that being here for days didn't even raise a flag for me. But calling me soft? That ruffles a couple feathers.

"Soft?" I scoff and arch my back a little bit. And I am certainly not flexing for the guy. "I'm not soft."

"Nah, but shoveling snow and helping thy neighbor is a different set of muscles, city boy."

"Screw you."

He chuckles.

From the hallway Izzy says, "Mr. Dillon needs the soap, Dad." She pads out into the family room wearing a one-piece fuzzy outfit with a rainbow horn sticking off the hood.

I tilt my head to the left, then the right, trying to figure out what the hell she's wearing.

"It's a onesie with a unicorn head," Miller explains. "They even come in adult sizes if you want one."

"We gots Penny one for Christmas. We're twinsies," Izzy screeches much too loudly for this time of day.

Picturing Penny in any costume sends my mind straight into the gutter.

"I don't understand the agreement between Ash and your grandfather," I say. Redirecting us back to safer territory seems like the only option.

"Izzy, sweetie. Go get dressed. We'll drop you off with Penny and the boys before we head out to check on Chance Lake." He doesn't even finish speaking before she's off and running back the way she came. "She hates being an only child."

I'm not sure if he says it to himself or me, so I don't comment, and after a minute, he turns to me with a giant mug of black coffee. "I don't have cream, and I ran out of milk, but sugar's on the counter."

I take it gratefully.

"To answer your question," he says. "Remy's looking for someone to be as invested as he was. In this place. In Chance Lake. And in the kids themselves. He isn't just looking for money. He's searching for a successor."

"And it's not you?" I ask over Ashton's words screaming in my head.

"The owner, well, let's say he's old school, and this isn't a business to him. It's a way of life."

"I already told you, I don't have the capital, and I can't be self-employed. I have Izzy to think about. Health insurance alone would break me if I didn't get it through the school. If the right opportunity came about and I could work here with benefits though? I'd be on it in a heartbeat. I grew up here. So many kids grew up in this building so their parents could work."

He walks across the room and picks up a large photo album. "Remy has been free childcare for Chance Lake since before I was born. I bet there's not a single person in this town who hasn't had dinner catered by him at least once when their parents couldn't make it home in time."

Heat fills my chest. Remy is what Ashton's dad was to me as a kid.

Every inch of the photo album is covered with photos. Page after page of kids' faces with a man who has a kind smile and grumpy eyes. He gets progressively older as I flip through.

"He sounds like a hero." I pause on a photo of a younger Miller and the man named Remy.

"To some of these kids, he is."

"Then why wouldn't the town approve his plans? It doesn't make any sense."

Miller shrugs. "Thirty years ago, it was a different town. Half the businesses now are owned by people forty and under. It's a younger demographic. If he was physically capable of the campaigning and labor required, I have no doubt he'd get it passed today."

"So there's a town vote or something?"

He scrubs a hand through his hair. "Chance Lake has its

own bylaws, so they essentially make up their own rules, to a certain extent. It's governed as a 'community of entities.'"

He holds up his hand to ward off any questions. "Don't ask me what that means, I have no idea. The town fully embraced love and peace in the sixties. They ousted the mayor and all traditional leadership, and now it takes town meetings with a majority vote to put up holiday lights, get a park bench, or open a new business. You have to fit the 'vibe' to be approved. But at its core, this town is made up of a group of people who care about where they live and the people in it."

"Hmm."

"Yeah." He rocks back on his heels but stays silent. He's allowing me time to work through something I have a feeling he already knows.

"And Ashton can't get the votes because he doesn't live here. Even though he still owns a property in town?"

"Right. And while Remy liked Ashton…"

A protective streak flares in my chest. "What?"

"I mean, have you seen Ashton? He isn't exactly the town jock. He even said he can't make a basket to save his life."

Relief washes through me that the hesitation isn't about him personally. Ashton is a great man, but an athlete he is not.

Laughter starts in my gut and works its way up my body until it bubbles in my throat. "That's true. So what happens next?"

"Well, it seems like Ashton and Remy have a plan. They just don't feel like sharing it yet, so we wait."

Fucking Ashton always has a plan, but now, maybe I do too.

"Yesterday, you said Ashton's been trying to get Penny and me together for years. What did you mean?"

"I have a feeling if Eddy hadn't forced your hand, you still would have wound up in Chance Lake eventually."

I scan the open folder on Miller's coffee table.

Dependent on D.O.H.

"Yeah, maybe."

Six months. He said he wants me to be here for half a year. That asshole had a plan all right, and he only told me half of it.

"Get dressed. We'll grab breakfast at Penny's."

My heart thumps against my chest cavity like a dog with an itch. Another meal in close quarters with my girl? My body screams hell yes, but my brain pumps the brakes.

"We can't show up unannounced," I argue, but the protest is weak.

"Welcome to small-town life, Dill. Trust me when I say this, she'll be expecting us."

I toss an incredulous expression his way, but he flashes a wide grin. "Well, she'll be expecting me because when life gets gritty like this, we're all the other has. She'll watch Izzy while I check on our neighbors."

That ache the size of the Grand Canyon in my chest keeps me from moving.

Miller watches me closely. "Penny's parents had her later in life. They passed away a few years ago."

"I know," I grumble. "She told me."

He smirks. "I forgot you probably know a lot more than I give you credit for. Three years of coffee dates is a long time to get to know someone."

I nod.

"Most of the friends she had growing up are still in town, but Eddy was really good at isolating her and the boys. I think it's how he hid his infidelity for so long, but she hasn't managed or is too embarrassed to try and rebuild the bridges he burned."

The coffee scalds my throat as I chug it down. I don't want to hear this shit from Miller. Freaking Matty Miller. I want to hear it from her. Straight from her.

"I'll be ready in five minutes," I say.

He gestures toward the armchair in the corner. "Those are all clean. Pick whatever you want, but it's going to be fucking cold, so dress in layers."

Beggars can't be choosers, so I nod in thanks and dig through a pile of unfolded laundry until I find a thermal and a pair of jeans.

I draw the line at wearing the guy's underwear.

"You'll want long johns too," he calls to my back, and I freeze in the hallway. "We're going to be outside all day. I'll run you over to Remy's for snow gear, but trust me, man. It's frigid out, and the radar shows a six-hour window before the next storm. Layers will be your friend."

Backtracking, I grab a pair of thermal pants from his pile and head into the bathroom. This time, I remember to lock the door.

CHAPTER 14

PENNY

"*A*ster? What are you doing here?" I open the door wider so she can scoot in next to me. Snow is frozen like icicles to the hair sticking out beneath her hat.

"We don't have heat," she says, shoving Marigold into my arms and dragging Dahlia behind her.

Do come in, my inner bitch says, but I learned a long time ago to keep her in check.

With a heavy sigh, I shut the door and shift the baby into the crook of my arm.

"Where's Eddy?" I ask as she starts to unbutton her coat.

Everything in my soul wants to hate her, but the mom in me keeps me civil. I don't know if she knew Eddy was married or not. He did. And she was an eighteen-year-old girl, not even a woman, when he knocked her up.

"He left an hour ago. Said something about finding someone to fix the heat, but…"

She doesn't have to finish that sentence. We both know he went in search of booze.

My gaze drops to the little angel in my arms with rosy, red cheeks and long lashes that flutter in sleep.

"Oh, you know what? I should probably wait at the house, right? Just in case Eddy has someone come to fix the heat?"

"Right, I'm sure he's all over it," Kai says behind me. Turning my head, I find him on his knees, helping Dahlia out of her coat. "Pull your arm through, Lia."

I don't have a chance to say anything before Aster is out the door and literally running from my house. It's probably for the best. She isn't fond of my boys, and she hates that they refuse to call their sisters by their full names. To them, it's Lia and Mari.

"We'll see her tomorrow or the next day," Kai grumbles.

I take a long breath and force my emotions down deep. Lia stares up at Kai like he's Santa, and it hits me then, but not for the first time, how unfair life can be.

Marigold tenses in my arms and lets out a wail that could wake the dead.

"Mari's here?" Gage comes running from the kitchen and slides across the floor until he stops in front of me. He holds out his arms in a gimme, gimme motion, but I usher him away from the door with my free hand.

"Go sit on the sofa, and then you can hold her while I make a bottle."

"Tweef," Lia whispers to Kai. One hand covers her mouth as she leans toward his ear. When she finds me watching, her eyes go wide like a little girl used to getting into trouble for speaking.

"Lia, you don't have to whisper here, okay?" I say gently.

She nods but looks to Kai and mumbles, "Marwe, tweef." She points to the baby in my arms and then to her teeth.

"Mari's teething? She's getting teeth?"

Lia nods, and I smile. "Thank you for telling me. I think I have something to help her, okay? Sometimes a little medicine can make them not hurt so much."

"No wonder Aster took off," Kai says.

I don't disagree, but I won't talk ill about her with him or in front of her girls. "Kai, that's enough. Why don't you find out if Lia's had breakfast?"

The door bursts open and almost knocks the little girl over as Izzy enters, covered in snow like the abominable snowman.

Taking hold of Lia's arm, I tug her into the hallway to make room, but it does no good as Miller and Dillon cross the threshold.

I suddenly wish I could bury my face in the snow to cool off. What the hell is Dillon doing here? Dressed like—like that?

Lia notices Dillon when he takes off his hat and catapults herself at his leg.

He stands frozen while we all watch.

"Dewey," she says quietly.

I forget how to breathe as he gently lifts her in his massive arms. "Hey, Lia." His voice is scratchy like he just woke up and hasn't had enough coffee, but he looks to Kai for confirmation that he got her name right.

Kai nods with a frown.

Is he jealous that Lia's attaching herself to Dillon? I search his face, but he gives nothing away.

Oh, this could be bad.

The last thing Kai needs is to feel like he's being replaced. Again.

Mental list four hundred and thirty-two, for today. Talk to Kai about his feelings.

"What's going on?" I ask.

"Dillon's going to help me with the roundup," Miller says.

"Roundup?" Dillon asks, but his eyes are on the little girl in his arms. She burrows into his side like a koala bear.

"We have a list of people we check on for holidays, inclement weather, that sort of thing. Then we'll make the rounds to make sure all the businesses around the green are prepared for the storms coming through," Miller explains.

"He can't go dressed like that," Kai says, pointing at Dillon.

"First stop after breakfast is Remy's. We'll grab him some gear and then head out. Are you helping me today, or does Mom need you here?"

Kai looks from Miller to me, then his gaze lands on Dillon, and again I can't read his expression.

"It's up to you, Kai. It might be good for you to get out and burn off some energy," I say softly.

His gaze flies around the house to his siblings and cousin, and Gage takes that opportunity to pull on Dillon's shirt.

"Hey, Mr. Dillon. 'Member me?"

Dillon's smile is wide and genuine. "You're Gage, and I'm Dill Pickle."

Gage doubles over laughing, and then he looks up to Lia in his arms. "Dill Pickle's funny, but I like Dewey better. Can I call you that too?"

Before I can answer, Dillon shrugs. "Sure, bud. Why not?"

"Okay, bye, Dewey. See ya." Gage barrels through the house, presumably to find Izzy at the TV.

Kai hasn't said anything, but his eyes haven't missed a second of everything happening. Once again, I'm hit with the fact that I don't know how to help my own son sometimes.

It's a heartbreaking realization.

"I can handle the kids, Kai. I'm working remotely every day this week, but Mr. Blaine knows what's going on. I'll be fine," I promise him.

He nods. "Okay." He takes Lia from Dillon's arms with a promise of food and walks toward the kitchen.

"Breakfast?" I ask. It comes out on a squeak, and I turn away from the guys, close my eyes, and shake my head.

Get it together, Penny!

Dillon's heat reaches me before I hear him. "You don't have to cook for all of us, Penny. I admit to ordering takeout most nights, but eggs and pancakes I can handle."

His hand lands on the small of my back as he turns sideways to pass me in the hallway.

"No, that's…"

He keeps moving. "Why don't you get work done that you can't do with a house full of kids? Miller can watch them while I make breakfast."

My mouth drops open, and my feet stop moving.

"Teamwork. It's a novelty, huh?" Miller whispers at my side. He takes Mari from me with a smirk.

"But I work in the kitchen."

"Then get to it." He gently nudges me forward. "As soon as we eat, we're out of here. The second storm might be worse than the first."

Swallowing hard, I pluck the hair elastic on my wrist, then shake out my hands and walk into the kitchen where my laptop is set up in the corner on a small card table.

Dillon and Kai stand together in front of the pantry door. Lia scoots past me toward the TV.

"I'll start the eggs and see if I can find some protein. Can you mix the pancake batter?" Dillon asks Kai.

"I can do a lot of things most kids won't do, Mr. Dillon."

Dillon's hand rises in the air behind Kai's back like he wants to reach out and comfort him, but he pulls it back at the last minute.

My stomach flips.

"I know you can. Let's get this done for your mom. One less thing she has to worry about, then we'll go take care of Miller's fucking list. Ah, sorry," Dillon grumbles, looking around the room, and Kai laughs.

"If you think that's the first time someone has sworn at me, you haven't met my dad."

Dillon's posture goes stiff, and his tone is low but controlled when he speaks. "First, there's a difference between swearing in front of you and swearing at you. I will never swear at you. Understood?"

Kai nods, and I'd be willing to bet he rolled his eyes, but Dillon doesn't let it faze him. "Secondly, call me Dillon. Mr. Dillon makes me sound old. And I will not swear in front of you again, either."

"Yeah, right." Kai laughs. "It's fine, really."

This time Dillon does reach for Kai. With his hand on his shoulder, I feel Kai's nervous energy from where I stand frozen in the doorway.

"You have no reason to believe me, but I keep my word," Dillon says with the patience and understanding of someone who hasn't always had an easy life.

Kai shrugs him off, and I feign a cough to announce my arrival. "You guys good?"

"Yeah," Kai says, but his voice is strained.

"Anything I can do?"

Kai inclines his head toward Dillon, but I don't understand the look they share. I scrunch my nose as I watch them.

"Nah, we've got it," Kai grumbles. "Mr., I mean, Dillon's right. You should get anything you can't do with crying babies done now."

Kai takes the Bisquick from the pantry, and Dillon moves to my fridge. He rifles through the contents and comes out with bacon and a package of sausage links.

I forget to breathe when he turns to me with them raised in the air. He should not look so right in my kitchen. He shouldn't feel so right in my space.

He can't feel so right in my space.

But he does. And it's becoming harder and harder to ignore.

"Okay to cook these?" he asks with a hypnotic rumble in his voice.

I purse my lips and nod. Afraid of what I'll say if I open my mouth, I keep nodding. He tilts his head, watching me, and the outside corners of his eyes crinkle when he smiles.

So, I smile back.

We just keep smiling at each other like a couple of fools.

"Work, Penny," he finally says. His voice is full of teasing that skates across my body like a feather and jolts me into action.

"Work. Right. Over here. Okay then. Let me know if you need anything. I'll be here. Working."

Turning my back on him, I mentally slap myself. I'm not someone who babbles like that. Not anymore, anyway.

Dillon Henry is dangerous to my entire being. He can squeeze my heart with a kind word. He can muddle my brain with a single smile. He can break me if I'm not careful.

I sit at my tiny table in the corner, and the sounds of a busy house engulf me. The girls babble. The boys laugh. Miller thumps around the house with heavy feet. But Dillon and Kai work in silence. They move around each other with ease in the tight space, and I can't take my eyes off them.

They look like a family, and it breaks my heart.

CHAPTER 15

DILLON

*S*wiping at the back of my neck for the twentieth time, I finally rest my forehead against the cool glass of the window.

Miller drives slowly with his plow lowered, though I still can't figure out how he knows what the hell he's plowing. There's nothing to mark the streets. He just inches forward like he has every bend and turn memorized.

Kai sits between us with his hands in his lap, and even though Miller sings whatever country song is on the radio at the top of his lungs, I have a feeling Kai doesn't hear a single beat. His eyes are glassy and focused straight ahead. The kid barely even blinks.

It's been a weird morning. Moving through Penny's home with him at my side unlocked something in my chest I haven't been able to get rid of. It's a constant buzzing that sends shocks of heat through every vein.

We pull into the TAC garage, where my Tesla sits untouched, and for the first time since I bought it, I'm overcome with a sense of guilt about the price tag it came with.

How many homes could that car heat this winter?

Guilt over things I've worked hard for has never been an issue for me. But today? Today, it hits differently.

"Why are we here?" I ask as we exit his truck.

"Remy doesn't do anything the easy way. His house is out back by the lake, but he refuses to put in a driveway, so to get through the woods, you have to take a four-wheeler or a snow machine," Miller says with a grin. "Have you ever ridden a sled?"

The buzzing in my chest gets stronger. "No," I say, grinding my teeth to keep from saying anything else.

"No worries." His eyes hold a challenge as he stands with his hands on his hips. "You can ride with Kai or me. Your choice."

He leads us to a bay in the garage with a handful of snow machines. I've never seen one in person, but the seat reminds me of a very wide motorcycle. Now I understand his smirk. I'll be on the back, holding onto whomever I ride with.

Awesome. Even my inner voice is full of snark today.

Even Kai is trying to suppress a smile.

"Can you drive this thing?" I ask him.

"Yeah." He chuckles. "Remy taught me after..." He tears his gaze away from mine. "After my dad left."

My fingers burn with the need to give fucking Eddy the finger and maybe a couple of black eyes.

"I'll ride with Kai." I slide my jaw side to side to work out the tension.

Kai looks at me with a questioning expression.

"I trust you more than him," I say under my breath. "Pretty sure Miller will do everything he can to dump me off the back of one of these things just to watch me tumble."

A grin appears on the boy's face. "Yeah, you're probably right."

"One hundred percent," Miller confirms with a laugh. "Let's get going. We've only got a few hours before the next storm."

Kai climbs onto a bright red machine and guides it down a small ramp. When he's outside, he scoots forward on the seat, then motions for me to follow him.

So, I do. I climb on behind him and trust that this kid won't try to kill me. As soon as I'm on, he relaxes into the seat. This must feel like freedom to him. I remember how much I needed that at his age. I also know that trust doesn't come easy to him; I can sense it. But he's trusted me twice now, and I don't take that lightly.

The ride to Remy's place is rough, though I doubt it's because Kai was trying to kill me. The terrain is unmarked, but they forge a path until we come to what looks like a lighthouse overlooking a lake.

What in the hell?

"Remy has a funny sense of humor," Kai calls over the wind that pummels us from across the lake.

"His house is a lighthouse? On a lake?"

"Yup." Kai stomps through the snow, and I follow in his steps since I don't have snow gear on yet.

Miller beats us to the door and opens it wide without knocking. I close the door behind us and take a deep breath of warm air filled with pine and apple pie. It's an odd mix that has my body relaxing before my mind catches up to it.

It smells like Christmas in here.

"It always smells like this. Year-round," Kai whispers when he catches me inhaling again.

"Huh." The circular room we're in looks like a storage unit full of apparel and gear for every type of weather, from fly-fishing poles to snow boots.

We all tromp up a spiral staircase to the third floor, where an old man sits on a stool near a window with a pair of binoculars held to his eyes. He's wearing a flannel shirt and jeans held together at the knees with duct tape.

Duct tape. He's sitting on property he must have dumped millions into over the years, yet he wears jeans that are probably older than me with holes covered in silver tape.

I don't understand.

"Remy, meet Dillon, the Westbrook friend," Miller says, leaning in to hug the old man.

"You're early," he says without looking at us.

"Actually, we're late. We stopped by Penny's first. She has Eddy's girls today too, so we helped settle them before we took off."

"Not you, Matty. Dillon. He's early. Wasn't expecting him till next month."

Miller turns to me with a wide grin but speaks to his grandfather. "You were expecting Dillon? Here?"

The old man finally turns my way and lowers the binoculars. He has round cheeks that are red from the elements and icy blue eyes that cut through my protective layers. His skin is leathered, like he's never met a bottle of sunscreen, and it makes him look older than his seventy years. I feel like a kid in the principal's office as he scans me from head to toe, but his expression stays the same. I have no idea what he's thinking.

"Yup," he says, then turns back to the window. "Not exactly what I was expecting, but we'll see how he does."

"How I do with what?" I ask.

"Finding your place," he says cryptically.

My place is with Penny. But I tame the forcefulness of that thought before it knocks me over.

"Why was he expecting you here?" Kai asks with a frown.

"I'm not sure, bud. But I bet it has everything to do with Ashton."

Kai turns away and crashes into stacked milk crates that have him hurtling toward the metal stairs. I move without thought and grab the back of his jacket just in time to keep him from hitting the floor.

"You okay?" I ask, lifting enough so he can find his feet.

His shoulders are tense, and his cheeks flush pink.

"Yeah. Thanks. I keep tripping over my own dang feet," he mumbles.

I snort and take a step back. "That's what happens when you go through quick growth spurts, kid. You turn into a baby giraffe for a few years."

Remy chuckles. "Already protectin'." He shakes his head, but he almost smiles as he says it.

"I didn't want him to get hurt," I mutter. Embarrassment and a sensation I can't place makes my spine tingle.

"'Cause you care. Nothin' to be ashamed about. It's about time someone was carin' on that family."

Kai jams his hands into his jacket pockets and stares at the floor. His lips are moving, but no words come out.

"Get him suited up to make the rounds," Remy says. "Levi told me that John was already on the roof again this morning."

"Jesus," Miller mutters, then looks at me and laughs. "Don't worry. You're about to meet a bunch of people. You'll learn their names eventually. John is an eighty-year-old man with two grown sons. They own the only restaurant in town, but John continues to climb onto the roof to shovel the snow off instead of waiting for one of his boys to show up and do it."

My mouth falls open in shock.

"He fell off twice last year," Kai says. "But he didn't even break anything. It's crazy."

He sounds crazy.

"Oh," Remy says with a chuckle. "Cassie and James were

at it again this morning, too. You might have to break them up if they're still snow blowing when you drive by."

"Ugh, not again." Miller grabs me by the elbow and guides me toward the stairs. "Cassie and James have…let's just say they have history."

"And dueling coffee shops," Kai points out.

"Technically, Books N'Beans is books and coffee," Miller corrects. "And Dough-Joes is a bakery slash coffee shop. They're separated by a salon and a huge misunderstanding none of us know about."

"How do you know it's a misunderstanding if you don't know about it?" I ask.

"Isn't a misunderstanding the only thing that could keep two people in love apart? What else would it be?"

As I descend the stairs, I scratch my head and look at Miller over my shoulder. "This town sounds like it has a ton of baggage."

"Baggage lets you know you're alive," Remy calls after us. "See you soon, Dillon."

"Bye?" Pretty sure I'll see him again.

While some might call it fate pushing me toward Penny, I know the truth. In my life, fate looks a lot like Ashton Westbrook.

MILLER'S TRUCK rolls to a stop in the middle of the street. We're the only idiots driving around in this shit anyway.

The snow comes and goes in waves, but the flakes seem to triple in size as the sky gets darker.

"What the hell are they doing?" I've got my nose pressed to the window like a kid seeing snow for the first time.

We watch as a hot pink snowsuit blows snow from a

bright red machine toward another plume of snow coming from the opposite direction.

A knock on the window startles me. An older woman with smiling eyes stares in. I lower the window.

"Abbie, what the hell are they doing?" Miller asks the woman.

She sighs and hands over a thermos and some paper cups. "James plowed Cassie's walkway, but she doesn't want any help from him, so she started snow blowing his sidewalk. Now they're just blowing snow back and forth while cursing under their breaths."

"How long have they been at it?" Miller sighs.

"Goin' on an hour and a half now. Well, this time. James ran out of gas and had to run home to fill up. While he was gone, Cassie worked her way down the entire street."

Miller curses under his breath, then jumps out of the truck. I watch as he walks first to Cassie, then to James, and then finally stands in the middle of them with his arms raised like he's brokering a peace treaty.

Hell, maybe he is.

He holds up his fingers, and it looks like he's counting to three. When his third finger raises, the noise from both snow blowers fades. The two enemies turn their backs and walk to their respective corners like it's an old-fashioned pistol duel.

"What the he—ck just happened?" I mutter. A gust of cold air sweeps into the cab of the truck.

"My guess is Miller told them to grow up and gave them each a corner of the green to clear. In opposite directions," the old woman to my right says. "He had to separate them like that over the summer at the Fourth of July party after James showed up. Unannounced."

I shake my head at the nonsense of it all. "The green?" I ask.

"It's what we call the town center. In the summer, it's all grass," Kai says.

Miller stomps his boots against the footrail of the truck, then climbs into the driver's seat.

"What was that?" I ask.

"Life. Messy. Complicated. Life." He grunts. Leaning forward and looking out my window, he asks, "Are the volunteers all set for the night at the firehouse?"

"All set. Two Reid brothers are on tonight. The other is manning the brewery," Abbie says, her eyes catching on Kai before a silent conversation happens between Abbie and Miller in one look.

"I'll drop these two off at home, then check on Three Brother's Brewing," Miller promises, and I suddenly understand the look. He's going to look for Eddy.

"You're a good boy, Matty." She thumps the passenger door three times, then steps back, and Miller puts the truck in drive while I roll up the window.

"You see, living in a small town isn't just about waking up and going to bed here. It's about the people who know your business. The ones who show up with casseroles when someone dies and cakes for birthdays. It's about the people who become your family," Miller says to no one in particular. "Even when you think all family can do is let you down. Small towns have a way of proving even the most cynical wrong."

His words could have been for Kai or for me. I think they hit us both in different ways.

At Heirlooms restaurant, I meet Lucas and Levi. After we help them clear a path to their barn and make sure the animals are fed and taken care of for at least twenty-four hours, we move on to the next item on Miller's list.

Then the next.

And the next.

Miller introduced me to each new person as a TAC-in-training but wouldn't tell me what it meant. Whatever it was, it seemed to put the community at ease around me.

It's late afternoon before we head back to Penny's house in silence. The scraping sound of the plow as it hits concrete picks at the scab around my heart. A wound I thought had scarred over years ago suddenly feels fresh and fragile.

I turn to look at Kai. I've done it a lot today. What would my life have been like without the influence of Mr. Westbrook? Where would I be?

I'd like to be that person for Kai. I just have to figure out how the hell to do it. And there's the TAC and the plans that have hovered at the edge of my consciousness since Miller handed me that folder.

I can be that person for Kai and his brothers. I know I can.

I glance at Miller, who is watching me and Kai nearly as much as he is the empty, snowy road. He raises his brow in a silent question I can't begin to decipher.

Maybe he's asking himself the same thing I am.

Could I be the man this family needs? Would Penny let me?

We pull into Penny's driveway, and I let Kai out but take my time heading to the house. My steps are heavy in the snow. They're weighted down by impossible questions.

"Penny will protect her boys first and foremost," Miller says as he rounds the truck. "But what she needs is someone who wants to be here. Do you want to be here, Dillon?"

Movement at the door catches my eye. Penny stands in the doorframe, hugging a squirming Kai. She lifts her smile to Miller and me, and my breath stalls in my lungs.

The warm buzzing in my chest spreads throughout my body at that smile, and I have a sense of belonging that I haven't had since I was a young boy. Young enough to believe in magic and not yet tainted by the realities of other people's choices.

I've always thought that a life full of choice wasn't for me. But maybe it's that the right choices haven't been presented to me yet.

For the first time I can remember, I want to make a choice. I want to choose Penny Mulligan, and I want to choose her boys.

CHAPTER 16

PENNY

Dillon and Miller stand in front of the truck with their hands in their pockets. Miller has his back to me, but Dillon? Dillon's face is a flurry of emotion as he watches Kai and me.

"Dillon did good today," Kai says, pulling free from a hug that has gone on longer than he'd like.

"Oh yeah?" I look back outside one last time, and when neither man moves to come in, I shut the door. "That's good, right?"

"We got through Miller's list in half the time, so yeah." He hangs up his coat and looks around. "Are you okay?"

I look down at my sweatshirt that has spit-up down the front and my sweatpants that are fraying on the thighs and at the cuffs. "Yeah, just another day."

He leans forward and pulls something from my messy bun. Pinching it between his fingers, he holds up a sticky piece of a teething biscuit. "Did…" He glances behind me into the family room and lowers his voice. "Did Dad show up?"

I smile sadly. "No, but Aster said she has a space heater and is waiting for him."

Kai's face falls. No matter how many times his dad disappoints him, there's still a sad little boy in there hoping for the best.

The front door opens, and rich, manly laughter fills my home. Miller stomps his feet on the porch and enters. Dillon does the same until we're all crowded into my six-by-six foyer.

All three of them share a look, then turn to me.

"Oh my God. It smells freaking amazing in here," Dillon says, pointing his nose in the air to get a better whiff. Then he leans forward into Kai's space. "Freaking isn't a swear where I come from. Is it here?"

Kai pales, then looks at me, and I shrug. "I mean, I don't want the eight-year-old saying it, but once in a while from Kai isn't the end of the world."

Kai's grin is blinding as color seeps back into his cheeks.

Dillon nudges him with his elbow. "I keep my promises, kid. All. The. Freaking. Time."

My son's head bobbles, and he averts his eyes.

Does Dillon have any idea how powerful that statement is for a family like mine?

Tears prick the corners of my eyes, so I quickly turn away from them. "I made beef stew in the slow cooker, and the bigger kids helped make rolls from scratch. It should be ready soon."

"We're going to shower," Miller calls as I retreat. My mind temporarily seizes on Dillon in my shower.

Using my soap.

My towel.

Gah. I move even faster so they can't see me fan myself.

"Ah, yeah. Okay. Show Dillon where everything is. Okay?"

"Don't you want to show me?" Dillon's husky voice murmurs into my hair.

I'm so startled that I nearly scream. I drag my hand up to

my chest like I can physically hold my heart in place as it tries to escape through my throat.

"Geez, Dillon." My voice is breathy as I turn to face him.

He's wearing a blinding smile and a thermal shirt with small patches of sweat on his chest and under his arms. Proof that he put in a full day's work with Miller.

Holy shit.

"S—Sorry," I stutter. "It's hot in here. Right? I'm not used to having so many people in my house. Maybe I should turn down the heat." I blink rapidly, then scan the room like a petty thief.

He takes a step forward. I take two back.

Looking behind him, I don't see Miller or Kai.

"They're taking the first showers."

"You won't have any hot water left if they go first."

His gaze rakes over me from head to toe, and my body flushes with embarrassment. Normally when Dillon sees me, I'm putting forth my best effort. I hate to admit it, but I get up an hour early on Wednesdays to put myself together. For him? For me? I don't know. But I always feel good when he stares at me with that look in his eyes.

But even as I stand here in holey pants and a vomit-splattered shirt, he has the same gleam in his eyes. Like he's mentally counting backward so he doesn't maul me right here on the floor.

Either I'm completely out of practice with flirting, or I'm in some serious freaking trouble.

"I think a cold shower is exactly what I need," he growls.

I gulp like a bullfrog, and he laughs. His tone is warm and inviting. It's a caress in the dark that reaches into the deepest parts of my being.

"Oh," is what I manage to say. "Right." I can't seem to string a sentence together, so I turn quickly, searching for a distraction. When I don't find one, I spin again and face plant against his chest. "Do you always move so quietly? Like a, like a…"

I tilt my head back to find him smiling down at me. His left hand lands on my hip, and he uses the index finger on his right hand to brush a piece of hair off my face.

"What are you doing?" I whisper, trying not to memorize how he smells. Masculine and spicy, with a hint of campfire. But not the stinky kind of campfire, the kind that reminds you of s'mores and hot chocolate. Where did his root beer scent go?

"I have no fucking idea," he admits. His gaze never wavers. He doesn't back away. We stand suspended in time while our breaths mingle like hot buttered rum on a cold night. Our scents meld into one.

"Why don't you smell like root beer anymore?" It slips out, and I wish I could hide because who asks that? But his eyes are alight with humor.

He reaches into his pocket and pulls out an old-fashioned root beer barrel hard candy. "I like that you noticed. It means you're as in tune with me as I am with you. I chew these suckers up whenever I'm nervous, I have since I was a kid. I crushed one in the elevator every time I came to see you."

With honesty shining in his eyes, he says, "I'm not nervous anymore, Penny."

I don't know what to say to that. He was nervous to see me? Him? To see me? He's completely ridiculous and smells completely delicious.

"I can't believe I'm so focused on how we smell."

His grin widens into a big toothy smile, and I frown a little.

"What?"

Dillon leans forward so the scruff of his jaw scrapes across the skin on my cheek when he speaks. "I love how we smell too, Penny. Like us. Like home. I like it a whole fucking lot."

And I'm done. My knees shake and threaten to toss me to the floor, but he tightens his grip on my hip and holds me steady. It's impossible not to feel every inch of his hard body standing like this.

Every.

Freaking.

Inch.

"What are you doing?" I repeat in self-defense. I need a defense here. I'm floating out in the sea of Dillon without an anchor to hold me steady.

His lips ghost over my cheek, to my temple, and then he takes a small step back. Then another, until he's leaning against the stove with his feet crossed at the ankles.

"Are you a planner, Penny?"

The sudden change of topic has my head spinning. Combine that with the loss of heat he created when he stepped back, and it's a wonder I can even form a coherent thought, let alone speak.

"Yes. I try to be. Why?" With three kids, I have to plan. I need to schedule and prepare for every eventuality. I make mental lists for my lists.

He knows this.

We've talked about it.

A lot.

On Wednesdays.

"I don't think I've ever had a plan. Not one that I made myself," he says lazily. Slowly. His Southern drawl is in full swing, like he has all the time in the world.

"I'm sorry?" I don't know what to say, so *I'm sorry* is what pops out.

His eyes crinkle when he smiles. "Didn't I tell you to stop apologizing?"

"Sor—Well, what would you like me to say?"

"I thought choices were for other people, but now I'm thinking that maybe I was waiting for the right choice to present itself."

What the what?

"I'm not sure I understand," I say. Needing something to do with my hands, I stab at the button on the slow cooker three times to turn it off.

"I like it here," he says, changing topics again.

Hello, cyclone. I can't keep up.

"I'm glad?" Where is he going with this?

"Are you?" His voice is low, nearly a whisper, and he's studying me with an expression I've never seen before.

Is he nervous?

The muscle in his jaw flexes. He's watching me watch him, and that flutter in my chest bursts into flames.

"I—I am," I stutter. "Chance Lake is a great community. Close-knit. Kind, for the most part. I'm happy you like it. Especially since you got stranded here because of my son."

"I have a feeling I would have ended up here eventually anyway." That small crease appears between his eyebrows. "Actually, I know I would have."

I tilt my head to the side and pluck the hair elastic that's a permanent fixture around my right wrist. "Why do you say that?"

"Ashton asked me to stay at his place. He wants me to take on an opportunity here. One that would remove me from Envision, get me out of the city and closer to you."

Mental list four thousand: have a word with Ashton.

"What kind of opportunity?" I ask. "There's not a lot of need for security here. There are more cows than people. I'm confused."

Dillon's body relaxes a little more as he leans against my stove. "I think Ashton likes to be a sneaky helping hand, especially if he thinks it's in the best interest of someone he cares about. I also think he's trying to play matchmaker. Possibly has been for a long time."

My heart rate picks up at his admission.

I know Nova likes the idea of Dillon and me, but I didn't realize that extended to Ashton. Nova is also aware of all the reasons it's a bad idea.

"He made a deal with Remy."

I blink at that information. "For the TAC?"

Dillon nods and watches me carefully. "But I think it all hinges on a missing piece."

My stomach flips. Sweat gathers in my hair at the base of my neck.

"What missing piece?" I whisper.

His eyes search mine. It's like he's pulling secret after secret from each of my irises, and no matter how hard I try, I can't close myself off from him. Not when he's opening himself up so completely.

It's terrifying and exhilarating and everything I can't have.

"Me. I think they want me here. Permanently."

CHAPTER 17

DILLON

I watch her closely for a reaction, and she doesn't disappoint. Penny's cheeks flush, and the pulse in the side of her neck throbs an uneven beat. When she licks those swollen lips, my entire body feels it.

"Here?" she squeaks. "As in here, here?" Her hands gesture around the small kitchen, and I struggle to keep my grin contained. But when her eyes go comically round, I let the smile out.

She's so damned sexy.

I glance through the open doorway to check on the kids. Gage, Lia, and Izzy sit with Mari in some sort of baby chair between them. Their eyes are glassy as they stare at the screen, and the tiny but annoying gnome that sits in my chest telling me families are for other people gives a rough kick against my rib cage.

I ignore the angry little chest-goblin and turn my attention back to Penny.

"Are we friends, Penny?" Maintaining this calm façade by keeping my voice smooth and even takes work. My heart is jackhammering against my chest, and my stomach twists like a tie-dyed T-shirt.

She nods three times, and I watch as her throat works to swallow. "Yes, of course we are."

"Friends tell each other the truth, right?" Never releasing her gaze from mine, I move a step closer. I can't help it. She hooked me years ago, and now she's reeling me in.

"Always," she says firmly. "Honesty is paramount, Dillon. I won't accept anything less from anyone in my life. Not anymore."

There's my sexy, strong woman, but the subtle reminder of her ex darkens my mood. What the hell did he do to her? But that's a conversation for another day.

I move forward again, happy as fucking sunshine when she inhales a shaky breath.

"Are we friends here, in your kitchen? Or are we still coworkers?" My voice dips lower, and she blinks. Her eyelashes flutter on her cheekbones like butterfly kisses I want to plant myself.

"We're not really coworkers, Dillon. You and Lochlan, yes. I'm an assistant, not—"

"Don't do that," I growl. That domineering tone flows through me, unexpected and focused on caring for the woman who cares for everyone else. "Don't diminish your role at the Bryer-Blaine. If you ask anyone in that hotel, they'll tell you who keeps the day-to-day running. Lochlan may make the decisions on paper, but everyone knows you're the one who executes. So do not downplay your importance at work, in life, or with me."

She gulps in that oddly endearing way she has, and my cheeks hurt from smiling so much. I can't help it. Now that we're out of the office, it's like her presence alone makes my lips curl into a smile every single time she's near.

"Okay," she finally says and steps back, but my body is so

in tune with hers that when her left leg shifts, so does my right one. We move in tandem like marionettes.

She holds my strings, and I never want them severed.

"So, Penny Mulligan." Her name is delicious on my tongue. "Friends. Friends who are honest. I'm going to be real fucking honest for a minute." I lower my voice to barely above a whisper, and she lifts her head up like she's straining to hear me. "You look gorgeous."

She snorts, then chokes and ducks her head, but we're standing so close that when she bends forward on a laugh, her forehead rests against my chest. She jerks back, but I crowd her even more.

"Right," she says. "With baby vomit on my shirt and a teething biscuit stuck in my hair. God, Dillon. I thought you were going to tell me my cooking sucked or something."

Why the hell can't she see what I'm seeing?

Irritation makes my scalp prickle, and I grasp her chin firmly between my thumb and forefinger.

There's no more keeping my distance from her.

"You could be wearing last week's pajamas and have liver in your hair, and I would still see the most beautiful woman in the room. You, Penny, are stunning in that gold dress I dream about. You're vexing in your pencil skirts. But this version of you? At home, relaxed? Real? This version is breathtaking."

I press my hips forward, wanting her to know what she does to me. "You're so mesmerizing that I can't think straight because all the blood in my body is rushing to my cock that's weeping for a taste of you."

Her breaths are shallow and fast. The color high on her cheeks makes me desperate to know how her body flushes in pleasure.

"Dillon," she says on an exhale. Her lips part, drawing my head closer to them.

When my mouth ghosts above hers, a whisper of a breath between us, I ask, "How's that for honest?"

She nods, and when she does, it brings her lips against mine. Her eyebrows shoot up in shock, but I won't waste this opportunity. The second she sighs into me, I slip my hand from her chin and wrap it around the back of her neck, holding her to me. No, not just holding her to me, but molding her to me.

Her entire body fits into mine like she was carved from my soul.

She has her reasons. Reasons a relationship is too complicated. But I have some reasons of my own. Reasons why this is exactly where I'm meant to be.

Perhaps it's time we came to an understanding. A meeting of minds to meld our opposing sides into one cohesive unit.

A gentle moan escapes the back of her throat, and I greedily swallow it down. She tastes of home-cooked meals and sex. A strange combination that has my head spinning in a lustful haze.

Baby giggles from the next room have us pulling apart. Her looking a little dazed. Me wanting to beat on my chest like a wild animal announcing that I've finally found my place.

"Dillon," she whispers, but I hold a finger to her lips to silence her.

"I'm going to be here for a while, and I know that was not taking it slow. But, baby, we've been taking it slow for years. So, give me a month. A month to try."

"Try what?"

Jesus Christ. Her voice is wobbly with wonder, and I'd give my left nut to know what she sounds like when she comes.

Focus, Dillon. Focus.

"A month to try. With you. With your family. No pressure. No expectations. Just me and you and them." I hook a thumb over my shoulder.

Penny shakes her head as her eyes go watery. "I can't, Dillon. I can't just try. They'll get attached. They'll feel let down and discarded when you go back to the city. I can't do that to them."

Rage burns in my veins. She's so sure I'll go back to the city. So sure I'll leave them.

Well, fuck that.

I just made up my mind.

"I'm going to be here, Penny. In this town. Your neighbor. Your friend. I can be their friend if we're together or not, and that will never change. I don't drop people. And I know from experience how hard it is to let people in when all you've experienced is the letdown from someone you should have been able to trust with your life. I would never cause them more pain. So let me be your friend when they're watching."

"And when they're not watching?" she whispers.

The anxiety that's normally squeezing my lungs like I'm trapped in a capsized boat suddenly rights itself, allowing my first taste of a new beginning.

"When they're not watching, let me show you what you've been missing." I lean in and kiss the corner of her mouth. Then kiss up her cheek to just below her ear.

"I think you'll be disappointed," she mutters.

I pull back enough so we're nose to nose. "Why do you say that?"

I know there's nothing she could do to disappoint me, but I need to hear what she's thinking.

"I met Eddy when I was fourteen. He's all I've ever known. He was my first kiss. My first date. My first—everything." She looks down but can only lower her eyes to my chin because I'm standing so close and holding her so tightly. "My first and only everything," she mutters.

My cock roars to life with this admission, and she gasps, but I don't pull away.

I inhale deeply through my nose until I'm sure I can control myself, then put my lips to her ear. "Then let me be very clear about something else, sweetheart." The low, demanding timbre of my voice sounds slightly unhinged. It surprises me, but when she shivers in my arms, I go with it.

"I'm going to erase all those firsts from your memory bank. Every."

I kiss her neck.

"Single."

My hips jut forward.

"One."

Pulling her earlobe into my mouth, I bite down gently, and her entire body shudders.

"I'm going to replace them with something better. And I know they'll be better because they'll all be focused on you. I get the feeling no one has ever taken care of you properly, Penny, and I'm going to fucking delight in changing that."

"But I…"

I flick her earlobe with my tongue, then pull away.

Wearing a smirk, I narrow my eyes. "I want to be your last first date. Your last first dance. Your last first fuck. And yeah, I want to be your last first kiss."

There goes that tiny frog-like gulp again. "But that would mean…"

I nod.

She shakes her head.

"But my life. Your life. We don't even kn—"

"If you're about to say we don't even know each other, I'm going to stop you right there because I know you, Penny. I fucking know you. Do you know how many Wednesdays we've missed in three years?"

Another head shake, but there's a flicker of acknowledgment in her baby blues.

She knows.

"Four. We've missed four. That means I've spent one hundred and fifty-two hours with you, not counting our out-of-office meetups at Ashton's house or Lochlan's parties. One hundred and fifty-two hours I've spent getting to know you. Listening when you speak. Hearing your words. Dreaming about your voice. Memorizing it all."

I take a step back, and she fills her lungs with air.

"I know you, and you know me."

"Dillon." She holds her fist to her chest like a shield as she speaks, so I give her a little more room. "My life? It's messy and complicated." She gestures to the family room, and some of the spark our kiss caused escapes, leaving sadness in her eyes. She stares at the floor, and I wish I knew what she was thinking.

"Sweetheart?"

She keeps her head bowed but lifts her eyes to mine.

"I grew up surrounded by chaos. I thrive in it. Just give me the chance to prove I can handle yours."

CHAPTER 18

PENNY

"'*Let me prove it,*'" I mutter under my breath. Dillon's words fly around my head like they're contenders in a fight club.

"'Just let me prove it.' Who says that?" I scoff, frustrated all the way to my fingernails.

"Apparently, someone who can get under your skin." Miller chuckles in the doorway.

I spin from the stove with my oven mitts on both hands. "For crying out loud, Mill. Why are you sneaking up on me?"

He pushes off the doorframe, takes the mitts from my hands, and then hip-checks me out of the way. Leaning forward, he takes the bread out of the oven.

Oh crap. The timer's beeping.

"I wasn't sneaking up on you," he says after he places the pan on a trivet, then presses the button on the stove to turn off the timer. "I told you the timer was going off, but you didn't hear me." He turns a devilish expression my way. "You were a little preoccupied. Want to talk about it?"

"No," I say too quickly.

"You sure?"

"No. Yes?" Dropping my face into my hands, I shake my head. "I don't know, Mill. I just don't know."

He grabs my hands and pulls them away from my face. Then bends at the knees, so I'm forced to look at him. "What don't you know?"

My brain seizes on memories from ten minutes ago. Right before Gage bounded into the room, breaking the spell Dillon had me under.

I purse my lips into a thin line and peek around his shoulder to make sure the kids aren't listening.

"Let me guess," he whispers. "Dillon being here, in your space, giving you bedroom eyes, has your fight or flight kicking in?"

"Bedroom eyes?" I whisper-screech. "Bedroom eyes? Are you kidding me? Do you think Kai noticed?"

Miller's expression softens. "No, Pen. I don't. I think Kai's too busy trying to navigate the teen years to notice, but me? Yeah, I noticed. I also noticed how he looked after Kai all day. How he made sure the ladder was secure before he let Kai climb up to reattach Mrs. Winters's holiday wreath. I noticed how he kept himself between Kai and the road when we cleared walkways. I noticed a lot, Pen. I don't think you need to keep your guard so high with him."

Tears make my eyes hot. Eddy doesn't even know where his kids are, but Dillon put himself between my son and the road to keep him out of danger.

How messed up is that?

"I know what you're thinking," Miller says.

"No, you don't."

"Try me," he goads.

"It's messed up, Miller. Eddy is messed up." Taking the sponge from the sink, I scrub at the counter with so much force my fingertips go raw.

"It's not easy," he agrees. "But Dillon seems to get it. Have you talked to him about his past? I get the feeling that dealing with Eddy isn't something that just comes naturally to him."

I chuck the sponge into the sink and cross my arms around my middle. "He told me his dad had issues with substance abuse and that he had to cut his mother out of his life when she wouldn't make healthy choices, but I didn't… I mean, we didn't…"

"You didn't dig deeper because you didn't want to be obligated to share," he surmises.

I clench my teeth, trying to keep all my emotions in check. "Yeah."

"Jesus, Pen." Miller surges forward and wraps me in a hug. "It's okay to let someone in. Not everyone is like Eddy."

"I'm certainly not," Dillon growls from behind Miller. With my head buried in Miller's chest, I can't see Dillon, but I feel him everywhere.

Miller roughly rubs his hands up and down my biceps, like he's shaking some strength into me, then steps back but turns to block me from Dillon's view. "Do you like Minecraft?"

"Mine what?" Dillon asks. His head tilts far to the right so he can see me, and I offer a watery smile.

"It's a video game that the kids love. Come on. Too many cooks in the kitchen and all that," Miller says, ushering Dillon ahead of him.

Thank God for Matty Miller.

WE'RE CROWDED around the table, Miller on one side of me, Kai on the other, and Dillon directly across from me.

The little kids are taking advantage of the full house and sit crisscross on the floor in front of the TV. Their bowls, hopefully, will remain on the coffee table. Ugh, the damage beef stew would do to the carpet out there. I shake away the thought and focus on my meal while the boys in front of me talk.

I try not to smile every time Kai injects himself into the conversation, but I wasn't anticipating Dillon encouraging him to participate either. As they recall every detail of their day, Dillon doesn't miss a chance to praise Kai or bring him in and ask his opinion. And then, every once in a while, I catch Kai staring at his bowl with a frown.

What's he thinking? Is this confusing for him?

Then he'll pop his head up like he's warring with himself.

Oh, God. Does he feel guilty for liking Dillon?

And then, sometimes, the fifteen-year-old in him can't help but bubble out.

"Who is the biggest celebrity you've ever had as a client?" Kai asks anxiously. "Any athletes?"

Dillon sits patiently and dips his bread into the stew while he thinks. I'm entranced as he brings a big glob to his mouth. How can he make chewing sexy?

When he catches me staring, he winks before turning back to Kai. "There's this thing called confidentiality. But maybe when you're older, I can get you on the payroll, and you can see for yourself."

"No. Way," Kai says in awe, and I bite back a squeak.

"What?" Dillon asks. "We've done internships before. There's a lot that can be done at Envision without ever going in the field." Turning back to Kai, he lowers his voice. "There is a certain New England Patriots quarterback who left the team a few years ago."

"The GOAT?" Kai whispers back.

Dillon shrugs but has a huge smile on his face. "His wife was attending the Met Gala, and they needed our specific brand of expertise."

"Holy crap. Mom. Did you hear that?"

Dillon must have seen Kai's room because it's covered in everything Boston sports has to offer.

"How did you end up a Boston sports family when you're closer to New York?" Stew dribbles over his lip, and I can't speak when his tongue comes out to lick it away.

"Gramma and Grandpa were from Rhode Island," Kai answers, utterly oblivious to my suddenly dry mouth.

Miller kicks me under the table. "You're drooling," he says with a cough, drawing Dillon's attention to me.

I'm going to kill Matty Miller.

"Me too," Dillon says, staring straight into my eyes.

"You too what?" Kai asks.

"Me too—I'm drooling over this stew. Does your mom always cook this well?"

Pride shows in Kai's squared shoulders. "Most of the time. She makes this one thing, pasta fugly or something, and it's so gross, but she says it's good for us."

It's good for them, and it's cheap to make. But I don't say that. I roll my eyes and dig into my stew that's getting cold because I can't stop staring at our guest.

"Is that right?" Dillon asks with a twinkle in his eyes.

"It's pasta fagioli, and it's not gross. It's…it just has a lot of canned beans in it," I explain.

"Beans, beans," Gage sings from the other room, and I drop my forehead into my hands.

Dillon laughs but finishes the song. "The more you—"

"Hey," I say, lifting my head quickly. "Don't encourage them."

"Toot," comes a chorus of giggles from the other room just as the baby starts to cry. She hasn't slept long enough. That means she'll either go right back down, or it will be a very long night for me.

"How come Aster hasn't come to pick them up yet?" Kai grumbles, and my heart pinches. I know he loves his sisters dearly. But he doesn't love that his sisters' parents take advantage every chance they get.

"If all she has is the space heater, it isn't safe for Mari," I say, placing a hand on his forearm.

I stand to get Mari but pause at the door when Kai clears his throat.

"I know," he grumbles. "I just…" Kai lifts his head and stares at Dillon like he forgot he was there. It happened to me earlier too. It's almost like he belongs here, and we forget. We forget that we're holding other people's secrets that fill us with shame.

Dillon watches him with nothing but patience and understanding. "People are flawed, Kai. All of us. It's how we hold ourselves accountable that matters. We can blame and shame and fight all we want, but at the end of the day, we can only do what we think is right. It seems like that's what your mom does every day."

That response makes me melt into a pool right in front of him.

"Yeah," Kai says with a wobble in his voice that sounds fragile.

"And just today, I've seen you do it too. You and your mom are making one heck of a family here. Your sisters are lucky to have you."

Kai's shoulders inflate at the compliment. It's like Dillon's words filled him with every ounce of confidence he's been missing.

A tear trickles down my cheek, and I quickly swipe it away, but Dillon watches it with a pinched brow.

He always sees me.

I duck my head and hurry to scoop up Mari and bring her to the pack 'n play set up in my bedroom.

This entire night has been a lot. Dillon in my home, in my

space and life in a way I never thought would be possible, has my mind a muddled mess of worries.

What if I let him in and he leaves?

What if I let him in and he doesn't?

What if I let him in and the kids don't approve?

Laughter rings out downstairs, and I hear them all singing about magical fruit. Dillon is the loudest of them all.

Or maybe, it's that I'm so in tune with everything Dillon Henry that his voice rises above all the others like he's singing straight to my heart.

He wants to be my last first kiss. How can that one statement start to mend the bits of my heart still shredded by broken promises?

CHAPTER 19

PENNY

Mari rests against my shoulder, and a tiny piece of me is happy she didn't stay sleeping when I tried to put her down earlier. Her little baby smell fills my nose as I rub small circles on her back. Kai is in the armchair to my left, watching the TV screen. Gage leans against me on my right, and Lia sits between him and Dillon, holding each of their hands.

Dillon's giant, and I do mean giant, hand cradles Lia's little one like she's made of porcelain, and I have to force my gaze to stay on the TV.

He never flinched when she attached herself to his leg after dinner or when she held out her hands for him to sit with her for the movie.

It causes a painful lump to lodge in my throat.

Landon, Izzy, and Miller are sprawled out on the floor in front of us on a bed made of pillows. Miller started snoring the second his head hit the pillow, and the other kids all curled around him.

It's crowded. And peaceful. And happy.

Mari hiccups in the way that babies do in their sleep. It

causes her little chin to tremble on a yawn, and her tiny fist stretches out next to my face, landing on my cheek.

Soft. Innocent.

It breaks my heart to know that her life will not be easy.

Before more tears can fall, I lean forward gingerly, and Gage lifts his eyes to me in question. "I'm going to put Mari down for bed," I whisper.

"Okay, Mommy."

The second I stand, he turns over and leans into Lia, and Dillon's left arm comes around the back of the sofa to rest on Gage's shoulder.

I'm frozen for a second, just watching how easily he's adapted to my messy life. I have to remember that it's easy in short bursts. Would he still be here if he knew that this is what life is like day in and day out? His right hand still cradles Lia's, but my gaze is on his left arm that holds both children safely. Protectively.

"Penny?" Dillon's whispered voice has my eyelashes fluttering to attention. "Everything all right?"

Throat locked, I simply nod and back out of the room.

"It's okay. She's probably going to her closet," Gage whispers, making every hair on my neck stand on end. "That's where she goes to cry when she thinks we can't hear her."

"Gage." Kai's voice is a warning that proves they all know my secret.

I'll need to talk to them about that, but right now, I hurry out of the room before anyone can question me. It isn't until I'm on the stairs that I breathe again.

I try so hard to hold it all together—this is proof that I'm failing at that too.

In my room, I close the door most of the way but leave it open a crack so I can hear anyone coming, and I stand next to the pack 'n play doing the mom-sway.

All mothers do it. That gentle sway of the hips from side

to side that instantly soothes the baby. Every mother but Aster, that is. She's tried, but she's jerky in her movements and on edge all of the time, and since babies feed off body language, Mari doesn't respond well.

"You're a great mom, Penny," Dillon says in a hushed tone that floats down both arms like a hummingbird hovering above my skin.

I swipe under my eyes, thankful for once that I'm not wearing mascara, then face him, but even I know my shaky smile can't hide my pain. Not tonight. Not when I'm so raw with emotions I never expected to feel again.

He walks forward with easy strides and wraps an arm around me and the baby. "You don't have to tell me, Penny. But I'd really like to be someone you can trust with your tears."

I inhale, and every muscle in my body quivers. "Trust is something I may not be able to give, Dillon."

"That's because you shouldn't. Trust isn't something given or taken freely. Trust is something that's earned. I want to earn your trust just like I want to prove to you that I want to be here."

Pulling out of his embrace is harder than it should be, but I do and shift to set Mari in her pack 'n play.

I take longer than necessary to tuck her in, running my hand over her wispy golden hair and down her cheek, loving how her little lips purse together, searching for something to nuzzle. Finally, I rest my hand on the small of her little back, feeling the gentle rise and fall of her breathing.

Dillon doesn't rush me. He doesn't move or say anything. He just stands where I left him, giving me the time and space I need to collect myself.

When I think I can face him without losing the battle of tears, I stand to my full height, cross my arms over my chest and turn to him.

His body is as relaxed as I've ever seen him. He's patient and kind and so freaking sexy. It's only now that I remember we're standing in my bedroom, only a few feet apart, and my gaze drops to my bed, thankful I made it this morning.

"Who takes care of you, Penny?" he asks. My name on his lips makes my core coil with need.

"I do. I take care of me."

He shakes his head and takes a step closer. "It's not enough."

"It's what I have. I'm all I have. Me and Miller."

"And me, sweetheart. For the foreseeable future, you have me. And if I haven't proven myself to you in one month's time, well, then I'll have to come up with a backup plan."

"You make it sound like you're planning to be around forever."

He takes another step and another until his warmth wraps around me like a heated blanket. "I like the sound of that," he whispers. "But we have to do things the right way."

"The right way?" Jesus. Why do I gulp every time his words affect me?

"I've waited, wanted, dreamed, and fantasized about you for three long years. I'm tired of waiting, Penny."

He's tired of waiting. What does that mean? He just said he would be here. Didn't he?

"I understand," I say with my eyes downcast, even though I'm more confused than ever. It's too hard to look at him. I can't afford to get caught up in the magic of the day, because that's all it is. Magic.

It has to be.

"I don't think you do."

Lifting my head, I crane my neck to look into his eyes.

"I've waited," he says again. "And I'm done waiting. I've been falling for you a little more every week, and now I'm going to act on it. But I'll go slow." He leans down and places his cheek against mine. "So, so, slow," he whispers. "Until I've earned your trust, your heart, and your body."

I whimper. Never before in my life has my mouth made that sound.

"Fuck me. I'm going to hear that little sound of yours in my head every time I close my eyes."

Maybe it's that I haven't been touched or loved in years. Maybe it's that even when Eddy would touch me, he never created this need that Dillon causes just by breathing. Or maybe it's that here, in my bedroom, for the first time, it feels like the happy home I've always tried to create is just within reach. Adrenaline races through my veins like a runaway car, and suddenly, I couldn't control myself if I tried.

Whatever it is has me throwing myself at him. My dirty clothes and unwashed hair are all but forgotten as he wraps his powerful arms around me and molds my body to his in the way he says he craves.

His mouth descends on mine like I'm the last drop of water on Earth, and my cheeks flush when my core flames with desire.

I never knew kisses could be like this.

I never knew anything could be like this.

Dillon's hand slides under my oversized sweatshirt. The feel of his palm on my bare skin has me shuddering against him.

"This isn't slow, baby," he growls.

"No. It's not." My words are a breathy, wanton admission. An admission that I want him as much as he wants me. An admission that I've lost all sense of balance around him, but I trust him to catch me.

Mari gurgles in her sleep, and he tears his lips from mine. His eyes are almost crazed. They're foggy with lust I've never seen in a man.

"Bathroom." He sounds urgent, demanding, and sexy as hell.

My brain isn't working, and before I figure out what he's saying, he's ushered me into my tiny bathroom and up against the door.

I moan when he pushes his thigh between my legs.

"This isn't slow," he groans, rocking his cock into my thigh. "But I don't want to stop. Please tell me you don't want me to stop."

"Don't—please don't stop," I plead.

His hand slides down my side, and I gasp when he cups me through my pajama pants.

"Damn it, Penny," he says through clenched teeth. "You're wet for me, aren't you?"

He grinds the heel of his hand against my clit, and stars erupt behind my eyelids. How is he controlling my body so quickly? I move against his hand, and I'm powerless to stop it. He grins and gives me the friction I need.

My stomach is in knots, and my clit throbs so painfully I could cry. I feel every beat of my heart in that sensitive bundle of nerves.

"I can't wait to slide my cock into this pretty pussy. I can't wait to make you mine. To watch you lose your goddamn mind and strangle my dick when you do it."

My eyes roll to the back of my head. I've only ever experienced dirty talk like this in my audiobooks, but they have nothing on Dillon Henry.

Every muscle in my core spasms as my orgasm spirals toward release. I'm so close. So, so close. It works its way through my body, and I just know that it will destroy me.

"Mom?"

Panic seizes in my chest as Landon's voice grows closer, but only a choked, frustrated sob escapes my throat.

Dillon presses hard against my clit, like he's demanding

my climax, and damn him if it doesn't wreck me. Right here, pressed up against the door, he pulls an orgasm out of me that makes my vision go blurry, and I'm helpless to do anything but suffer the pleasure of it.

"She's getting medicine for my headache. She'll be down in a minute," I vaguely hear Dillon reply.

"Can we have ice cream?" Landon asks. I can't tell if he's truly that far away or if my head is still swimming with pleasure.

But my brain is trying to fight through the fog, telling me my children come first. Not me. I can't be this selfish. I can't be what their father is.

Dillon presses against my clit again and grinds the heel of his palm back and forth, picking up the pace.

"She said yes," he calls to a chorus of cheers, and I'm nearly positive they're all coming from downstairs.

The upside to living in chaos is that Mari doesn't make a peep in the room next door.

CHAPTER 20

DILLON

I keep my palm pressing and sliding against Penny's fully clothed pussy. I missed her expression when she came because we were almost interrupted, but I'll never forget the muffled erotic sounds she made just for me. I need to hear them again. We'll have to talk about this later, but right now, I'm determined to see her when she comes this time.

I've never been with anyone this responsive. Is it because of me? Or because she's been neglected for so long? I want it to be because of me so badly my head spins. The idea of her being neglected makes my neck blaze hot, like it's being attacked by a million tiny needles.

She'll never come last again. Not if I have anything to say about it.

"They will always come first, sweetheart. Always." I grind the words out in time with my hand pressing into her. Her body convulses, and I know she's close. "But you will also come first to me. Give me what I want. Please."

Penny's legs buckle, but I hold her up with my thigh

pressed between hers. Her face is pale, and sweat dots her forehead. I crash my mouth to hers and slip my tongue in to savor the taste of her.

Her tongue is hesitant, but the second I find it, I coax it into my mouth and treat it as if it were her clit. I suck and flick mine against it as I pick up speed with my hand. She tastes like dark coffee and even darker promises.

I swallow the sounds of her pleasure and let out a groan when her hands push through my hair to tug on the ends. It sends a spark of pure lust straight to my cock, and my hips jerk in response.

Her heat soaks the cotton pressing against my fingers. I would give anything to strip her bare and bury my face in her sweetness, but I can't change course until I get her over the edge again.

My wants and needs will always come second.

This is all about her, not me, so I keep going even though my cock roars like it's wrapped in the most painful vise. I devastate her with my kiss and my palm. My fingers twitch and press to her opening, forcing the cotton to give a little with my thrust.

Fuck, I want to feel her heat.

With my free hand, I thrust my fingers into her hair and grip it tight to hold her face where I want her.

"Come, Penny. Come right now. Let me see your eyes as you let go for me. Only for me."

Her mouth falls open as her shoulders shake, and a tremor rolls down the length of her body. The faintest of flutters pull at my finger pressed to her entrance, making precome seep into my boxer briefs.

Penny climaxes in a torrent of spasms that feed my soul. I cover her mouth with my hand to muffle her cries of plea-sure, and I watch every detail of her face as it contorts, but I never let up the pressure on her clit. I wring every ounce of this orgasm I can out of her.

And when her glassy eyes blink to refocus, I don't give her time for regret. I take her mouth in a gentle kiss.

"That wasn't taking it slow, but this was the best night of my entire goddamn life. Please don't say you regret this, and for the love of God, let me do it again."

My desperation for her bleeds into my tone, and I don't give a fuck. I will drop to my knees to give this woman the world. "Next time, I'll make sure we're not interrupted because I plan to see and taste and explore every inch of you."

"Dillon, I…" Penny's voice is rough and ragged, like she's still trying to catch her breath.

"Will you give me a chance to fit in your life? If that means stolen moments against a bathroom door or holding you in your closet so you don't have to cry alone, that's what I'll do."

"But…"

"No buts, Penny. Unless you tell me right now that you don't want me. That you, not your life or your responsibilities, that you and you alone do not want me, I'm going to work for it. I'm going to work for you."

Something like fear flashes in her eyes, and it has me lightening my tone a little and cupping her jaw. "What? Tell me what you're thinking."

"Besides all my baggage, if you want to know *me*, I don't think I'll be what you're looking for. I'm not like Nova or Tilly. I'm forty-two. I've had three kids. The last time I dated…" She pauses and frowns. "Actually, I've never dated. I had a boyfriend at fourteen who turned into a fiancé at nineteen. We broke up for a few years, but I focused on college, and when we got back together, it was to get married."

Her face is still flushed a beautiful shade of red, and I

can't help the ridiculous urge to sink my teeth into her milky flesh, to mark her as mine. But even though she's never been more beautiful, I wasn't wrong. There's fear in her eyes that I don't understand.

"What are you trying to say, sweetheart?"

"I—I have scars and stretch marks. Lots of them. My body sags, and it looks like Freddy Krueger took his knives to me in places. I don't know how to date, and when you see me, really see me"—she sweeps her arms down her midsection—"I don't look like the women you're used to dating."

She's insecure about her body. That's why she clutched my T-shirt to her stomach all those months ago.

That fucker really messed her up.

The sadness and disappointment in her eyes nearly rips me in two.

"Baby," I murmur, "you've known me for years. How many dates do you think I've had in all that time?"

"That's not what I'm saying."

"I know it's not. But guess. For me." I catch her gaze, and a contented smile tugs at the corners of my mouth.

"I have no idea."

"One. One coffee date that lasted twenty-six minutes because I couldn't stop thinking about you. You're not going to scare me off with your insecurities. I can handle scars, Penny. In fact, I look forward to finding them. Tracing them. Exploring them. And then making you love them too."

She scoffs. "Never going to happen. Eddy wouldn't even look at me. He said I was damaged goods. And that was before I had kids."

I involuntarily squeeze her chin and force myself to relax before I hurt her.

"Rule number one, Penny. Unless it's an emergency with your kids, never say his name to me right after I make you come. Rule number two, always remember that I'm not him. I don't care if your entire body is a mass of snarled scars. I'm here for you. I like you. All of you. Not just for what you can offer with your body. I'm here for this," I say while splaying my hand across her heart. "I'm here because of this."

Tears fall down her cheeks, and she looks to the side.

She really tries hard not to cry in front of anyone. What strength does it take to smile through pain just to make everyone else around you comfortable?

"We have to get back downstairs," she whispers. She's pulling away, and I allow it.

"I know. But remember this, every time I see you. Every time I'm near, I'm going to be counting down the minutes until I can bury my face between your legs, until I can lick every scar on your temple of a body, and I do mean every fucking time. So when you see me, and you worry that I won't like what's under these clothes?" I press my cock into her hip and grind. "Just know that I went home tonight with this in my pants. Because of you. For you. And when I finally get myself off? It will be to visions of you."

I step back, then catch her when she falls forward. Pride cheers loudly in my mind when her legs wobble for a minute before she gets her bearings.

"And for the record?" I lower my voice, and it takes on a gravelly texture. "I love how you come for me, sweetheart. I look forward to doing it again and again."

Leaning forward, I kiss her on the forehead, and then because I need her to know how much I mean every damned word, I grab her ass with both hands and squeeze. Hard. Pulling her flush against me again as I do.

"Okay?" I ask with a grin that makes me feel twenty years younger.

"You're asking me if I'm okay after all—after all that?"

"Yes."

Her head does a weird twirl. Like she wants to shake her head no and yes at the same time and it ends in some version of a circle.

Good.

Sometimes, she needs to get out of her head, and I'm just the man to take her away.

"I'll meet you downstairs," I say, ushering her to the left so I can open the door.

"Dillon?" she whispers.

I glance over my shoulder and give her a soft look. "Yeah?"

"You just had one of my firsts."

What? I scratch at my jaw, trying to figure out what she's talking about. The way her face flushes tells me it's something big.

"What's that?"

She nibbles on her bottom lip. Fresh heat flushes across her cheeks. "Um, that," she says, gesturing to her body.

Turning around, I walk back to her and keep my voice low. "You mean you never fooled around through your clothes when you were a teen?"

Penny bites harder on that lip, and worry starts to worm into my chest. When she won't make eye contact, I take a deep breath. "Penny?"

She searches behind me in the hallway, probably to ensure we're still alone. "No," she says quietly. "No one's ever made my body do—that before."

Understanding slams into me like a bullet.

Sweaty fucking Eddy never made her come.

I have a lifetime of fuck-ups to undo, but I'm more than up to the challenge.

"My hands are very excited to have had that pleasure,

Penny. And thank you for trusting me with that information."

Kissing her forehead one more time, I turn to head down the stairs.

"My life is complicated," she says to my back like the words are a reminder for herself. "I'm constantly protecting my boys from more heartache. It's eighteen-hour days and—"

"I'm not here to make it more complicated, Penny. I'm just here for you."

With that, I leave her standing in the hallway. Happy to have had one of her firsts. Relieved that she isn't throwing me out. And for the first time in my life, excited for the future and all her firsts I can have.

THE KIDS ARE HAVING a sleepover on the family room floor, and I'm contorted like a pretzel on Penny's sofa above them. The house has been quiet for a couple of hours now, but my thoughts are loud until Gage sits up.

"Dewey?" he whispers with an urgency that makes my gut clench.

I slide off the sofa, then walk on tiptoes through the mass of bodies. When I reach him, I have to crouch in a weird position so I don't fall on anyone.

"Hey, buddy. What's wrong?"

"Dewey?" he says again, and my heart does a pitter-patter it's growing accustomed to around these little people.

"Yeah, Gage, I'm right here. What's wrong, buddy?"

He rubs his eyes with the heel of his hands and looks at me. Then he does it again, and I try not to laugh.

"Are you okay?" I ask again.

"Yeah. I was makin' sure you were still here." He lays back down and is out in seconds.

I can't breathe. I can't move. I don't even blink. But my hands shake, and my head pounds with his words. This kid just carved my heart straight from my chest and is now using it as a pillow.

It belongs to him now.

Standing, I stay perfectly still until I'm sure my legs have stopped trembling, and I can make it through the maze of limbs without hurting someone. Then I make my way to the sofa with my brain running at warp speed.

Ashton made a deal with Remy. A deal that obviously includes me, and once it's done, he'll leave Envision behind.

Is it possible he knew all along that this is where I belong?

Can I belong here in such a short amount of time?

Is it really that fast, though? I've been pining for Penny for years. I've gotten to know her. I've fallen for her in so many ways.

"Go to sleep," Miller grumbles from his spot on the floor.

"Why didn't you go across the street to sleep?" I whisper.

"Why didn't you?" he chuckles softly.

We had both said the snow was too thick, and we were too comfortable to go out in the freezing cold, but I have a feeling we both had very different reasons for staying in our uncomfortable positions.

I didn't leave because I needed Penny to know that I was here, really here. Especially after what we did in her bathroom. And I suspect Miller stayed to make sure she was okay too. He's been good to her, and for that, he'll always be a friend.

He did give me the side-eye when I returned to the living room. And he didn't hold back a chuckle when she followed a short time after, looking thoroughly spent. But he also looked genuinely happy. For all the crap in her world, she's always had Miller.

It seems like the entire town has Miller. It makes me wish I could do something to help him.

"That's what I thought," he mutters when I don't answer. "Go to sleep, Dillon. It's going to be a long and bumpy road."

"I'm not afraid," I say more to myself than anything. And I'm not. I never pictured a family, but now that I'm here? Now I don't know what my life looks like without them in it.

CHAPTER 21

DILLON

"*D*o you know how to use a plow?" Miller shouts over the engine of his truck a week later.

He wasn't kidding about the snow, but I'm also not fooling anyone. I could have gone back to the city days ago. I just couldn't make myself leave, especially with Penny working from home.

But why would I? Even sleeping on Penny's sofa is better than my empty apartment. And I have to say, I never pictured myself as a cuddler before, but who knew? I can't get enough of her plastered to me, which I do every chance I get.

"Not a clue," I yell back.

He climbs into the cab and gives me a quick lesson on plowing. "Start with the parking lot," he says, gesturing to the empty space outside the TAC. "You can't hit anything here, and you'll get the hang of it before we make the rounds. The radar says we have two days to get this shit clear before the next storm."

"Jesus. Is it always like this out here?" Not that I'm complaining. Keep snowing, motherfucker. I'm finally warm.

"No. We haven't had storms like this since the late

nineties. It's like Mother Nature is in cahoots with Ashton, isn't it?"

My gaze automatically flies across the field to Penny's house, not that I can see it over the mountain of snow we plowed to the edge of the property. Kai went back a few minutes ago to stay with the kids so Penny could run to the grocery store. She refused to take money from me, and it pissed me off.

But I'm really beginning to love small-town life because Miller said I could call Hazel at the general store, and prepay over the phone.

Where the hell else can you do that?

I know Penny will be pissed, and I must be a sick bastard because I'm excited to see her reaction.

"Romeo, you good?" Miller teases.

Snapping my face forward, I grunt. "Yeah. I'll clear this. Then what?"

"Then we make the rounds just like yesterday. Remy said two more families are without heat, so we'll make sure they're all set. He's inside getting the cots ready in case we have to open for shelter."

"You mean you take people into the TAC when stuff like this happens?"

"Yeah." He shrugs. "It's what we do and part of the reason the TAC is so important."

Unease sits in my chest like a lead weight because I know not everyone would run the TAC as Remy does, and that would be devastating for this community.

But I could. I could make this place what it was always meant to be.

Miller hops out of the truck and jogs to the side of the lot. He nods and gives me a wave, so I slowly step on the gas and lower the plow. It's rough going the first few passes, but when I make my fifth turn, Miller is nowhere in sight, so I assume I've got the hang of it.

Clearing the parking lot doesn't take as long as I expected, but it's still half an hour before I put the truck in park and climb out.

How the hell can I be sweating after driving a truck?

The sound of…something, something that I shouldn't be hearing, has me spinning in place.

Landon is running at full speed toward me in his pajamas. No coat. No hat. And by the way he's sliding down the mountain of snow, no shoes either. A fear I've never known reaches into my chest and rips it wide open. I take off at a dead run and meet him at the edge of the property.

"Landon, what are you doing? What's wrong?" I try to look over him, but I can't see a damned thing. The snow is piled too high on this side of the property.

"My dad, Kai," he gasps. "Lia. The car." The kid is out of breath, and tears have frozen like tire marks on his cheeks.

Ripping off my jacket, I lay it on the ground, move him on top of it, then place my hands on his shoulders, and wait until his eyes focus on me. His words are a jumbled mess of syllables I can't make out, mixed with sobs and choked sounds that turn my stomach.

"Something's wrong? At your house?" Thankfully, he nods in confirmation. I give him a squeeze and attempt a smile. "Miller is inside. In the office. Do you know where that is?"

"Y—Yes," he cries.

"Good." I turn around and squat. He hops on my back like it's natural. No, he hops on my back like I'll protect him, and it makes me dizzy. His feet are so frozen from running through the icy snow it looks like razor blades have cut him open, and I bite back a curse. I stand with him on my back and run as fast as I can to drop him at the front door of the

TAC. I hate leaving him alone, but my gut tells me to get back to Penny's house.

"Go find him. Tell him what's happening. I'm going to your house to check on Lia. Okay?"

"Kai. Dad." His entire body trembles.

"Landon? Go. Okay? Everything will be okay. I promise."

He doesn't respond, but he turns and runs into the TAC. I run across the abandoned lot. It's faster to go the way Landon came than to drive the truck back down the road. I scale the pile of snow, and when I get to the top, I don't feel like the king of the mountain. I feel like the lord of impending doom because I find Eddy with his hands on Kai in front of Penny's house.

Nothing matters but getting to Kai. The closer I get, the louder their words become.

"You can't take her, Dad. You shouldn't be driving." Kai's voice slaps me across the face, and I move impossibly faster.

Eddy's words aren't clear enough to make out. But the grunts from Kai's exertion tell me that he can't fight him off much longer.

"Let him go," I roar when I'm within striking distance.

Kai's head snaps up, and Eddy's lolls to the side, but he doesn't let go of Kai's torn shirt.

"I said, let. Him. Go."

"Who the fuck are you?" Eddy spits. Or at least that's what I think he says. It comes out in a slur of syllables.

Stepping forward, I wrap a hand around Eddy's wrist and squeeze tightly enough to feel his bones crunch together before he finally releases Kai's torn shirt.

Eddy swings at me, and I duck. Kai's eyes are on me. Eddy's off-balance, and his wind-up is so blown out of proportion that he strikes Kai just below his collarbone with enough force to knock him back.

It happens in horrifyingly slow motion. Kai staggers back

—one step. Then two, and then he collapses, hitting his head on the post of the mailbox.

He crumbles like a stack of blocks. I shove Eddy with all my might and race to Kai. I'm on my knees when the first trickle of blood hits the snow.

Oh my God.

"Kai?"

His eyes flutter, but he doesn't move. I can hear Eddy cursing, but he doesn't come near Kai, so I ignore him. Time rolls over in slow motion while I search for the cut on his head. Long moments that cause my fear to roar in my ears like an avalanche. I'm sure I don't breathe until I find where the blood is coming from. Thankfully it doesn't appear to be too big but…

"Lia. She's…" He tries to sit up, but I hold him still.

"Stay down, Kai. You have a cut."

His eyes are wide and alarmed. "Lia's in the car. He's…" Suddenly I understand what he's saying, and I gently release my hold on him. Jumping to my feet, I see Eddy fall into the driver's seat.

"Oh, shit."

A car honks wildly in the background, but I move without thinking. He cannot take Lia in that car. She might not survive it.

I reach the car in seconds, but I hit a patch of ice and slide before coming to a stop. It's enough of a delay for Eddy to turn the ignition, but I claw for the door. His blurry, startled eyes look up at me when I rip the door open, and he snarls something I can't understand.

That's when I catch sight of her tangled hair and hear her soft whimpers in the back. She's not even buckled in, for Christ's sake.

"Get out of the car," I growl.

"Make me," he spits.

So I do. I drag him from the car by his collar and pin him to the ground. Eddy kicks and gets me right in the nuts, but I don't loosen my hold. He manages to buck in my moment of weakness though and gets a hand free.

He's all limbs and hatred as he swings at me. His free fist connects with my eye, and it's all the shit I'll take from him. I land one hard blow to his face. His nose erupts. It's broken, for sure. He rolls to his side just as Miller jumps out of his truck.

Right behind him is the sheriff.

And Penny.

I shake out my hand and stand. I don't regret hitting the asshole, but looking around at the pale faces, I do regret letting the kids see me like this.

The kids.

Making eye contact with Penny, I say, "Kai. He's hurt."

All the color drains from her face, and she runs forward. Miller opens the back door of Eddy's car, and Lia jumps out in her princess PJs and runs to me. I scoop her up like I've done it a million times and tuck her into my side, trying to keep her little legs covered.

The sheriff steps forward, shaking his head.

Landon drops to his knees beside Penny in the snow, crying and explaining what happened as Eddy rolls around in his own blood, yelling about pressing charges.

Sheriff Jacoby listens for a few moments before he places handcuffs on Eddy, then puts him in the back seat of the police car.

"Penny?" I ask, lifting Landon out of the snow with one arm wrapped around his belly while cradling Lia in the other. She won't look at me, and my gut twists.

"I think he's okay. He needs a few stitches," she says distractedly.

"Mr. Henry?" Lifting my head, I focus on Sheriff Jacoby's

angry face. "I hate to do this, but I saw ya hit him. He wants to press charges, so I have to take you in too."

"No," Kai screams.

Landon shakes against my body, and Lia sobs.

Gage stands on the porch in a T-shirt that says Not Today, barefoot and crying. "Don't take Dewey and Dad."

"Can we get them inside? I don't want to do this in front of them," Sheriff Jacoby says under his breath.

"Lenny, you're not putting him in the same car as Eddy," Miller rumbles as he takes Landon from my arms. "Just take Eddy in and then come back for Dillon. I'd bring him in, but we don't have a big enough car for all six kids and us. You know this is bullshit anyway. Dillon was protecting these kids and himself."

The sheriff nods and backs away. "I know, Matty. But the law is the law." He faces me and looks genuinely apologetic. "For what it's worth, you'll be in and out in no time. But I have to take a statement, and there's a process."

"I understand," I say tightly.

When I turn back, Penny has Kai on his feet. He's pale and unsteady, but it could have been so much worse. Fuck. My stomach clenches. It could have been so much worse. She's taken off her jacket and is holding it to his head. He shouldn't need more than two or three stitches, but the kid is a bleeder. It looks much worse than it is. I'm proud of my girl for holding it together.

She cries in her closet when she thinks no one's listening. Gage's whispered secret hits hard.

Not anymore, she won't. Not if I have anything to say about it.

CHAPTER 22

DILLON

The sheriff said I'd be in and out, but it's been almost two hours. Two hours without a damned update on Kai because I have no fucking idea where my phone is.

At least he kept his word and didn't put me in a cell with Eddy. I'm not sure I could have controlled myself. For the first time in my life, I fear I could actually kill someone.

Instead, I'm pacing a conference room that's seen better days and smells faintly of urine. There are light gray cement walls and a blue-speckled floor that looks like it was new in the sixties, and the folding chairs aren't any better.

I'm climbing the damned walls in here.

The door finally opens, and I'm speaking before anyone can enter. "How's Kai?"

"Well, you've got your priorities straight. I'll give you that," Remy says, stepping into the room and letting the door shut behind him.

Oh, no.

"Hi, Remy. Do you know how Kai is?"

He nods. "Take a seat, champ."

Champ? Really? What am I, ten?

I take a seat.

"Kai is okay. Physically, anyway. He's home now with Pen and Matty."

He takes the seat across from me. His kind eyes, wrinkled with age, hold a million stories and it makes you want to open up and tell him all your secrets. It's unnerving and comforting at the same time.

"I hate that Kai saw me like that. So out of control. I've never felt such anger," I say quietly.

"Anger and fear often smell the same," he says, settling deeper into the metal chair.

"I was terrified," I agree.

"'Cause you love hard."

"I—"

"And you know this kind of pain."

"Jesus."

"I can see it in your eyes. I can also sense that you're a good kid."

I bite my lip instead of telling him I'm almost forty.

"Do you know what Chance Lake, Faith Falls, and Hope Hollow all have in common?" he asks.

"Really shitty town names?" When he doesn't answer, I say, "They're the three towns connected to the TAC."

"Connected by the TAC," he corrects.

"They're still terrible names."

"Are they? I don't think so." He lowers his elbows onto the table and suddenly appears tired. Bone tired. The kind that comes from years of carrying the town.

"Chance, hope, faith," he says, ticking them off on his bony fingers. "They're all dependent on someone else. You can have hope for a better life. You can have faith in a better life. You can even leave it up to chance, but without the missing piece, they're just empty wishes."

"But you still have to work to make them happen." I'm not really sure where this conversation is going.

"Yup. But everyone needs someone to survive, too. Not everyone has someone."

I stare at him as pieces of the puzzle form in my head. "You became their someone," I say with a hint of awe in my voice.

"I became their someone. It's important to have a safe space to land."

My throat feels itchy. "What are you doing here, Remy?"

"I came to see if you care enough to work for it."

"I care." I release a heavy breath. "I care," I repeat, holding my head in my hands.

"I know you do, but I'm not talking about the TAC."

That has me lifting my head a little too quickly. My neck crackles, and I try to sit back in my chair. "What are you talking about then?"

"Penny. Those kids. The town. Stepping into someone else's shoes is one of the hardest things to do. You're a leader. You were never meant to follow. But you've been wandering without direction for some time now."

"Let me guess. You had a talk with Ashton?"

"No, I looked into your eyes."

I pinch the bridge of my nose and count to ten. If he's about to tell me he's some kind of fortune teller or something, I'll officially think he's off his rocker.

"Okay, I'll bite. What did you see in my eyes?"

"Myself," he says as carelessly as you would toss an empty box into the recycling bin. "I focused on the wrong things for so long that I lost the one pure joy in my life before I ever got to appreciate her."

A jolt of pain has me rubbing my fist into my chest just above my heart. When I find him watching the movement, I drop my hands to my sides.

"I'm sorry for your loss." The sadness that fills my heart at his words is surprising.

"It was forty years ago now." He speaks with a gentler tone, but he's not looking at me. He's staring at something I can't see with regret filling his eyes.

"Forty? That's a long time."

"It's a long time to be alone, yup. But you know how that feels, now, don't ya?"

That question makes me shift in my seat uncomfortably. "It hasn't quite been forty years for me, Remy."

He leans back, folds his arms over his round belly, and then kicks his feet out in front of him. It's a relaxed position, almost like he's going to sleep. But he just stares at me.

And stares.

And stares.

"Ah, Remy? I'm kind of on a time crunch here. I need to see Kai. And Penny. All the kids. Even fucking Miller."

"You know what's funny about that statement?" His eyes crinkle at the corners.

"What?" I'm about to start pacing again when he speaks.

"The first person you said you needed to see was Kai. Not Penny."

He's right. I wait for the guilt to come, but it never does.

"They're a package deal," I say, "and he's so young. I made him a promise I think I might have broken. I don't really remember, but I need to make it right."

"I think when a man can love another man's child as much as his own, he'll never let them down. That's what Kai needs. That's the kind of man that family needs. That's the kind of man my town needs. Are you that man, Dillon Henry?"

There's so much pressure and responsibility in his statement that I pause. Not because I don't want to be, but because I think I want it more than anything in the world.

But can I do it?

"I've heard you grew up much like Kai is, Dillon." He sighs, and it hits hard. He's tired, but he keeps pushing on. "I did too, back in the day. It's a cycle that's hard to break, but sitting here with you now, and seeing the way you want to protect those kids, I believe in you, son. You're just what we need."

My breathing gets shallow, and my throat closes up. This old man is going to make me cry right here in a county jail. And I think he's laughing about it.

I look over, and sure enough, he's laughing at my tears.

"They don't make you boys like they used to." His chuckle dies down to a happy smile. "And I think that's for the best. You'll do better than the generation before and encourage the next generation to do the same. You have heart, Dillon. You have love and loyalty. You can do this. If you want it."

"I want it," I hear myself saying. There was no thought, no pause. I want it. Then reality sets in. "But only if we can bring Miller on full-time. Whatever he needs to make that happen, we do."

Remy pulls a handkerchief from his chest pocket. "I think that's a fine idea," he says, then scrubs the cloth over his face to hide the emotion peeking through. "I'll have all the paperwork ready for ya over at the TAC. What are your plans?"

What are my plans?

"I need to make sure Penny, Kai, and the kids are okay, and then I'll go to the city and pack a few things. I have some loose ends to tie up with Envision and my condo so it might take a couple of days. Then I guess I'm moving to Chance Lake."

A weird tingling sensation takes over my entire body. I'm happy. I'm scared shitless, but I'm happy and excited—more than I ever remember being in the past. Like I'm finally alive and full of possibilities and my body is responding to it.

"Well, there's a truck outside waiting for you. It's not fancy, but it'll get you where you need to go. When you get back, we'll get started."

I'm already on my feet, anxious to get to Penny's house, when he stops me.

"I believe in you, Dillon. But this is a major life change that doesn't just affect you. It affects Penny, her kids, and everyone in town. I know you want to run off and be that girl's hero, but don't. Go to the city. Take the time to really think about what this means, and then, if you still want it all, come find me."

"But, Remy, I have to see Penny before I leave."

"Call her. Take the time to think. Make sure it isn't only high emotions that are propelling you. Take the time, Dillon."

"I hate leaving without seeing her," I say.

"If you come back, you'll never have to leave her again."

"I'm coming back. There's no doubt about that."

Remy smiles. Pulling a real smile from this old man feeds my soul and makes me want to do it again. "If that's so," he says clearing his throat and adopting his signature grumpy tone. "The faster you leave, the faster you can come back."

This time when I reach for the door, he doesn't stop me. One step after another, I race to grab hold of my future.

CHAPTER 23

PENNY

Miller says something, but I'm not paying enough attention to comprehend his words. We're all piled in my family room, waiting for the call from the sheriff's office to pick up Dillon. He's been gone for hours.

Maybe they released him, and he's already halfway back to the city. I wouldn't blame him for that, but I would have at least liked to thank him.

"Penny?" Miller says, obviously not for the first time, and I realize I've only been half listening.

"I'm sorry," I say with a shrug.

"Did you hear what I said?"

I shake my head and peek at the kids. Mari is asleep upstairs in my room, and Kai is resting in his, but the other four are across the room playing, even if they're a bit subdued. Kai ended up with three stitches and enough anger to light the entire state. Landon hasn't said anything since we got back from the hospital. Gage, Izzy, and Lia have been abnormally quiet, but they seem to be bouncing back better than the older two.

"I said, Eddy is getting more dangerous. He's gotten progressively worse over the last few months, but now it's scary. He could have killed them if he got them in the car today."

My vision tunnels as my greatest fear flashes before my eyes. Right now, I have no protection for them. He's their father. And I have zero rights when it comes to the girls. They're not mine.

"I don't know what to do." I choke back a sob and turn my head to hide my expression from the kids.

"You do know, Penny. You just have to do it. It won't be pretty, and Eddy will be pissed, but you have to get full custody now. He can't have access to them unless he gets well."

We've been barreling toward this truth for about a year now. But in the last few months, something has changed. It's time to accept that the Eddy I once knew is no longer there. I don't know the monster he's become, and it's my job to protect my family.

"I know." I blow out a deep breath. "I was hoping I could save a little more for a lawyer before I called, but you're right. It's time."

Knock. Knock.

My eyes flash to Miller's. "Is that Dillon?" My voice is fragile as hope consumes me.

Miller shakes his head. "Lenny said he'd call when he can release him." He stands and walks the few steps to my front door.

Maybe I'm still in shock because it didn't even occur to me to answer my own door.

"Came to get the kiddos," Remy's throaty voice calls out. The sound of three hard claps tells me they're hugging. Remy always gives three rough pats when he's ready to be done with a hug.

"Thanks, Rem," Miller says. "Did you hear anything?"

Remy tries to lower his voice, but his hearing isn't what it used to be so a whisper to him is loud chatter for everyone else. "Eddy's in it this time. Child endangerment. Abuse. That's some shit."

"What about Dillon?" I stand quickly and cross to them, hoping to keep as much from the kids as possible. But children are intuitive little things, and when I look down, all eyes are on the door.

"Haven't heard," Remy mutters, but his gaze flicks away quickly.

My chin quivers, and he pats my shoulder like a father unused to tears. "Let's get the kids over to the TAC to run around. I've set up the Boy Scouts' campground in the auxiliary gym and the blow-up movie screen Ashton bought too. They can camp out there for a few hours while you sort ya"—he gestures toward my tears—"stuff."

Some of the tension bleeds from my shoulders knowing I'll have a little time to process everything without having to be strong for the kids. Somehow Remy always knows what we need, even if he doesn't know the details of it.

Miller moves beside me to pack a backpack for the kids, and Remy steps closer. "Aster isn't at the house," he mutters. "Have ya seen her?"

"What? No. She said..." He shakes his head to cut me off.

"Word is, Eddy was on a bender, mouthing off about how she took all her stuff out of the house. I went over to check before stopping by here. She's gone."

She's gone.

And I have her girls.

My knees wobble, threatening to buckle and throw me to the floor.

I'm barely getting by with the boys, and they're in school

most days. How will I care for two more who need full-time childcare too?

"We'll figure it out, Penny," Miller mumbles beside me. "I got you."

"We always do," Remy agrees.

The three of us share a look, but only Remy looks convinced.

❧

STRAPPING MARI INTO THE BABYBJöRN, I pat her back and sway side to side. "Why haven't they called yet?" I ask Miller.

Without the little kids here, I can unload a little of my worry. Kai had a headache but, luckily, no concussion. He's upstairs watching TV in my bed while the littles are terrorizing the small gym of the TAC.

"I'm not sure, but Dillon has a lot of resources. I'm sure whatever's happening, he has it handled."

"I'm scared, Miller. About everything."

"I know, Pen." He glances at the staircase and then stands in front of me. "I think you need to call that lawyer, though. Like, tomorrow. Find out what your options are."

"Options?"

He glances down at the sleeping baby on my chest. "For the girls. You can't just hold on to them until Aster decides to show up. What if something happened and you had to take them to the hospital? How are you going to work? There's a lot to figure out."

"I'm barely holding it together," I admit, and my lip trembles.

"I know. And you know I'll do whatever I can to help. We'll do this together, like we've done everything else since Izzy was born. Maybe I can talk to Remy about suspending your lease on the land for a few months."

God, the lease. Remy owns the land, and until recently, he's been amazing.

"What's that look?"

"What look?" I duck away so he can't search my eyes.

"Jesus, Penny. What is that look?" He points a finger at my face.

"Remy—" My stomach plummets. I don't want to tell Miller this. "Well, he's raised my lease three times this year. He must be hurting more than we knew."

Miller's face goes harder than I've ever seen. "Who told you that?" He's seething mad, so angry that spittle flies from his lips. Unease makes my stomach turn.

"Aster did. Eddy and I share the land, so we split it. I was late with mine this month. That's why he went to Lochlan's hotel in the first place."

"Penny." He pinches the bridge of his nose. "When was the first increase?"

Mari wiggles in the baby carrier, and I adjust her with a hand under her little bum. "Ah, I'm not sure. I'd have to check. About six months ago, maybe? Aster told me Remy came by, and she relayed the message."

"Fuckers. The both of them. From now on, make your payments directly to Remy. I don't care what Eddy says. Okay?"

"What's going on?" That unease in my stomach sizzles up my spine until I think the nausea might win.

"Pen, I help Remy with the books. I know for a fact he hasn't increased your rate. Ever."

My head spins like I might pass out, and I grab hold of his arm to keep upright. How could I have been so stupid? Shouldn't I know better than to trust them?

The phone rings next to the TV, but it barely registers. When I make no effort to move, Miller reaches down to answer it. It's another sign that I'm not thinking clearly.

"Hello? Yeah," he says, and I move closer, trying to hear who it is. "For how long?"

"Who is it?" I mouth.

"Then what?" He turns his back on me, but I walk around him to face him. He spins again to get away from me.

"What the hell, Miller?" I whisper-yell, then tug on the hair elastic that's always been my nervous habit.

"Are you sure?"

I wave in front of his face, and he once again spins away from me. I stomp my foot, and Mari gives a disgruntled baby cry but settles quickly.

"Make damn sure you know what you're doing before you come back here. There's no turning back once you do this," he mutters.

Silence.

"Fine." I watch in irritation as he replaces the phone.

"Seriously, what the hell, Mill? Who was that? What did they say? Who is doing what?"

"It was Dillon."

That's it. That's all he says.

"Why did he call the house phone? Why didn't he call me? Where is he?" Each question has my voice pitching higher. "Is —is he okay?"

Miller nods abruptly twice. "He lost his phone in the scuffle. I have to go dig through the snow for it." He turns to look me in the eyes. Really looks me in the eyes, then says, "He's on his way back to New York."

My mouth opens, and my lungs seize like I'm drowning. I can't get any breath in or out. "Oh," I finally whisper.

I knew it was coming. I've told him all along my life is too messy. Too complicated. Too much. I'm too much. Isn't that what Eddy always used to say?

"Right," I nod. Blink. Then nod again. But I'm not really looking at anything as my eyes blur. "That makes sense. Get home before the next storm sets in. I—I'll have to thank him for his help on Wednesday."

My stomach plummets to my toes like I took a punch to my gut, and I can't catch my breath.

Wednesday.

Oh, no. I can't see him on Wednesday.

"Miller, I—I can't see him at work. Not after what happened in my bathroom. Not after what he saw here. Oh my God. What have I done?"

"Sit down," Miller commands.

I rest my ass on the edge of the sofa and recline like I was dropped there so Mari can sleep against me.

"I don't know what happened in your bathroom," Miller says with a teasing lilt to his voice. When I look up, he's smiling.

"Why are you smiling? The kids. The kids are going to be heartbroken. They didn't get to say goodbye. Maybe we can FaceTime a thank you when we find his phone. Oh, his phone."

I try to stand, but he places a hand on my shoulder to gently push me back down.

"I don't think you'll need to FaceTime him."

All the blood drains from my head, making me woozy. "After all, all of this," I say, waving a hand around my house. "He doesn't want to see me again, does he?"

Miller drops onto the sofa next to me.

"Just the opposite, actually."

My head snaps to him so fast my dirty hair whips Mari in the face. I brush it away quickly and pat her back while staring open-mouthed at Miller.

"What are you talking about?" I hate how my voice trembles. Hate those tiny grains of hope that seep into each word.

"Remy bailed him out of jail and didn't tell us." He leans

back and wraps both arms along the back of the sofa. "Seems he made a deal with your lover boy."

"What kind of deal?" I can barely get the words out. They sound small and fragile.

"One that has him driving like a bat out of hell to New York to pack his shit."

"Pack?"

"Pack."

It takes more than a minute for my brain to understand.

"He's moving to Chance Lake. At least for now," he says smugly.

If I weren't already sitting, I'd definitely fall over.

"I mean, I knew…" What? What did I know? "I knew," I try again. "That Ashton wanted him to stay for a while, but I assumed he'd commute. Or—or…"

"Or move into one of the apartments at the TAC to be closer to you. Looks like you snagged yourself a white knight, missy."

"I didn't ask for one," I say numbly.

"Does anybody ever ask for one? Or do they just ride in on their Tesla when you need them the most?"

I give him the side-eye but can't find a response. Do I want a white knight?

Yes, you idiot. You want that white knight like you want your next breath, but only if it's Dillon.

We sit in silence for long moments. Long enough for Miller to get antsy. He's never been good at sitting still.

"I don't even want to know what happened in your bathroom." He grins.

A laugh bubbles out of me. Just because Dillon is supposedly moving to Chance Lake doesn't make all my problems disappear. If anything, it makes them more complicated, but I can't help feeling like maybe, just maybe, I won't be so alone anymore, either.

CHAPTER 24

DILLON

*R*emy's truck is about a hundred years old and shakes like it'll fly right off its frame when you go over fifty miles per hour, so the drive back to New York is long.

Too fucking long.

The sheriff assured me Eddy would be drying out in detox for at least a few days and then hopefully in jail even longer, but my skin burns like someone's holding a match to it when I think about Penny and the kids home alone with him still so close.

I tug on the ends of my hair, trying to focus and get my shit in order, but the only thing I can think, feel, or see is them.

All of them.

As mine.

The image of Kai falling into the iron post of the mailbox pops into my brain, and I hit the steering wheel. It'll be a nightmare that replays on repeat for the rest of my life. My heart stopped when I saw his blood, and a protective rage sent fire through my veins, as violent and unforgiving as lava.

Is it normal to have these thoughts after such a short time?

If it's not, I'm pretty sure I don't even care.

This is how I feel. It's real, and honest, and mine, and no one can take that from me.

The ancient phone Remy left for me to forward my calls to vibrates on the seat next to me, and I look down at a number I recognize on the screen. Ryder. Good. I need to talk to him.

"Hello," I bark. My emotions are too high for anything else. Not when every reaction feels like not enough.

"Heard you're a free man. Mind telling me why you're getting arrested in some small-ass town I've never heard of?"

"Ryder, if you tell me Ashton has already called you, I will lose my goddamned mind."

"I won't tell you then."

No point in trying to tame the growl that comes out of me. But this is how Ashton keeps those he loves safe. Wouldn't I do the same for Penny and the kids?

Stupid question. I'd do anything I could to keep them safe. And I will. As soon as I get back to Chance Lake.

"What's going on, Dill?" Ryder's voice is missing his usual light tone. He actually sounds concerned.

"You're getting a permanent promotion. Effective immediately." I'm not ready to explain what's going on in my mind. Not until I can explain it to Penny first.

Silence.

"What did you do?" he asks warily, and I picture him scanning his desk for our lawyer's information. It makes me lay down a little of the bite in my words.

"They need me, Ryder," I finally say. "And honestly, I need them too. I can live off the money I've made at Envision for the next thirty years. I don't need that job. It was just a time-filler."

"And you have a trust fund." He chuckles dryly.

"Had. I had a trust fund."

Slowly the pounding in my ears eases until it's just mild anger living inside of me like a living, breathing force of nature.

"What did you do? Give it away?"

"I bought a giant warehouse."

"For forty million dollars?" He chokes on the words. "Is this because of your Wednesday girl?"

"Some of it," I admit. I wait for some kind of shame or worry to hit, but all I feel is blinding love.

"So she finally caved, and you're what? Going steady?"

"Not exactly," I hedge.

"Jesus, Dillon. You're doing this without a commitment? What happens if things don't work out?"

"Then I will spend the rest of my days looking out a lighthouse window with a pair of binoculars."

"Did you get punched harder than they said? You're not making any sense." Ryder definitely sounds concerned now, and if I were in his shoes, I would too. But he'll understand someday.

"It makes perfect sense, actually." Looking over my left shoulder, I put the blinker on and change lanes in this godforsaken city before continuing. "And since Ashton is such a busybody, you can call him for instructions on your promotion. It'll give him something to do."

"Hey, I'm not going to turn down more money. I was already doing your job anyway."

"Screw you."

"Hey, Dill?"

"Yeah?" I ask as the stop-and-go traffic finally starts to clear.

"I'm happy for you. I haven't seen you care about anything this much the entire time I've known you."

I let out a harsh breath and tell him the truth. "I haven't. This is where I'm supposed to be, Ryder. I know it."

"Well, then give them hell out there in the boonies! I'll catch up with you when you come into the city."

"Thanks, Ryder."

"Anytime."

I toss the phone onto the seat and a few turns later, I take a right into the valet of Lochlan's hotel. He's my first stop. I need to let him know that one of my guys will take over our Wednesday meetings for a while.

If not forever, the tiny goblin in my chest shouts, causing palpitations I can't control.

It should be too soon for thoughts like that.

Thoughts of forever and fairytales.

But fuck me because that's all I see.

And I really love what I'm seeing.

It's late when I pull in, so the normal guard isn't on duty, but everyone in this building knows me. And I'm guessing the giant black eye I'm sporting is why everyone is giving me a wide berth to enter.

No one says a word as I take the elevator to Lochlan's private floor, where he lives with his family.

When the elevator dings, I march with a singular purpose to his front door just as it opens.

"Dillon?" he asks, obviously surprised to see me. He glances down at my clothes, then back up to the shiner, drops the garbage bag he was holding just outside the door, and then opens it wide to allow me through. "What the hell happened to you?"

"Are we friends?" I ask instead of answering.

"After three years, a few weddings, some parties, and…" He sighs heavily. "Yes, Dillon. We're friends," he says.

I've never in my life met someone so opposed to friends.

"Good, because I need you to trust me when I tell you that Ryder is taking over for me at Envision, and he's as good as I am, if not better."

"Take a seat," he says, gesturing toward the sofa in his open-concept penthouse apartment with views of Gramercy Park.

He walks around the kitchen island and bends down out of sight. When he stands, he has an icepack in one hand and two beers in the other.

Huh. I never pegged Lochlan as a beer guy. He must read my expression because he almost, *almost* cracks a smile.

"Considering you're dressed like Old McDonald, I figured beer was the right call," he says dryly.

A bark of laughter escapes me as I accept the ice pack gratefully. My eye was starting to throb. I place the open beer he hands me between my legs because even the smell of it makes my stomach sour. I'm not sure why I even accepted it.

"What's going on?" he asks in a tone that tells me he might already have an idea.

"How much do you know?"

"Well…" He unscrews the top on his beer, then sits across from me. Even at home at almost eight o'clock at night, the guy is still in his vest and dress pants. I don't understand him. "I know Penny called to say she had a family emergency and needed some time off."

"Her ex is a fucking nightmare," I blurt.

"So I gathered." His voice is sharp and tight, like a protective older brother seeing his baby sister in a circle full of men.

"And he's putting them in danger. He tried to drive, wasted, with his four-year-old in the car. He tossed Kai around, ripped his shirt, then shoved him back so hard the kid hit his head and tore his scalp open."

"Obviously, you're telling me this as…" This time he does smirk.

"As your friend." I glare.

"Because…" he drawls.

"Because Penny is my friend too," I say, then exhale heavily as my shoulders slump forward. "And I need some advice. I know it's fucked up because she's your employee. And I know it's fucked up because we're coworkers."

He stays silent, allowing me to think out loud.

"But I don't think I give a shit, Lochlan. I've skirted around this for years. I like her. I like her a lot. And I really like her kids. Ashton, the prick, was making deals left and right trying to get me to Chance Lake, but really, he was setting traps to push Penny and me together, and I don't want to fight it anymore. I want to be there for her and her kids. I want her messy hair and her vomit-covered sweatshirts."

Lochlan scrunches up his nose.

"I want to be able to kiss the haunted look from her eyes and take on some of her burdens. I want it all, and to have it all means I can't be your point person at Envision. I don't even like working at Envision."

That last bit surprises me, and I sit back in stunned silence. I take a long pull from the beer he handed me as a diversion while I digest all the words that fell from my lips, but it transforms to acid in my gut, and I set it down on the coffee table before I get sick.

I've never been a big drinker, but after seeing Sweaty Eddy Demon-Fucker with Kai, I'm not sure I'll ever have the stomach for it again.

Sweaty Eddy Demon-Fucker.

I almost snort. I'll have to make a conscious effort not to call him that in front of the kids. I suspect it'll be an excruciatingly difficult task.

When I think the built-up rage has subsided enough for me to behave like a normal human being, I lower the ice pack to find Lochlan smiling at me.

"What?" I ask tentatively.

"Took you long enough, you arsehole."

I blink. Then blink again.

"What?"

"I'd have fired you a year ago if I'd known that was part of the reason you weren't pursuing Penny."

My jaw nearly hits the floor.

"You've never needed my permission," he continues. "I'm the one who married my event planner, and everyone around you has known how you feel about her for years. It's not a surprise, but if I have a choice, I'd rather not lose Penny. Even thinking about finding another assistant makes me bloody raging mad, so I need her to help me find her replacement."

"No," I say quickly. "She needs this job. She isn't going anywhere."

"Not yet, but you know how those Westbrooks are. They're always a step ahead of you with a plan or a hug."

That makes me laugh. "Yeah," I agree because it's true.

"How closely did you look at that deal Ashton was working on?"

A headache attempts to break free at that question. I rub my temples. Admittedly, there wasn't much in the way of fine print anyway. I trust Ashton and made a verbal agreement with Remy, so the details are still in negotiation.

"I've only seen the big picture," I say with a heavy sigh. "Everything has been a clusterfuck since I got there. I haven't had time to hash out the details."

"I suggest you do. I think what you find will be beneficial for you and Penny. And it means I'll get to keep her on my payroll."

Various scenarios run through my head. "You're going to build Remy's hotel. You've been in on this the entire time. You prick," I mumble, but there's no heat in my words. Maybe it'll come when I have time to think about how underhanded Ashton can be, but I don't have it in me right now.

"Not the entire time. But yes, I'll build the hotel, and Penny will run it."

My gaze snaps to his. That's more than being an executive assistant. "What are you saying?"

"Penny will have the chance to run that hotel. It's not so big that she can't learn on the job. I know she can handle it, and honestly, she's up for the promotion anyway, but I'd like to be the one to talk to her about it if you don't mind. The rest is all you, but the hotel is my news."

"Fair enough." But my mind is still processing everything that's happened in the last twenty-four hours. Staring at him, I shake my head. "I'm moving to the country."

"Sounds like it," he says with a chuckle.

"I've got a shit ton to do before the next storm hits." I stand and hand him the ice pack and the mostly full beer.

After seeing flashes of my childhood in the eyes of Penny's kids, even looking at the beer makes my stomach lurch.

"Good luck," Lochlan says with a genuine smile. One of the few I've ever seen from him unless his wife was around. "Let me know if I can do anything at all. And I mean anything. Penny is part of my family. I want to help if I can."

When I turn to look at him, his face is full of concern and honesty. "I will, Loch. Thank you."

"You know, I've heard that you and my wife grew up in a very similar situation as Kai."

I pause on the other side of the coffee table. I've never

been one to share this shit, but I do know a little about Tilly's childhood.

"What about it?" I ask.

"Like I told Kai, I can only go by what she's told me, and based on that, I'm really happy to see you finally having some agency over your life."

I rub at my forehead with my thumb and forefinger. "What do you mean?"

"Tilly said that it's pretty common for adult children of alcoholics to go with the flow, and that they're usually trying to broker peace so they never truly go after what they want. I'm happy that you're going after what you want now. That's all."

I think about his words. Was I just going through the motions and letting Ashton guide my future?

Probably. I hadn't ever thought about why that is before, but it makes sense.

"Yeah, I guess I am too. Thanks, Loch."

He offers a curt nod, then ushers me out his door. "Toss the rubbish in the chute on your way out."

I leave with a sense of purpose buzzing through my body like a hive protecting their queen, and with happiness in my heart, even if I am taking out the man's trash.

That went much smoother than I had anticipated.

It's like all the stars are finally aligning for us. All the stars, or all of Ashton's meddling.

And I don't even care how we got here. I'm just happy that we did.

PENNY

"This place is disgusting." Miller gags behind me.

Remy and Kai have all the kids at the TAC, even the baby, so we can't be here long even if we wanted to be.

"Just grab anything you think the girls might want or need. I don't have the money to replace everything."

"Where the hell would Aster have gone to? She doesn't have any family around here that I know of. And who walks away from their kids?" he rants, shoving crib bedding into a trash bag.

"She's just a kid herself," I defend, unsure of why I'm doing so.

"Maybe when she had Lia, but she's twenty-two now, Pen. Time to grow the fuck up."

"Lochlan said Dillon paid him a visit the other night," I say to change the subject, but I'm also fishing for information. I haven't heard from Dillon since he was arrested two days ago, and that pit of worry sits in my gut like a lead weight.

"Yeah? Remy said he showed up at the TAC at five this morning with a truckload of shit."

My hand stills in the laundry basket I'm digging through, searching for the girls' clothes. "He did?"

"Yup." Miller looks at me with a grin that lights up his eyes.

"I think I like him," I whisper. Knowing my face is heating from within, I start stuffing the bag I'm holding with Lia's clothing again.

"I think you do too."

"I haven't been with anyone—anyone but Eddy."

"Jee-zus," Miller grumbles. "Are we about to have a sex talk?"

"I haven't had sex with him, Miller. He just—" I pause and tug on my ear that suddenly feels sunburned. "He just did things to me."

He lets out a groan of irritation, though he's watching me closely.

"Penny, you know I love you, but you have got to get some damn girlfriends."

"It's not. I mean. It's not that I don't want them..."

His posture softens, and he nods before speaking. "Eddy isolated you when you were together—don't let him do it to you now. You used to have a ton of friends. You used to love having people around. Find that girl again, Penny. She was a lot of fun, and I think you'd like her. Skylar is back in town. You should go visit her."

Guilt makes my hands twitchy. It's an emotion I know like the back of my hand these days. Sky and I were really close growing up, though I'm a few years older than she is. But in the end, I chose Eddy, and we lost touch.

"Maybe." Even I'm not convinced by my tone.

"Ugh," Miller groans, pressing his fingertips into his eye

sockets. He's such a drama queen. "Fine. Until then, I'll be your Gilmore."

"Gilmore?" I laugh.

"I want to be Lorelei though. You're Rory, or Emily, just not Paris. Jesus, Pen." He runs a hand roughly through his hair. I don't even fight the smile. Who knew big bad Matty Miller was a closet *Gilmore Girls* fan? "Just don't drag it out, okay?" he groans. "And for what it's worth, I think Dillon is a good thing."

"Yeah?" Heat spreads down my neck as I fight to control a grin. Even the tension in my back and shoulders starts to release.

How can Dillon do that to me when he isn't even in the same building?

"Yeah. You deserve to be happy, and you deserve to have a partner. If he wants to be and do those things for you, I think you should let him try."

"He said he wants to try."

"What do you want?" he asks, studying me carefully.

What do I want? It's been so long since anyone's asked me that question. It takes me longer than it should to verbalize it.

"I don't want to feel like I'm drowning in guilt and fear anymore." Admitting that out loud unlocks something in my chest, and my breaths become shallow.

"Then let him in."

"It's not easy dating with kids, Miller, you know that."

He sits down on the sofa, then jolts upright with a curse when cans crunch beneath him.

"You've kinda skipped over a lot of the first date stuff, Penny. He's met your kids. He likes your kids. And most importantly, he's good with them. You've spent years with Mr. Wednesday, now get to know him as Dillon."

Pulling the strings of the trash bag, I glance around the

stale, musty room. "Would you let someone into Izzy's life so easily?"

"Oh, make no mistake, Penny. There's nothing easy about this. But he's here. He's in it, and it doesn't appear that he's leaving anytime soon. But to answer your question?" His face changes like he's watching a memory only he can see, and a hint of sadness filters through his amber eyes. "Yeah, I would. Life is too short to go it alone. We need love in our lives. It's what keeps us going."

"How do I know it won't end up like this?" I ask, sweeping my hand around Eddy's home.

"Penny, seriously? You're not fourteen anymore. You've experienced what you don't want in your life. If any piece of you thought for a second that Dillon could end up like Eddy, you wouldn't have allowed that little bathroom rendezvous of yours."

My knees buckle at his words, and he gives an uncomfortable chuckle.

"That good, huh?" Then he holds up his hands. "Never mind. Forget I asked."

But I'm already speaking. "It was like nothing I've ever experienced." He pinches the bridge of his nose but doesn't stop me. "He just—with his hands. And I had my clothes on. But I, God, Miller, I couldn't even stand after. And then when I tried to—"

"I've got the picture," he interrupts, then looks to the ground with his hands low on his hips. The slow head shake comes next, and I know he's contemplating how deep to go in this conversation.

"That's how it's supposed to be, you know?" He lifts his gaze but keeps his head bowed, like this really is embarrassing for him. "That fluttering in your belly? The lightning bolts that shoot through you? That's what shared intimacy does to sex." The word "sex" gets caught in his throat, and he coughs and then rolls his shoulders. "Damn it, Penny. This is like having a sex talk with your little sister. I'm really freaked the fuck out right now."

Unexpectedly, my laughter rings throughout the dirty house. And it feels so damned good. "Miller! How are you going to have a sex talk with Izzy if you can't even talk about it with me?"

"Easy. Izzy isn't having sex until I'm dead." His face is set in hard lines. This sweet man believes his own bullshit.

"Well, I'll make a deal with you, then. When the time comes, you talk to my boys, and I'll talk to Izzy."

He wraps me in a brotherly hug while holding his hands away from my body because we're both covered in grime from poking around in here for so long.

"Deal," he finally says softly. "We're family, you and me. We'll figure it out. I've got you, Pen."

"Got you too," I whisper, nodding into his chest.

When he steps back, his signature crooked grin is in place. "I have a feeling I'll make out pretty good in this deal, though."

"Oh, yeah? Why's that? I have three boys. You'll have to teach them all how to use a condom, but I'll only have to have that conversation once."

The sound of a door slamming in the driveway has me spinning around and leaning down to look out the window. Fear that Eddy's home slams into me until Dillon comes into view, stomping through the snow with a scowl on his face.

Miller leans down next to me. "That is why I think I have the better end of this deal. If you think that man will let anyone but him play daddy, you've got another thing coming."

The door bursts open, and Dillon's wild hazel eyes cut straight to mine. The air that swirls around my feet is frigid, but my body is on fire.

"What are you doing here?" he asks, looking from me to Miller and back again.

"Getting the girls' stuff. I can't afford to replace it all," I explain as Miller says, "Aster skipped town."

"It smells like a college bar in here," Dillon says, closing the door behind him.

His nose scrunches up in disgust, but there's something else lingering in his eyes. It's understanding and sympathy. I know a little about his past, but watching emotion cloud his eyes, I know I was lying to myself. I want to know everything about Dillon, not only what you can cover on hour-long coffee dates.

"Let's get everything you need so we don't have to come back," he growls. His eyes appear haunted as he looks around the small house.

"We?" Miller teases.

"I'm here, and I'm here for good," Dillon replies, leaving no room for argument, but his eyes never leave mine until Miller nudges him in the back and hands him a bag.

"Start loading up the truck. We can wash everything at the TAC before taking it to Penny's place."

"Dillon, your face. Are you okay?" My voice shakes. The closer I get to him, the easier it is to see the dark, angry bruise on his cheekbone in the dim lighting. His eye is still a little swollen and bloodshot, but his expression is determined when he looks at me like he can read my deepest fantasies and slay the dragons that keep me up at night.

"I won't pull away if you want to kiss me better." A slow grin spreads across his face, showing perfectly straight teeth and that damned dimple of his. I'm pretty sure he short-circuits my brain.

It takes a minute for his words to register because I'm so focused on his blindingly white teeth, but his smile ignites sparks in my chest. He leans down into my space, and I gently lift my lips to his battered cheek. The second they touch his skin, rough with days-old scruff, electricity zaps through my body. He's a live wire lighting up my world.

His exhale whooshes over my face like a weighted blanket that calms my nerves. "We have a lot to talk about, but I'm fine, sweetheart. I want to know how Kai is doing and that you're okay, but I want to have all of these conversations when we're not standing in this hellhole. It—" He shudders before he refocuses on me. "It brings back a lot of bad memories. No kid should have to grow up like this, Penny. I know that more than anyone could ever understand."

"Is it too much for you?" I try so hard to keep my voice from trembling and fail miserably. "This is what my life is like right now, Dillon." That familiar pang of shame has my stomach churning and sweat beading the ridge of my spine.

"Penny?" I lift my chin, and he captures my lips in a chaste kiss. "You could never be too much because every piece of you I get makes me ravenous for more. I'm here for you, but the last place I want to do anything is in your ex-husband's filthy home. Can we get out of here?"

"Yeah." I sigh against his chest, not even realizing my body had melted into his until he runs his hands down my back. "They don't have as much stuff as I thought." I step back and look around, but he keeps me close.

Dillon squeezes my waist, and a shimmer of self-doubt creeps into my tired mind. What does he think when he touches me like that? Because he definitely has a handful of me. But when I look up, his expression is only filled with love and concern. It's enough to make my weary emotions cross signals until I no longer recognize what it is I'm feeling.

"What do they need?" he growls. "Make a list, and I'll get it to your house as soon as possible."

He moves, but my feet don't seem to be working. "This isn't your responsibility to fix," I say gently.

"And it's yours? The boys should go without because your ex-husband can't handle his shit? They're little girls, Penny. They can't need that much. Just make a list and let me do this for you."

"Take the help, Pen," Miller yells from the back of the house before walking to the door and heading out into the winter wonderland that refuses to stop dumping its white glitter on us.

When I still don't move, Dillon leans down, and suddenly I'm airborne with my ass in the air and my forehead flopping against his back.

"Dillon!" I screech. His hand lands hard on my ass, and I'm knocked speechless by the tingling sensation racing through my body that I've never, ever felt before. Even Miller's low chuckle does nothing to help me out of the weird fog settling over my body and brain.

I bring my hands around to massage my ass, but Dillon beats me to it. It's not meant to be sexual—at least, I don't think it is—but my mouth is dry, and my panties are damp.

What. The. Hell?

"I'll lock up," Miller says from somewhere close by. I'm still upside down and can't get my bearings.

A hand lands on my lower back, and then Dillon slides me down his body with eyes that sparkle like he knows what I'm thinking. "Oh, my sweet girl. The things I'm going to do to you."

His voice is dark and smooth. Like expensive chocolate that has me licking my lips for a taste of every last morsel.

"Not now, Romeo. We've got to get the kids from Remy. The old geezer is probably ready for a nap," Miller says before climbing into the cab of his truck.

That's when I notice Dillon's got a new SUV. "New wheels?" I ask with a shaky grin. He's standing in front of a gunmetal gray Suburban that looks to be brand new. "Kai is never going to let you live this down. He knew your other car wouldn't cut it in this snow."

Dillon presses a button, and the engine roars to life. "We couldn't all fit in my Tesla, smarty-pants. And I'm not built for a minivan."

"You riding with me or Romeo?" Miller shouts from his open window.

"I've got her," Dillon answers for me since my lips are no longer working. "But I'm meeting with Remy in an hour." He returns his gaze to me. The intensity in his features wraps around me like a hug. The odd sensation that he can sense my darkest fears unnerves me, and I turn my attention to his new truck as he continues his conversation around me. "I have some stuff to talk to you about, too, Miller. Can you be there?"

Miller's laughter fills my ears, but I'm singularly focused on Dillon's new vehicle. "You need me to drive you over there on one of the sleds. But yeah, I was supposed to bring his groceries over later anyway. Ten bucks the old man planned that too."

Then Miller pulls out of the driveway, and I'm left staring at Dillon's SUV. I don't notice that he's closed the distance between us until his warm breath lands on my heated skin.

This time when he kisses me, it's deep and demanding. He's asking for ownership of my pleasure, and my responding sigh tells me everything I need to know.

I'm in over my head.

His tongue presses at the seam of my lips, and I open on a whimper. He explores and works every inch of my mouth until I'm gasping for breath, but I kind of miss his root beer flavor.

"A lot is coming our way, Penny," he says against my lips. "It won't be an easy few months, but I'm all in now. Everything I have. Everything I am. It's here." His warm hands hold my freezing face, and his fingers flex against my scalp with each declaration. Like he's promising everything my wounded-little-girl heart ever wanted.

But my grown-up heart is hardened through layers of betrayal. It's made me wiser and safer.

He knows it, too, because he doesn't give me a chance to answer. Instead, he releases my face and takes my hand. He's leading me to the SUV when his steps falter.

"C—Can I see Kai?" He stumbles over the words like he thinks I'll say no, and my chest expands painfully.

"Of course you can, Dillon. I don't even know what would have happened if you hadn't been there. I don't know how to thank you for that. I haven't been able to sleep because how do you say thank you to someone who may have saved your child's life? Nothing seems good enough."

"Baby," he says like it's painful. "The only thing I'll ever want from you is a chance. A chance to be who and what you need. And a chance to be what and who your children deserve."

I scratch at my throat like I can't breathe. His words, they seem too good to be true. But he's here, looking at me like everything he says is the truth.

And what shocks me the most is that I want to believe him.

He reaches over and takes my hands away from my neck. "Just a chance."

"Just a chance," I repeat because my mind is trying to make a list. A list of ways this could go wrong and ways I could get hurt, but it won't quite form. For the first time in my life, making a list won't save me.

"Let's get out of here. I really do have to get to Remy's, but I want to make sure I have time to speak with Kai before it gets too late. It's important."

That makes everything running through my mind come

to a screeching halt. "Is everything okay?" My thoughts immediately jump to lawsuits, jail time, and my ex.

Dillon squeezes my hand. "Everything's fine. I'd just like to speak with Kai."

"Sure. Of course." He opens my door, and I slide into the plush leather. I've never felt anything so smooth.

The drive to the TAC is short, and it's over before I'm ready. But Miller's right. Gage alone is enough to have Remy regretting his very generous offer of babysitting, again.

As we pull into the parking lot, I glance around in confusion. Four brand-new vehicles with paper license plates are lined up in a neat row at the front door. They have "TAC Athletic Complex" on the side in bright kelly-green lettering.

He squeezes my hand and flashes me a smile that I'm certain has broken some hearts. Then he dips his head forward like he's embarrassed, and a lock of golden-brown hair falls into his eyes.

"I told you. Lots of changes." Then he's out of the SUV and standing in front of it with his hands in his pockets. He's studying my reaction with a sheepish expression on his face.

What in the fresh hell is happening? He's been gone two days, right? Not two weeks?

Mom-brain has me actually questioning that since Mari was up most of the night.

He finally rounds the SUV to my side, opens the door, and holds out his hand. "Trust me, sweetheart."

Three little words that have held no weight my entire adult life buoy me like a life raft in the middle of the ocean. I have no option but to hold on to him for dear life.

DILLON

Just before we reach the TAC doors, I release Penny's hand. I think she's agreed to give me a chance, but I'm not willing to set us back by pushing too hard in front of her kids.

The door opens before I can reach for it, and Miller lets out a long, low whistle. "City boy has some connections. He didn't even buy them from the Brandts. He shipped them in from Bevvy, two towns over," he says to Penny with a nod toward the assortment of vehicles.

I seal my lips shut tight to keep from cursing. They were supposed to deliver those straight into the garage.

Before he can say anything else, I try to make light of it and fill her in without overwhelming her. "Well, as the new owner of the TAC, I can't be seen supporting the Brandts now, can I?"

It's meant to lighten the mood, but she pales, which means I'm fucking it all up.

"You bought the TAC?" she whispers, a beautiful crease appearing between her eyebrows. The smallest imperfection, and I have an overwhelming desire to soothe it away.

"Well, not yet," I say, tugging on my jacket zipper and dropping my gaze. I'm suddenly boiling in my own sweat. "The paperwork will take a few weeks. But we have an agreement in place." Stepping into the entryway, I mutter, "Sort of."

The sound of Mari crying sends all three of us in that direction, and now I know I wasn't imagining the dark circles under Penny's eyes. She's done a good job of hiding them with whatever makeup women use to do that shit, but I feel it now in her hunched shoulders and how she shuffles her feet instead of walking with her usual purposeful stride.

Before we enter the auxiliary gym, I wrap my arm around her shoulders and lower my mouth to her ear. "What's wrong, baby?"

Her eyes widen as she glances around, but I know I kept my voice low enough for no one else to hear.

"You can't. We have to…"

"We have to talk. And we will. But make no mistake, I'm here to try for you. That makes you my baby, my sweetheart, my fucking queen. It makes you mine if you'll have me, and it definitely makes me yours. Now tell me what's wrong."

"Nothing." But the weight of her sigh could knock over a brick house. "I'm just tired. Mari's teething. She was up all night."

Placing both hands on her shoulders, I turn her to face me. "I'm here now. I'll help tonight." She tries to pull away, but I move in tandem. "Let me speak to Kai, deal with Remy and Miller, and then I'll be over with dinner. Okay?"

Even if she wanted to fight me on it, I think she's too tired and stressed to do it, so she nods.

With a final squeeze on her upper arms, I let her go and watch as she enters the gym. Gage is running in circles with Izzy chasing him. Kai sits, swaying Mari on his shoulder.

Landon, Lia, and Remy are seated at a card table with papers strewn about.

But my eyes keep drifting back to Kai. So much responsibility is thrown at this young boy's feet. Penny tries to shield him, but like a lot of kids who grow up like him, he feels a responsibility to the household that won't allow him to be a kid.

If I do one thing right with him, it has to be teaching him to enjoy what's left of his childhood. He deserves that and so much more.

Penny heads straight for Kai and Mari, lifting the baby into her arms before saying something to him and pulling him in close.

My chest pinches watching them, and my breathing shallows with a need to wrap them all up in my arms and put them in a bubble. My bubble.

"You are so fucked," Miller whispers at my side.

"I am," I say through the purest smile I've ever worn. "But I'm going to need your help." We're standing in a similar stance—side by side with our arms crossed over our chests, but I turn my head to face him. "A lot of help."

He looks from me to the family spread out in front of us, then finally to our surroundings. "You're going to get me in over my head, aren't you?"

"Abso-fucking-lutely." I grin. Cursing seems to be our love language. "Can you handle it?"

"Guess we'll find out after you tell me the plan instead of just throwing a challenge at me."

I clap him on the shoulder. It's a friendly reaction that should surprise me after trying to keep my circle small for so many years, but it doesn't. Miller is a friend. And if I have my way, he'll also be part of my family.

"I need to speak to Kai. Can you get everyone over to Penny's, and then drive me to the damn lighthouse?"

He chuckles and meanders over to Izzy. His laughter is light and unfettered, but I'm not naïve enough to believe he doesn't carry his own demons.

Demons.

My eyes immediately fly to the banners hanging all over this place. That is going to change. Now.

I stride to the closest banner and rip it down. The sound is like nails on a chalkboard and echoes loudly in the gym. Everyone turns to me.

"We're rebranding," I say, trying to keep the emotion from my tone and watching Kai's expression closely. When I think I see the first hint of relief wash away the sadness that boy carries like a noose, I rip another one down. "Have at it, kids. Put it all in a pile by the door."

The little kids run through the gym, excited by the possibility of destruction without consequences, and they have no idea of the deeper meaning happening above their heads.

With their laughter in my ears, I walk to Kai. My palms are sweaty, and I'm surprised to find I'm nervous. I rub them on the ass of my jeans just as I reach him.

"Hey, Kai. Can I talk to you for a minute?"

His eyes shift from his mom to me and back again. She must nod behind me because he mimics the motion before turning his eyes to mine.

"Sure."

I bite the inside of my cheek as his posture sinks, and I turn to Penny to figure out what the hell I did. She gives a shrug that I think is supposed to be encouraging, so I plow forward.

"Can we sit?" I ask Kai, and his shocked expression tells me he isn't used to having choices.

Neither am I, kid.

"Y—Yup." He backs into the chair he was in with Mari. I

pull another folding chair over to face him and place my forearms on my thighs.

He sits farther back in his chair with his hands in his lap like I'm making him more nervous, so I just blurt it out.

"I think I owe you an apology."

"What?"

"Why?" Miller asks, obviously eavesdropping.

"Dillon?" Penny says softly, but I hold up my hand to silently beg them all to stay out of it. If I have any chance with Penny, I need to win their trust.

Trust from each of them.

"After I saw what was happening the other day, I don't remember much but an impulse. A need more powerful than myself to keep you all safe. It's like I blacked out, but I need you to understand that I don't take my actions lightly. I would do it again if I had to, but I don't willingly choose violence. Ever."

I search his face, noting the first signs of stubble on his upper lip. In some ways, he's still a baby but forced to act like a man.

Kai's eyes water, but he blinks away the tears. When he opens his mouth, a thick string of mucus stretches between his open lips, a sure sign he's on the edge of what he can handle. He closes it without a sound, swallows, and tries again.

"You didn't do anything wrong, Mr. Dillon. You did what I couldn't. You kept Lia safe." He looks away like he's ashamed by that admission.

The air couldn't have been sucked from the depths of my lungs more painfully if someone had stabbed them with a knife.

Penny steps forward, but my eyes cut to hers, and I silently ask for a chance. A chance to have this conversation with her oldest son. She nods with a trembling chin.

"First of all—" My voice cracks. In the background, Remy tells the younger kids that he has ice cream in the kitchen. That man is a goddamned savior. "First of all, that's not your job, Kai. You were put in an adult situation, and you did protect her. You kept him from getting in that car and driving off. You stalled him long enough for me to get there. You did everything you possibly could, but it wasn't your job."

"She's my sister," he says with an edge to his voice that I'm not sure how to handle. Where am I going wrong?

Then it hits me. He's a little protector because it's all he's ever known. He doesn't have the healthy boundaries fathers are supposed to set.

So I try again. "When she's older and starts dating, that's the kind of protecting big brothers are supposed to do. Keeping her safe in a situation like we were in? That's not on you."

I shake my head while biting my tongue to keep from saying anything negative about his father. It's so fucking hard, but that's not what he needs from me. When he shifts in his seat, I work up the courage to continue before I lose him.

"But helping you protect your family is not what I'm apologizing for."

He frowns and looks at his mother. I follow his gaze to find Penny and Miller staring at me with twin expressions of confusion.

Leaning forward, I wait for Kai to look at me again. "I made you a promise, Kai. And I keep my promises, remember?"

He lifts his hand to scratch the side of his head but doesn't say anything.

"I'm apologizing because I don't remember what I said. It

was a moment of panic and true fear, and I don't remember what I yelled at your dad."

Kai's shaking his head, but this is important to me.

With the clarity of the rising sun, it hits me that he is important to me.

All of these people. Even this town. It all matters to me. This is what Remy was talking about. This is who I am now, their someone.

My body fills with a purpose I've never had. I've drifted through adulthood with no compass.

Until now.

They're my true north. My home.

"I don't get it," he says, and I blink out of the thoughts invading my mind. He looks at his mom.

We all do that. Look to Penny for guidance. For confirmation. She's our lighthouse, calling us all home. I offer her a small smile before returning to catch Kai's eyes on me.

"Kai." I sigh and look to the floor. Shame hits me hard, but I'll show him that I mean what I say and do what I mean. "I don't remember if I swore in front of you, and if I did, I broke my promise. I don't do that. Not ever, so if I did, I'm sorry."

Penny makes a gurgling sound, and Miller mutters something under his breath, but Kai stares at me like he's seen a ghost.

It's silent in the gym, and I can hear everyone's breaths as they slowly sync, slowly becoming one.

Whole.

Together we feel whole.

"For Christ's sake, Dillon. You were arrested and put in jail, and you're worried about saying a fucking curse word?"

I turn to Miller with a smirk. "It's important, potty mouth. And I wasn't really put in jail. I didn't even go behind bars. I just sat in a corner for a few hours." I raise my brow to get my point across, then return my gaze to Kai.

"You—You didn't swear. I don't think. I don't remember," he says honestly.

"So, if I did, you'll give me a pass and help me turn this place around?" I say, gesturing to the gym.

"Did you really buy it?" he asks cautiously.

I nod.

He looks at his mom. "Can I talk to Mr. Dillon? Alone. For a minute," he adds when her eyebrows pinch together.

Miller ushers Penny out of earshot with a warning glance for me.

I'm all in now.

"Are you doing this because you like my mom?"

Oof.

"That might be part of it. She's been the best friend I think I've ever had. But I'm also doing it for the other kids who need this place and for myself. I needed this place when I was a kid, and I sort of had that with Ashton's family. But truthfully, I wasn't happy in the city, and I think I can be here."

"Don't hurt her," he demands. He sits higher in his chair and puffs out his chest.

"I'm going to try hard not to. And I'll do my best to always be honest with you. I'm serious about this place, and I'm serious about building trust, Kai. That's the only foundation we can build on."

He bites his lip and watches me. It's like I can feel him fighting. Fighting the desire to believe me, fighting the anger that's been swelling inside him for years, and fighting the exhaustion of living the way they have.

"Listen," I say when he remains silent. "I know trust isn't something given easily, and honestly, it shouldn't be. Trust is something you earn. I told your mom the same thing, and now I'm telling you. I want the chance to earn that trust, but I've never been around that many kids. So if I mess up, I'm hoping you'll tell me. This only works if we're a team, and I've heard you're a pretty amazing team player."

His eyes widen slightly. "What's going to happen to my team?"

There he is. The kid he's supposed to be. The worries he's supposed to have.

"Your team is going to win the championship, and I'm going to help you do it."

"W—What do you mean?"

"If I hadn't been trying to hurt my father when I was younger, I probably would have entered the NBA draft before my senior year of college. But that was his dream. It was mine at one point, but he pushed so hard and only wanted me for what he couldn't do that I lost the love of the game and quit."

"You gave up the NBA? Are you serious?"

I get it. To a fifteen-year-old, that sounds insane. But if you don't love something with your whole heart, you can't give it your full effort. And the NBA required all of me.

"I didn't love it anymore, Kai. I resented it. I resented what it stood for and who it made me. I also didn't want to make my father proud of me anymore. Once I had that realization, I quit. I didn't want to do it for him, and I haven't felt the itch, that buzz that goes through your body, for the game again. Until now."

His eyes drift to the pile of ripped paper and torn banners. "My dad isn't going to like this."

"Probably not," I agree. "But that's a worry for me, not you. Whatever comes, I can handle it. And as far as this place?" We both look around the rundown gym. "Teamwork makes the dream work. Are you in?"

I stand and hold out my hand. Cautiously he does the same. His hand is tentative and limp in mine, so I release it.

"Try that again," I say, holding up my hand a second time.

Confused, he places his palm in mine, and once again, I release it.

"Again." This time when he puts his hand in mine, I squeeze it. "Always go into a handshake with confidence, Kai. You shake hands like you mean it. Like you belong, because you do. No matter where you are in life or who you're shaking hands with, at the end of the day, we all put one foot in front of the other. Believe in yourself, and let your strong handshake portray that."

He pulls his hand from mine and squares his shoulders. After a beat, he holds his hand out again. This time when our skin connects, his handshake is confident. He doesn't try to squeeze the life out of my hand, but he does hold it firmly, and the tiniest smile tugs at the corner of his lips before he brings his eyes back to mine.

"Good. That, my friend, is your first lesson in becoming a man."

"Thank you, Mr. Dillon. For everything."

"Call me Dillon or Coach. Mr. Dillon sounds like a pickle company."

As I'd hoped, he laughs, and the tension leaves my shoulders. When we turn, we find Penny and Miller watching us. Their expressions are different, but the emotion is the same.

I just built one more layer of trust.

CHAPTER 27

DILLON

"Hop on," Miller laughs, hooking his thumb over his shoulder.

"I can't believe I'm doing this," I grumble as I sling a leg over the back of his snow machine.

"Hold on, sweet cheeks." He guns it, and I almost topple off the back.

Dickhead.

Luckily, the ride to the lighthouse is easier this time around now that a path has been made by so many trips and a break in the snowfall.

When he finally slows to a stop, I hop off and remove my helmet. As I'm handing it to him, I ask, "Why a lighthouse, though?"

"Remy was in the Navy. When he started the TAC, he realized not everyone had a talisman to call them home. He recognized that more parents were being forced to work multiple jobs just to survive, and many of the kids in this area seemed lost. He's always told the town that the lighthouse was a safe place to center yourself when you feel lost at sea. I have no idea how many people he's taken in over the years or how many people he's helped get back on track, but if I had to guess, I'd say it's in the hundreds, and they all came here first."

"Do you know why he does it? Why he gives so much of himself?"

Miller shrugs and looks at the lighthouse. "Because he can. After the Navy, he became a mechanical engineer who created a device that helped release certain weapons remotely. He knew enough to trademark it, so when the Navy came calling, he cashed out. He does what he can because I think, like you, it was something that was missing in his life."

I don't have a response to that, so I follow him into the lighthouse, and up the spiral stairs, wondering again how Remy gets up and down these every day.

If he hadn't left the TAC early, I would have come with him. One of these days, I need to see if he's in any danger climbing these stairs multiple times a day.

"Rem? We're here," Miller calls out as we reach the top.

Remy is at the window with binoculars pressed to his face. This seems to be the only place he sits.

Curiosity gets the best of me. "What do you watch up here?"

The old man doesn't turn to us, but he answers in a voice gruff with age and wisdom. "It's huntin' season. I'm making sure those damn Brandt assholes don't try killin' my wildlife again. This is a protected area. Protected by me for over fifty years. And now it'll be protected by you. It's all in the paperwork."

For the second time, I try to imagine myself sitting up here, watching for hunters, and almost laugh. I think I can fall back on my security company training for this one and install cameras and sensors throughout the property.

He finally spins on his stool to face me. His face is wrinkled with age, but he's spry for as old as he is, and his eyes tell of more stories than I can fathom. He's also still wearing the jeans with duct tape, and I wonder if I should buy him some new ones until the cash transfer hits his account.

Remy misses nothing, though. "See that pile over there?" He points to a shelf overflowing with denim.

"Yeah," I reply.

Miller laughs. "Those are all the clothes we've bought him over the years for birthdays, Christmas, Father's Day, you name it. They all have tags on them still."

Tilting my head, I wait for an explanation.

"There isn't anything wrong with these, champ. You youngsters are wasteful, but in my day, you wore things until there was nothing left."

I cross my arms over my chest, and a smile slides across my face as I wait for him to continue. It's been a long time since I've been called "champ." Or young. Yet he does it every time he sees me.

"Arrogant too," Remy mutters, and I widen my eyes in surprise. He holds nothing back. "Why would I wear a new pair every day when some folks come through here with nothing but the shirt on their backs? The whole world needs to think of others a little more than they think of themselves. Imagine the difference it would make."

I nod, and he turns his attention to Miller. "Did you agree?"

"To what?" he asks. His eyes roam between Remy and me.

"I didn't have a chance to tell him yet," I say.

"Well, get to it then. I don't have all day. I don't want to end up on the wrong side of the grass before we get you squared away."

Miller and I chuckle because he literally does have all day, and the more I get to know him, the more I realize he's stubborn enough to outlive us all.

Remy taps the window behind him with his binoculars and gives the universal sign to wrap it up with his finger.

Miller laughs even harder when he sees my expression. But as soon as I take a deep breath, the laughter dies on his lips, like the last leaf on a maple tree.

"I need your help," I admit. It was harder to say those words than I care to admit. Growing up, I had Ashton's brothers and the rest of their family. As an adult, I learned to watch my own back.

I'm not used to needing anyone.

"So I gathered." Miller sighs and flops down onto the sofa. Remy perches like a bird, watching closely for his turn to step in.

"What are you asking of me?" Miller looks around the room nervously.

"You know the town, the people," Remy answers before I can. "You gotta help him get the votes."

"More than that," I say. "I need you full-time. It seems Ashton is willing to put money in but can't commit his time. I can put the money in, and I have the time, but I can't do this on my own. Not the scope of work we all have in mind."

Miller drags a hand through his hair. "You know I love this place, but I have Izzy. I can't leave the school gig. I need the insurance."

"Done," I say and widen my stance. With my arms still crossed over my chest, the first beads of nervous perspiration cause my shirt to cling to me. I really can't do this without him. Miller stands to face me and adopts a similar pose. "What else?"

"What else? What do you mean, 'done?'" Miller sputters, and Remy turns back to the window.

I'm really going to have to look more closely at those contracts. There's not a chance in hell I'll spend my days sitting up here waiting for someone to ambush me in fatigues and deer piss.

"Times have changed, Miller. To run this place, we'll need full-time employees. That means I'll offer you health, dental, vision, life—whatever kind of insurance you need, we'll offer. How much do you make as a gym teacher?"

"Physical Education teacher. The gym is where the class happens," he grumbles.

I'll give him that, but it will always be gym class for me.

"How much?" I ask again.

"About forty-five thousand," he mutters, then turns his back and paces the round room.

"I'll offer you one-twenty-five per year with a buy-in package. It's similar to what Ashton did for me at Envision Securities. Twenty-five grand will go to the buy-in, leaving you with one hundred thousand a year gross, but you'll own a stake in the TAC."

"It keeps it in the family," Remy says, nodding his head.

Miller bites his lip, and his eyes narrow as he thinks. "What does that entail? I still have to take care of Izzy. What about summers?" His voice breaks, possibly from nerves. "What exactly are you asking of me?"

"Technically, you'll be a VP. Functionally, you'll help me run the day-to-day after you help me win over the town. As far as Izzy goes, we'll offer childcare, summer camps, after-school programs—all of it. I'm going to ask Lochlan's sister-in-law to come into town this week. This is her specialty. She sets up child-focused community centers in areas where they either can't afford one or it simply doesn't exist. Your hours may change, but the heart of the TAC stays the same. If that means Izzy's running around here with Gage after school, then that's what it means."

He clears his throat, and his posture stiffens. "Are you doing this because of Penny?"

"I'm doing this to help her, yes. But I'm also doing it for the kids who grew up like me with abusive parents and need something to hold on to. I'm doing it for me too. I need this. I need a purpose that's not just about collecting a check."

"And if things don't work out with you and Penny? Then what happens?" There's a hard ridge of doubt in his tone that sets my teeth on edge, and I move forward so he can search my eyes.

"If you think I'm going to dump my entire net worth into a project and then walk away because 'things don't work out,' I haven't earned your trust yet. But make no mistake, I will. And to be clear, Penny is it for me. I don't give a shit if I have to wait another three years. She's it. If she decides I'm not hers? It'll fucking suck, but I want her happiness more than my own. I'll bleed out before I hurt her."

Miller steps up to me, so we're only a few feet apart.

"Boys," Remy interrupts, like he's spent his life breaking up fights.

"One fifty, and you have yourself a deal." Miller keeps a straight face for as long as he can, but a grin breaks free after only a few seconds.

"Deal. We start tomorrow. If you have to finish out the school year, I'll need your afternoons, maybe some nights and weekends. This will move fast with four crews working around the clock to have the TAC, or at least the gym, ready for the summer sneaker circuit leagues. Ashton and Remy have had the leg work done for months. The sneaky bastards were waiting for the right time to strike."

"And it ends up being sweaty Eddy who gets you here," Miller says, shaking his head. "I'll make the schedule work. How will this affect Penny?" he asks, and I decide I really do like this guy. He puts his family first, his entire family, and that includes Penny.

"Lochlan has a long-term plan he'd like to discuss with

her. In the meantime, I'll learn to take care of a baby and a four-year-old during the day while we do this, so she can continue to work."

"Got the paperwork she asked for from the pro bono attorney. She's gotta go to the judge a week from Monday for temporary custody of the girls," Remy says, then returns his attention to the window.

Pro bono? Hell no. If she needs a lawyer, we'll get her a damned lawyer. But something niggles at the back of my mind. Something telling me she hasn't thought of herself in a very long time.

"Did anyone ask if that's what she wants?" I rub my chest.

"They're her son's sisters, Dillon. Wouldn't you do the same thing?" Miller asks, but his expression says he's as worried as I am.

"But she needs to have a choice," I argue.

"She got one. I spoke to her in the gym," Remy says. "I offered to take the girls in. She politely declined."

Is there anything that gets past this man?

"Satisfied?" Remy asks. His body vibrates. He's tapping his toes, and there's a light in his eyes that wasn't there before.

He's as excited about this new venture as I am.

"For now," I say. My mind is on Penny, though.

"We're really doing this?" Miller asks.

"Looks like it." I give him my complete attention now. "Thank you, Miller. I think we're really going to make a difference here."

He holds out his hand, and I shake it. "I know we will," he says, but emotion chokes him up. "You've already made a difference, you know?"

"What difference?"

"In our lives. You more than tripled my salary. Do you have any idea what that will do for my life? And you love

Penny. Whether you acknowledge that or not, I knew it the second I saw you teaching Kai how to execute a proper handshake. All those things matter, Dillon. You are making a difference."

Now it's my turn to suck down the emotions. I clap him on the shoulder, but it's Remy who breaks us up with a huff.

"Get outta here, now. No one's got time for ya blubbering. But, Dillon?" Remy calls. "That folder on the table is Landon's. He left it here. I think ya should take a look. Seems like he could use someone too."

Worry seeps into my heart, and sweat trickles down my back as Miller and I hurry to the folder, elbowing each other out of the way in our race to reach it first.

I get there half a second before he does and flip it open. We stare for a long moment.

Inside are…drawings. More accurately, sketches. I've seen something like this before in Nova's studio when she was designing a dress. But he isn't sketching clothes. He's drawing buildings and their interiors.

"Holy shit," Miller whispers. "He's drawn the TAC."

"That fucker Demon Face told that boy that only pussies draw stuff like that. I'm sure there's more to it than that, but he keeps that part of himself hidden from the world now. Whatcha gonna do about that?" Remy stares at me with such intensity I feel the challenge of his words all the way to my toes.

"I'm going to fix it," I promise. "And then we're going to offer him an internship."

Miller's eyes slide to mine. "He's eleven years old."

"Exactly the age when childhood dreams start to die. But this?" I say, waving around his folder. "This is too much talent to be lost because of a misogynistic asshole. Even if that asshole is his own father."

"Proud of you, Dillon. Now get the hell outta here. I got

shit to do," Remy rumbles. But his words catch, and he turns away. It's the only show of emotion he's willing to give, but it's like a cannon shot straight to my heart.

I'm not sure the last time anyone said they were proud of me. It was probably when Ashton's dad was alive. That means I was a teenager. Maybe that's why it hits hard when he says it now.

With his words weaving through my heart like the magic from a wizard's wand, I try to thank him, but he waves me away.

This town. These people. This family. They might need me, but I need them more.

CHAPTER 28

PENNY

My front door swings open, and Miller walks in with four large bags full of food from Buttery Kuts, an amazing steakhouse in the next town over. I've only been there once years ago, and Eddy ordered for me, but I've dreamed of going back.

I had a salad while my mouth watered as steak after steak passed our table. It was only later that I realized he'd ordered the cheapest things on the menu, all so he could say he'd taken me there.

That's when Eddy had been worried about appearances.

The scent of butter and spicy seasonings makes me salivate until my mind catches up with my senses.

"Miller, what are you doing?" I hiss. "I know for a fact that neither of us can afford to eat at this place." What in the actual world is he thinking?

His smile is blinding as he leans down to kiss the top of my head. "Things change, Penny. Karma has a way of working out where to send the blessings, and today the blessings come straight from your crush."

"Dillon paid for this?" I'm not sure what emotion I'm feeling. Anger because he has already paid for my groceries twice this week. Melty because he must have remembered me mentioning steak was one of my splurges. And fear because all good things have a habit of coming to a painfully abrupt halt. And they all war for top billing in my heart and mind.

"He did, but I would have." Miller sets the bags down on my small table and his energy is electric when he turns around. "He also gave me a new job. Triple what I was making teaching, with some ownership in the TAC. Penny, what he wants to do?" Excitement pours from him as he nearly bounces on his toes, like a toddler about to get cotton candy for the first time. He clasps his hands over mine with a sudden seriousness, so I have no choice but to look into his eyes.

"What Ashton has been planning? It's going to change this town. It's going to change our lives." Half of his sentences end like a question, almost like he can't believe it himself.

He's so geared up and—and happy. I'm actually speechless.

"I mean, Jesus, Pen. I only skimmed the surface of the plans that Ashton and Remy gave Dillon. I don't even know when Dillon had time to go through them, but he marked them all up with different colored pens and sticky notes to build on their already impressive ideas. It's like the guy hasn't slept in days. You would have been proud of his color-coded notes too."

His blinding smile makes the corners of my lips twitch. His energy is infectious right now. "Penny, the changes Dillon added are—I don't even know where to begin. What he wants to bring to this town? It's like he's lived here his entire life and knows exactly what it lacks."

"He did?" I can't seem to formulate my thoughts into a coherent sentence.

"And I'm not supposed to say anything, but I think good things are coming your way too."

I hate surprises, and I can't control the full-body flinch that has me curling in on myself. My last surprise was walking in on my husband with an eighteen-year-old—in my bed—while my boys were asleep.

"What do you mean?" My voice shakes, and I withdraw my hands from his. I stare at a point on the wall to have something to focus on.

He bops me on my nose with his finger. "I don't know the details. You'll just have to wait and see."

"I don't like people making decisions for me." I've spent too many years without the right to make my own choices. I won't go through that again. Not even for Dillon freaking Henry.

This makes Miller freeze on the spot. "Pen? I don't know Dillon as well as you, but I bet my life he'll never take away your choices."

Guilt claws at my neck as unbearable heat rises across my skin. Miller's right. It's not how Dillon or Ashton operate.

"I have so many questions," I mumble.

Miller glances around my small kitchen and tilts his head to the side. He does this when he's listening for little ears. When he's sure we have a modicum of privacy, he leans toward me but still whispers.

"You know who you have to ask those questions to, right?"

"Yes." Crossing my arms over my chest is a defense, but I'm no longer sure who I'm protecting myself from.

"Well, I happen to know that he's probably just finishing up contracts over Zoom with Ashton and your boss. I also know that he was going to shower and then come over here." He makes a show of looking around my small home. "But there's not a whole lot of privacy around here. If you need privacy..."

He waggles his eyebrows at the word privacy, and it's so ridiculous I can't hold in the laughter. It whistles through my nostrils and is not at all cute.

"I can feed the kids and get everyone to bed," he says, moving to the bags of food. "And I bet if I tell everyone about my new position, it'll even give you an excuse to be away for a few hours. You know, since your boss is involved and all."

My mind races faster than my pulse. I don't know what's happening. I've never felt so out of control. But Miller's right. I do need to have a lot of conversations with Dillon. Conversations about us, about life, about the TAC.

But most importantly, about how amazing he was with Kai today.

The weight of it all makes me lightheaded. So many questions. So many changes. If I give myself time to really delve into everything, I'm afraid I'll never surface.

I nod before I've made my decision. When I look up at Miller, his expression is soft and kind.

"You deserve happiness, Pen. Remember that."

"Are you sure? You have them all? Mari is still—"

"Izzy was colicky for what felt like years, remember? I can handle this. You're not the only supermom in town."

I can't help it. I scoff. Loudly. "Hardly a supermom."

"Someday soon, you'll see what the rest of the world sees. And I think if Dillon has anything to say about it, he's going to be the one to open your pretty eyes."

I blink.

He winks.

I open my mouth, but I don't know what to say to that.

"Go," he says, shooing me toward the door. "I'll handle the hellions. But, Penny? I'll still gut him with my bare hands if he hurts you."

Miller's tone is easy, but I know he means it because I would do the same thing for him.

~

I WALK across the street instead of driving around the block to the TAC's driveway. I need the time and freezing temperatures to cool off. I can't walk in there before I've collected my thoughts. I don't want to say something I might regret.

Plus, Dillon shoveled a path through the mountain of snow separating us, making the walk easy because that's Dillon.

It's how he's always been. Isn't it?

How many times over the last three years has he shown up for his meeting with Lochlan with something for me that he just happened to think I'd like?

My boots crunch in the icy snow, and each step brings forth a new memory.

The donuts from the place in Brooklyn that I know for a fact was out of his way.

The book I was excited about and impatiently waiting to release that he somehow managed to get his hands on early, then said he'd remembered me saying something about it.

When I said I wanted to get an air fryer, but they were so expensive. The next week he showed up with one in a battered box, but the fryer itself was brand-new and untouched. He'd said he'd had it for years and never used it. But I'd always wondered if that was the entire truth because when I got home, it was Miller who pointed out he'd never seen damage on a box quite so perfectly spaced before.

Never, ever forgetting my coffee order.

Binge-watching my favorite shows so we could talk about them together.

My heart is in my throat when I reach the TAC. And

when I get to the bottom of the stairs that lead to his new apartment, I'm finding it hard not to fidget.

I unwrap the scarf covering every inch of my face except my eyes, and a cloud of warm air puffs into the night sky.

Before I can talk myself out of this, I clomp up the steps, removing my hat and fluffing my hair as I go.

Breathe in for three. Exhale for four. Paisley's one attempt at teaching me yoga on the green over the summer runs through my mind, and for once, her breathing techniques help calm the shakiness overtaking my body.

Then I knock, three quick, hard pounds before I can chicken out.

There's movement inside, a crash, Dillon cursing softly, and my entire being unwinds.

His door opens, and surprise flashes in his expression before he relaxes into an easy smile.

But it's not his face I'm looking at.

Once again, he's standing before me in a towel. I'd have to be dead not to remember the last time we were in this position.

But this time, things are different.

Everything is different.

I'm different.

I don't know what comes over me, but I fling myself at him. Again. He catches me easily, and the door slams shut behind us as he pulls me in out of the cold.

He's too tall for me to reach his lips, but I claw at his neck in desperation anyway.

One of my hands lands on his bare chest, and he hisses through clenched teeth. "Jesus, Penny. Your hands are like ice."

I cringe and start to pull back, but his hands clasp over mine and hold them to his bare skin.

"You're hot," I say with my eyes still glued to where he's holding my hands to his chest.

"Fire and ice, baby. You can never say they don't go together again because this feels pretty damn perfect to me."

Every question, every conversation we need to have pounds against my skull, but I don't listen to any of them. Instead, I focus on the smallest voice I have. The one who speaks my wants and needs. The one who's usually buried so deep I don't even recognize it as my own anymore.

Tonight though? Tonight she's loud and fierce, and she's the only one I can hear. This tiny voice that lives deep in my soul says to take what I want, so I do.

Leaning forward, I watch his eyes as my lips land on his pec just above his heart. I can't help myself—my tongue slips out to taste him. I've never felt so powerful or free.

This is what confidence does to you.

"Fuck," he groans, and his cock responds to me. It's hard and heavy even against my thick down jacket.

I feel like a queen. For the first time in my life, I ask for what I want.

"Dillon." My lips brush the skin of his chest as I speak.

"What do you want? Tell me," he demands. "I'll give you whatever you ask for."

And at this moment, I know that to be true.

"You," I say simply. "I want you."

CHAPTER 29

DILLON

My chest expands to three times its normal size at her words. "Say it again," I growl.

"You," she whispers. The confidence of a moment ago is vanishing as her insecurities creep in. I can see it in her sky-blue eyes. And in the way the specks of silver that shine in her irises like stars on a clear summer night begin to fade.

Bending my knees to lower myself so we're eye to eye, I search her face. "Use your words, pretty girl. How do you want me?"

Her cheeks burn a sexy red that creeps down her neck. I reach out to undo her zipper and then toss her jacket on the floor beside us. An oversized T-shirt and leggings are the uniform of moms everywhere, but I never gave them much thought until now.

In her gold dress that lives rent-free in my mind or T-shirts and leggings, she is my every fantasy.

"I—I mean, we have a lot to talk about."

I trail my fingers up her arms and watch her skin pebble in my wake. I don't say anything until I reach her neck. Then

I wrap her ponytail around my fist and gently but firmly tug her head back, so she's facing the ceiling.

Her surprised gasp makes my shaft twitch against her, and I smile.

"We do. Is Miller watching the kids?"

"Yes," she whispers.

"Good. We have so much to discuss. But right now, I need to hear your answer. How do you want me right…" I place my lips at the hollow spot below her earlobe and lick. "Now." I graze my tongue down her slender neck and, with my free hand, reach around to grab her ass.

"Oh, God," she moans when her belly rubs against my throbbing cock, and I squeeze harder.

"You can pray all you want, sweetheart, but tonight I'll be the one answering them. Open your eyes, Penny."

She obeys immediately, blinking like she hadn't realized they were closed.

"I have every inch of your face, every freckle, every curve committed to memory." I gently give her ponytail a tug that exposes the column of her neck even more. "Now I want to learn the rest of you. Can I do that?" I slide my left hand up her ass and under her sweatshirt until I find bare skin. "I want to make you feel so good that when you pray the next time, it's my name that slips past your lips."

She nods, but that will never do.

My hand moves higher, taking her T-shirt with it, but this time she hesitates, and I stop my upward motion immediately. Fear overrides her pleasure, and she removes her hands from my chest to hold her shirt in place.

"Talk to me. Trust me to make this good for you. Trust me to worship your body. Your heart. And your soul."

"I do," she says, and I believe her.

She swallows. "There's a lot of scars."

"So you've said." I place my lips on her cheek because I

love how she shivers when I speak softly in her ear. "And I look forward to showing you how to love every single one of them."

"How can you say that?" Her fingertips give the slightest pressure against my chest, and I freeze, then release her. I won't push if she isn't ready.

Putting a couple of inches between us, I let her see the truth as I say it. "Because there isn't an inch of you I'm not already programmed to love."

Our life is full of bombs ready to detonate, but I just tossed a live grenade into her heart, and I don't regret it.

"Let me show you." I step forward and reach for her ponytail again. Using my fingers, I massage her scalp.

"Yes," she moans.

"Yes, what? Be specific," I growl. I like to be in control in the bedroom. I always have. But it has never been an all-consuming desire that burns through my skin to my core as it does now.

"I want to make you feel good."

"Tsk, tsk, tsk, sweet girl." The hand under her shirt slips free, and I land a hard smack on her right ass cheek.

"Jesus," she mutters into my chest.

"Try again," I demand.

"I—I want…"

The confusion in her voice makes me smile. Her first lesson will be putting herself first, and I am up to that fucking challenge.

"I want to make you feel good," she says again.

Smack. Smack.

This time my hand lands in quick procession, then I squeeze and massage her plentiful cheek.

"What? What do you want me to say?" She's breathing heavily.

Jesus. How quickly can I make her come?

"Oh, Penny. I want you to say all sorts of filthy things. But for starters, I want to hear you say that you want me to make *you* feel good."

"Yes. Yes, I want that," she says so quickly a dark chuckle shakes my torso.

I raise my hand to spank her again when she opens her mouth to speak. "I want you to make me feel good," tumbles from her lips.

"There she is." Without warning, I lift her by her thighs. She wraps her long legs around my waist, and my hips give an exploratory thrust that wedges my cock between her ass cheeks. Greedy little bastard. "How long do we have?"

"Um." She bites her bottom lip, and my vision glazes over, imagining my dick between those rose-colored gates. "A few hours, I think."

I'm already moving toward the bedroom but also shaking my head and muttering under my breath. "That's not enough time for what I want to do to you, but I'll do my best."

When we reach my bed, I'm grateful I'd finally made it with sheets today. There's no reason to unpack. Not when Miller and I will have to move out of these apartments soon so the contractors can meet their ridiculously tight deadlines.

I lower her to the floor, and she flashes me a deer-in-headlights expression. "I've only been with…"

"Do not say his name right now," I grind out. "I know you've only been with him, and that alone has me a hairsbreadth away from losing my damn mind because this, tonight, will be your last first time if I have anything to say about it. I'm going to erase every first he ever gave you, and I'm going to replace it with memories of me. Of us. And I'm going to fucking love defiling you that way every chance I get."

Her eyes are so wide that I can't stop the lecherous grin I give her as I slowly guide her to the bed.

"Say yes."

"Yes," she says without hesitation, and I drop my towel.

Penny's eyes drop to my dick, and it twitches under her perusal, but when she licks her lips, it jerks up and bounces against my stomach.

"Holy hell," she whispers.

I step forward so it's level with her face but not quite touching and bend at my waist. "What did I say, baby? When you pray, you pray to me."

Her mouth drops open, and I take full advantage. My lips cover hers in a dominating kiss that still manages to have a softness to it. The softness is all her. She's the softness to my hard edges. My tongue dives in, searching, exploring, savoring her sweetness, and I groan into her.

"I'm going to undress you now." My lips land on hers before she can reply, and I work my hands under her shirt, lifting as I go. I use the tips of my fingers to dance patterns up her spine.

Her body shudders as I lift the T-shirt over her head, then clench my teeth when I get my first look at her pale blue bra and tits that almost spill out of the cups.

I watch her eyes as I use my pointer finger to trace the edge of her lacy bra over the mound of one breast to the valley between and up over the other side.

"You're so damn beautiful," I murmur. There's a sense of wonder in my tone, and I hope to God she hears it. She's simply the most precious soul I've ever encountered. And I need her to be mine.

"Dillon," she whispers, pressing up to place her cheek on mine as she says it.

I pull back to stare down at her body. She hollows herself

out, trying to appear smaller, but I drift my fingertip down her sternum to her soft belly.

Her shoulders tense when I circle her belly button.

I intentionally crowd her, so she's forced back onto her elbows. Her legs hang off the edge of the bed and I straddle them. Standing there, I scan her body. The small scars on her left side form a half-moon shape—a remnant from some surgery I don't know about yet—and over her stomach that once housed three boys.

"I would have loved to see you pregnant." The words slip from my mouth, but I don't regret them. "Unhook your bra."

Penny reaches up to the triangle of satin between her breasts with two hands. "Ah, there are scars here too."

Confusion sets in, but I force myself not to frown.

What the hell kind of scars does she have on her tits?

"They're pretty terrible," she says, staring down, and I doubt she's seeing anything but her own insecurities.

"Did someone hurt you?" Murder runs rampant in my veins. I'll fucking kill Eddy.

Her head snaps up to meet my fierce expression. "No. God, no. Nothing like that. Eddy and I split up for a while before we got married. I used the time to work on myself. I— I hated my boobs." She looks anywhere but at me. "They were always too big for my body and my back hurt all the time. And people looked at me differently no matter how conservatively I dressed."

Reaching forward, I place two fingers under her chin and lift. When she finally drags her eyes to mine, I hold her captive. "What happened, sweetheart?"

"I had a breast reduction," she says with a shrug. "I was happy at first, but then Eddy and I got back together. He said they looked like a science experiment gone bad. He always wanted me to keep a shirt on after that."

How could she have ever been with someone like that? It doesn't seem to fit the woman she is today.

As if she could hear my unasked question, she says, "I didn't have very good self-esteem growing up. And with Eddy, I don't know how it happened. It was easy, and I was happy enough. Then week by week, I lost myself. It got to the point where I really thought I was losing my mind. Now I know I was just losing myself because that's how he wanted me. He twisted things up so much that I couldn't remember how to breathe without him giving me permission."

I lift my thumb to swipe softly across the bottom of her cheek while I calm my heart rate and choose my words carefully.

"Okay, let's backtrack. You were happy when you first had the surgery. What about now that he's out of the picture? How do you feel about them now?"

I have a feeling I already know, but like everything else with us, we'll need to retrain our brains from what we thought we knew to what's factual.

She shrugs, and I have no doubt that if I wasn't holding her chin, she'd look away. As it is, her eyes scan the entire room.

"I don't think about them anymore, just like I don't think about the C-section scars that left weird dimples along my pubic bone. Or the robotic scars from gallbladder surgery. Or…"

"Or the scars on your heart that keep you from building new memories."

This time, when she looks at me, her expression is so full of shuttered emotion my chest actually aches.

Penny nods, and I run my thumb along her bottom lip. "Do you want to make new memories? With me?" I keep my voice low so she can't hear the desperation in my tone.

"I do."

The instant her words hit my ears, a crooked smile tugs at the right side of my lips.

"I do too, and I'm going to show you how to love every inch of your body, Penny. I want you to love it like I do. All of it. Are you ready for that?"

She nods again, and I hitch one eyebrow. "Words, baby. Just because you're sitting on your ass doesn't mean I can't reach it."

Penny yelps and leans up quickly. My arms cage her in on either side though, and she can't sit all the way up.

"I'm ready," she whispers, raising her hands to cup my cheeks.

"Take off your bra," I say again. This time the strain in my voice entangles every part of my body. It's there in every tense muscle, every misfiring nerve cell, and especially in my cock.

With my eyes trained on hers, she lowers her arms and undoes her bra. Her breasts fall free in my peripheral vision, but I keep my focus on her face.

"Scoot yourself up the bed." I don't give her any room, so she has to shimmy herself up a few feet, and I follow her like a predator.

Placing one hand on the bed beside her ribs, I lower my body to hers. The weight of us presses her into the bed, and a delicious moan breaks free from the back of her throat.

"I'm going to stare at your tits now. And when I'm staring, I want you to feel my cock against your leg. See what the sight of you does to me. Feel it. Understand?"

"Yes," she gasps when I slide my dick along her thigh.

And finally, finally, I get my first look at my Penny. As expected, I jerk against her leg. The weight of my erection throbs in time with my need.

"Fuck, Penny. Just fuuuck." It's all the words I can form before I dart forward and take her peaked nipple into my mouth with a deep pull. She jerks against the bed as I blindly grab for her right tit, and when I find it, I pinch her nipple with the same aggressiveness as my tongue on her other side. I flick, and suck, and bite until her hips lift, seeking the friction I can't wait to give her.

I find the scars that run down the center of her breast and all along the underside with my fingers. Then I trace one with my tongue and her fingers land in my hair.

"Someday soon, I'm going to fuck these magnificent tits, and when I come all over them, you'll see how amazing I think they are."

I'm ravenous for her body and don't wait for her to say anything before popping her other breast into my mouth. This time when I bite down, I make sure to leave a mark.

My mark.

"God, Dillon," Penny whines below me, and I memorize the sound.

All finesse has vanished as I surge up to plunder my tongue deep into her mouth. My desperation for her to clamp around me has my hands fumbling for purchase, and my groin grinding into her leggings-clad pussy.

While my tongue searches and savors every corner of her mouth, my hands slide down, down, down until I slip beneath the waistband of her leggings and cup her bare ass.

For a moment, we simply grind into each other, mimicking what's to come, and I fight the urge to rut. I flip my wrist and tug her leggings down a few inches.

I pull away when I can't get them any lower without breaking the kiss. Penny's eyes are glazed over with a lust I feel on a molecular level.

"I'm going to fuck you, Penny. And I'm going to make love to you. I'm going to ravish, and regale, and worship every goddamn inch of you. And when you scream my name, you'll mark me as yours. I've been tested and I'm clear. I haven't been with anyone since I met you."

I wait for my words to sink in. That's right. I've been celibate since I met her, and I can't wait to break this dry spell. Her mouth falls open, but when she bites down hard on her bottom lip and stares at me through long, fluttering lashes, I'm hit with a wave of lust that steals my breath.

"Me either. I mean, I haven't been with anyone else."

"Do you want me to use a condom?" I will, but it'll be torture to go find one right now.

"I mean…" She leans up, and I scoot lower down her legs. So low that I can lean down and plant an open-mouthed kiss on her pussy even though it's still mostly covered by black stretchy Lycra. When I blow hot air into the material, she moans.

"No. Just you," she pants. "I can't get pregnant. I needed a hysterectomy after Gage. It's not possible anymore." Sadness washes over her face as she watches me closely.

Does she really think kids would be a deal-breaker?

"It's a good thing you already have some pretty incredible kids, then."

Before she can get lost in her head, I yank her leggings down to her knees. It takes some effort to tug off her boots, but once I do, I strip her bare.

"Holy hell. You're perfection."

CHAPTER 30

PENNY

*D*illon growls the word perfection like a dangerous animal announcing its kill. Any lingering doubts I have about his sincerity are lost as he lazily scans my naked body.

His cock jerks against his stomach, and he reaches down absentmindedly to give it a rough stroke.

My throat goes dry as I watch. It's the most erotic thing I've ever witnessed.

"You like watching me touch myself?" His words skate over my body like a caress, and I press my legs together. The pressure and need building have my clit throbbing. Actually throbbing.

I didn't know that was a thing.

"Open your legs," he commands.

I hesitate for half a second while my mind wars with my body. Why do his commands set my pussy on fire when I fight tooth and nail for independence in every other facet of my life?

"Stop thinking so hard. Just let go. With me, you can always let go. I might want to control your body and your pleasure in this bed, but outside of these four walls? Sweetheart," he groans, and my core clenches. "Baby, outside the bedroom, you own me. Own. Me. Your choices, your decisions, and your life are yours. I just want to be a part of it."

My legs are scissoring in front of me. When I realize what I'm doing, I suck in a breath.

"You fight every day. Your mind never shuts off, and I want it all, Penny." His hand gives another harsh tug, and my heart rate increases to a near-painful rhythm.

"I want your overcrowded worries and your hidden desires, but most of all, I want your happiness. And in our bed, I want to overwhelm every other thought, so for a few minutes, all you think about is me. That's what I want. I want those few minutes when we're joined as one. The rest of the day? The rest of your time? I'll share you. Hell, I'll drop to my knees out there and happily have you make every goddamn decision."

"But in here?" I whisper, and a lascivious grin appears on his face as he crawls back up my body.

"In here, let me take it all away. Let me carry your burdens and guide your body in all things pleasure. I'll spend eternity showing you how fucking special you are."

He gives a gentle thrust. The blunt head of his penis rubs against my clit, and I gasp.

"I think you need me to take control in here, so you can fully let go. Please."

His words are hoarse, like he's fought an uphill battle his entire life, and he's finally cresting the precipice of home.

Am I that? Am I home?

"Tell me you want that, Penny. Tell me you want all of that."

"I want it." I gasp in shock that his tiny thrusts have my tummy fluttering already.

"Thank you," he says, staring into my eyes with an intensity that threatens to burn us. The emotion in his tone is my undoing, though. When he lowers his lips to my skin and traces small circles with his tongue down my body, I know I'll never recover from this.

"Spread," he orders with a tap to both thighs.

I obey, and a string of low curses leave his lips. Before I can figure out what he's saying, his tongue darts out over my pussy, and in one long lick, he tastes me.

"Oh, God. Oh, God," I chant. Somehow, my fingers have clenched in his hair. When his tongue flicks relentlessly against my clit, I cry out.

I have the sensation of floating right out of my body. I'm incoherently moaning, but when his teeth scrape against the sensitive bundle of nerves, and he thrusts two thick fingers into my channel, my torso lifts off the bed.

I can barely breathe.

For once, I'm not focused on my to-do list, or the way the skin of my tummy sags over my C-section scar. I'm not worried about money or my ex. My only concern right now is coming. On Dillon taking my orgasm like it belongs to him.

And really, doesn't it?

Just when I think I'm going over the edge, he eases back. I blink a few times to focus my vision, and when I stare down my body, I find Dillon watching me with a smile that hints at what's to come.

"Tell me what you want." He strikes as soon as he's finished speaking and sucks my clit into his mouth. It borders on brutal in the most inviting way.

The pull from his lips sends a ripple of lust through my entire body.

Then he stops, and an honest-to-goodness whine of protest escapes my lips. "Wh—What are you doing?" I cry.

He digs his chin in closer to my skin and his tongue slips

inside me. He circles his entire face, and the flickers of orgasm threaten to burst before he moves away again.

"Dillon," I sob. "Dillon, please."

A growl that's neither human nor beast erupts from somewhere deep inside him. "Jesus Christ, do I like my name on those pretty lips."

Another lick. Another suck. Another finger.

Then he stops.

I'm bordering on real tears now but can't form one coherent word.

"Tell." He gives my pussy a lazy lick.

"Me." His finger curls deep inside me.

"What." His tongue flicks like it's in a race against time.

"You." His growl vibrates against my clit.

I'm close. So, so close that a tear breaks free.

"Want. Tell me what you want." A devious curl of his lips tells me he knows exactly what he's done to me.

He's done the unimaginable.

He's taken my worries, my fears, and my insecurities. He holds the weight of them, so all I can do is feel.

"You," I scream. "I want you, and I want to come. Please, Dillon. Please."

My eyes squeeze shut, and he moves over me. His thumb rests with heavy pressure against my clit and the thick head of his cock breaches my entrance. I'm lost. He's my only anchor, and I wrap my legs around his back and pull him into me.

"Fuck. Fuuuck," he groans.

One thrust, and he's inside.

Two thrusts, and my vision blurs.

Three thrusts, and I'm gone. Body, mind, heart, and soul erupt in a chorus of orgasms so powerful I'm incapable of thought.

I hear myself chanting Dillon's name as he moves above

and in me like he has all the time in the world, but my body is somewhere else. I'm not with it. I'm having a sexual out-of-body experience, and I don't ever want to return.

He taps my clit, and my eyes surge open.

Oh, shit.

"We're not done," he says. "I could die today with your pussy clenching the life out of my cock, and it wouldn't be enough. It'll never be enough. You—"

He thrusts in a steady rhythm, and I give an exploratory clench of my inner walls.

Dillon freezes. His eyes narrow on mine. "Do that again," he demands through clenched teeth, so I do.

Kegel exercises do work after all. I clench until I'm shaking, then release him. Dillon's eyes darken, and his thrusts falter.

"Again," he hisses.

Even in my lustful haze, the power I have over him right now is intoxicating. I squeeze him again and see the first drops of sweat roll down his neck. It's the only indication that he's struggling to hold himself together.

I do it again, and this time roll my hips until his head drops back. Curses and prayers mix into one stream of consciousness as he drops his head back and stares at the ceiling. The entire time, he keeps an almost brutal pace in his powerful thrusts, and Lord have mercy, I love it.

Apparently, I like fucking even more than making love.

Who knew?

I roll my hips and grind into him. When he withdraws, I follow, and whatever cord of control he had snaps.

Dillon drops over me, hooks his arms under my armpits, and holds my shoulders. It brings our faces together, and it gives him leverage to tug me to him.

There's no mistaking he just took back control, and the image of him above me has me licking my lips.

Yeah, Dillon Henry knows what I need.

A deliciously dirty fucking.

But it's like he can read my mind because when he grins, he eases up, so the gentle glide of his cock is torturously slow. It gives the added effect of his pubic bone lazily grinding against my clit, and I don't know if I should cry, plead, or just lay here and take it.

"There's time for fast and dirty." He punctuates each word with a forceful thrust. "And there's a time for making love." This time, he slows down his movements, but they are no less impactful. My body is overloaded with sensations and doesn't know which one to reach for. "But tonight? Our last first time? Tonight, we're doing both."

It's the last thing he says before he alternates deep, hard thrusts with gentler ones that touch my soul on a cosmic level. Each sweet plunge is accentuated with a devastating kiss, and every lancing impale lodges me deeper inside a world where only Dillon and I exist.

I can't keep up, and my body is cresting on the verge of an Earth-shattering orgasm. Dillon must feel my walls contracting because he pulls back a mere inch to watch my face. "Come for me, sweetheart. Give me your everything, and trust me to hold you together."

His words are my undoing because I want that. At the end of the day, I just want to know that someone will be there to catch me if I fall.

And by the look in Dillon's eyes, I'll have to cut out his heart before he ever lets me fall. So I let go.

I come so hard I think I black out, and when I come to, Dillon is right where he said he'd be—holding me to him like he can fight my demons while seducing my fantasies.

For once in my life, I fall asleep with only one thing filling my brain: Dillon Henry.

CHAPTER 31

DILLON

Penny moves to the stove in her small kitchen, which is currently overrun with people. Lochlan is here, and so is his sister-in-law, Eli.

It's been seven days since she gave herself over to me. Seven days of feeling a love that burns so brightly from within, I'm half convinced if you look too closely, you'll see the charred remains of my self-control.

She moves with grace, a peacefulness to her that I've never noticed before, and pure loving pride surges in my chest.

I watched her closely the first time she fell asleep in my bed. The calm that came after our coupling washed away my remaining fears. Fears of being enough. Of being able to give Penny and her boys everything that they need.

Now, whenever I look at them, all I see is a family—my family, if they'll have me.

We'll need to talk to her boys soon. After she came to me last week, I couldn't leave her side. The boys think I'm sleeping on their sofa because of the construction set to start next week at the TAC, but truthfully, as soon as she moved

Mari to Landon's room, everything changed. The second Penny has settled for the night, I stalk the empty hallway until I'm at her door, climbing in beside her, and holding her until the sun comes up.

Yes, there was a night of panic when Gage woke from a bad dream. Luckily, I heard the door opening and rolled out of bed onto the floor and out of sight before he caught me.

I can't help the grin that appears thinking about that now, but I don't want to sneak around. And I don't want Kai to think we're lying to him, either. He's old enough to feel that betrayal like another hit to his heart, and I promised to be honest with him.

"Dillon?" Eli's no-nonsense tone cuts through my wayward thoughts.

"Huh?" It takes more effort than it should to tear my gaze away from Penny to Eli, but when I do, I find them all watching me with varying degrees of annoyance.

"Think you can give me your attention for a whole five minutes there, stud muffin?" Eli asks, and Penny drops a pan onto the stove.

I'm standing before Penny turns around, but then she flashes a startled look my way, and I freeze. "Sorry," she mutters. "The handle was slippery." She lowers her gaze quickly before I can read her expression, but that doesn't stop the deep blush that instantly rises on her cheeks.

Penny has a little jealous streak in her.

I like it.

"Dillon," Eli warns again from my right, so I give her my undivided attention. "Matt—"

"Miller," he corrects. "Matt Miller, but everyone calls me Miller."

Eli narrows her eyes, then carelessly blows air up her face to push a few stray strands of hair off her forehead. "As I was saying," she begins again. "Matt—"

"Miller."

"Matt," she grinds out, and I raise a brow at Miller.

Eli doesn't appear to be the type to back down. I wonder how far he'll push her. When he doesn't say anything, her lip curls a fraction, as if signaling victory.

"Matt Miller called the special town meeting for Thursday. That gives you three days to learn about everyone in town and what they like and dislike. Who they're related to and how. What they do for work, and how we can exploit that for the TAC. Basically, you are going into that meeting like you've lived here your entire life."

"But Miller actually has lived here. Wouldn't it be better for him to take the lead on this?" I ask. Glancing around the room, I find Lochlan wearing an expression that asks the same thing.

"No," Eli says with no room for negotiation as she rounds up another pile of papers from Penny's table. "Everyone knows or will know that you're the new owner. They need to see that you're invested. It's our job to introduce you as a valuable community member and show them what the expanded TAC can offer them. Miller will warm them up, but you have to be the one to close the deal."

"Eli's right," Penny says, plucking on the elastic around her wrist. She's leaning her ass against the kitchen sink, wearing black leggings and my old college T-shirt that falls to her knees, but it's her posture that I can't stop watching.

Penny is relaxed, and although the edges of worry creep in late at night after the kids are in bed, she isn't drowning in fear anymore.

Is that because I'm here?

Because Eddy's in jail?

Because Aster still hasn't returned?

I want it to be me so fucking badly I can taste it.

Her lips curve into the gorgeous smile I saw underneath

me last night, but then she hitches one eyebrow, and I realize she's waiting for a response.

I zoned out. Again.

This isn't a great look for me.

"She said you're the new Remy. Jesus, Dillon. What's gotten into you?" Lochlan mutters.

"More like who he's gotten into," Miller says under his breath. Penny gasps, and I react with a sharp jab of my fist to his bicep.

"Grow up, Miller."

He turns around and drops his fist to my thigh, causing a charley horse to erupt in the muscle.

I bounce on one leg, trying to work out the tangle in my other thigh, and Miller stands opposite me, rubbing his bruised bicep. When our eyes meet, we burst into laughter.

"Is this what working with you every damn day will be like?" He laughs, but the question stirs something in my chest.

I shrug, remembering what growing up around Ashton's family was like. I was always there, on the periphery. No matter how hard they tried to bring me into their circle, it was always just out of reach.

But this? This feels like my own version of the chaos that swirls around big families. Chaos, and love, and hope.

"Yeah," I say with a hint of insecurity. "This is exactly what it's going to be like. And I'm looking forward to every single second of it." My eyes roam from Miller to Penny and back again. "This is where I belong."

Penny purses her lips to keep them from trembling, but Miller charges me like a bull and wraps me in a hug.

"Bloody fucket. I thought only the Westbrooks were huggers. Is there a worldwide hug initiative I'm not aware of?" Lochlan's crusty tone lacks its usual tartness. Even he's been sucked into the world of chosen family, demonstrative men, and the women who keep us in line.

"Here," Eli says, tossing a packet my way. "This is what I could gather. Have Matt and Penny fill you in on every detail about every business owner. You need to know if they take out the trash on Tuesdays, when they have lunch with their girlfriend, and even when they take a shit. Trust me on this. Knowing them better than they know themselves is the only way you'll get this passed on your deadline."

I flip it open to a spreadsheet. Businesses, their owners, ages, and their families are all neatly color coded.

Penny crosses the space. I don't have to look up to feel the air shift. I just know when she's coming to me. I'm proven right a second later when the scent of peonies fills my nostrils.

She runs a slender finger down the column labeled: TAC Propositions.

"You're going to offer them all space in the TAC." It's not a question. Her voice is soft and full of emotion as she reads our plans.

"Basically," Eli explains. "It's most similar to a franchising opportunity. The hotel will need a restaurant, so we'll offer the kitchen to Heirlooms. The entire complex will need coffee, so we'll split that up between the two weirdos dueling it out over coffee shop real estate on the square."

"You even have Tanks on here. What can Kyle offer? He owns a gas station and a mechanics workshop. I can't imagine there's a huge need for those services," Penny muses aloud.

"Not for the customers of TAC, but with the expansion, we'll have a fleet of machinery that needs upkeep," Miller says, taking ownership of this piece of the deal. I sit back with a sense of pride as he explains what we want to offer everyone in town. "We're hoping to design the children's play space within the TAC like a gas station or workshop. All the ball pits, trampolines, etc. can be done in a Tanks theme. We'll also hire Kyle to run routine maintenance throughout the property."

Lochlan watches me from across the room with an odd expression marring his face, but Penny speaks, and I'm drawn to her like a ship seeing the lighthouse after a long journey. I can't help but drift toward her.

"And Chancy's? Karma? Even Three Brothers Brewing? You have roles for all of them too?" There's wonderment in her tone that heats my blood. I like making Penny proud.

"Yeah," Miller says, practically salivating over the information like a six-year-old Saint Bernard. "Chancy's will have retail space in the hotel lobby and the athletic complex. The Brothers can set up a bar in the hotel and a small tasting brewery in the TAC's food court."

He flips through the papers until he finds the one he's searching for. "Paisley will have studio space where she can teach yoga, boxing, or whatever the hell she's into at the time. The parents who come to these weeklong tournaments always look for things to do outside their child's sport. We're bringing it all to them within one complex."

"How will you have space for all of this?" Penny asks, turning her questions on me.

I shrug. "We're expanding, baby."

Her eyes go wide. I've been so good about keeping us under wraps, and I go and blow it with one single word.

"Well, that answers that question," Lochlan grumbles. Penny opens her mouth, but I'm not sure what she intends to say. Lochlan doesn't give her a chance when he says, "It's about damn time." Getting to his feet, he smooths down his vest—which has no wrinkles—and opens a folder of his own. "That brings us to you, Penny."

"Me? What about me?"

"You've been a particularly good assistant, Penny. You've saved me from myself more times than I can count, and at the Bryer-Blaine, we reward loyalty and service like yours."

He's so prim and formal, but Penny sways a little on her feet, so I wrap an arm around her waist to hold her steady against me.

"What does that mean, Lochlan?" she asks with a shaky voice.

He slides a piece of paper across the table. Penny and I look down at the same time. I know what it is. It takes her a few minutes to read it.

"I'd like you to run Apex. It won't be as big as some of the other Bryer-Blaine properties, but it's a branch into something new—something more family-friendly. If Apex works well here, we'll look into expanding with you as an integral member of the team. I'm asking you to lead this endeavor, Penny."

Penny shakes her head, but no sounds come from her mouth. I gently massage her back, trying to coax some words out of her.

"Lochlan, I don't know the first thing about running a hotel. I'm your assistant. I do assistant-y things like make coffee and file paperwork."

I open my mouth to dispute her utter lack of belief in herself, but Lochlan, not unkindly, holds up a hand to stop me.

"That's not exactly true, and I think if you looked around the Bryer-Blaine you'd see why. You know how every piece of that hotel operates. You researched, you learned, you dove in headfirst to know my company better than most of my top-tier executives."

"No, I learned what I had to do so if something went wrong, I knew the steps to fix it before I had to bring it to you."

"Exactly. You've freed up so much of my time, and for that, I'm grateful. I also dread finding your replacement when the time comes, but that's a different conversation. What I'm saying is, you know that hotel from the ground up. The Apex will be smaller, a starter hotel, if you will." He smirks, but she doesn't return any expression at all. In fact, Penny looks like she's seconds away from throwing up.

Pressing on her shoulders with both hands, I guide her into the chair. "This is good news, Penny. Think about how nice it will be to just go across the street to work instead of taking a two-hour train ride?"

She turns her teary eyes on Lochlan. "I truly don't think I'm qualified for this, Lochlan. I appreciate the opportunity, but I'm terrified I'll mess it up."

"That's what life is all about, Penny." Lochlan floats gracefully into the chair beside her. "Being scared and doing it anyway. This position will ensure you can comfortably provide for your boys on your own. You'll be closer to home. And it will open a whole new world to you when they've left the nest. This is for your future as much as your present."

"I wouldn't even know where to begin," she admits.

"I'd never throw you in without a life vest. I'll work on this with you over the next few months, and when you're ready, you'll take over on your own. But this will also mean working very closely with these two idiots every day."

Lochlan glares between Miller and me before returning his attention to Penny and lowering his voice. "Will you be able to work for the foreseeable future with Dillon by your side? I know things are…personal, and believe me, I'm happy for you. But if it doesn't work out…"

She glances around the room and a low growl rumbles in my chest. "Y—Yes, I can work with them."

My lips curl into a snarl as I glare at Lochlan. I'm baring

my teeth like an actual wild animal, but I can't control the fury taking over my body.

I know he's looking out for her best interests, but I hate the stab of pain his words cause.

He may not believe I'm all in with Penny, but I'll show him. I'll show this entire damned town that Penny Mulligan was always meant to be mine.

In work, in life, and in love.

I actively work at relaxing my balled-up hands, but Eli notices and flashes a mischievous grin. "And on that note, take me back to the city, Loch," she demands with an air of happiness that doesn't quite sound real. "I'll be back for the town meeting, but my job is pretty much done here. Do everything in those folders, and you've got this community in the bag."

CHAPTER 32

PENNY

Someone—probably Dillon—knocks right at six thirty. I'm still going over all the rules with Kai on the upstairs landing when Gage opens the front door.

"Gage!" I'm too tired to even voice my exasperation at this point, but I still hurry down the stairs. My youngest son has one speed: get it done and think about it later. "You cannot just open the door." The words die on my lips when Dillon walks into the foyer.

His black peacoat hangs open, revealing a baby blue button-up with the top two buttons undone. He slides off his coat and hangs it over the staircase railing. The first thing I notice is that the sleeves of his shirt are rolled up to look effortlessly casual, with a touch of businessman, but it's the damned veins in his thick, muscular forearms that have me stumbling in the hall.

I reach them just as Dillon goes down on one knee in front of Gage. "Hey, pal. Thought your mom talked to you about opening the door for strangers?"

Gage laughs. "But you're not a stranger, Dill Pickle."

The corners of Dillon's eyes crinkle with a smile he's

trying to hide as he watches my son. "But you didn't know it was me. It could have been anyone."

"It's six thirty," Gage whines. "You always come right at six thirty. I was watching the clock, and when it said 6-3-0, you knocked on the door. I knew it was you, Dewey."

How do you argue with that face? Or with Dillon's every time one of them calls him Dewey?

Dillon must think the same thing because he ruffles my little guy's hair, then places a heavy hand on his shoulder. "Let's try harder to remember, okay? Your mom wants to keep you safe."

"Yes, sir," Gage murmurs, and my eyes go wide.

"Sir?" I mouth to Dillon as Gage runs off again. This time Dillon flashes a devastating smile.

"Guess my Southern charm is rubbing off on him a little after all." His eyes flick back and forth between mine. It's like every word he's thinking is projected through hazel irises that look me in one eye, then the other, and back again at a rapid pace.

His eyes are saying he wants to kiss me. Devour me. Savor me. He purses his lips, and mine part on a breathy exhale. That's exactly what he's thinking. His heaving chest and flexing fingers tell me all I need to know about his tightly held self-control.

I have to have a talk with Kai. Soon. Landon and Gage are younger, and I'm not even sure they would care if I were dating someone. They don't have as many memories as Kai does. But Kai. Ugh! My heart hammers against my chest.

Dillon looks around at the piles of shoes on the floor. I've noticed he does this every time he walks in, and shame makes my shoulders tense.

Why didn't I think to clean up? I knew he was coming. Gage was right. He's shown up every single night right at six thirty.

"D—" The words get caught in my throat, so I cough to clear it. "Does the mess bother you?" I stare at the floor, unable to meet his eyes.

That was a huge mistake. Because there's a pile of dirty socks in the corner, and oh, God. There's even one hanging from the ceiling fan when I look up. Gage! He's started using them as slingshots.

I avert my gaze and hope he doesn't look up, but then I find individual packets of Cheez-Its, open and spilling onto the floor under Landon's backpack. I turn quickly and put my back to it, only to find a handful of Nerf darts scattered across the bottom stair.

This is my life.

His heat leaches into my back, and his deep inhale in my hair wills me to turn around.

"There's not a single thing here that bothers me." His words are so soft I can barely hear him, but he's close enough to smell the minty freshness of his toothpaste.

I lift my face to his, and my tummy does the excited flip that only he can cause.

"I like the piles of shoes," he rumbles. "I don't know what it is about them, but it makes this feel like a home to me. It's always just been my shoes. One or two pairs. But these?" He gestures to the pile of cleats, sneakers, boots, and slippers scattered beside the front door. "These look like happy dinners and loud nights. Busy car pools and exhausted but beautiful moms. When I take my shoes off here and place them with the pile, it gives me something I didn't know was missing."

My eyes sting as I ask, "What's missing?"

He drops his forehead to mine before answering. "You. Your kids. This place. It's home and love, and everything I never knew I wanted."

I drag in a ragged breath, and he pulls back to give me

space. I want to answer with something as special, something worthy of the truths he keeps laying at my feet, but my mind is blank. All I have is this feeling deep in my chest that's screaming at me to listen. To listen with my whole heart. To tell him that he's home.

But before I can find my courage, Gage slide-tackles Dillon's legs and nearly takes him out.

"Gage!" I yell, just as Dillon performs a genuinely impressive high kick and then spins out of my ninja's way.

Dillon lands with a dull thud and a grin that matches Gage's. "I think we should add wrestling mats to the TAC. This kid needs to work off some energy."

It's true. Gage is a lot for anyone, but a single tear finally falls when I register that Dillon didn't say any of that unkindly. He said it like he's looking forward to giving Gage that outlet. Like he's impressed by my little boy's endless bouts of energy. He leans down, hauls Gage over his shoulder, and dumps him on the sofa.

"No more sliding in the house. You could hurt someone."

"Okay," Gage says.

I haven't moved. Haven't managed a thought. Even my endless to-do list is silent.

Dillon's shoes on the hardwood tell me he's headed back this way, but then I hear Gage again.

"Hey, ah, Dewey?"

I take a quiet step forward and peer around the doorframe to the family room.

"Yeah, pal?" Dillon gives Gage his full attention.

"Are you a grandpa?"

And just like that, all the warm, cozy feelings bubbling below the surface burst like they were shot out of a cannon.

We go through the same thing every year. I'm about to interrupt when Kai bumps my shoulder. I was so focused on Gage, I didn't hear him come down the stairs.

"Maybe he'll have a solution," Kai whispers. "He seems to be fixing everything else." His tone tells me something is off, and I'm once again reminded that there are never enough hours in the day.

Now is the time to have this talk with him about Dillon, but I chicken out and instead ask, "How do you feel about that?"

Kai shrugs. "He seems nice. But promises this big rarely come true, so we'll see, I guess."

I swallow past the lump lodged in my throat like a jagged boulder. "Not everyone breaks promises, Kai."

I swear my teenager rolls his eyes harder than a bowling ball.

I glance over my shoulder at Lia, who is still coloring at the table. She hasn't even noticed Dillon yet. How much life did that little girl learn to block out?

"Nope. Not a grandpa," Dillon says with a chuckle, drawing me back to them. "Why do you ask? Am I getting old? Gray hair?" He runs a hand through his thick, brown hair. "Potbelly?" He places both hands on his perfectly flat and muscular midsection, but bounces them like he's Santa holding his pants in place.

Gage laughs, but it's half-hearted, and Dillon can tell.

"What's up, Gage?"

"Nothing."

Dillon looks left to right like he's searching for the missing piece, then eventually walks to the sofa and plops down next to Gage. "Feels like it might be something. Wanna talk about it?"

Gage shrugs, and every ounce of mom guilt I've ever experienced begs me to intervene, but something holds me back. That piece of me that wants Dillon to fit in our world pleads for me to give him a chance. Even Kai's hand, gripping my forearm, seems to tell me to let it play out.

So I do. I stand and watch, with Kai to my right, as Dillon pulls pain from Gage's little heart.

"Tomorrow's Grandparents Day at school."

It's the first time Dillon has searched for me. When his eyes land on mine, I gently shake my head no, then circle my fingers, hopefully signaling that our only family lives in this house. Us and Miller, anyway.

"Ah. I see. And you don't have any grandparents?"

Gage shakes his head but doesn't lift his eyes. He watches the blanket he's pulling pills from like it's the most interesting thing in the world.

"Hmm."

"Remy said he'd come with Izzy and me, but Izzy's always gotta share him, so I said I was fine."

"But you're wishing you had someone to go with you?"

Another two-shouldered shrug from Gage. "Maybe," he says quietly.

"You know, when I was growing up, I didn't have anyone to go to my stuff either."

Gage's little head snaps up to stare open-mouthed at Dillon. "You didn't?"

"Nope. Ashton's mom and dad always stepped in, but it wasn't the same as having someone there just for you."

"Yeah." Gage sighs too heavily for an eight-year-old. "It kinda stinks."

"So, tell me the rules of Grandparents Day. What do you do? Is it only grandparents that go?"

"Benny Bird had an auntie come last year. They come and have lunch in the cafeteria with us. Then we make a picture together and the kids get to go home early with them. It's okay. Mrs. Danforth said I can have extra recess."

Dillon frowns. "Oh yeah? Just you?"

"Everyone else has someone. Don't tell Mom, though,

'kay? I don't want her to feel bad 'cause she's got to work with Mr. Lochlan tomorrow."

Gage bounces like he's about to stand, and I shuffle back with Kai in tow, so we're just out of sight but close enough to hear Dillon's next words.

"Gage? Look at me, buddy." There's silence for a few long beats. "You have someone, okay? You're never alone. And don't worry about Grandparents Day. I think it might be the best one ever. You'll see."

"He's gonna do it," Kai whispers at my side. "He's going to do Grandparents Day." The genuine shock and awe in his tone has that mom guilt rearing to life again.

"I think he'd do just about anything for all of you," I say. Turning to face him, I find him watching me with his bottom lip between his teeth.

There's a war raging in his bruised heart. The little boy in him wants to trust and believe in everyday magic, but the boy who has seen too much knows what happens if you believe too hard for too long. I hate that I've failed him this way, but I have no idea how to fix it.

Dillon strolls into the foyer with a wide smile and reads the room like there's a flashing neon sign over our heads. "I'm earning trust one day at a time," he says, staring at Kai. Turning to me, he relaxes when our eyes meet. "How do I go about getting on the list for Grandparents Day?"

CHAPTER 33

DILLON

Kai watches me with a mix of anger, interest, and confusion as Penny tells him the rules and what to do in case of an emergency for the third time since I've been here. His eyes have that glazed look about them that makes me think he could recite this particular speech in his sleep.

"I put Mari down in her pack 'n play. As long as Gage doesn't wake her up, she should stay sleeping until I get home. Landon can help get Lia to bed, so it's only Gage you have to—"

"Penny?" I interrupt. "We'll be less than ten minutes away, and Remy is across the street with Izzy. I think Kai can handle it." It's a fine line that I walk. I'm still not sure what or where my place is as far as the kids are concerned, but if I want to make a life with all of them, I have to test my boundaries a little.

"I know." She sighs, then pinches the bridge of her nose. "But he's only fifteen. And there are two more kids here now, and…"

"And he can handle it," I assure her. "You know he can."

She nods with a weary smile for Kai. "I know you can handle this, Kai. I don't think there's anything you can't do if you set your mind to it. There's just a lot on our plates, and I hate that I'm burdening you with babysitting on a school night."

He shrugs but can't quite hide a shy smile. "It's okay. I finished my homework." His eyes cut to me with a frown, then he turns back to his mom. "It sounds like this is an important meeting for everyone in town. You can't miss it."

Penny closes the distance between her and her oldest son. She takes his cheeks in both hands and stares into his eyes long enough to make the teen uncomfortable. Then she leans in and kisses the side of his face.

"I'm proud of you, Kai. You're growing up to be an amazing young man."

His chin trembles, but he juts it out in protest. "Thanks, Mom. I'm trying. I want to show Landon and Gage something—something different."

Penny sucks in a breath that seems to stall deep in her lungs, so I step forward. "I think acknowledging what and how you want to be at a young age is something to be proud of, Kai. Sometimes in life, we're shown the darkest corners of humanity so we can choose the light. Your future is as bright as you want to make it. No history, or family genes, or even circumstance can change that. Your future and your brothers' futures are what you make out of them. From what I've seen so far, you'll be a fine leader in whatever you choose."

Kai takes a wobbly step back. "Th—Thank you."

His reaction reminds me what it's like to be fifteen and so unaccustomed to receiving compliments that they hit like a tsunami when you get one.

"My life was a lot like yours growing up, Kai, except without the siblings. The similarities between your childhood and mine make your life shockingly familiar to me.

From the sport you love to the choices our fathers made, but I'm proof that even if the apple falls from the same tree, it's what you make of it that matters. You are your own man, and you're responsible for your own choices."

Kai stares at me like he wants to believe me but can't quite bring himself to do it.

I understand that war all too well.

"Trust—"

"Is earned," Kai says. "Yeah, I heard you. You guys better get going or you'll be late." He walks backward until he reaches the family room door, then turns and practically sprints away from us.

"Thank you for that. For everything, really." Penny's soft voice finds its way into my heart. It beats a steady rhythm like a siren's song whenever she's close.

"I'd like to tell him that we're dating," I blurt in a hushed tone. "I don't think we should sneak around. He's old enough to understand, and I don't want to ruin the fledgling trust we're building."

"I know," she says, but she sounds defeated. "But I should be the one to talk to him first. I'll need to check in with all of them."

"Soon, Penny. I'm not trying to rush you, but I'm serious about being here with and for you. I don't want to start something with him on a rocky foundation."

She nods and reaches for her coat. "I'll talk to them this weekend."

Taking the coat out of her hands, I hold it up so she can slip into it, then I grab mine, and we walk out the front door. I wait on the stairs while she locks the door behind her, and after checking the windows for little eyes, I take her hand.

The innocent touch doesn't feel so innocent when I've spent all day wanting to hold her.

"It's fucking brutal seeing you all day and not being able to touch you."

She expels a puff of air with a shaky laugh. "I'm glad it's not just me."

Opening her door, I wait for her to sit, then lean in. "It is most definitely not just you. I've had a steel rod in my pants all day because of you. I ache to hold you, and that's not a line. My hands shake when you're near. My heart beats so rapidly I'm convinced it's trying to bust free to reach you. Not touching you, kissing you, holding you is the hardest damn thing I've ever done."

"I know," she whispers.

"Soon, right? We'll stop hiding soon?"

"Yes," she agrees. "Soon."

It's the best I'm going to get right now, so I round the hood of the SUV and get in. Unless Miller was screwing with me, we're in for a doozy tonight.

THREE BROTHER'S Brewing is on the other side of a heart-shaped lake, and there's a single covered bridge to get to it. It's such a pain in the ass to get out here that I half expected the place to be empty, but I'm shocked to pull in and find a full parking lot.

"Is this because of the meeting?" I ask, pointing toward all the cars as I creep along toward the back of the lot, searching for a space big enough for the Suburban.

"Maybe a little," Penny says. Her tone is distracted. "This place always has a crowd, though. The Reid brothers do a good job of community outreach."

Interesting. I file that away to use later.

"Are you worried about the kids?" I ask after pulling into an open spot far from the building.

"No. I mean, a little, but I do know Kai can handle it." She picks at the sleeve of her winter coat.

I slide my hand over the console and rest it palm-up on her thigh. Her shoulders drop, but she places her hand in mine.

"Then what's bothering you?"

"I think I'm nervous about making anything official."

"Anything, meaning us?" Tension flows through me as I wait for her response.

"Anything meaning anything, but yes, including us. Eddy has burned so many bridges and pissed off too many people. I've just laid low, trying to avoid the fallout of every epic disaster, but now with the TAC, and you... I don't know. I worry people will have a lot of things to say, and most of them won't be good. I don't want to put the boys through the gossip mill any more than they've already been. This is a small town. Everyone has something to say, and not all of it's good-natured. Does that make sense?"

Unfortunately, it does.

"It does." I sigh. "But you can't live your life running from his shitty choices either. Build your life to fit you and the kids the way you imagine it. Not how you think others expect it. The expectations of strangers should never weigh heavier than your own."

Her smile is uneven when she looks up at me through thick lashes. "You're pretty smart, you know that?"

"I have my moments." Turning my head, I peer out all of the windows. When I'm sure the coast is clear, I lean my face toward hers. "I need to kiss you now. And then I want to watch your eyes darken when I tell you all the ways I imagined defiling you today."

We move at the same time. Our lips crashing into each other. Teeth, and tongues, and lips meld into a sexual dance of desire and greed.

My tongue traces her lips, and she whimpers against me, but my phone is vibrating in my pocket nonstop, and I'm willing to bet it's Miller.

"We don't have time to do all the things I want to do to you right now. But please do not torture me with so many hours between touches ever again. I'm going at your pace, baby, but we have to keep moving forward. Okay?"

Penny's phone vibrates in her hand, and Miller's name flashes on the screen.

"Okay," she agrees. "We should go in. He's been trying to call for a few minutes." Her phone screen goes dark, so she puts it in her purse, and we head toward the bar to find him.

We don't even make it to the front door when Miller rushes to our side. I know immediately that something's wrong.

"Miller?" Penny asks. Her body goes rigid, like she's preparing for a hit.

I can read a room pretty well, but Penny knows Miller.

"What's going on?" I ask.

"Why didn't you answer your damn phones?" He runs his fingers through his dark brown hair, roughly tugging on the ends. "I wanted to warn you."

"Warn us?" My voice is stronger than I feel.

"It's Eddy," Miller explains. "He's here."

"What the actual fuck?" I bellow. "What do you mean, he's here? Why isn't he in jail? Why didn't Penny get a phone call? He put her children in danger. Doesn't she, at the very least, deserve a heads fucking up?"

Miller holds up his hands, and Penny gently reaches for my forearm. I relax immediately.

"Don't shoot the messenger," Miller says, but by the deep scowl on his face, he isn't any happier about the situation than we are. "Town gossip says he got out on a technicality. How many lives does demon fucker have?"

Too many. I don't say it out loud, though.

"I'm going to be fighting to correct Eddy's selfish mistakes for the rest of my life," Penny whispers with a shaky voice.

"You won't be alone," I promise. Turning to Miller, I ask, "What's he doing here?"

My shields climb higher, as if I'm actually doubling in size with armor so thick I can protect us all while I wait for him to speak.

"Town meeting," Penny says, obviously forgetting for a moment that I haven't learned all of Chance Lake's quirks yet.

"The Reid brothers offer dollar pints to encourage people to volunteer and be involved in the community." Miller fills in the gaps. "Eddy always takes advantage of their kindness."

"Sweetheart?" I lower my mouth to her ear, knowing she's spouting off all the reasons she's failed in one of those checklists she's always making. "Put the list away for now, okay? I've got you. I promise. We came here on a mission, and nothing, not even your ex-husband, will derail that, but I need you to stay close at all times. I don't trust him, and I won't be able to focus if I'm worried about him cornering you. Promise me?"

"He's right, Pen." Miller also seems taller as he comes to stand to our left.

We flank Penny like two protectors.

"I know this is your battle," I tell her. "We'll let you fight it, but every queen needs an army behind her. Everything in me will always protect you, but only if you can't do it yourself. You fight whatever battles you need to, but let us support you."

"Romeo's right. It's not that we don't think you can do it, because I've had a front-row seat to your strength for the last ten years. I know you can. But that doesn't mean you have to."

Miller hooks his arm through Penny's, and I hold her hand tight against my forearm. My legs tremble, my ears ring, and a whirlwind of emotions flows through my body, overriding all my senses. Eddy is done messing with my girl.

"I don't deserve either of you," Penny says like she believes those words down to her very core.

"Bullshit," Miller mutters.

"You, my queen, deserve the world and then some. And I look forward to helping you believe that," I say in the commanding tone I only ever use in the bedroom.

Her enchanting body shivers against mine.

Oh, the things I'd like to show her.

Heat spreads across her cheeks, and Miller chuckles like he can sense the direction of our thoughts.

"You two are good for each other. Don't let Eddy mess that up. You ready?" Miller asks, peering over Penny's head at me.

But my eyes don't leave Penny's when I say, "Yeah, I'm ready. Let's do this thing."

CHAPTER 34

DILLON

The three of us walk inside the brewery arm in arm in arm like we're entering a battlefield as a united front.

I spot Eli immediately, and she moves to stand on the other side of Miller, though she keeps a healthy amount of space between them.

"Remember, we're here to win them over. Part of that will be showing them how you handle adversity. Especially Penny's sleazeball ex-husband," Eli says with a shudder.

I can only imagine what he's said to her.

"Where is he?" I growl through clenched teeth but keep a pleasant expression plastered to my face.

"To your right. All the way around the bar in the corner. We're set up in the tasting room. We can head straight there," Eli says. She doesn't wait for us to agree. She just moves efficiently, expecting that we'll follow.

We do.

All eyes are on us, and I'm thankful that most seem friendly. Miller has moved from Penny's side to walk behind us, but I have yet to release her hand. It's probably drawing whispers from every table we pass, but I don't give a fuck.

Penny walks with a smile and a wave for a few people, but every once in a while, she'll squeeze my hand. Like she's drawing strength from our connection, and I'll be damned if I'm the one to break that.

We enter a large room with giant stainless steel silo-looking containers behind a glass wall that runs the entire length of the room. I'm assuming this space is usually filled with tables, but it's been cleared, and in their place are metal folding chairs set up in long rows like you'd find at a back-yard wedding.

Eli walks us to the front of the room, where a long folding table has been set up facing the chairs on the left side. In the middle stands a podium, and on the right is a smaller table with a laptop.

Penny notices me taking everything in. "Grady, the oldest Reid brother, moderates, I think, and Mrs. Winters sits over there transcribing the meeting. Though her notes are gener-ally more gossip-based."

"Speak of the devil," Miller chuckles as a behemoth of a man reaches us with purposeful strides. With his thick beard and muscular chest hidden beneath a blue checkered button-down, I can't decide if he's in a motorcycle gang or a busi-nessman.

The man extends a hand to Miller. "Miller, good to see you." His tone is gruff, like it's rusty after years of being unused, but it also carries a hint of familiarity that comes with lifelong friendships. "How's Izzy?"

"She's good. Crazy, but good," Miller says with an easy smile.

Grady steps forward and places a chaste kiss on Penny's cheek, and my knuckles crack with tension. All eyes turn toward me.

"Stand down, growly bear. We've known Grady our entire lives. He's like a brother," Miller says. He's teasing me, but it does nothing to ease the tension making the vein in my neck throb like a volcano nearing an eruption.

"Good to see you, Penny," Grady says, ignoring me. "You know you're always welcome here. You didn't have to stop coming to the town meetings just because Eddy is a dirtbag. We've always been Team Penny. You know that, right?"

Penny blinks rapidly and swallows hard before even attempting to speak. Maybe this guy isn't so bad after all.

"Thanks, Grady. Sometimes it's easier to remove yourself though. You know?"

"I get it," he says. "Just promise you won't hide forever. No one blames you for his choices."

Miller throws a playful punch into my arm while laughing at my scowling face.

"No, but the Brandts will surely use it to their advantage every chance they get," Penny says. She drops her head to look at the floor, and I hate that anyone can make her question herself.

"Leave the Brandts to me. Once we get the approvals, things will change around here." I vow.

Grady crosses his arms over his broad chest. I'm not going to lie—the guy is an intimidating fucker, but when it comes to Penny and the kids, I would fight the devil himself if I had to.

"Small-towners don't usually like that much change, newbie. But I hope you have a plan because Duncan Brandt is out there running his mouth like he runs around on his wife. I have no room for that kind of shit in my life. So, if your plan can knock him down a few pegs, you've got the support of my family and me." He doesn't smile exactly, but he does finally hold out a hand.

Yup. I could probably be convinced to like this guy.

I reach across the empty space and shake his hand.

"I'm Grady. You'll meet Adam and Harrison later."

"Dillon Henry. It's nice to meet you, Grady," I say, narrowing my eyes when he squeezes my palm a little harder than necessary. I refuse to back down and give it right back to him.

He finally lets go of my hand and says, "I'll let you know how I feel about meeting you after you do what you're promising, newbie."

I'm used to this kind of grumpy asshole who's not really an asshole at all. Does he know that everyone around him can see him for the giant teddy bear he tries to keep hidden?

"Fair enough," I say.

"Get set up." Grady motions toward the table. "I'll ring the bell in five to round up the troops."

"Thank you, Grady." Penny moves quickly and wraps the bear in a hug.

He pats her back awkwardly, and Miller laughs while setting up papers on the table. When I'm within earshot, he whispers, "Grady's a good guy, but settling back here in Chance Lake sits right up there with peeling off your finger-nails one by one for him."

"Why is he here then?" I ask, watching his retreating form.

Miller shrugs. "Some hurts are too painful to share, even with friends. Whatever sent him running home has the true Grady shuttered behind so many layers of solid steel, it would take a blowtorch to even melt the surface."

My chest pinches for the pain he's hiding. I hope he finds his second chance.

If there's anywhere it can happen, it's here. Chance Lake is a fortuitous name because I think an entire generation of Chance Lakers are about to get their second chance at a new beginning.

~

"Mrs. Walker," Grady says for the fifth time, but the older woman steamrolls right over him.

We've been in the meeting for thirty minutes, and so far, Grady has played judge and jury for two neighbors fighting over a shared tree. He's promised to go to Mrs. Winters's house to look at her fence so her dog, Pepper, will stop escaping and peeing on Mr. Morgan's snow-covered bushes.

Now he's listening to Mrs. Walker plead her case for a town-funded book club called Sexy Scenes and Sips.

Penny leans in to whisper in my ear, and my eyes catch on sweaty Eddy Demon-Fucker as he stomps over to the small tasting bar in the corner. He slams his empty pint glass on the counter, drawing attention from anyone within earshot.

I ignore him and focus on how Penny's hot breath makes my cock twitch in my jeans.

"Mrs. Walker likes steamy romance books. She got Mr. Walker hooked on them too, but he won't admit it. She said reading them together changed their sex life and scarred their two adult kids for life."

Maneuvering my face so I'm now at her ear, I say, "I'm all for experimenting with you. Just say the word."

Her pretty face immediately pinkens, and when I stare back out at the crowd, I find Mrs. Higgins, the owner of Heirlooms restaurant, watching our every move. After she holds my gaze hostage for a second too long, she winks and flashes a wicked grin. A single nod, and it feels like approval.

It's shocking how much that means to me.

Placing my hand on Penny's leg, just above her knee, I gently squeeze as Grady promises to look into the book club options.

"Now," Grady says with a sigh so heavy his shoulders

drop three inches. "This meeting is actually about the TAC and its new owners. Matt Miller is on board over there full-time, and Penny Mulligan will be heading up the new hotel."

"If it's passed," a slimy-looking man sitting in the front row says with a snarling smirk, and I know from my research that it's Duncan Brandt.

"Well, Duncy," Grady taunts, "that's the point of this meeting—to see how their plans will benefit everyone in town, not only a single family."

"It's Mr. Brandt," Duncan seethes.

"Mr. Brandt, if you're nasty," someone coughs from the crowd. When I meet the eyes of a man who can only be one of the Reid brothers, I raise a brow in silent appreciation. He shrugs and smiles like he lives to stir shit up.

"I think now is a good time to turn over the podium to Miller and"—he pauses for effect—"Mr. Henry," Grady announces with an antagonizing flourish that's completely unexpected from the growly biker slash accountant.

I can't stop the chuckle that rumbles in my chest. He really does like to rib that asshat Duncan. Grady just went up a few hundred points in my book.

Miller takes his station at the podium like we'd planned for this portion of the presentation. Eli said his lifelong relationships will put people at ease instead of just throwing me at them. She's right. As I watch the crowd's excitement rise to match Miller's, I can almost taste change in the air.

He gestures wildly with his hands when he explains certain programs he's especially excited about. The tone of his voice goes higher when he discusses the change we want to be for the entire community.

When Brandt interrupts for a third time, Miller slams his fist on the podium, and I take that as my cue to step in, but not before Miller gets a parting shot. "You've gotten rich on the backs of good people in this town. You hide and hoard resources while climbing over every one of your neighbors. We believe we're stronger together, and the success of one can be a win for all. Your time as the dictator of Chance Lake is over."

"Highly doubtful," Brandt replies, unfazed.

But Miller's response has everyone else whispering in their seat.

Placing a hand on the podium, I give Miller's shoulder a squeeze before sliding into his spot and adjusting the microphone.

"Hello. My name is Dillon Henry. I'm the new face of the TAC, but by no means does that mean I'm doing this on my own. I'm investing millions of dollars that were left to me with one stipulation: That I use it for good. I can't think of a better good than investing in the lives of youth who grow up like I did."

People are paying attention, which was my goal for this first part of my speech.

"Ashton Westbrook has matched my investment. Lochlan Blaine has agreed to run the hotel as a Bryer-Blaine property. That alone gives it a legitimacy we couldn't have gotten on our own. Miller will be my partner in all things day-to-day, and is also investing, so he has a stake in making this work."

My gaze drifts over to where Penny sits, toying with the ever-present elastic on her wrist, and I give her a comforting smile.

"Penny Mulligan," I continue, "will oversee the hotel and everything that comes with it. But the rest is up to us. I hope that as a community, we can unite to make this the premier destination for youth sporting programs around the country."

I take a moment to collect my thoughts before continuing and use that time to make eye contact with a few faces in the crowd. "A project this size has a million moving pieces that have to work in harmony to succeed. I want you all to be a part of that. Not only will the TAC bring jobs to the area, but business owners will have a fair shot at expanding within the property's walls."

"How so?" someone asks from the back of the room.

"Well, we'll need a restaurant at the hotel. Heirlooms will have the first right of refusal for that space. The same goes for concessions within the hotel and inside the event spaces.

"Exhausted parents always need coffee, so there are plenty of opportunities for both coffee houses to have a place. We have plans and proposals for all businesses within the Chance Lake borders. From Tanks to Chancy's, we want you to be a part of this success. The reason people keep coming back to this little town is because of its people. Now, I want to bring you and your energy to the TAC."

"What if we can't afford to branch out?" a man asks from a middle row. I think it's Kyle Caldwell, the owner of Tanks, but it's hard to tell with his ball cap pulled low.

It's a good question. "The TAC can only be as successful as its people. All of its people. There will be concessions and opportunities for all who want and need to be a part of changing this community for the better."

"Why should we trust you? How do we know you're not just a suit waltzing in making empty promises?" fucking Duncan asks. If he thinks he can create a divide just because I'm new in town, he doesn't have a goddamned clue how deep my investments go that have absolutely nothing to do with dollar amounts.

I tilt my head and take strength from Penny's kind eyes staring at me like I'm responsible for every ray of light in her life, and I speak from the heart.

"I'm here for the long haul, Duncy." This earns me a chuckle from the crowd. "I'm invested. The kind of invested that doesn't come from a bank, but from the heart. I won't be leaving unless I'm taken against my will. This, Chance Lake, the people, this is the home I've always been searching for."

My eyes never drift from Penny's as I speak, and her eyes sparkle with a mix of love and fear that catch in the overhead lighting.

Eli hip-checks me when I don't notice her at my side. I walk toward Penny, and Eli takes over.

"Hello, I'm Eli Camden. I'm a consultant for Mr. Henry and company because I specialize in after-school programs for underprivileged youth. And I can tell you from personal experience, I've never seen a more committed group of people. They want this for you as much as they do for themselves, and they're playing the long game. No shortcuts will be taken, but I can also tell you that all who want to be involved will have the opportunity." She pauses to make eye contact with as many in the crowd as she can.

"We're working out those details now, and all we need from you is permission to break ground. Someone within the TAC will be reaching out to each business owner over the next two weeks so we can get all the information to the architects. We're not asking for an investment from you yet, only a verbal commitment to consider it."

"And a vote allowing us to proceed," Miller interrupts.

I stand behind Penny with my hands resting possessively on her shoulders as Grady returns to the podium.

"Thank you, everyone," Grady says into the microphone. "And thank you, Miller and Mr. Henry, for your transparency. Unless anyone has questions related to the ethics of this project proceeding, I think we can call a vote. Am I correct in assuming that someone will be available to answer more questions this evening?"

"Yes," Miller speaks up. "We'll all be here for a couple of hours."

"Great." Grady knocks on the podium, and all eyes return

to him. "All in favor of allowing the TAC to proceed, please raise your hand."

Nearly every hand in the room goes up in a flash.

"All those opposed, raise your hands."

Three hands lift. Duncan's, Eddy's, and someone in the back I can't see.

"Majority rules. Mr. Henry, you're good to go."

Miller crashes into my side and wraps me in a hug.

"That's it? There are no papers to sign or anything?" I ask.

"There will be eventually for the state, but the town puts everything to a vote. We're good to go!"

I shake my head as an odd lightness eases over my shoulders. When has anything ever been that easy?

The thought instantly vanishes when I lock eyes with Eddy, who is stewing in the corner with another beer in his slimy hands.

He pushes off the bar like he's coming for me, but another Reid brother steps in before he gets far. They're not close enough to hear their words, but there's no mistaking the giant Reid hand pressing into the center of Eddy's chest. Grady joins them a second later, followed by the third brother.

They close ranks around Eddy, and by the set of Grady's stance, I'm assuming he's laying down the law of his land here in the brewery.

It makes me appreciate Grady and his brothers all the more. They're good people. My kind of people. Studying the ones who are scattering throughout the room, I've never felt more at home in a group of near strangers.

If ever I needed a sign that I was on the right path, this would be it.

CHAPTER 35

PENNY

Stress is exhausting. It's been an hour since Dillon finished his speech in which he essentially outed us in front of everyone, and people are finally starting to ease back on the questions.

Most didn't even ask about the TAC—they were too interested in our new resident to be bothered by business.

I don't blame them, either. Dillon is a fascinating subject I thoroughly enjoy studying.

But I've had an uncomfortable awareness all night. The kind that happens when you know you're about to be attacked, but you don't know where it's coming from. It's making my head pound from the muscles bunched at the base of my skull. Eddy hasn't approached me, but I don't think that's for lack of trying.

I know I'll have to speak to him eventually, but not tonight. Not when I have to go home and care for his daughters, one that has yet to sleep through the night. Not when it's time to have a conversation with our eldest son about Dillon.

My head spins, and my mental lists begin to form again.

- What does Eddy want from me?
- Keep an eye on him so he can't get to the kids.
- What will he do when he approaches Dillon?
- Are people still judging me based on Eddy's decisions?
- Protect the boys and their sisters at all costs.
- The kids come first. Always.
- Confirm that Miller can still watch the girls tomorrow so I can go in to work.

They pull me from the conversations happening around me until all I hear is one cruel voice telling me I'll never measure up, that I'll never get anything right.

"Dance with me," Dillon whispers into my neck. I hadn't even noticed him approach. "You're lost in lists again. Dance with me."

My eyes dart around the room, trying to gauge who's watching us or if it matters. "Dillon, I…"

"It's just a dance, Penny, not a public claiming." He says it nonchalantly, but I hear the hint of pain he's trying to bury deep down.

Guilt, my lonely friend, consumes me. In my quest to do this the right way, I only focused on how that looked for me and the boys.

How could I have been so selfish?

I never once acknowledged what holding him at arm's length would do to him.

My insides churn like I'm on some awful amusement park ride that spins and spins but never goes anywhere.

Decision made. I have to give him what he's given me so freely—all of me.

"Maybe it's time for a claiming," I finally say before nerves can talk me out of it.

I love how his eyes darken, and that rumble in his chest vibrates through my body.

"Be very careful what you ask for, Penny, because if it's in my power, I'll move heaven and Earth to give it to you."

"I—I know you will. I trust you, Dillon."

He steps forward until our bodies are almost flush, and the background noise falls away. It's just him and me in this moment.

His tone changes to the one I dream about late at night, and my panties dampen at his demand. "Tell me what you want."

One of his large hands lands on my hip, and I fight to focus. "I want to be yours. For real."

Dillon's other hand cups my face. "It's always been real for me. It's been real since the first time I met you." Then his lips are on mine.

He has more control than I do because I'm trying to climb him like a tree, but he's holding me stationary. And while there's nothing chaste about this kiss, it is tamed down, presumably for the audience we're sure to find when we lift our heads.

Always protecting.

I shiver beneath his touch. Maybe it's always been real for me too.

I don't know how long we stay like that, wrapped in each other, but all too soon, he pulls back so we're nose to nose.

"Hi," he whispers as the sounds of the room slowly start to worm their way into my consciousness.

"Hi," I whisper back.

"Dance with me?" he asks, and I'm done fighting him. How can I when he spends all his time fighting for me?

I nod, and he takes me by the hand. He leads me through a crowd of smiling faces, and I'm surprised to see they all seem genuinely happy—for me.

I lose track of Eddy though, and my steps falter.

"What's wrong?" Dillon asks low in my ear.

"I lost track of Eddy. I need to keep an eye on him so I know he isn't trying to get to the kids." Fear makes my words tumble out at an alarming rate.

"He's at a table along the wall. Farthest away from the front door. If he leaves, I'll know it."

When I look up at him with startled eyes, he kisses the tip of my nose.

"I'm pretty fond of his kids. If you think I'm going to let anyone, even him, do anything to hurt them, I need to work harder to prove myself."

My heart melts right there on the dance floor.

I'm in love with Dillon Henry. Hopelessly, helplessly, endlessly in love. I can't even pinpoint a time when it happened. Somehow over the last three years, it just came to be my truth.

He pulls my body flush to his and guides us to a slow song I recognize. "You're Beautiful" by James Blunt. Dillon sings softly with his chin resting on the top of my head. My ear is pressed to his chest, and his heartbeat engulfs me in the love he shares so freely.

To do:

- Talk to Kai.
- Help him understand Dillon's role in our family.
- Tell the other kids.
- Finally, finally, tell Dillon that I'm in love with him.

The song ends, but Dillon doesn't release me. We sway together song after song until I'm a vibrating ball of wants and needs. Being so close to him without fear is short-circuiting my self-control.

I'm on a new mission. I can't tell him I love him until I have all my ducks in a row. But maybe I can show him?

Pulling away, I search for Miller. I hold up a finger when Dillon leans in to ask a question. "I'll be right back."

I cross the room like my ass is on fire. "Miller? Can you keep an eye on Eddy for like ten minutes? I have something I—ah—want to show Dillon."

Miller covers his ears with both hands, but his grin is as wide as the Grand Canyon. "I don't need details, Pen. I've got Eddy. You do you." He glances over my head and chuckles. "Or maybe him." He nods his head toward Dillon, and an honest-to-God smile makes my cheeks hurt.

I smack Miller in the gut, then turn back to Dillon freaking Henry. Taking his hand, I lead him toward the restrooms. When I was younger, there was a closet back here that never did lock. Hopefully, the Reids haven't fixed it.

The loud sounds of the happy bar are muted when we enter the darkened hallway that smells faintly of stale beer and the bleach they use to clean it up.

"Where are we going?" Dillon asks with humor lacing the words.

I scan our surroundings like a bank robber on a heist until we come to the door I'm searching for. I test the handle and sigh with relief when it swings open.

Dillon is still holding my hand, so I tug him inside. As soon as the door closes, I spin and lean into him with so much enthusiasm, he hits the door with a dull thud.

"What are you doing?" His grin is evil. He knows exactly what I'm doing and is more than into it. His dick pulses against the zipper of his jeans, and I look up at him with wide eyes.

"I want to show you something," I say. He lowers his mouth to my neck and kisses a line along the sensitive skin there. Tilting my head to the right, I angle myself to give him better access. "I have some things I need to cross off my list before I can do what I want to do," I say in a rush. "But I wanted to show you. Show you how I feel."

His smile curls against my neck, and he bites down gently. "How are you going to do that?"

I lift shaking hands to his belt, then glance at him through my lashes. I pause, waiting to see if he'll stop me. I've never initiated an encounter like this.

Am I doing it right?

Before the doubt can creep in, he's cupping my face. "I don't want you kneeling on a dirty floor to prove how you feel about me. You are my queen, Penny. That means when you kneel for me, it will be on satin pillows, not a cold cement floor."

His words lance my heart but encourage my hands to move at a frenzied pace.

"Penny," Dillon whispers when I lower his zipper. "Not here, baby." Then he groans, and it spurs me on.

I reach into his boxer briefs and release his cock that's already peeking through the top.

"Goddamn it, Penny," he hisses through clenched teeth. "Are you sure? This is what you want? Don't do this for me. If you're going to suck my dick right now, it's because it's something you want. Do you want my cock?" he asks before pushing my hands away and grabbing himself.

I'm already nodding as I sink to my knees. He takes two long, rough pulls on his very impressive length before rubbing his palm over his tip. I lick my lips, greedy in my need for this.

"Words, Penny." He sounds tortured, and his hand jerking his long, hard shaft picks up speed.

"I want to suck your dick," I say in a rush. And then he's there. Rubbing his tip along the seam of my lips.

"Look at how pretty my crown is resting against my queen's lips," he growls. "So fucking pretty."

I open my mouth, but he continues to outline my lips, so I stick out my tongue.

"Oh, baby. You're ready to play today." He smacks his length against my outstretched tongue, and just when I think he won't actually let me suck him off, he guides himself to the back of my throat.

I have little to no experience with this. Does it matter? Even thinking about doing it with Eddy always made me gag before I reached him, and he'd get so pissed off I wouldn't see him for days.

"Stop thinking, Penny. Just focus on breathing because I've dreamed about this for so long that I won't last."

His thrusts are just on this side of being too rough, and my traitorous body responds. My clit throbs, and my entire body sizzles with so much sexual desire I might burst into flames.

Dillon reaches the back of my throat, and I try to swallow against the intrusion.

"Shit, Penny. Shit, your fucking mouth is heaven." He eases back, and I gasp for air. "Play with my balls."

Reaching between his legs, I cup him. What the hell do I do with them now? When he doesn't offer any direction, I use the pads of my fingers to explore his body.

When I hit a particular spot, he hisses. "Right there. Jesus Christ. Press right there." I follow his command, and the first shot of salty cream hits the back of my throat.

It's—different and not nearly as unpleasant as I'd thought it would be, but when I look up into his eyes that are hooded with lust? I'm done.

Dillon Henry is my new favorite flavor.

He comes with a string of mostly incoherent curses, but

when his dark eyes find mine, he hooks me under my arms and lifts me to my feet.

"That was an appetizer," he whispers darkly. "I hope you're able to be quiet because the things I'm going to do to you tonight will wake the dead otherwise."

Dillon tucks his still-hard cock into his pants and adjusts his shirt. Turning his attention to me, he leans down to brush off my knees. That's when I notice some kind of oil stain on my kneecaps.

"Oh my God. I kneeled in something. Everyone will know what we were doing. Oh my God!"

"Relax, Penny."

The door behind him tries to open, and he pushes it closed with his back.

"Jesus Christ. Not again," Grady bellows from behind the door. "I swear to the devil himself, if I find another condom in the mop bucket, I'll burn this place down myself."

My eyes go wide as Dillon listens to make sure Grady has moved along.

"My knees," I plead.

"It's dark in the bar. No one will notice. We'll just make a quick escape, okay?"

"Okay. Yes, that could work," I admit. It is dark out there.

"And, Penny?" He waits until I look up at him, and when I do, his expression softens. "I love you too."

CHAPTER 36

DILLON

"*I* love you too."

Well, shit. Did she just suck all my brain cells out of my body too? That's not the way I meant to tell her, but I guess in the name of claiming and all, I'm done holding back with her.

"Dillon," she says with a sexy sigh.

I lean down quickly to place a sweet kiss on her lips. "When you're ready. Not until you're ready." My eyes search hers, but all I find is love. I don't need her to say it before she's ready because I can feel it in every touch, every glance, every word.

Our love transcends paradigms. It simply exists, like something tangible I can hold on to.

She pulls me to her, and this time, her kiss bleeds with equal parts affection and lust. I accept it all like a starving man.

When she's breathless, I take her by the hand. "We should get out of here before Grady comes back." Her eyes widen in shock, and I chuckle. "Did you forget where we were?"

"Yes," she says quickly. "You have the ability to make me forget myself."

"You're welcome," I moan into the back of her head as I open the door around her.

We make it two steps into the hallway before we're face to face with Eddy. Miller's nickname suits him better than I'd realized.

He stands there with a dirty shirt and pit stains visible under both arms. Even his hair appears to be sweating. Is this what alcoholism does to a person?

I left home before I saw my father get to this point. How freaking terrifying it must be for the boys.

"Such a whore," he slurs and stumbles while reaching for Penny.

I pull her behind me and let him stumble past us in the narrow space like we're circling each other. One hand holds Penny's hip behind me, and the other is held out in a stop motion.

Apparently, sweaty Eddy doesn't read universal hand signals because he moves forward until my palm is pressed to his chest.

"Simmer down," I growl.

"What did you say to me?" he spits out.

"I said, simmer. The. Fuck. Down."

The fingers holding Penny in place press into the inch of exposed flesh hard enough I might leave bruises. I attempt to loosen my grip, but it seems to be directly tied to the fear firing to life in my heart.

I'm not scared of Eddy. Physically, I could take him with both hands tied, but he has the ability and the carelessness to cut Penny and the kids down to their very souls.

Any kind of pain on my watch is unacceptable.

Forcing my hand to press harder, I give him a gentle nudge. "What do you want, Eddy?"

"What? You playing house with my family? Now ya think you can order me around like your own personal grunt? Not happening. You might be able to get my whore of a wife to drop to her knees, but my kids are mine." His words mash together, but I'm fluent in asshole.

I begin to shake with a rage I haven't felt since the last time I saw my own father.

"You hear that, you cunt? Those boys are mine. I picked up Aster today over on Douglas Street." Penny gasps, but he steamrolls over her. "We're comin' for the other ones too."

My vision has gone red, but I'm trying to control myself. Hitting Eddy again won't solve anything, even if every bone in my body is aching to make contact.

"You won't step foot on Penny's property," I growl. "If you want to see any of her children, you will go to court and ask for that right. As of now, seeing them is not an option for you."

I turn my back on him but keep my ears peeled for any movement as I usher Penny forward. It's not until we hit the crowded bar that I hear him.

"Well, look at that," he bellows as the song fades. "My ex-wife isn't so innocent after all. She drops to her knees for money and then has the nerve to brainwash my boys against me. Hey, Penny? Maybe if you'd sucked my cock once or twice instead of lying there like a dead fish, I wouldn't have had to dip my stick somewhere else. Our family fell apart because of you. You remember that you, sl—"

Fuck the appropriate thing to do. I charge this asshole, intent on killing him, but Grady beats me to it and knocks him out cold with one mighty punch.

I stare at him in disbelief, then down at the knocked-out Eddy.

"Don't look at me like that, newbie. He can't use it against me, but if you'd killed him, he would have used it to hurt her," he points to Penny, who stands alone in the center of the room with tears shining in her eyes and her chin trembling with the effort it takes to not fall apart in front of everyone.

"Or"—he lowers his voice—"he would have used it to keep you from those boys. They need a good influence. Don't make me regret stepping in."

He turns and steps over Eddy, grumbling about getting a new lock for his utility closet.

Two men push me out of the way and lift Eddy off the floor, but my attention is on Penny. On the hurt he caused. The embarrassment of this situation is written on her reddened cheeks and sad eyes.

When I go to her, Miller meets me inside the circle of people. He should have been watching Eddy. My entire body shakes with rage at him, at sweaty Eddy, at the entire fucking world.

"I'm so sorry, Pen. Mr. Higgins was choking on a chicken wing again, and I lost track of Eddy while giving him the Heimlich. Again. Do not listen to that asshole. None of that is true, and you know it. Do not allow him to drag you under again."

It irks me a little less knowing that Miller hadn't just forgotten, but I'm still pissed. I take Penny by the shoulders and turn her toward the front door.

A vaguely familiar woman rushes to me, hands me our jackets, and gives Penny a look I can only describe as understanding.

I nod in thanks and wrap my coat around Penny. I don't have time to screw around with getting her arms in hers. Then I lead her out of the brewery.

She doesn't speak until we're sitting in the cab of my SUV. "He's always going to hurt us."

There's no emotion in her words. They're flat and lifeless,

like he siphoned her spirit straight from her body with his bullshit.

"He won't." I can't stand to see her like this, so I put the vehicle in reverse and start the short drive home. "He won't." It's a vow, a promise. It's one I intend to keep. I reach over and take her small hand in mine, but it lies limp. Linking our fingers together, I hold her tight.

"You're not alone anymore, sweetheart. I'm in this with you, whatever you need. He will not ruin our lives. I won't let him."

"What about the girls?" she asks through a choked sob. "If Aster's back, God. Those poor babies. They're never going to know what safe feels like. And it's so much worse than I feared."

I glance over at her before returning my eyes to the road. "What do you mean? How is it worse?"

"Douglas Street. Eddy said he picked her up on Douglas Street."

I glance over and she's shivering, but not from the temperature. No, this is the kind of shiver that comes from true fear.

"You only go to Douglas Street if you're looking for drugs, Dillon. All this time, I thought she was suffering some sort of depressive episode, but what if she's been on something and I missed it?"

Penny's words shred my heart to tiny bits and set them on fire. I keep imagining Lia holding onto my leg like a lifeline, and now I'm the one who can't keep the tears from falling.

This entire situation is fucked, but it's not hopeless. I won't allow it to be.

"It's not your fault, Penny. It's not. You've done everything you could do. Those girls will know what it means to be safe and loved if it's the last thing I do. Please just trust me, baby. I don't have all the answers right now, but I will. I fucking will."

~

WHEN I PULL into Penny's driveway, all the lights are off except for the entryway light.

Thank God.

I don't know that either of us has the energy to put on a happy face right now.

We walk up her front steps in silence, but our connection is secured by the warmth of her palm in mine.

There's a lifetime of baggage to work through, but as long as we have this connection, we'll get through it together.

She unlocks the front door, and we enter. It takes my eyes a second to adjust to the dim lighting, but when they do, I find Kai sitting on the stairs. His eyes burn a hole straight into our joined hands and Penny breaks the connection immediately.

The weight of his stare hangs heavy around my neck. When he lifts his gaze to mine, his eyes are full of nothing but pure hatred and anger that he doesn't know what to do with.

I recognize it because I lived with it for years. When the mistakes of our fathers trickle down to corrupt our lives, it feels like hell has opened up and claimed every inch of you with razor blades.

"It's true," Kai points an accusing finger at Penny.

He's radiating anger like a force field.

"What's true, Kai?" Penny's throat works hard at keeping her voice steady.

Kai scoffs and holds up his phone, where a video from the bar plays.

Someone recorded the entire damn mess.

"It's not bad enough I have to go through life with everyone treating me like I'm already Dad, but now everyone at school knows my mom gets it on with strangers in dirty bar bathrooms," he yells.

"Watch your tone, Kai. Your mother didn't do anything wrong. You don't know the entire story." Penny flinches at my words, and the first fissure crackles in my heart.

"You are not my father," he screams. "I don't need one, and even if I did, it wouldn't be you. Why are you even here? If all you want is my mom, why spend so much time hanging around here? We don't need you, and I don't want you here."

"Kaiser," Penny says sternly. It's one of the few times I've heard her use a mom voice with him. "That's enough. Dillon is a—he's a guest here. He's been a wonderful—friend. You need to apologize right this second."

"Friend?" he scoffs again. "Friend? Do you think I don't hear him sneaking out of your room every morning? Do you think I don't notice the way he looks at you? At us? Like we're a family that needs saving. You always said we weren't a charity case, but did you ever tell him that?"

"I said enough," she fumes, and her body begins to tremble even more. "I get that you're angry, but I work too hard for you to disrespect me in my own home. You have a right to your feelings, Kai, but you do not ever have the right to take them out on anyone else."

I watch it all unfold in front of me. A witness and not a participant. Another crack bursts in my heart.

"So, you're going to choose him just like Dad chose Aster. Aren't you?"

Penny's hurt gasp cuts me wide open.

"He broke us, but at least he had the decency to come clean when confronted with the truth. You're both cowards." He spins on the stair like he's going to walk away, but I catch him by the elbow and hold him in place.

With him standing on the second stair, we're eye to eye.

"Dillon," Penny pleads.

"If you think what your father did was brave, then you have more growing up to do than I realized." Kai's eyes rage with unspoken words. "This isn't a drive-by for me, Kai. I've said that I'm all in. With your mom, your siblings, and you." He rolls his eyes and tries to pull free from my grasp, but I keep him still so we can finish this conversation.

"Did we sneak around for a while? Yes, we did. Because your mom loves you enough not to bring a string of people who will hurt you into your lives. Someday, when you're done being angry at the world and start taking responsibility for what you can control, you'll understand that."

"Dillon, please let me handle this," Penny tries again.

"I love your mom, Kai. I love your siblings, and I love you. I think I have for a long time, but trust is earned. You may push, but I promise you, I'll keep showing up. Over and over again until you believe me."

"Just go away," he spits. "I don't want a father figure. I don't need promises. I don't need anything from you except for you to leave and never come back."

"That's one promise I can't make," I say calmly.

The rage that's burning inside him bursts free. "If it was him or me, who would you choose, Mom?"

"Kai, you're angry and upset. Don't make this worse for your mother."

"Stop telling me what to do."

His voice is so loud that a door opens at the top of the stairs, and then Landon is standing there, clutching Mari to his chest, watching this mess. Fuck.

"Who do you choose?"

"I'll always choose you, Kai. You know that." Tears stream down her face as she speaks, and my heart spirals toward a very painful collision. I don't know how to fix this.

"Then break up with him. Tell him to stop coming here. I already wear Dad's crappy life like a beacon, begging jerks to come for me. Don't make it happen because of you too."

This time when he tugs, I let him go, and he takes the stairs two at a time.

"It's okay, Landon. You can go back to bed," I call up to him. "Kai is upset. It'll all work out tomorrow. Can you put Mari back in her pack 'n play?"

Landon nods. He doesn't seem convinced by my words, but he returns to his room, and then it's just Penny and me and a chasm of regret.

As soon as we hear the click of Landon's door, Penny breaks down. The sound of her sob brands itself to my aching heart. I wrap her in my arms and carry her to the sofa.

"Shh, sweetheart. It's going to be okay."

She sniffles and shakes her head while her tears soak my shirt.

"I promise you, it will be okay."

"I—I can't do this to him, Dillon." Each word sounds like it's been ripped from her throat.

My hand freezes on her back. That sounds an awful lot like goodbye.

"What do you mean?"

"I told you. I've told you so many times. I'm their mom and their dad. I'm their everything. I can't cause them more pain. They can only take so much."

"And what about you? What about your needs?" My throat closes up as she slides off my lap to sit next to me.

"My needs don't matter. I gave up my life the second I became a mom."

"We'll figure it out. We just need time."

"How? How will we figure it out? Eddy is going to always be around, causing pain. Kai is so angry that he doesn't even know how to let anyone in. I don't know how we find a way through that, Dillon, not without hurting him more. I'm sorry…"

"Don't," I growl.

"We can't—"

"For fuck's sake, Penny. Don't do this." Panic and fear invade my body, and my hands shake.

"The timing. It's… I… We… I have to put them first."

"I know that, and I respect that. But what I won't do is throw away the best thing that's ever happened in my life because a fifteen-year-old doesn't know how to work through his emotions yet. I won't do that, and you can't make me. One day Kai will realize that I'm not the enemy. Until that day, I'll be here, helping you, loving you, and being your friend if that's all you can give for the time being. But I'm not going anywhere. Not unless you tell me you don't love me."

"I can't ask you to do that. I don't even know how long it will take for Kai. I can't ask you to wait."

"Penny, I've been waiting for you for three years. I'll wait for another three and then another if that's what it takes. My home is where you are, and that isn't going to change."

The air is too thick to inhale. "But can I ask something? About Kai?" Each word is more painful than the last.

She nods without looking at me. "What?"

"Has he talked to anyone? A therapist, maybe?"

She shakes her head, and another tear falls free.

"I think it might help him. He has a lot of big feelings and a lot of guilt built up inside of him. That kind of energy is toxic and needs an outlet. He'll probably hate it at first, but I think it's important."

She nods again while swiping at her eyes. "I'll see if I can get him an appointment," she hiccups.

We sit side by side, staring into the silence for long minutes. Like we both know things will change when we move, but neither of us is ready.

Neither of us wants this.

I try really fucking hard not to resent the hell out of Kai right now. But I have faith that he'll come around. It's just going to be a goddamn nightmare getting through this mess.

Finally, I sigh. We're only holding off the inevitable. "I'm going to sleep like shit tonight. I've gotten used to holding you."

Penny's shoulders shake with silent tears.

"Please promise me something?" I whisper.

"What?" she asks. The emotions clouding the word make it nearly unrecognizable.

"Promise me that if you're going to cry, you'll call me. I can't take the thought of you crying alone in your closet. Please don't do that to me, baby. If you need to cry, let me catch your tears, even if it's through the phone."

"God, Dillon. Why do you always say these things? It would be so much easier if you were pissed off right now."

"Oh, don't mistake my silence for contentment. I won't be happy again until we've come out on the other side of this. But I mean it when I say I will wait, Penny. I'll wait forever if I have to because no one else can own my heart. Not when you hold the key."

She leans forward and puts her head in her hands. I wrap an arm around her shoulder and tug her into my side. Kissing the top of her head, I make a final promise.

"We will get through this. It's going to hurt, but I'll be waiting for you at the finish line."

When I stand, she lifts startled eyes to mine, and then she stands too. Her steps are heavy, like her legs have filled with lead, as she follows me to the front door.

"Where are you going?" she asks, barely above a whisper.

"I'll stay at the TAC tonight. Tomorrow I'll talk to Miller about moving into Ashton's place with him and Izzy."

"I'm sorry. I…"

I place my pointer finger over her lips. "We're done apologizing for things that are out of our control. This isn't the end of us, Penny. It's a speed bump on our path, nothing more."

A tear slips down her cheek, so I lean down to kiss it away. I refuse to believe this is the last time I'll have that right, but for all my forced positivity, I know my heart will break the second I walk away. It no longer beats a steady rhythm unless she's by my side.

"I love you." With a parting glance that guts me, I step out into the chilly night, knowing nothing is right in my world.

I've never been a praying man, but for the first time in my life, I send up a little prayer for our hearts.

CHAPTER 37

PENNY

I lie in bed, watching the numbers on the clock tick away. There was no sleep for me last night. Not when my bed smells like Dillon. Not when my fingers keep clawing at my chest to ease the ache there.

I never knew love could hurt so much.

It never felt like this with Eddy. With him, it was just pain for what he put my boys through.

Remembering Dillon's expression when he told me he loves me has me choking down another sob, and I bury my face into his pillow.

How long can I cling to the scent of him before that's gone too?

Eventually, the alarm goes off, and I drag myself from bed. My head rages like the worst hangover of my life. Everything hurts, my stomach is threatening a revolt, and the cobwebs in my mind keep multiplying.

Standing in the hallway, I poke my head into each of the kid's rooms—except for Kai's. He locked me out.

I hear the ding, ding, ding of a video game that means

Gage is downstairs. He's physically incapable of sleeping in. I'm surprised he even stays still long enough to sleep.

I'm halfway down the stairs when there's a gentle knock on the door. My heart skips a beat the closer I get, but Gage comes flying around the corner before I can see who it is.

"I got it, Mom!" He flips the lock's latch and opens the door with so much force that the wind blows my hair around my face. "Dewey! What's in your hair?"

Dillon's face lights up at Gage's excitement. "Well, it's Grandparents Day. I figured I could at least play the part."

Peeking around the door, I take in the full picture, and I laugh despite myself. He looks like he went thrift shopping at Remy's boutique. His pants are at least three inches too short and four sizes too big. He has suspenders holding them up over a flannel shirt that looks surprisingly good on him.

But it's his face that keeps me frozen on the spot. He's wearing a pair of glasses I'm reasonably sure he doesn't need, and he has white powder falling onto his shoulders. But it's the dark circles under his puffy eyes that match my own that cause my heart to riot against my chest cavity.

I'm hurting him too.

"Did you— Did you put baby powder in your hair?" I finally ask.

"Good morning, Wednesday Girl." He hands me a large coffee. I've never wanted to smile and cry at the same time as much as I do right now. Is that a thing? Maybe a smry? "I know it's not Wednesday, but you're going into the city today, and I told Miller I'd handle the girls so..."

He shrugs but hesitates on the porch.

Remembering myself, I move out of the way and let him in.

"Are you really coming to my school today?" Gage asks, bouncing on his toes.

"If that's okay with you," Dillon says.

"Heck yeah! Oh, man. Everyone's going to be so jelly. I gotta go eat. We cannot be late today." He darts off toward the kitchen, and I know I'll be cleaning up cereal for a week, but I can't bring myself to care.

"What are you doing here?" My voice doesn't know which emotion it wants to share, and the words come out in a mangled mess.

"Yeah, what are you doing here?" Kai demands from the stairs behind me.

It's like a switch flipped in him overnight. He's been a little standoffish with Dillon, but he's never been outright rude before. If I didn't know better, I would have even said he liked Dillon a few days ago.

Maybe Dillon's right about therapy. Kai's anger needs a target, which seems to be painted on me and Dillon right now.

Dillon takes it in stride, though. He crosses his arms over his chest with a small frown forming on his face. He looks ridiculous and utterly perfect at the same time.

"I'm here because I made a promise—"

"And you keep your promises, yada yada yada. Yeah. I've heard that before."

"Kaiser. That's enough. In this house we choose kindness, and if you cannot think of something nice to say then you will keep your mouth shut."

My son glares at Dillon and mimes locking his lips.

"You're right. You have heard it before. At some point, you'll have to stop blaming your father and take responsibility for your own life, and maybe then you'll realize that not everyone will disappoint you."

"You're a dick," Kai spits.

"Kaiser." I suck in a sharp breath and my heartbeat rushes in my ears. This isn't my son. "Go to your room and be prepared to hand over your phone. You're grounded."

He stomps up the stairs, complaining the entire way about my loyalties.

When I think I can keep my composure, I turn back to Dillon. "I'm so—"

"Don't do it, Penny. You do not need to apologize for him. He'll do it when he's ready. He's a good kid going through a rough time. He doesn't know how to believe in me yet, but I will keep showing up until I'll prove to him that I'm not going anywhere."

My chin trembles, but if I allow myself to break now, I may never be able to fix myself again. I stare at him and the shadows hiding behind his eyes.

Do I look as lost as he does?

"Until we figure out a way forward, we will continue with our plans. But as…" He swallows hard, like he's forcing down a rotten egg. "But as friends."

"What does that mean?"

"That means I'll have a severe case of blue balls until you're comfortable being mine. It also means that on the days you work, I'll come here to help with the kids. If I have to do stuff at the TAC, I'll take the girls with me, and I'll get the boys off the bus."

"Are you sure you never wanted kids of your own? You're pretty good at this whole parenting thing." It's so easy with him. Everything is easy with him, except, apparently, being with him and not alienating my oldest son.

"I learned from a very young age that blood does not make a family, Penny. It seems to me you have a pretty good one here. I just need to figure out how to make myself a more permanent fixture."

He's interrupted when Landon walks down the steps with a weary expression. When he reaches us, he gives Dillon puppy dog eyes that make my mommy heart clench. "Mari's still asleep." His tone is so sad, and I hate myself a little more for it. His worried gaze switches to Dillon. "For what it's worth, I like you, Dillon."

He inhales a sharp breath before speaking. "I like you too, Landon. In fact, I have something to talk to you about too."

My middle son's expression changes instantly. "Me?"

"Yeah. I found this over at the TAC." Dillon hands over a folder I hadn't noticed under his arm, and Landon's face pales. I'm reaching for it before I can form words, but Dillon's next sentence stops me. "You're incredibly talented. I love that you have so many ideas for the TAC, and I wanted to see if you might be interested in a junior internship."

Landon's hands shake on the folder. "I—I'm not sure I like doing this anymore," he says quietly.

"Landon?" Dillon pauses until my son lifts his head to meet his eyes. "Don't let the words of others ruin the dreams you have for yourself. If that is something you're interested in, even a little, I think you should explore it. You can't teach talent like that." He points to the folder in Landon's hands, and this time I do reach for it.

Of all the things I was expecting, sketches of the TAC and the hotel were not it. Not just sketches though—detailed, amazing sketches.

"Lanny, you did this?" The nickname he asked me to stop using when he turned ten slips free. He's my baby, and I missed all of this.

My son stares at the floor.

"Why didn't I know? Do you like doing this? Dillon's right. These are incredible."

"Dad said drawing was for pu—other people. He said I couldn't do it, or everyone would think I'm a freak."

Dillon's chest rumbles, Landon's eyes droop, and my anger flares.

"Your dad doesn't have a clue what he's talking about, Landon. Dillon's right. If your dad's words made you rethink something you love, then let's talk about it. Don't give up on something because he chose to be cruel instead of supportive."

"Really?" his little voice asks.

"Really," I say vehemently.

"Will I get to watch them design the hotel?" Landon asks Dillon with love in his eyes.

"As long as there are no safety issues, you can shadow any part of the process you're interested in."

Landon launches himself and wraps Dillon in a hug. Dillon returns the embrace, but his eyes stay on me. "We're going to be okay," he mouths.

And as he says it, everything in me wants to believe him.

"Go get ready for work, Penny. I've got the kids," he says when Landon releases him.

"But Kai…"

"If Kai doesn't want to ride to school with me, he can take the bus. He's a big boy, Penny. He might just need to learn a few lessons on his own."

"Okay," I say and head up the stairs. My lists are loud in my head, but the one thing that's the loudest is Kai.

- Am I doing right by him?
- Is it too soon to bring Dillon into our unit?
- Will he hate me if I can't give Dillon up?

The last one haunts my every waking moment.

LOCHLAN ENTERS his office and pulls up short when he sees me. "Penny? You look like bloody hell. Are you sick?"

"No, I'm fine." Fine. Fine. Fine. Keep chanting it, and maybe it'll be true.

"Listen, I may not understand women, but the one thing I've learned being married to Tilly is fine is never fine. What's going on?" He crosses the room and sits on the edge of my desk like a protective older brother.

"Kai's getting teased at school about Dillon and me. He had a major freak-out and basically told me to choose him or Dillon."

Lochlan frowns and rubs his thumb and forefinger along his jaw. "Penny, I'm about to say something you won't like, but I'm saying it as your friend, not your boss."

Squaring my shoulders, I prepare for him to tell me I'm not in the right mindset to take on all this new responsibility right now.

"Kai is a teenager in a bloody awful position, but he's still a teenager. Teenagers are known for making shitty choices. I know. I read it in that damn parenting book Tilly made me read. Why are you allowing him to make this call?"

His words leave me speechless. Lochlan is not an *advice-giving* kind of guy. He's a *keep your personal life personal* type of guy.

He stands and tugs on his vest. He's upset—for me. "I've known you for years now, Penny, and I've never seen you happier than you've been the last few weeks with Dillon. That should count for something."

"It does count. And I'm not letting Kai make the decisions, but I need to be mom and dad first. I have to be supportive of his feelings because no one else will."

"No one?" He stares at me and shakes his head. "You weren't here when Kai showed up a while back, but I saw Dillon's face. He's been pining for you and all that comes with you for years. And if I know him, he's beating himself up over Kai. You can be supportive while still doling out tough love. Don't let the misdirected trauma of youth dictate your future."

My phone chimes with an incoming text. Glancing down, I see it's from Remy, so I open it and promptly fall back against my chair. Lochlan walks behind me to see what's making my hands shake and my eyes misty.

Remy sent me a picture of Dillon dressed as a grandpa with Mari strapped to his chest, sitting on the floor in a sea of eight-year-olds, reading a book.

His message simply reads: Some fights are worth the battle.

Lochlan pats my shoulder. "That looks bloody awful. If he's willing to entertain a gaggle of kids, he's certainly going to put up a fight for you. Just be careful how long you keep him at arm's length. Eventually, there will be nothing left to grab ahold of."

He walks into his office, leaving me alone with my thoughts and a picture I already have memorized.

Being a single mom is so damn hard.

- Can I have Dillon and not hurt Kai in the process?
- Can I help Kai, or has his father already doomed his childhood? And how big of a part did I play in that if he did?

CHAPTER 38

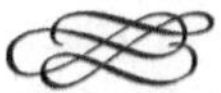

DILLON

The days are starting to bleed together in one endless pit of angst. My time is filled with TAC meetings, decisions, and three days a week, playing daycare with Mari and Lia while Penny works.

Despite Eddy's threats, neither he nor Aster has shown up at Penny's house, even after they were served with a letter stating Penny had full guardianship until a hearing next month. I'm still beating myself up over not being able to go to the courthouse with her. The only thing I could offer was a decent attorney.

And she's still refusing to let me put in a security system, so I drive by like a stalker to keep an eye on them when I technically have no reason to be there.

I don't want a reason. I just want to belong with them.

The last two weeks have been a living nightmare. Every time I'm close to Penny, my throat burns. I can tell she isn't sleeping, either. The circles under her eyes have returned and, in the mornings, they're rimmed red like she's been crying all night.

But she hasn't called me once. She's shutting me out, and

it's hurting her as much as it is me. The only exception was when she called to say thank you for the lawyer.

Kai still won't look at me. His anger has settled all the way to his bones, and even though I know it's not me or Penny he's really hurt by, I want to shake him a little every time he ignores me.

The one shining light is that my relationship with the other kids has grown stronger. Like a living, breathing thing, I soak in the love they express greedily.

Every time Landon shows up with a new sketch to show me, pride beaming in his eyes.

Every time Gage tells me he misses playing with me in the morning.

Every time Lia wraps her little arms around my neck so tightly, I worry she'll break.

And every time little Mari gives me a toothless smile.

My heart expands beyond the limits I thought I had. These kids have buried themselves so deeply in my life that I can't imagine a day without them.

Hopefully, it won't come to that. But God forbid, if Penny doesn't let me in, I will never be able to walk away from them. Blood or not, they're mine. My love for them is different than my love for Penny, but it's no less powerful, and it hit me just as fast.

"Dillon?" Miller calls from somewhere within Ashton's house. Construction is happening around the clock at the TAC now, so I'm even more thankful for this place. A construction zone is no place for Izzy. "Dillon," he calls again, and I hear the strain in his voice this time.

I'm barreling out of my room and down the hall a second later. He's standing at the bottom of the stairs like he saw a ghost.

Fuck.

There are times in your life when you see someone and

just know. You just know that something awful, something life-altering has happened.

It's in Miller's face now.

Dear God, let them be okay.

"What? What is it? Are they okay? The kids? Penny? What the hell, Miller? What's wrong?"

He backs into the wall as I crowd the landing.

"E—Eddy's in jail."

The air whooshes from my lungs like a popped balloon.

"He was driving…"

Every muscle in my back tightens, and my spine goes rigid. Fear makes it hard to breathe. Miller is shaken up, with blurry eyes and trembling hands. I count to ten to give him time to tell me what the fuck happened.

"Aster. She was in the car."

My knees lock, and the vein in my neck throbs.

"He said she took some pills, then told him she wanted the girls to be happy, right before she grabbed the steering wheel." He sucks in a ragged breath that's so choppy I'm afraid he'll choke. "They hit a parked police car before crashing into the Bowens' fence. His truck rolled three times before it caught fire. Eddy wasn't wearing his seatbelt and was thrown from the truck. By the time he regained consciousness…"

Oh, God. Aster wasn't a great mother, but no one deserves this.

"He—he couldn't get close enough to know if she made it out, and the police officer on the scene never had a chance to get to her because the car ignited almost immediately. The flames were too hot. When the firemen finally made their way down the embankment, it was too late. She—she's gone. And Eddy is in more shit than he can ever get out of. His blood alcohol level was three times the legal limit."

I place my hands on his shoulders. It's an oddly intimate

gesture, but this man is part of my new home. He has a place with me. For the first time since I was a child, I embrace how the Westbrooks championed found families. Miller is my friend, my brother, and right now, he's hurting.

"Are you okay?"

"Yeah," he says quietly. "It's just such a shock. And fuck, Dillon. Penny. The kids. This will bring a shit show of epic proportions down on them."

"We'll protect them as best we can. Does Penny know?" My throat burns, thinking she might have gotten this news with no one supporting her.

Miller shakes his head. "Not yet. She took Lia for a well-visit with the pediatrician. It happened at the county line on the other side of town, so I don't think the news has spread this far yet. The sheriff heard it on the scanner and called me after he got the details."

"Okay," I say to buy time as I formulate a plan in my head. "We need to get to Penny before someone else does, and we have to get the kids from school. They can't hear this kind of thing from anyone but Penny, and with social media these days…"

"Agreed." We share a look that lets me know we're on the same page. "I know things are rough with Penny, but the fact that you didn't even hesitate right now? That means more than you could know. I'm in your corner, Dillon. The road is going to knock you around a bit, but stay the course. I've got your back."

I clap him on the shoulder and then step back. "Thanks, man." He can't know how much I appreciate him right now, but I do. It's an amazing feeling knowing someone has your back. "Same goes for me."

He nods, and we walk into the family room.

"I'll go get Penny. Can you get the kids from school? You must be on some kind of list or something, right?" I ask, grabbing my shoes by the door. A pair of Izzy's red boots are thrown carelessly in the corner, and I take a steadying breath.

I need this mess in my life. I need Penny's chaos and piles of shoes. I won't stop until this family is mine in every single way.

"Yeah, I'm the emergency contact. I'll go get them now. Meet you back at Pen's?" He's already heading for the door.

I'm right behind him. "Text me the address of the pediatrician. I'll get there as soon as I can."

"Thanks, Dillon."

"This's what families are for, right?"

Miller pauses halfway into the cab of his truck, and his expression changes in an instant. "Yeah, that's what we're for." He lowers himself to the seat, then pops back out. "Glad you've joined our pack."

Before I can respond, he slams his door and backs out of the driveway. A second later, my phone dings with a text. The address. Plugging it into my GPS, I take off to find my girl.

I also send up my second prayer this month. Dear God, please don't let this destroy them.

I PARK RIGHT NEXT to Penny's car. According to Miller, she should be almost done, so I figured it was better to catch her this way than storming the doctor's office.

I've been having conversations with myself, testing out the best way to deliver this news, but I keep falling short. There's no easy way to say this.

The door opens, and Penny emerges with Mari on her hip and Lia's hand in hers. She stares down at a chatty Lia, then tips her head back in laughter. It's the most uninhibited I've seen her in weeks.

She's beautiful.

I watch them while trying to keep my breaths even. Penny's complexion complements her golden-brown hair, and while the girls have lighter hair and olive skin like their father, Penny's nurturing nature would make anyone passing by think these are her girls.

And now they might be. Forever.

How does she carry the burdens of others without being crushed by the weight of them?

She's more than my queen. She's a goddamned superhero.

Penny looks both ways, instructing Lia to do the same, and then they cross the parking lot. When they're close, I step out of my SUV, unintentionally surprising her. There's the flash of happiness before it retreats into sadness, but it's that flash that gives me hope. It's that flash that tells me we'll get through this.

"Dillon? What are you doing here?" she asks.

Lia looks up at my name, and a smile that outshines the sun stretches across her face when she spots me.

Will I ever tire of that purity? Knowing I can make someone so happy just by existing? I know I'll never take it for granted.

"Dewey!" Lia screeches. When they're close enough, Penny lets go of the little girl's wiggling hand and she runs straight for me.

"Penny, the kids are okay," I say, scooping Lia up in my arms. I inhale her scent, strawberry shampoo, shocked to find comfort in it.

"Oh, God. That's a precursor to something not being okay, isn't it?" Penny's chin quivers as she watches me.

I swallow a ball of sawdust that's lodged in my throat and nod. "I need you to come with me."

She doesn't hesitate. She unlocks her car and attempts to remove Lia's booster seat with Mari still in her other arm.

I place a hand on her shoulder, and sparks light up my skin even through the thick down coat she's wearing.

"I have car seats already, Penny."

"You do? Where did you get them? I don't have extras." She appears confused but grabs a couple of bags from her back seat that I take from her.

"This SUV has had car seats since the day I bought it. Call it planning ahead."

My joke falls flat, though, and we get busy buckling the girls into their seats. I turn on the ignition and press a few buttons to stream the movie *Trolls* for Lia, then turn around and hand her a set of headphones.

The little girl's entire face lights up as she pulls them over her ears. When I'm confident she's settled, I turn back to a frightened-looking Penny.

I can't keep the boundaries between us. Not right now. Reaching over, I take her hand in mine. My thumb rubs gently over the soft skin between her thumb and forefinger.

"Dillon," she chokes out. "You're scaring me. Is it Miller? What's going on?"

"No," I say quickly. "It's not Miller. He's on his way to pick up the kids. We'll meet them at home."

She drags in a shaky breath that causes my eyes to grow hot, like I'm staring directly into the sun.

"There was an accident," I finally say. "Eddy and Aster."

Her entire body freezes. I can't even be sure she's breathing until she speaks. "What happened?"

Penny's eyes glaze over, and her chest rises and falls too quickly as I relay Miller's message. Fear, anger, and pure, unadulterated pain filter across her features in the few minutes it takes me to recite this terrible tale.

I hate hurting her like this, but watching her emotions

play out, I know I'm the only one who could do it. She's mine, and right now she needs me.

She spins in her seat to stare at the two little angels, happy and safe in my backseat. When Lia notices us watching her, she waves with two hands and a giant smile.

Penny's hands fly up to her mouth to cover her choked sob.

"I have to keep them, Dillon. I don't know how I'll manage, but I have to. They can't go into the system. They're my boys' sisters. What am I going to do? Oh, God. Kai. Kai. Any of these kids could have been in that car. What if…"

I grab the back of her head and pull her close enough to rest my forehead against hers. I breathe in and out slowly until she matches my rhythm.

"But they weren't, Penny. They weren't because you were taking care of them. They're okay because they have you. They have us. It's going to be fucking brutal, but we'll figure it out."

Her shoulders shake as the weight of this horrific situation hits her.

"We have to head home. What do you need?" I ask, silently praying she says she needs me. She doesn't, though.

"There's no handbook for this kind of thing. I— I'll need to have different conversations with each of them, I think." Her eyes scan back and forth, but I have no idea what she's searching for. It's like her eyes move with each thought she has, and my heart aches knowing I can't fix this for her.

"Kai will need more details than Gage, and Landon is too smart not to piece things together, but he's still only eleven." She rubs a hand under her nose, so I dig around in the compartment on the driver's side door and pull out some napkins.

She takes them and turns to rest her head against the window.

I put the SUV in gear and start driving home. It's a short drive that we make in silence. When we arrive, Miller's already inside.

Penny grabs the door handle, but I place a heavy hand on her thigh to hold her in place. "You're not alone. Remember that, okay? You don't have to be everything to everyone. Miller and I are here for you all. Go inside. I'll get the girls and meet you in there."

She squares her shoulders and lifts her chin. When her lips tremble, she presses them into a thin line. With one rough swipe under her eyes, she blinks away any remnants of tears and slowly makes her way up the steps and into her home.

A LOUD CRASH sounds from overhead that has Miller and me on our feet, but neither of us attempts to go to them. Kai has been yelling and screaming for over an hour about everything and nothing, but Penny's voice has remained calm and steady as she talks him through it.

Her strength might be my undoing.

Everything in my soul is begging me to race up those stairs and take this burden from her. To fix it. Fix everything. But I can't. Not yet. I've never felt so goddamned helpless as I do right now.

"He feels broken, and he's lashing out," Miller mutters at my side. He has Mari curled up on his chest, and I'm momentarily struck by how natural he is with her.

"I know," I say, scrubbing a hand over my face like if I can just rub hard enough, it will wash away the helplessness that's consuming me. "I hate this. All of it."

The other kids pretend to be focused on the screens in their hands, but I know better. Even Gage is silent and still.

Kids truly are energy vampires. They feed off the vibe of every room they enter.

"I know," Miller says. His tone is compassionate, but his face is hard. He steps closer, so we're shoulder to shoulder. "If he weren't already in jail, I think I'd kill him myself."

Same, man. Same.

My eyes snag on Landon, sitting alone in the corner. He tries to mask his fear, but it's palpable. I cross the room and settle on the floor, resting my back against his chair.

"My dad did something again, didn't he?" Landon whispers.

I won't lie to him, so I nod even though I'm not sure it's my place.

"Does it make me a bad person if I hate him?" His voice trembles at the words, and I let my head fall back so he can see the truth in my eyes.

"No, Landon. That makes you human. We're not defined by our circumstances but by the choices we make. We can't control the choices of others, but we can control our own. We will always be here to help you make good choices, okay?"

"You promise?" It's a whispered request that's full of fear. "What if Kai makes her..."

"Landon? Look at me." He drops his watery eyes to mine. "I bought that building over there," I say, pointing in the general direction of the TAC. "That is where I'll be until I retire. Regardless of what happens within these walls, I will always be available to you. I promise. And I never break my promises."

"Sometimes..." He looks away, and his cheeks flush red. "Sometimes I wish you were my dad."

My gut hollows out at his words. A full-body tremor makes its way through me like a giant wave, and I can't control the tear that slips free.

"The thing about family is—" I cough to clear my throat. I need this to resonate with him, so I get control of my emotions and make my voice as strong and clear as possible. "Family is what you make it, Landon. Sometimes the families we're born into are not the ones that can support our souls. It's not only blood that creates a family. If you learn anything from me, I hope it's that."

Kai chooses that moment to barrel down the stairs. He's so out of control he misses a couple and lands at the bottom with a thud. Venom shoots from his wild eyes when he sees Landon and me.

"Why are you always here?" he seethes, stepping closer. This isn't the kid I first met. This is a kid so shattered by broken promises that he can't find his way out of the dark.

I stand and move to him with a relaxed stride. "Just because something's hard doesn't mean you get to walk away. This," I say, motioning around the house, "is hard. Really freaking hard, but someday you will realize that some men do keep their promises. And I will be the one to teach you. I don't care if it takes three months or thirty years. I'll be here."

His expression flashes from confused to angry to sad and back again in the span of seconds.

"I don't need you," he bellows before running toward the door, grabbing a jacket on the way and sending backpacks crashing to the floor.

Spinning on Miller, I ask, "Where's he going?"

"Let him be. There isn't much trouble he can get up to out here. Let him cool off, and then I'll go looking for him."

Penny is standing on the stairs wearing exhaustion like a heavy cloak. Her eyes are on the door, but when she notices me staring, she looks at Landon.

"Hey, buddy? Can I talk to you for a minute?" she asks.

Landon stands slowly and walks toward the stairs, but at

the last minute, he turns and wraps his arms around me in a solid embrace.

A strangled cry has me looking up. Penny has shaking hands over her mouth, and tears that won't stop sliding down her cheeks.

Leaning over, I kiss the top of Landon's head. "I'm always here, okay?"

He nods against my stomach, then pulls away and follows his mom up the steps.

The rest of the night goes more smoothly. I'm not sure what she said to Landon or Gage, but they return to the family room a little sad but calm.

It's almost two hours before Kai walks back into the house with a red face and no voice. It's like he went out into the field and screamed his throat raw.

Watching him head upstairs, I wonder if that's just what he did. I wouldn't even blame him.

"I'm going to keep them out of school the rest of the week," Penny says from the kitchen, but her voice is flat. She has no energy to feel anything anymore, and it shows in her monotone sentences.

I don't know if she's talking to Miller or me, but we both give her our attention. "And I'm going to hold off on telling Lia until I can talk to the pediatrician. I don't want to traumatize her any more than I have to."

I'm drawn to her like a magnet, and there's no use fighting it. When I pull her into a hug, she clings to me like I'm her lifeline.

I rub her back, and she shakes in my arms. Miller keeps the kids busy in the other room as we just stand here. I hold her until her tears dry. Until her body stops trembling. I hold her like I'll never let her go, and someday that will be the truth.

CHAPTER 39

PENNY

One week blends into another, and before I know it, it's been almost two months since Aster's funeral. Two months of walking around in a daze. Two months of custody hearings, finding a new normal, and outbursts from Kai. Two months with Dillon on the periphery of my life.

I got Kai into a therapist a few weeks ago, but so far, he's rejecting everyone and everything he once loved. I haven't even seen him with a basketball in his hands for weeks.

Our home that has always been filled with love is now a cesspool of tension and anxiety. Landon retreats to his room the first chance he gets. Gage is abnormally calm.

It wasn't supposed to be like this.

"Mom?" Landon whispers and gently places a hand on my arm.

I startle and jump. The spoon in my hand is frozen in midair.

It takes me a second to process his worried expression. Then I realize tears are falling from my eyes.

I drop the spoon and quickly wipe them away. "Sorry,

buddy. I was lost in my head. I don't know what this is about." I laugh with no humor as I point to my face.

Landon shoots an angry glare at his oldest brother.

"I'm okay, just tired. Emotions get the best of us when we're tired." I offer a smile, but I know it's not fooling anyone.

"What?" Kai shouts at his brother.

"Boys."

"You. You did this to her," Landon shouts. "Even when dad was terrible to her, we never saw her cry. Now she can't control it and it's because you took away the one thing that made her happy. You took Dillon away from us all. He doesn't sleep here anymore because of you. And even after all that, he still keeps his promises to all of us."

"Fuck you," Kai says, his words full of venom and without a hint of remorse.

Lia whimpers and seems to shrink in on herself.

"Kaiser." I'm out of my chair with my palms planted on the table for support before my next breath. Emotions run haywire through my body.

"Never. You are never to swear like that in this house. I've raised you better than that. I know that things are hard for you, but guess what? You're not alone in this grief. We're all hurting. Step outside of your own walls for two seconds and see how this has affected your siblings. How it's affecting me. This isn't just about you."

The front door bursts open at the end of the hall and Dillon stomps through it. I can tell by his expression that he's on a mission. He doesn't stop until he reaches the table. As always, he reads the tension in the room.

"What's going on?"

"Kai swore at me, and he's making Mom cry," Landon says.

Dillon turns a dangerous expression on Kai. His face is all

hard lines and throbbing muscles as he pulls a root beer barrel from his pocket. No one says a word as he stares at Kai and crunches angrily on the hard candy.

"Dewey," Lia claps happily with open arms, waiting for him to go to her.

"Hi, princess," Dillon says gently, but the tension in his body is still ready to snap.

Even Landon lit up at the sight of him, while Gage holds out his hand. Dillon's eyebrows relax when he reaches into his pocket and pulls out more candies. He sets one in front of each kid's plate. "You can't eat it until after dinner."

They all nod happily, then his posture shifts again, and he turns his scowl on Kai.

"This ends now. Get your coat on," he demands.

Kai looks scared but defiant and sits back in his chair with crossed arms.

Dillon goes to him and leans down into his face. "Unless you want me to call the sheriff myself, you will get your coat on. Now."

"I—I didn't—"

"Save it, Kai. I have cameras all over the TAC. Do you really think there's anything that happens there that I don't know about? I own a security company, for crying out loud."

"What's going on?" Nerves settle deep in my gut.

Dillon pauses to smile at each of the kids, who are all staring at him, then turns back to me.

"Penny, he's gone too far this time. I know he's hurting, but I'm tired of sitting back and watching him lash out at everyone except the one person who should be on the receiving end of his anger." He turns a foreboding expression on Kai. "Now, Kai. I mean it. You do not want me to help you out of this house."

Kai stands, knocking his glass over in the process, and

stomps to the foyer. Landon is quick to jump into motion and mops up the spilled water with his napkin.

Dillon rounds the table and holds up his phone.

"No. Oh no," I gasp. On his phone is a photo of one of the new TAC vehicles painted with the words "go home" across the side. Deep gouges run along the length of the SUV. "He did this? What am I doing wrong? Why can't I reach him?"

I turn my back away from the kids so they can't see the new tears forming. Dillon stands in front of me and gently places his lips on my cheek.

"I have an idea. I just need to take him somewhere for a little bit. He'll fight it, but trust me enough to do what's right for him."

"W— What are you going to do with him?"

"Give him an outlet for the rage rotting inside him." The front door slams shut, and Dillon searches my eyes. "Trust me," he pleads.

"I do trust you."

"He won't be in any danger, and I'll bring him home when he's ready." And with that, he makes his way around the table, kissing all the kids' heads. My kids now.

"Bye, Dewey. I wub you."

He pauses at the door and turns to smile at Lia. "I love you too, princess." He makes a point of catching each of their eyes, then says, "All of you."

God help me because I know it's the truth.

MERCIFULLY, the kids all go to bed without too much of a fuss. I'll need to figure out a more permanent situation soon, though. There are not enough bedrooms for everyone. Mari is in with Landon and Lia is on the bottom bunk in Gage's room.

I'll add it to my list of worries for another day.

Right now, I'm curled up in the chair near the window that faces the TAC. A million scenarios run through my head, but I still have no idea what Dillon is doing with my son.

Because I'm watching the window, I see Miller pull into my driveway. I stand quickly to let him in before he wakes up the kids. Mari has been an especially light sleeper lately.

I open the door before he can knock.

"What are you doing here?"

He walks past me and tosses his jacket and shoes before heading to the family room. I shut the door and follow him.

Miller plops down on my sofa and spreads his arms wide. "I'm here to check on you. I was with Dillon when he watched the security footage."

I walk to him and sit on the other end of the sofa. I'm exhausted to my bones. The kind of tired you only feel when you allow your body a moment to rest, but when you do, it overpowers you.

"I can't believe it, Mill. This isn't Kai, but I don't know what to do."

"I agree, it isn't Kai. Not the Kai he can be, anyway. I know he's a good kid, Penny, but you can't keep coddling him either."

"I'm not," I say defensively.

"You are. And I know why you're doing it, but the more you let him push, the more he's going to take. He feels out of control, so he's trying to control anything he can. But you are the parent. You have to take control and show him how to manage it."

"How?" I choke out. "How do I do that?"

"Well, letting Dillon take Kai tonight was a good start. But really, what you should do is get your head out of your fucking ass."

My jaw hangs open. "Please, tell me what you really think."

"I will. Because I love you, I will. For starters, have you looked in the mirror lately? And I'm not talking about your ponytail or spit-up on your shirt. I'm asking, have you really looked at yourself lately?"

"What is your point, Miller?" He doesn't need to know that I avoid the mirror like the plague.

"My point is that you're a walking, breathing billboard for heartbreak and sadness. But it doesn't have to be like that. Dillon's still here. He's still trying. You're hurting everyone around you by keeping him in this weird version of a friend zone slash stepparent. He's doing everything right, and you're not."

"I'm trying to do the right thing for my kids." The excuse sounds hollow even to my own ears.

"Don't you think Dillon is too? Have you thought of it that way? There are a million different things he could be doing right now. His to-do list is longer than the Nile. But where is he tonight? He's helping your son exorcise his demons. He's doing it because he loves Kai as much as he loves you."

Tears appear to be my default these days. I lift my legs to rest my chin on my knees. Everything is so out of control.

"And Penny, I think when you find someone who loves that deeply, that freely, without asking for anything in return, you open your heart and your life, even if it's hard. Especially if it's hard. Because those hard times will be so much more manageable with a partner by your side."

"What do I do about Kai?" I ask because I'm not sure how to respond to his Dillon comments.

"Honestly? At this point, I think he needs Dillon. Dillon's strong enough to survive the storm and carry your family out on his shoulders. Let him do it."

I suck in a ragged breath. "You make it sound so easy."

"Oh, Penny. It is easy. Choose love. Choose it, live by it, and receive it. The first step you have to take is to acknowledge that you're helplessly in love with him, and then choose to accept his love in return."

I close my eyes for long minutes as Miller's words run through my head like the pieces of a Scrabble board.

"I need to head back. I left the high schooler next door babysitting Izzy. Do you need anything before I go?"

I stand with him, and he wraps me in a hug. "No, I think I'm okay."

"You will be," he promises.

"How did you get so smart?"

"Sometimes it's easier to see through the storm when you're not the one in it." He gives me a final squeeze before releasing me and heading toward the door.

"Thank you, Mill," I call after him with a whisper yell.

He winks. "I got you, but I'm still going to encourage you to find some girlfriends to hash all this out with next time. I'm out of my element here."

"Got you too. And, Miller?"

"Yeah?" He flashes a devastatingly handsome smile, and not for the first time, I wonder if he's as lonely as I am. Or I was, maybe.

"You're the best girlfriend I've ever had."

He chuckles, then has a coughing fit when he tries to stifle it. I hurry to him and usher him out the door before he wakes up Mari.

"Waaaaa," Mari cries, right on cue.

I'm halfway up the stairs when Landon walks out holding her. When I get to the top, he hands her to me.

"I agree with Miller, Mom. You deserve to be happy, and Dillon makes us all happy."

The little spy has always seen and heard too much.

I kiss him on the cheek. "I know, buddy. I've got some stuff to work out. You all have just been my only priority for so long."

He shrugs. "Dillon says it's okay to take care of your needs sometimes. Self-care, I think he called it. Maybe you should be your priority too."

My smart little boy.

It isn't until he's back in his room and I'm rocking Mari that I latch on to what he said. What the heck were they talking about that Dillon had to give him permission to take care of himself?

There's so much more to Dillon Henry than I could have imagined. And maybe Miller and Landon are right. I'm miserable. Dillon's miserable. We're all walking on eggshells around here. Dillon might be the key to happiness for all of us.

I vow to find out. Tomorrow, I'm making some changes.

CHAPTER 40

DILLON

e walk into the garage of the TAC. I've moved all the vehicles outside, and only the vandalized one remains. But that's just the backdrop. The real reason we're here, I hung from the ceiling before storming over to Penny's house.

"I don't know how to fix that," Kai says with his chin held high, but there's a slight tremor to his words.

I'm not looking to scare the piss out of the kid, but he needs to understand the damage he's done—not just to the SUV but to his family too.

I walk past him, close enough that he steps back, and head to the utility cart against the back wall. I pull out a pair of boxing gloves and toss them at his feet. Then I grab the wraps and cross back to him.

For the first time in weeks, Kai's mask falls. "I don't know how to box, and you outweigh me by like a hundred pounds."

Damn him. Forty pounds, maybe fifty, but not a hundred. I roll my eyes in a way that would make any teenager proud.

"You're not boxing with me. Hold out your hand."

His eyes widen when I grab his arm and begin to wrap his

wrist and knuckles. When one is finished, I move on to the next one, then step back and point at the gloves.

"Put them on," I demand.

I stand guard with my arms crossed over my chest and a neutral expression on my face as he fumbles his way into the gloves. When he has them on as best he can, I tap the bottoms with a rough thump to make sure they're all the way on, then I wrap the Velcro tightly around his wrist.

He's silent when I do the other one.

"Listen, I'm sorry, okay? I went too far." He says the words, but I don't believe he feels them. Yet. He will by the time we're done though.

I don't reply. I simply move to stand behind the bag. There are no weights to hold it steady, so I stand behind it and hang onto the sides, anchoring it for him. And hopefully, give him a way to reach for the kid I know him to be.

"Hit it."

Kai doesn't move.

"Hit this bag, Kai."

He still doesn't move.

"That rage sitting in your chest? That thing that makes you pop off at your brother? That thing that beats inside you like a spiteful, hurtful entity will rot you from the inside out if you let it. But what you haven't figured out is that it's not your weight to carry."

He watches me with wary eyes.

"Hit the bag."

Finally, he moves forward slowly, gives it a half-hearted punch, and then drops his arms to his sides.

"When that anger coils in your stomach, who are you mad at? Picture this bag as their face, then hit it."

His eyes widen, then his eyebrows droop into a frown. "So, if I'm most mad at you, you want me to pretend it's your face I'm hitting?"

"If I'm truly the one you're—"

He hits the bag with his entire weight behind it. Kai steps back and a flash of shame flickers in his eyes that are so much like his mother's.

"Again," I say. "Whoever is causing you pain, get it out here. If it's me, fine. But the longer you hit, the more you'll know who you're really upset with. Don't lie to yourself when that happens just to spite me. Again."

He hits the bag. Left then right. Right then left. He never takes his eyes off me. We go at it for close to thirty minutes before he clings to the bag, gasping for breath.

I return to the utility table and grab the water I placed there earlier. I raise it in the air to squirt it into his mouth, but he rips off one glove and does it himself.

When his breathing returns to normal, I grab the bag. "Again."

"I just…"

"Again," I bite out.

Kai narrows his eyes, adjusts his gloves, and attacks the bag with as much vigor as before.

"Every hit. Every jab. Think about that thing that sits in the back of your mind that you're too scared to acknowledge. You are stronger than your fears."

His eyes drop from mine, but I don't miss the tears pooling in the corners of his.

For the next hour, we're silent as he hits the bag. Sometimes consecutively, sometimes with a brief pause in between, and sometimes he kicks it. It's like I can see the wheels turning behind his sad gaze each time he makes contact.

I'm not naïve enough to think this will solve everything, but I do think it's going to break past the barriers he's built so high they've been impenetrable—until now.

He drops his hands and gasps, "Water?"

Reaching down, I pick up another bottle and hold it out to him.

He tentatively opens his mouth, and I nod. The goal isn't to break him down more than he already is, so I squeeze the water into his mouth. I need him to realize I'm not the enemy.

He backs off when he's had enough. "Thank you," he mutters under his breath.

I set the water down and hold the bag. "Again."

This time when he steps up to the bag, his punches have less fire behind them. He hits, and hits, and hits until the tears fall free. When he collapses into the bag, I grab him by the elbow. Leading him to the back wall, we both slide down it to the floor.

Kai's head lolls to the side. The kid has to be fucking tired. He exorcised a lot of demons tonight.

"I'm afraid people will always think I'm like him," he finally admits, so quietly I have to strain to hear him.

"I used to worry about the same thing. My dad was a violent drunk, Kai. I left home as soon as I could. My mom loved who he once was and took him back over and over again, but I couldn't live like that."

He angles his body to rest his cheek against the cool cement wall and watches me.

Dragging my gaze from his, I stare straight ahead while I collect my thoughts.

"The thing is, life is all about choices. Only you can choose who you're going to be. The opinions of others are none of your business."

I hear a muffled chuckle and turn to face him.

"What? I saw it on a tea towel once. It stuck with me." I shrug and rub my palm over my chest. Even the smallest smile from him makes my heart flutter wildly in my chest. "Your dad may have given you your last name, but it's up to you what that's going to mean. He chose to live in a way that brought shame to the name. You can be the one who makes it respectable again."

He turns his head toward the damaged SUV and drops his sad eyes to the ground.

Remorse, that's what I wanted from him. Remorse will lead him back to being the Kai that everyone loves. It means that the good kid is still in there. He was just muzzled by pain.

"I wasn't mad at you. I was mad at..." he says softly.

"I know."

He lifts his head to look at me, and I exhale a heavy sigh, then smile.

"I know," I repeat. But I leave it at that. The feelings between a father and son in situations like this are tumultuous. Kai will have to decide on his own if he can forgive his father or if he has to forget him.

"Why did you do it?" he asks. "I was horrible. Why are you sitting with me instead of in the sheriff's office?"

"One of these days, you'll realize that I know what I'm talking about sometimes. I'm here because I said I would be. Not all men leave, and not all men break promises."

He's fighting back the tears, so I look away to give him some privacy.

"I love your mom, Kai. And I love you kids, too. You aren't making it easy, but that doesn't make it any less true."

I hear him suck in a breath. "I know."

It's not exactly the declaration I was hoping for, but it's a start.

"You'll need to do an apology tour, you know?" I ask on a sigh, letting my head fall back against the wall.

"Yeah, I know. And Dillon, I am sorry about the SUV. Chase suggested it, and I don't know. It just felt good to break something."

I turn to him with a serious expression. "The next time you want to break something, or the next time you want to lash out at someone who loves you, you come here and lash out at that." I point to the bag. "That is the only acceptable outlet for rage like this, do you understand? You have the opportunity to choose the right path. I hope you're going to take it."

"I'll try."

"And you'll mess up," I say. "But I'll be right here when you do. If you could keep the mistakes to toilet papering houses or something less expensive, I'd appreciate it, though."

He winces. "I don't know how to pay for that."

"We'll get an estimate from Tanks, and then you'll work off your share of it here."

Kai nods, and it's like I can see the noose he's been wearing around his neck finally slip free.

"I am sorry, Dillon."

"I know, kid. I appreciate that, but do you want the truth?"

He nods.

"The truth is, I was more upset that you let a Brandt in here. I grew up with friends who were more like family, and they taught me everything I know about love. It's not the people you share DNA with that make a family. It's who holds your heart when it's breaking. It's who stands by your side, even when you make a really bad mistake. And family is about loyalty above all else. You chose enemy sides, kid. That hurt."

"You're going to make us a family, aren't you?" He sounds resigned, but not really unhappy either.

It's so unexpected I laugh. "If I get my way, yes. I want to marry your mom one day, Kai. I want to go to your games and watch you graduate from high school. I want you in my life as much as I want your mom. I know that's hard to understand, but it's the truth."

"I believe you," he says, exasperated, and I'm thankful for the normal teen snark. It means I reached him. "But I didn't choose the enemy. Not really, anyway. Chase isn't like the rest of his family. We've been friends since kindergarten. He's always been there for me, but his dad pits him against me on the court. His dad is a different kind of evil. Chase is counting down the days until he can leave."

I think about that for a minute. Just another kid stuck in a life made by their parents' poor choices.

"Okay, I trust you. If you say Chase is a good kid, I believe you."

His head snaps up to look at me. "You do?"

"Remember when I told you trust is earned?"

"Yeah," he grumbles.

"Well, I'm still working on earning it. But you earned my trust the day you showed up at your mom's office in the city, and you trusted me to get you home. It has never wavered. I believe you, and I believe in you. Chase is welcome here anytime."

His mouth hangs open, and he looks away, but I don't push anymore. It's been a rough day, and I'm willing to bet the mental gymnastics he put himself through were a lot more taxing than the workout he pushed his body through.

I know I need to get him home before the crash settles in, but for a moment, I just sit here in the peaceful calm beside a young version of myself.

My heart skips a beat. The fluttering in my chest tells me I'm alive, but more importantly, it tells me that this is where I'm meant to be.

Reaching over, I undo his gloves. He lifts his arms to remove the wraps and winces.

"You're going to be sore for a month." I chuckle.

"Great," he mumbles. "Hey, how did you know to do this?" He gestures to the punching bag.

I shrug. "I didn't, but nothing else was working, and it wasn't that long ago that Ashton went through something he could only work out by hitting stuff. I took a chance."

"I liked him," Kai admits. And it hits me then—Ashton was another man who left. Why didn't I get that before?

Kai and Ashton built a strong bond while Ashton lived here, but when he moved to California, because that's what was best for his family, it left Kai feeling abandoned again.

"I know you do, kid." Emotion clogs my throat. "He likes you too."

"I know," he says, but I wonder if he really does.

"Let's get you home." I stand and hold out my hand to help him off the floor. He sways on his feet when he stands, and I wrap an arm around his shoulders to steady him, and I'm thankful when he doesn't shrug me off. "You pushed yourself hard tonight. Things are going to hurt. Memories, thoughts, hearts, souls, and your body will hurt sometimes, but you don't have to experience it alone."

We exit the TAC, and he nods thoughtfully, but doesn't respond. Then I drive us back to the house. He makes it up the steps on shaky legs, and Penny rips the door open. She's beautiful even when she's so worried she's bitten her lip raw.

Kai walks to her and places a kiss on her cheek. "I'm sorry, Mom. For—" He glances over his shoulder, and I tuck my hands into the pockets of my jeans. "For everything."

Penny stands in shock as he brushes past her and up the stairs. Now it's my turn.

I walk up the steps and don't stop until I'm in her foyer and kicking the door shut.

"What did you do?" she asks. Her gaze flips from me to the stairs.

"I helped him exorcise some demons. It's not a miracle

fix. He still has shit to work out, but maybe now he'll be more open to the process of therapy."

"But how?"

I scan her head to toe, and my heart thunders in my chest. I'm home.

CHAPTER 41

PENNY

ONE MONTH LATER

"Gage!"

He zips down the short hallway on some kind of hoverboard Dillon got him for his birthday and crashes into the wall.

Mari army crawls across the floor toward him, and I suck in a breath as I race to her. Holy crap, I need to babyproof. It's been a long time since I had a crawler. I scoop her up off the floor and set her back down in the gated safe area of my bedroom. This time I make sure the gate is latched. It's meant to keep her in and Gage out while I'm doing laundry, but it figures that he would be her favorite person in the world. She drags herself to him every chance she gets.

The front door opens, and Dillon walks through with Kai talking animatedly about The Celtics versus The Hornets. I don't even know who likes which team anymore since they're constantly switching back and forth. But I sit at the top of the steps and watch them.

Was it really only a month ago that my life fell apart?

Things are not perfect by any means. Kai still has bursts of anger that seem to come out of nowhere, but now he has the tools to combat them. That's where they're coming from. Dillon now takes Kai to his therapy sessions at Dillon's request.

The time alone in the car on the thirty-minute drive to the therapist's office is helping them bond, and Kai wasn't opposed to it.

"Mommy," an excited voice calls from the bathroom. But it's a voice that has always called me Penny.

Dillon and Kai look up the stairs at me. The family therapist said it might happen, but I'm still not prepared for it.

Dillon takes the steps two at a time and holds onto my biceps. "It's okay."

"Yeah. I know." My heart's about to sprint out of my chest. "It's just that it makes it feel real."

"Mommy," Lia calls again.

"It is, Penny. It is real. Trust it."

I bite my lip at the same time as I pat down my hair. Why am I so stinking nervous? Dillon gives me a gentle nudge and I walk the few steps it takes to get to the bathroom. Lia is standing at the mirror, covered in makeup and a smile that will surely break hearts one day.

"I is so pwetty." She beams the words to me like sunshine.

Laughter bubbles up my throat. "Yes, sweetie. You are so pretty. But we don't need quite so much lipstick. This is—" I swallow past the nerves. "This is Mommy's for work. We can get you your own play set sometime though, okay?"

She shrugs and hops off the stool. "Okay."

I stand, unblinking, as she dances her cute little booty right out of the room. And then I catch my reflection in the mirror. Leaning in, I look at myself. I really examine every inch of my face.

For so many years, I avoided ever looking, but for some reason, I like what I see when I do it today.

Huh.

I smile, making the crow's feet at the corners of my eyes more prominent.

And I like them too.

I exit the bathroom with a smile that makes my whole body happy, and Dillon is waiting for me. "You okay?"

"Yeah." I smile and mean it. "I am."

He grins and stalks toward me until I'm flush against the wall. His hands land on my face, fingers twisting into my hair. Then his lips crash into mine.

I moan into his mouth. I can't help it and don't want to, except Lia is running around and probably smearing lipstick everywhere.

"Landon wiped her face with a baby wipe after she hugged him and got lipstick all over his jeans," he says, hovering over my lips. "Miller's coming over tonight."

"Oh, okay."

He pulls back but doesn't release my face.

"He didn't say anything when I saw him earlier," I murmur.

"That's because I asked him not to. Not until I was sure my plans would work out. I was just waiting for Kai's driver's ed schedule."

"Huh? What does driver's ed have to do with Miller coming over?"

"Because he's staying the night. Here. With the kids." He enunciates every word by slowly sealing our bodies together. I frown, and his smile grows wider. "It occurred to me yesterday that we've been to hell and back, but I've never taken you on a proper date. I'm aiming to fix that. Tonight."

A million scenarios run through my mind, but I can't stop my gaze from drifting toward Kai's room. After a few family sessions, we've stopped asking his permission for things concerning my relationship with Dillon. I wouldn't say he's done a complete one-eighty, but he's close.

Dillon takes a step back and chuckles. "I spoke to Kai on the drive today. I asked him to help with the kids tonight because we're going out. He said, and I quote, 'Sure, it's not like I have any plans for the rest of my life.'"

Because yeah, he's still grounded for the SUV damage he caused.

Anxiety slowly bleeds from my tense shoulders, and my body softens as I stare up into Dillon's eyes. "We're doing an overnight?"

"We are." He grins and I feel it everywhere.

"What do I need?"

"An outfit for dinner and nothing else. After I feed you…" He leans in. His hot breath hits my ear, and a shiver skips down my spine. "I'm going to feed on you."

My core clenches at the possibilities, and Dillon groans like he can feel it too.

"We leave at five," he says before walking away.

I check my watch. That leaves me three hours to primp, pack, and pray. I pray every day that this isn't a dream because, on the good days, it's like I'm living inside a rainbow.

WE'RE SEATED at a VIP table tucked into the corner at the back of Buttery Kuts Steakhouse. If we weren't sitting here, I probably wouldn't have even known it existed. I'm trying to remember when I told Dillon the name of this place, but I can't recall it.

"Did I tell you that I've always wanted to have a real meal here?"

Dillon's jaw twitches, like he's clenching his teeth, and his nostrils flare on a deep inhale. He stands and slides his chair along the round table until he's seated next to me instead of across.

He reaches for my hand and brings it to his lips, where he places the most delicate kiss. It's such a contrast to how he is in the bedroom that I might swoon a little.

He's doing this, all of this, for me.

"I told you I wanted to be your last first everything. The last first kiss. The last first orgasm."

He grins when I cross my legs.

It's dangerous being in public with him and no kids. The sexual energy flies out of him like a torpedo.

"Well," he says, then he flicks my hand with his tongue like he does when he goes down on me, and I wiggle in my seat. "I decided there are some firsts I want to erase from your memory. Like coming here and only getting a salad."

I narrow my eyes. "Miller ratted me out."

"Miller loves you and wants what's best for you. But yes, he told me about this place and recommended this specific table for the"—he glances around the secluded space—"privacy."

"It's nice. Like a private room, but…not." My gaze follows his to see the sheer pillowy panel that covers the narrow entrance. "Do you ever wonder if Miller's lonely?"

He sits back in his chair, and his eyes trace every inch of me. "Are you turning into a lovesick matchmaker now?"

My crossed legs are not relieving the pressure that's building.

When I don't answer, Dillon sighs. "Sometimes. But I'm also a firm believer in everything happening for a reason. His girl is out there. He'll find her."

"But what if he needs a push?"

He shrugs and licks his lips, and all thoughts leave my head.

"Penny?" he rasps, then moves his hand to my thigh. Very high on my thigh. When he flexes his middle finger, he brushes against my clit. To anyone watching, it seems like he's innocently resting his hand on my thigh.

But he's not. He is definitely not.

"Huh?"

His low chuckle vibrates against my arm.

"Do you want to spend our night alone talking about Miller's love life, or do you want to spend it talking about what I'm going to do to you? In explicit detail. While you eat whatever the hell you want."

"Oh, God." I swallow and squeak simultaneously. "Um, option two, please."

"Tsk, tsk, tsk." His tone has gone low and gravelly and so sexy a whimper tries to escape me. "You know what my rule is." He raises one eyebrow, and my mouth goes so dry you'd think someone stuffed me with cotton balls.

I reach for my glass of water with shaky hands. His finger presses harder against me.

"Dillon," I hiss after I drink like a dehydrated marathon runner. "You have to move your hand."

His grin grows slowly until it practically reaches ear to ear. But it's the way his eyes seem to glow when he's like this that makes me squirm in my chair.

"Do you want me to move it because you're close to coming and worried about what people will say?"

Flick.

Flick.

Oh no.

"Or do you want me to move it because you don't like it there?"

"I do. I do like it, but…"

Flick.

Flick.

Flick.

My stomach clenches with need.

"You know what I want to hear," he rumbles near my ear. He leaves his head there like he's telling me a secret, but all he's doing is breathing on my neck.

How is that so hot? How is his freaking breath making me even hornier?

Flick.

Flick.

"D—Dillon," I pant. My sight has gone a little hazy, but as I scan the restaurant through the sliver of an opening, I don't find a single person watching us.

"The tablecloth covers the table on the other side. They can't see anything but me whispering in your ear. Tell me what I want to hear."

"I want to talk about what you'll do to me," I say in a rush that expels my breath like a yoga exercise.

"That's my girl," he growls.

Flick.

Flick.

Flick.

I turn my head and bite into Dillon's shoulder just as the first sparks of light form behind my eyes.

He twists his hand and pushes it deeper between my legs, forcing them open. And then I'm coming. Silently sobbing the scream I want to let loose into Dillon's shoulder.

"Fuuuuck, baby, yes. You come so sweetly for me." He sits up straight with a pleasant expression, like he's about to play bingo at an old folks' home. How does he do that? "But when we get to our room? I want to hear you screaming my name so loudly they call the cops. I'm going to make you come on my fingers, my tongue, and my cock, then I'll do it again. I have three years of fuckery to make up for, and I can't wait."

My mouth hangs open, and he chuckles.

"My queen. My partner."

"If I'm a queen, then you're the king of dirty talk. Seriously, I think I could come just listening to you talk about it."

He narrows his gaze like I laid down a challenge. And to him, maybe I did.

"We'll test that theory too." He drops his dirty-talking voice and says, "I love you, Penny."

Each time he says it, it's like the first time.

"I love you too." I watch his eyes as I say it, and his reaction doesn't disappoint. They flash like a neon sign, and he leans over to kiss me.

A kiss fit for public.

A kiss fit for a queen.

CHAPTER 42

DILLON

I'm on her the instant the hotel room door closes. My dick has ached for the last hour, but I don't regret it. Watching Penny lick chocolate sauce off her spoon was foreplay.

Can room service send just chocolate sauce?

Her heaving breaths hit my neck as she kisses me as high as she can reach. I bend my legs, wrap my arms around her ass and lift her to me. She tightens her legs around me like we've done this for years.

She licks a line down my neck while I walk us to the bed. When I reach it, I lay her down gently with me on top of her.

Cupping her face, I kiss her lips sweetly. Chastely. "I love you."

"I knoooow," she moans when I grind my hips against her. So I do it again.

"We're wearing too many clothes," she breathes.

"Let's fix it then. I told you, all you have to do is ask, and I'll make it happen." I slide off the bed and rip my clothes off like they're about to catch fire.

Then I put my hands on Penny's ankles and slowly skim

up her bare legs. When I reach the hem of her dress, I slide my hands up farther and take the dress with me.

"I like this dress," I admit.

"Me too." Her eyes are hazy with lust, and it drives me insane.

Slow is not going to be the name of the game tonight. I push her dress up over her head and take a minute to appreciate her lingerie. Running my finger along the edge of her panties, I ask, "Are these new?"

"Yes."

Good girl.

I surge forward and place an open-mouthed kiss over her pussy.

"Ooh. Oh, Dillon."

Is there anything better than hearing your name on your woman's lips? If there is, I have no fucking clue what it is.

I tug her panties down her legs and toss them aside and allow my hands to roam all over her body as soon as she's almost naked. I can't decide what I want to do to her first until my eyes catch on her tits. Decision made. I pull the cups of her bra down, baring her beautiful, full breasts to me.

"So. Damn. Perfect," I murmur, a hint of awe in my tone.

"Please, Dillon."

"Please, what?" I ask while circling her clit with my tongue but never quite touching it.

"Please fuck me." She's writhing beneath me now.

"Such a dirty girl. I like you needy in here. It's sexy as hell."

"Dillon, I swear to God…"

She doesn't finish that sentence because I breach her opening with two of my fingers. The moan that escapes will be the soundtrack to the rest of my life. When I realize I'm grinding into the bed like a horny teenager, I remove my fingers, rise up onto my forearms and crawl over her, settling between her legs.

My cock glides easily through her wet pussy. She's so damn perfect.

She opens her mouth to say something, but I use that moment to slide into her.

I didn't think I could get any harder. I was wrong. Knowing how wet she is and that her desire matches my own is the sexiest damn thing I've ever experienced.

I push forward until I bottom out inside her, where I pause, staring at her while we exchange breaths, and memorize this moment like a snapshot.

And then I rut into her. I swear, this woman makes my control snap just by breathing.

The sound of skin slapping rings in my ears, and Penny's legs quiver as they press into my sides.

She's so close. So close to coming, I have to grind my teeth so her body doesn't send me over the edge before she explodes. She's bearing down on me so hard I almost see stars. But she needs help finishing.

She needs me.

"I've got you, Penny." I snake my hand between us and rub her clit in the fast side-to-side motion she prefers.

I reach my other hand up and place it around her neck. Her eyes go wide with surprise, but it's washed away as fast as it came when her eyes roll back and her body shudders around me. I squeeze just enough to drag out her orgasm but not hard enough to leave marks.

"Jesus, Penny," I roar, slamming into her one last time. My cock twitches and jerks inside her where my streams of come mark her as mine. Sliding my dick out, I watch for the moment my come seeps out of her. "Fuuuck, yes." I slip back in, rocking in and out at a lazy pace.

Her walls press against me with the last of her orgasm,

and I drop on top of her. If I could stay buried inside of her like this for eternity, it wouldn't be long enough.

I open my eyes a few minutes later and am shocked to find I've fallen asleep. Penny is lying on her side, completely naked, watching me.

"You've changed our lives, you know that, right? Just by being you. You're the thread that wove through our tapestry and brought us back together. You made us whole again." Her tone and watery eyes suggest she's been thinking hard about this for a while, but she's too far away from me to have this conversation.

I rectify that by pulling her flush against me.

"That goes both ways, though," I say, my voice gruff with sleep. "I didn't even know I was lost until you found me. I've never felt so whole, so right, as I do when I'm with you."

She smiles with eyes that light up my world, and I kiss her. I'll always kiss her better.

"Move in with me. All of you, move in with me." Well, fuck. What is it about her that makes me lose my damn mind and spew every thought in my head? I hadn't planned to blurt that out while we're naked in bed, but here we are.

Her hand moves to her chest, and she blinks too fast.

"What?" she whispers.

"I want you. I want you and your messes all the time. Not just for visits or the occasional sleepover. I want my toothbrush sitting next to yours in our bathroom. I want Gage's dirty socks on my floor and Landon's easel taking up all the space in the kitchen. I want to trip over Kai's sports equipment, and I want my shoes to be in your pile. I want it to be forever, so move in with me." She's still blinking too quickly. "Please," I add as an afterthought.

"But isn't it too soon? That's a big change for the kids."

"Sweetheart, I've wanted forever with you since our very first goodbye in Lochlan's office. We've been building toward this for years, so no, I don't think it's too soon. And the kids? Yes, it'll be an adjustment, but the book I'm reading says that kids are really resilient. If we build a happy, healthy home where they know they're safe and loved, it doesn't matter where they go to sleep at night."

Shit. Now she's crying.

"You're reading a book?"

I twist my lips into a frown. "Of everything I just said, the one thing you comment on is the book?"

"What book are you reading?" She's teasing me, but when she bites down on her bottom lip, I know it's a serious question.

"A book on parenting, or stepparenting, I guess. I hate the word step," I growl. "It insinuates I'm not fully invested."

"It does?" Penny bites down harder on her lip, and visions of sucking on it flood my brain, but this is too important of a conversation, so I force the images back.

Get Penny to move in with me, then we can fuck.

"I just don't like the term, but the book has been helpful, I guess. I'll never tell Lochlan, though. He'll never let me live it down."

Penny runs a hand up my chest, and she gives a little push before climbing on top of me.

Jesus, this view though. Okay, maybe fuck, then get Penny to move in with me.

"We won't call you a stepparent then."

She rolls her hips, and I have a hard time following her words as her wetness coats me.

"What will you call me then?" My voice sounds like a broken garbage disposal, but if she keeps moving like this, I won't be able to talk at all.

"We'll call you ours."

Record scratch. Nails on the chalkboard. Knife on a glass plate. Everything stops.

"Say it again."

"We're yours, and you're ours." She looks to the ceiling like she's sending up a prayer.

I send one up too.

Dear God, please forgive the shit you're about to see.

"I guess that means our living situation will have to change."

Did I hear her correctly?

"What?" The word comes out sharp and loud. It has to, in order to drown out the noise filling my head.

"We'll move in with you. Or you can move in with us. Where will we…"

I surge to a sitting position and take her with me. She rests on my lap with her legs wrapped around my back.

"Where we live isn't important. It's semantics. What matters is that you're finally, finally mine."

I lift my hips, and my cock slips inside her. It's the best homecoming I've ever experienced.

This isn't fucking. This is making love, and it's goddamned amazing.

My last thought before I explode inside her is: My Wednesday girl is now my forever girl.

CHAPTER 43

DILLON

ONE MONTH LATER

"**A**re you sure you want to do this?" Miller asks from the passenger seat.

We're sitting in the parking lot of the state penitentiary. Miller's just along for the ride since he came to check on the progress at the TAC, then found out where I was going. If he calls himself my emotional support buddy one more time, I might deck him, though.

"No, I don't want to do it. I have to do it. He's facing a trial for manslaughter. The last thing the kids need is to watch this play out."

"So you think bribery is the way to go?" He holds up his hands in defense. "I'm just asking."

"It's all I have. I'll hire him the best criminal defense attorney I can find, and in return, he'll sign over all parental rights for all five of them."

Miller winces but recovers quickly.

"He doesn't deserve any rights, Miller," I grind out.

"It's not that. I'm thinking about what it would be like to

360

never see my little girl again."

Now I'm pissed.

"You and Eddy? You're not the same. Not even fucking close."

He undoes his seatbelt, settles back into the leather, and closes his eyes. "Okay. Good luck."

"You're staying out here?"

He opens one eye and squints at me. "I'm too pretty for prison."

When he winks at me, I shake my head and exit the car.

Fucking Miller.

I'm escorted to a room that's nothing like the TV shows. This room has sofas and tables. There's even a box of toys in the corner.

But it's the smell of ammonia and bad decisions assaulting my senses that I'll never forget.

The door along the back wall opens, and Eddy is escorted in. When he spots me, he drops his head back and stares at the ceiling.

"Just my fuckin' day," he mutters. The security guard urges him along, and he finally sits across from me at the dirty table I'm purposely keeping my arms off of. "What the hell do you want?"

I clench my teeth and focus on breathing. Getting into a fight with this asshole will not do anything constructive.

"I'm here to talk about the kids," I finally say as pleasantly as possible, but there's still an edge of ice around my words.

"Why isn't my cunt of an ex here to talk? They're her kids too." He bares his teeth, daring me to do something.

I sit on my hands so I don't.

"Don't talk about my future wife like that."

"Ah, I see. Sloppy seconds. There really is someone for everyone, I guess."

I growl. I don't mean to, but he's poking the bear and knows it.

"Penny isn't here because she's at home taking care of her kids."

"That's her job," he says with a scoff.

Pick your battles. Pick your battles. Pick your battles. I chant until I know I can form words that aren't going to end with us fighting to the death.

"I'm here to offer you the best attorney money can buy."

This has him sitting up taller in his chair. "Bullshit. Nobody gets nothin' for free in this life."

"Oh, it's not free. It comes at a cost much higher than money can buy."

"What are you talking about?"

"I'll hire you an attorney, the best I can find, if you sign over all parental rights to Penny." Then I can adopt them. I don't say it out loud, but it sounds off loudly in my mind. "It's a good deal. Even if you do get out in a few years, you'll only ever be allowed supervised visits. Penny will make sure of that. And you'll have to be sober to see them."

"I am sober, asshole."

Only because being in prison forces it.

I start a new mental chant. Do not roll your eyes. Do not roll your eyes.

"It's a good deal. You'll never have the relationship you could've had with those kids, so cut them free and give them the opportunity to have a happy, healthy childhood."

He sits back in his chair and studies me. The minutes tick by on the clock on the opposite wall like a bomb about to explode. We don't speak for a full five rotations of that second hand. But when he does, I know there's no redeeming this asshole ever.

"See, I've been sittin' here trying to figure out why you're so invested in this. I know you're fucking my wife…"

"Ex-wife."

"But I've had her. That pussy isn't worth it, so it must be something more…sentimental, shall we say?"

He says it with a sneer that sets my teeth on edge.

"You wanna adopt them. That's what this is. Well, guess what, asshole? I'm not givin' them up. Not ever. They'll wear my name and follow the same path that my father and I did. The Damon name will never leave them. Those ungrateful assholes can carry around the shame of being my children, it'll make 'em stronger. Build character. Ya know?"

I slide a piece of paper across the table. "Take the deal," I grind out.

He uses one dirty finger to slide it back to me. "I don't think I will. Those kids are Damons, and they always will be."

I stand and take the papers with me. Before I reach the door, I turn to him. "They may carry that name, but I'll make sure we change the stigma behind it if it's the last thing I do. Those kids will never carry the burden of your shame. I won't allow it."

His laugh is wet and raspy. "What are ya? God? You won't allow it. Get the fuck outta here. I'll fight for my rights to those little peckers just to spite ya."

I'm at the table and in his face in the blink of an eye. "Spite me? Spite. Me? I will fight to the death for these kids. Come at me, come at them ever again, and I will end you." The security guard takes a step closer but doesn't interrupt us. "Understand me? You can rot in here, bitter and petty as hell. I will find a way to make sure those kids, my kids, are never ashamed of who they are. I can promise you that."

I step back and watch his face contort as he processes my words.

"Your kids…"

"And let me be very clear on this. Unlike you, I *never* break my promises. Sit and spin, you fucking asshole."

Fury rampages inside me as I leave the prison. He's hurtful just to be hurtful. There's no reasoning with a person like that.

The SUV door practically bounces when I rip it open, and I slam it shut once I'm in.

Miller doesn't even open his eyes. "Didn't go well?"

"How do you share DNA with that fucking twat-sucker of a scumbag dingle-dicked asshole?"

I know I'm not making any sense. There are a million emotions warring in my head right now, but anger outweighs them all, and I pound my fists on the steering wheel.

Miller sighs and pulls his seat upright. "There are laws in Connecticut, you know."

I spin to glare at him. Of course I know there are laws.

"Get to the point."

"One of them, in particular, is about incarcerated parents. I'm not a lawyer, but I think I read something online about parental rights and how they can be revoked if there's no contact for a period of time."

I'm speechless. Truly speechless.

"You knew this the entire time and didn't think to say anything? What the actual fuck, Miller?"

He shrugs like he didn't just waste half my day.

"I sat in there biting my tongue, and it was all for nothing? What is wrong with you?"

"It wasn't for nothing. Eddy's scars go deep, and I don't think he'll ever change, but as a single dad, I had to be sure. I don't take stripping fathers' rights lightly."

Miller's left eye twitches. I have a feeling there's much more to being a father and his right to be a single one than I know about.

"I held out my last hope that he'd put his children first. I needed to be sure that there was nothing good left in him before I encouraged you to adopt those kids and make it right."

"Make what right?" I almost don't recognize my voice. It's wobbly from these interactions I haven't been able to process yet.

"They're your family. Adopt them and make it right. Give them the happily ever after. Protect them. Love them. Fight for them."

"That has always been my plan, Miller."

He nods but remains silent.

For the first time since I met Miller, I feel like I don't really know him. Not fully. He hides a world of hurt behind good deeds and a charming smile. Maybe Penny was right. Maybe it's time for Miller to find love.

I process everything from Eddy to Miller on the long drive home. Miller closed his eyes and fell asleep as soon as we hit the highway.

When I finally pull into Penny's driveway, I find Gage tussling in the mud with a foam roller.

"Ah, hey, buddy. What are you doing over there?" I ask when I step out of the SUV.

He grins like he's the luckiest kid in the world, even if he is covered in mud. "I'm practicing tackling. I wanna play football."

Internally I groan. The one sport I was never particularly good at. "Looking good, kid."

"Thanks," he yells, then piledrives the foam roller.

I have to get that kid some gym mats before he hurts himself.

I trudge up the steps, suddenly exhausted. Exhausted but happier than I've ever been. When I step through the door, I trip over Kai's basketball shoes and smile as I kick them to the side. Then I remove my own shoes and toss them into the pile.

Who would have guessed that a pile of shoes would make me happier than I ever remembered being?

Picking up Gage's sweatshirt, I hang it on the hook, then call out, "Honey, I'm home."

And home has never felt so right.

CHAPTER 44

PENNY

"Why would you put the store over there?" Dillon asks Landon. They're sitting side by side on the sofa. Dillon has his feet propped up on the coffee table with Mari fast asleep on his chest. It's quickly becoming her favorite way to fall asleep.

It's mine, too, if I'm being honest.

Landon moves another sheet of paper onto Dillon's lap. He's literally covered in them as Landon explains his ideas, but he never once shuts Landon down. If anything, he's encouraging him by taking him to the TAC any chance he gets.

Dillon lifts his head from the paper he's studying and finds me standing in the doorway.

"Hi," he says softly.

"Hi."

"Hey, buddy," Dillon says, looking down at Landon with more love than I've ever seen from a man. "Why don't you see if you can figure out the waterfall thing for the hotel? You had some good ideas earlier. I bet if you sketch it, you'll come up with something that will blow Lochlan away."

"Yeah?" Landon asks excitedly, but he's already scooping up all his papers. He runs by me with his arms full. "Hi, Mom. Bye, Mom."

Dillon lifts his free arm and pats the space next to him. "Come here."

I can't deny this man anything, so I go and cuddle in next to him. I rest my head on his shoulder and stare at Mari's chubby little face. I know someday these girls will ask tough questions about their mom, but until then, I hope we can provide them with a happy, peaceful home.

Dillon tugs on the hem of my shirt—his UNC T-shirt that I wear like a security blanket now. It's my favorite.

"Nothing makes me happier than seeing you in my clothes, but this one? This one makes me want to do very naughty, very dirty things to you," he growls.

Gage runs into the house and slams the door shut behind him, interrupting us before that line of conversation can turn me into a puddle of longing.

I smile as we listen to him hopping around in the entry-way. We do have a happy home, and it's mostly peaceful, that's all I ever really wanted.

"He's covered in mud," Dillon says.

"I know." I laugh. "And now he's stripping naked in the foyer." Sure enough, a naked bum runs by a second later, then scoots upstairs where we hear the water turn on.

"I think I found us a house today," Dillon says out of the blue.

With my hand on his chest, I push back to look at him. "You did? I've been looking everywhere. I haven't found a single thing. Chance Lake isn't exactly a hotbed of real estate activity, I guess."

He smirks and butterflies flutter in my belly. I don't even try to hide my smile. "Well, tell me. Where is it? I literally couldn't find anything."

"You didn't see this one because it's not on the market," he says with an easy swagger that has my heart racing.

"If it's not for sale, how will we get it?"

"We ask."

"We ask? Dillon, you're not making any sense."

"Do you like Ashton and Nova's house?"

I place my hand on his forehead. "Are you feeling okay?"

He traps my hand and brings it to his lips, where he places a kiss on the center of my palm.

"Do you like Ashton and Nova's house?" he asks again.

Finally, when he just stares at me expectantly, I sigh into him. "Of course I like their house. It's beautiful. Why?"

"Because it's ours."

I have a hard time making sense of his words.

"What do you mean ours?"

"Well, technically mine, but what's mine is yours so…"

He flashes me a lazy smile, but there's nothing lazy about my thought process right now. No, my thoughts are flying around my head like people in a dark maze—I can't find my way out.

Finally, finally, Dillon takes pity on me. "Somehow, Ashton snuck that into the TAC deal. I don't know how I missed it because I combed those contracts myself. But he sent me a copy of the deed transfer when I asked if we could stay there."

"But he loves that house," I say when something like hurt settles in my chest.

"That's what I said. But their life is changing as quickly as Nova's couture line, and he said as much as he loved it, it wasn't their forever home, but it was important to him that it stayed in the family because a lot of healing happened there."

My hurt feelings intensify and suddenly I know why. "Why wouldn't Nova have told me this? She's one of my best friends. We don't talk nearly as often as we did when she lived here, but we still text."

"I think that's Ashton's doing too. It's like he had this planned out the entire time, and we fell right into it like puppets. I'm sure Nova didn't mean to hurt your feelings."

"I'm going to miss knowing they could just pop up anytime. I don't have a lot of friends." Admitting that out loud makes shame flare to life in my mind.

"Yet, Penny. You don't have a lot of friends yet. When things settle down, you'll be having wine nights with every female resident over twenty-one. I heard that Sexy Scenes and Sips will be up and running by the end of the month." He waggles his eyebrows at me as he says it.

My shoulders shake with laughter. He's ridiculous.

"So, what do you think?" he asks.

I think he's unbelievable. I think he's amazing. And I think I made the best decision of my life when I finally let down my walls.

"I think we could be happy there," I whisper.

Really happy. The kind of happiness that lasts forever.

"I'm thinking we can get movers here early next week to pack up and move everything."

My eyes nearly bug out of my head. "Sometimes I forget that you don't have to worry about things like money." Embarrassment heats my cheeks. Talking about money always makes me uneasy. It's a side effect of always being poor, I think.

He grips my chin between his thumb and forefinger. "Neither do you, Penny. What's mine is yours, and what's yours is mine. That's how this works."

I snort. "You're getting the short end of that deal."

The seriousness of his expression sobers me quickly.

"That's where you're wrong. I'm getting you and these guys," he says, nodding toward Mari. "That's priceless, so I am definitely the winner here." He leans over to kiss me, and Mari lets out an unhappy cry.

"She doesn't like sharing you." I laugh while he adjusts her. She snuggles into the crook of his arm, and her eyes flutter in that way that babies do. Like they're too tired to stay awake, but too stubborn not to fight it.

"She'll get used to it," he promises. "There's enough of me to go around."

Scooting closer, I rest my head on his shoulder again. I lay there, listening to the sounds of a happy home. There are too many kids for it to ever be truly quiet, and I'm already dreading the day that it is.

Contentment washes over me. The kind of contentment that makes you sink your feet in and grow roots.

This is what happy feels like. My eyes flutter like Mari's and I allow myself to drift to a peaceful sleep while Dillon stands guard.

~

"I can't believe he got movers and a small army of people to come here to pack and move our entire lives in just seven days," I say as they organize the remaining boxes.

"You can do anything if you're motivated enough. He was very, very motivated." Miller gives me a grin.

I let out a heavy breath and look around. It almost looks like we never lived here, so maybe it's okay to leave all the bad memories behind and only take the good. That's the thing about starting over. You choose how you want it to go.

A mover sets a box of Miller's belongings down on the floor. We decided this was the perfect place for him and Izzy, and since Ashton's house is still furnished, we left all the big stuff for them.

Miller bumps my hip with his. "To new beginnings."

I rest my head on his shoulder. "To new beginnings."

"I still got you, you know?"

"I got you too, Miller. Always. You're my family."

He clears his throat like he's uncomfortable before tugging on the collar of his shirt, then pulls away just as a car door slams outside. A second later, Gage comes barreling through the front door.

"Mom. Mom. Mom."

"I'm right here, Gage."

He spins and charges me. I've learned to brace myself for impact with him, but maybe someday he'll learn to take it easy when he's excited.

"Mom, there's a gigantic bathtub at our new house. Well, Uncle Ashton's old house, but ours now. It's huge. And it has jets that make bubbles. Jets, Mom!"

Miller and I both laugh, and it's so damn good to laugh for a change. When I catch his eye, I wink. "We're going to be okay, Mill."

"Yeah," he says, mussing Gage's hair. "I think you're right."

Just then, I catch Kai coming down the stairs holding a box. Huh. "Did the movers miss one?" I ask.

He shakes his head, and the tears he's trying desperately to hold in slip free. Miller nods in my direction and escorts Gage into the kitchen.

"What's this?" I ask.

"I've been sitting up there for hours," he confesses. "Just sitting there looking at this box. I don't want it, but I can't make myself throw it away, either. It makes me so angry but also super sad, but also it, I don't know, it's like a piece of me or something. Like my history."

I flip open the top of the box and see what he's so torn up about. Pictures of him with Eddy before things got bad. Trophies he won with Eddy there encouraging him. It's all in there.

Jesus. It's like someone turned the power off to my heart and I don't know how to jumpstart it. "That's tough," I say gently. "I understand why you'd want to get rid of it and why you might want to keep it. You're the only one who remembers life wasn't always bad."

"It wasn't bad, Mom, not always, it was just hard. You were always there for us."

Now it's my turn to cry.

"Yeah, it was hard. But now the decision to have a relationship with your father is yours to make. I'll support you either way, but it's okay to hang on to the few good memories you have of him too. All those memories make up the fabric of your life. They're part of your story and what makes you you. And I think you're pretty terrific."

"Mom," he groans, then rolls his eyes. "You were doing so good until you got all corny on me."

"It's my job to be corny sometimes."

"I still don't know what to do with this stuff." The sadness in his voice cuts me deeply. Seeing your baby hurting and not being able to fix it is a special kind of hell.

"Why don't I hang on to it? I'll put it in the back of my closet, and if you ever decide you want it, you come and get it. Okay?"

"Yeah, that's good." He shoves the box into my arms like it might explode.

"Oh, okay. Are you good now? With everything?" I move around the room and set the box down next to the front door so we don't forget it.

"Yeah, I am. I really am," Kai corrects before I can interrupt. "Dillon's a good guy. He makes everyone happy. I—I'm sorry I tried to make you choose between him and me. I don't know. I don't know why I needed to hurt you so badly."

"Like begets like. Hurt begets hurt." He stares at me with a blank expression. "It means misery loves company. You were hurting, so you wanted the one you're closest with to hurt too."

"You're weird." He looks at the floor, and I realize how quickly he's growing up.

He'll be gone in a few years, and it eats away at me that I allowed our lives to get so out of control for so long. This mom guilt is a real bitch.

"Anyway, I am sorry," he says again, and I wrap my arms around him. He's so much taller than me now, but I soak in the embrace for as long as he'll let me.

"I know you are, Kai. But it's in the past. We don't need to look back to know where we're going. I love you, buddy. So much." I get choked up at the end and blink away tears.

"I love you too, Mom."

Dillon walks by but stops when he sees us. "Hey, Kai, sometimes you have to tap out, or she'll stand there all day hugging you."

"Tap out?" Kai asks. "Like in wrestling?"

"Yup. Just like that."

I don't have to see Dillon's smile to know it's there. It warms his voice.

Kai taps my shoulder three times, and I begrudgingly let go. Whoever invented that rule should be punished.

"Told you so," Dillon says as he enters the family room. "You guys all set? I asked Miller if he wanted help unpacking, but he said he was good."

I look around with a hint of sadness.

It's not like this is the last time I'll ever walk into this house. Miller lives here now. I'll be here all the time, but it's the last time I'll look at it as the woman I once was—a newly single mom of three, scared to death that I wouldn't be able to provide for my boys—that I wouldn't be enough for them. But when I leave this chapter behind, I'll be the woman I was always meant to be. All because the man standing by my side was strong enough to support me while I found my way.

"Yes, I'm ready. You ready, Kai?"

From my son's expression, I get the uncanny sensation that he's having a very similar conversation with himself right now.

"Yeah, I'm ready," he says, and this time he stands a little taller. He even walks out of the house like he's a little lighter, a little less haunted.

Dillon wraps an arm around my shoulder and walks with me to the SUV, where he already has the other kids buckled in.

"We're going to be all right," I say.

"More than all right, sweetheart. We're going to be whole and happy—I already am." He kisses my forehead, then searches my eyes. He does this a lot, always checking in on me, and I've never felt more loved, safe, or happy.

"Come on, let's go start our next chapter." He leads me by the hand and stands guard until I'm safely in my seat.

Like turning a page in a book, I look forward to the future. I'm leaving behind what doesn't suit me anymore and carrying the love and light that makes me me.

Sometimes it's okay to walk away from what hurts you, and believing that has made me a different person. I'm stronger than I've ever been, but more importantly, I believe in myself with my whole heart.

"New beginnings and next chapters. What do you think will come next?" I ask when Dillon climbs into the driver's seat.

"I'm thinking a little enemies to lovers or maybe a hot neighbor vibe."

I look at him like he's crazy.

"What?" He shrugs. "One of the Westbrooks married a

romance author. It was an education, to say the least. But that's my prediction."

"Why?" Kai asks from the back seat.

A mischievous grin appears on Dillon's handsome face. "Because I didn't tell Miller who was moving in next door."

"What? Is someone moving into Dad's old house? It's kind of a dump," Kai says.

"And it always smelled weird," Landon pipes in quietly. He's always been an observer, and my mama heart expands seeing him come out of his shell. That's all because of Dillon.

I have so much to be thankful for.

Dillon looks at Kai in the rearview mirror. "We cleaned it up and made some upgrades too."

"So, who's moving in?" I ask.

That smile full of trouble is back. "Paisley," he says. "Paisley is moving in tomorrow."

Kai and I both burst into laughter. Everyone in town knows how Miller feels about her—everyone except Paisley.

"Well, this should be interesting." Kai laughs.

"Chance Lake, the official home of the second chance." I laugh, but no one joins in. Party poopers.

"Mom joke," Kai says while trying to hold in a smile.

Dillon reaches across the console and holds my hand. "I'm pretty fond of a second chance myself."

Me too, Dillon. Me too.

EPILOGUE

DILLON

ONE YEAR LATER

$\mathcal{I}$f someone told me a year ago that I'd be walking into a pharmacy one town over to help a sixteen-year-old buy condoms, I would have laughed in their face.

But here we are.

I'm not sure who is more horrified, Kai or me, but we've made it this far, so we're doing it.

"Why are there so many options?" he whispers. "Seriously, is this necessary?"

A month ago, I would have said no. But when he asked if I'd help him find a tux for junior prom, I decided this would be part of the deal.

I remember what I was like at sixteen. The memories make me shudder.

"If you're not mature enough to buy condoms, you're not mature enough to have sex," I say.

"I'm not having sex," he mutters.

"Yet. But you will, so I'm making sure you're prepared."

Kai's head is on a swivel as he scopes out the aisle around us like we're doing something wrong.

"So how do I know what ones to get?" He sounds as panicky as I feel.

"They come in sizes. I have no idea how big your junk is." Kai's face pales, and I amend that sentence quickly. "And I don't need to know. You must have an idea if you're small, average, or large, and I understand the temptation to say you're large, but trust me on this, you want the right size."

He swallows hard, glances around the aisle, then reaches forward and grabs a box of regular Trojans.

"Good choice," I say, then immediately wipe the sweat from my forehead. I'm also positive that my cheeks are as red as his.

"Kai?" a girl's voice asks from behind me.

I watch Kai's eyes go horribly wide right before he slams the box of condoms into my chest.

"H—Hi, Lilly," he says, stepping around me.

Keeping the condoms at my back, I turn to see who he's talking to.

A pretty girl with bright blue eyes and auburn hair is smiling up at Kai like he's her hero, and something in me settles as I watch them.

Kai has had a hard few years, but I know in my heart he's going to be just fine.

"Dillon, this is Lilly. Lilly Reid. Lilly this is, he's my, he's ah, this…"

What to call me is still something we're working on, so I interrupt and introduce myself.

"I'm Dillon Henry. It's nice to meet you, Lilly."

"You too. Wow, Kai," she says looking from him to me. "You look just like your dad." Kai tenses next to me. I know there are still times he worries people will think he's like

Eddy, but she puts that idea to rest with her next words. "I mean, look at you two. You even have the same messy hair."

"Lilly?" A low growl comes from the end of the aisle as Grady stalks toward us.

"Grady," I say in greeting, and the connection hits me. "Is this your daughter?"

Grady's lips press into a thin line before speaking. "No, she's my baby sister. She was in boarding school in Maine until a few months ago."

"Lilly goes to school in Hope Hollow now," Kai says quietly.

I watch Grady's eyes as he scans the shelves behind us and narrows his eyes. "Nope," he says gruffly. "Nope, not gonna happen. Lil, we've got to go." He grabs the girl by the arm and starts to drag her away.

I chuckle until I realize that might be me in ten years, and then I think I might be sick.

"I'll see you soon," she calls from under her brother's arm.

When they're out of earshot, I lean into Kai's space. "That's who you're going to prom with?"

He nods, unblinking, as he stares down the empty aisle.

Now I do laugh and clap him on the shoulder. "Good luck with Grady. Let's get these and get out of here."

His face goes a shade whiter, and I take pity on him. "I'll carry them to the register."

Kai walks away like his pants are on fire.

We reach my SUV and climb in. I turn on the ignition, but I don't back out of the lot because something's bothering me.

"Hey, Kai?"

He turns a weary expression my way.

"You wanna talk about what happened in there?"

Kai blinks and faces the windshield with a shrug.

"That's not the first time you've had trouble introducing me," I gently press.

Another shrug. "I just don't know what to say. You're doing all the dad things, and Dad is, well, he's where he is."

Eddy's trial ended three months ago and now he's serving a ten-year prison sentence.

"I get it," I say. "The littles call me Dewey, but I understand that's easier for them. You're older, and you've had more life experiences. It would be like me suddenly calling Remy dad or grandpa."

"Dewey doesn't feel right," he agrees. "But it's hard. I know you love me like a dad is supposed to. You're a dad in all the ways that matter. I don't know why it feels so weird to call you Dad. Sometimes, like in there, it's weird to call you Dillon too though."

"Kai." I heave a deep exhale. "I don't care what you call me, or how you introduce me. All that matters to me is that you know how much I love you."

"I do," he grumbles.

"Then how you introduce me doesn't matter. Introduce me as your dad, your stepdad, or your Dillon. It's no one's business how our family works as long as it does work. And sometimes it will be easier to say this is my stepdad or dad. Sometimes Dillon will work better. But however you introduce me, just know this—you will not upset me, nor will you hurt my feelings because I know how you feel about me. That is all that matters, okay?"

He nods and runs a hand through his mop of hair. "Yeah, okay. Thanks, Dillon."

"You got it, kid. Now, tell me about Lilly."

Kai's face turns an unflattering shade of red, so I put the SUV in drive and pull out onto the street before he begins talking.

"I like her," he says shyly, and I flash him a knowing smile.

"Good. I'm happy for you then. And I'm always here if you have any, er, questions. Okay?"

"I know, Dillon. Thanks."

This family gig is the best thing I've ever done, and sometimes it's also the hardest. But I wouldn't change it for the world.

~

Penny

"TELL me again why we're hiking out to the lake?" I ask. Dillon leads the way with Mari in the backpack carrier while the boys help Lia keep up behind us.

"Because," Dillon calls over his shoulder, "Remy bought a houseboat he plans to live in. I promised him we'd come to see it."

He pops his third root beer barrel into his mouth, and unease worms into my gut. It's been a long time since he's used that particular crutch.

"What's he going to do in the winter? The lake will eventually freeze over," I say to break the silence that fills my mind with anxiety.

Dillon turns to flash a wicked grin. "Guess we'll find out."

It's not a long or even a difficult hike now that they've put in a dirt driveway, but I'm not exactly dressed for it in my sundress and flip-flops.

We reach the clearing a few minutes later to find an empty shoreline. Dillon stands at the water's edge with one hand blocking out the sun. The boys arrive next to me with Lia a second later.

"Looks like they're in the middle of the lake," Kai says, pointing toward the water.

I squint and still only see shadows. The sun is so stinking bright.

Kai drops his backpack and after digging through it, comes up with a pair of binoculars. He looks through them, then gives a thumbs up.

Before I can ask what he's doing, he says, "Yup, they're out there. Look, Mom. Miller's waving a sign at you."

"What? Why would he have a sign out there?"

"Who knows? It is Miller we're talking about," Dillon grumbles.

"Look, Mom." Kai shoves the binoculars into my hands.

It takes me more than a few seconds to get the dang things to focus, but when I do, I follow the outline of the houseboat until I find Miller, Izzy, and Remy on the deck, waving wildly.

Miller's holding his own binoculars and waves at me, so I wave back. "He's such a goofball." I laugh. Then I see that he's pointing to Remy and Izzy, so I scan to my right.

Izzy is holding a sign that says *yes* while Remy holds one that says *no*. "What are they doing?"

Then Miller moves in between them, holding a sign that says *or*.

Lowering the binoculars, I turn to ask Dillon what the heck they're doing out there, but everything freezes the second I turn.

Dillon is down on one knee with Kai and Gage on their knees to his right. On his left, Landon and Lia are in similar positions, and each of them holds a peony, my favorite flower.

Then Dillon holds something out in his palm, and tears wet my face.

"Penny." Hope and awe give his words a gravelly texture. "You hold this family together with love and sheer stubborn will. You've given me more than I could have ever hoped or dreamed for. Now I want to make it legal. I want to make you mine—all of you mine. Forever."

Dillon leans forward to make eye contact with each of the kids. Landon smiles and gives a thumbs up, then helps Lia do the same. He turns to the right, and as Kai lifts his hand to give a thumbs up, Gage starts shaking his flower in excitement. He sends flower petals flying through the air.

"We're getting married, Mom," Gage yells, then jumps into the air, and Dillon's shoulders shake with mirth. "We're going to get handsome clothes on, and we get rings, and presents, and…"

"Gage?" Dillon says through bouts of laughter. "I think you're getting things mixed up."

"No. No, I'm not. We're getting married, Dewey. All of us. That means we're a family. Benny Bird told me so. Do we get new names too? Benny told me his name used to be Freeman. Now it's Bird 'cause he got a new dad. What's ours gonna be?"

At some point, I've drifted closer to them all until I'm standing directly in front of Dillon. I've never felt so freely happy in all my life.

Dillon smiles up at me, then shrugs and pops open the box he's holding. "Looks like we're getting married." He grins. "If you say yes, that is."

"Yes! Yes! Yes!" Gage screeches. "We say yes!"

Kai finally gets a hand on Gage and somewhat contains him while I sink to my knees to face Dillon.

"What do you say, Penny? Will you marry me?"

I can barely see him through the tears I can't control. But I've been nodding for a while now, so I say the only thing I can. "Yes. Yes, I'll marry you."

He leans forward and wraps me in a hug that has me tumbling into him.

Gage explodes and runs in circles around us.

Kai and Landon stand back with smiles on their faces as they hold Lia's hands.

We look like a family.

Dillon stands and helps me up in the process, then reaches out and takes my hand. When he slips the enormous princess-cut diamond onto my finger, it's like the final tethers tying me to my old life are finally set free.

"I love you, Penny," Dillon whispers.

"I love you too. So much I'm afraid I'll wake up someday and this will all be a dream."

"No dream, sweetheart. This is the most awake I've ever been. Before you, I was sleepwalking through life. You've opened my eyes to what I was missing."

Gage barrels into Dillon's legs right then, and he has to take a step back to keep his balance.

"Hey, buddy," he groans.

"She said yes. We said yes. That means we're married," Gage yells. His volume rises with each word like the excitement is working through his little body.

"So, what's our name gonna be?"

Dillon glances around at all the children's faces before settling on Kai. "Well," he says, never taking his eyes off Kai. "We had the conversation a few weeks ago about me adopting you guys. And I want that more than you'll ever know. But names are a tricky thing. At least, they always have been for me."

His words break, and emotion wells in his eyes.

"You see, I've never had an attachment to Henry. But that doesn't mean you guys feel that way about Damon. So, I think it should be your choice what you want it to be. But for me? I'm actually thinking Mulligan sounds good."

It takes a few breaths for his words to register, and when they do, I spin so fast my ponytail whips him in the chest.

"What?" I ask with a shaky voice.

Dillon shrugs. "Mulligan literally means 'a do-over,' Penny. And I feel like this, all of you, are my do-over in life, like a new beginning. And this way, the kids won't feel like they're choosing between their dad and me." He can't quite control the growl that escapes with the word dad.

A few months ago, Eddy was singing a different tune about parental rights after his attorney told him he would still owe back child support when he gets out of prison.

A month later, we got all the paperwork in the mail, and then we spoke with each kid separately so they could think about the adoption on their own terms.

"You want us all to be Mulligans?" Kai asks with a furrowed brow, like he's thinking really hard about something.

"No," Dillon says. "I want you to be whoever feels right to you, and it's not a decision you have to make today. We have plenty of time for you to think about it. All of you," he says, smiling at the other kids. "I'm just telling you what I would like. Your last name doesn't change who you are to me. It won't change how I love you."

"I wanna be a Mulligan," Landon says quickly, and my tears flow faster.

"Me too," Gage sings.

All eyes turn on Kai, but once again, Dillon knows just how to handle this.

"We won't make any decisions today—"

"I think I'd like a do-over, too," Kai says quietly. "Mulligan sounds like me."

Dillon and I stand in silence looking at Kai as the other kids pull snacks and drinks from their backpacks. Lia isn't as quiet as she used to be, but she reads the vibe of every space she enters in seconds. If she isn't sure how to feel, she remains completely silent.

We'll speak to her privately at home. She's still too young to fully understand what we're talking about.

"Are you sure?" I finally ask. "We won't pressure you, and we'll respect whatever decision you make."

Kai nods twice. "I'm sure if he's sure." He gestures to Dillon.

"I've never been more sure about anything in my life," Dillon says confidently.

My eyes drop to the ring he just placed there. The weight of it grounds me to this moment.

"We all have to make choices, right?" Kai asks quietly, but he's staring straight at Dillon.

"Yeah, kid. We do." Dillon's words are choppy. Like he's forcing them out through a sea of emotions.

Kai nods again but drops his eyes to the ground. "Then I choose Mulligan. I—I choose you, Dillon."

Dillon takes a shuddering breath next to me, then he whooshes past me and slams into Kai with a giant bear hug.

"I choose you too, Kai," I hear Dillon whisper. "I choose all of you. Forever. I promise you that."

"I know," Kai chokes out while pulling away. "I know," he says again before turning to join his siblings.

With Mari babbling happily on his back, Dillon walks to me with love in his eyes.

"What about you?" he asks. "Are you okay with Mulligan? I know I should have discussed that with you first, but when Gage pushed, it just slipped out. It's something I've been thinking about for a while, though. With my childhood the way it was, I never wanted to be a Henry anyway, so it doesn't matter to me, but I know your parents were pretty amazing, so it just felt right."

I'm nodding into his chest as he wraps me in a hug.

"Mulligan is great, Dillon. It's perfect, actually. My parents would have loved you."

He leans down to kiss the top of my head. "Then let's spend the rest of our lives making this do-over the best one anyone has ever had. Together. Forever."

Tilting my head up, I find him staring at me with so much love he's vibrating with it. "I love you, Dillon. You've taught me how love should be. You've given me a gift I've been missing for a long time—unconditional love, and I'll never be able to thank you enough for that."

"I love you too, sweetheart," he says gently. Then he sweeps his arm out like he's wrapping all our kids up in this embrace. "I promise to love all of you until my last breath."

And I see it in his eyes.

Dillon never breaks his promises, so forever is what we'll get.

BONUS SCENE

MILLER

"Congrats, Dill. I'm really happy for you," I say, then clap him on the shoulder. "You're good for her. For all of them."

"Thanks, Miller."

We're standing on the edge of the dance floor in the center of the largest white tent I've ever seen. Their wedding was beautiful—not that I ever doubted it. Dillon would have turned the world inside out to give Penny this day.

"It's been a wild ride, that's for sure. And I couldn't have done any of this without you. You know that, right?"

"Don't bullshit a bullshitter. You would have found a way with or without me," I chuckle. But it's the truth.

"Maybe," he concedes. "But it sure as hell has been a lot easier with you. And a lot more fun too."

I'm about to tell him to go dance with his wife when Paisley's wild hair catches my eye.

"Why the hell is she carrying a tray that weighs more than she does?" My voice is a possessive growl I have no right to.

Dillon watches me closely. "She said she needed the hours and asked if she could work the wedding."

"She was working at the dog groomer's this morning and at Three Brother's Brewing last night and she taught six classes yesterday at Karma. Is she trying to work herself into the damn ground?"

I don't wait for Dillon to answer. Instead, I stomp through the center of the dance floor. It's twelve long strides before I'm lifting the tray from her arms.

"Hey," she hisses. "What are you doing, Matty?"

"You're going to kill yourself with this thing." Turning away from her, I walk to the back of the room where tables are set up.

I don't have to turn to know she's following me with a pissed-off expression on her face and her fists at her sides, ready for a fight. That's how it always is with her. Push and pull. Tit for tat. One day, one of us will snap, and I hate to admit that I'm looking forward to that day.

Her hand lands on my forearm, and I spin back to face her.

She opens her mouth to speak, but I cut her off. "Why are you running yourself into the ground?"

She blinks and snaps her head back like that's the last thing she expected me to say. "What are you talking about?"

Paisley attempts to reach around me and grab the tray I just set down, but I move to block it with my body.

"Matty! I need to work. Get out of my way."

"Why? Why do you need to work so many hours?"

Frustration blooms on her face. "Are you stalking me?"

A small smile tugs at my lips. "Maybe. Now answer me. Why are you working seven hundred jobs?"

Her hands fist at her sides and I feel her sneer like a kiss. "I need the money."

"For what?"

She attempts to sidestep me again, but I move with her, and she lets out an annoyed huff.

"That's none of your damn business, Matty. Just…" Her voice breaks, and I watch as her throat works hard to swallow. Something simmers to life in my chest that I haven't felt in a very long time—a feeling of rightness and forever.

"Are you in trouble?" I ask, lowering my voice.

Her angry gaze snaps to mine. "I'm not in trouble," she says through clenched teeth, "but I'm running out of time, and I need this money, so please, please get out of my way and leave me the hell alone." The way her voice catches even through her self-righteous rage is like a knife to the heart.

"Running out of time for what? What is going on with you?" Now that I have her cornered and questions are flying from my mouth, I put it all out there. "Why do you hate me so much? Why are you always such a pain in my ass?"

Paisley's beautiful face contorts as if she's in pain. "I—I don't hate you, Matty," she says quietly while staring at the floor. When she lifts her gaze to mine, time stops. "I just can't be anything to you."

Leaning into her space so we're eye to eye, I stare her down. "Why? Why me? You've made friends with every other goddamn person in this town. What makes me different?"

Her head shakes, and it's the first sign of softness I've seen from her. "It's not you, Matty. It's me. It's who I am."

We're so close that her breath skates across my face. "Who. Are. You?"

She's quiet for a long moment, and when she looks back at me, I find something too close to fear in her eyes. "I'm Bella's cousin, and—and I have my reasons. I can't get close to anyone, so please just leave me alone."

I'm stunned into silence and stand frozen as she reaches around me for the tray. At least she removes some of the dishes before walking off on shaky legs.

She's Bella's cousin? Bella, as in Izzy's mom? I guess that's a good enough reason to stay away, but I know it's not the whole truth. Bella wouldn't instill the fear that's swallowing Paisley whole.

"Sometimes, you need to make a plan to get what you want," someone says behind me.

Pinching the bridge of my nose, I turn to the stranger inserting himself into my business.

"Dexter Cross." He holds out his hand and begrudgingly, I shake it.

He's a friend of Dillon's. Part of the whole Westbrook group that moves like the mafia.

"Matty," I say, never removing my gaze from Paisley.

"You like her," a soft, female voice says to my left.

Dexter wraps his arm around a very tall, willowy blond woman.

"I'm Lanie," she says with a shrug and a smile that could grow angel wings on the devil himself.

I'm not in the mood for small talk, but there's something about these two that requires I give them my undivided attention.

"She seems like she's carrying the world on her shoulders." Lanie's observation is dead-on. "And that can be a very lonely place."

"What you need is a plan," Dexter repeats.

"Fine, I'll bite. What kind of a plan?" I ask.

"Oh, for fuck's sake. Not again," a man growls on the other side of Lanie.

Before I know what's happening, I'm surrounded by a handful of men I know to be Westbrooks.

Maybe Dillon's adopted family really is in the mafia. Where there's one, there's a hundred of them.

"Whatever, Easton," Dexter says. He rolls his eyes, but his smile never leaves his face.

"If you like that woman, stop screwing around and go get

her," Easton grumbles. "Otherwise, Dexter is going to turn your story into a fairytale and before you know what's happening, you'll be doing shit you never dreamed you'd do."

"Like you did," Lanie says, wearing a saccharine smile.

"Listen," I say, not even sure who I should be addressing at this point. "I appreciate whatever it is you're trying to do here, but Paisley has her own demons and she's made it clear she doesn't need me to slay them."

"No one needs you to slay their demons, Matty." Lanie places a hand on my forearm. "That's not how it works. Sometimes the monsters we run from can only be exorcised by the person running, but that doesn't mean we don't need someone holding our hand while we do it."

Her gaze drifts through the crowd, landing on Paisley. "It's a hard thing to be completely alone in life. After a while, you forget how to trust and the foundation you've always clung to begins to crack."

"You sound like you're speaking from experience." My throat is dry and scratchy, and I swallow hard. There's something about this woman that sucks you in, makes you want to listen and believe in the goodness she exudes.

She flashes me a genuine smile. "It wasn't that long ago I was running from my own monsters, Matty. Dex couldn't fight them for me."

"Not for lack of trying," Dex grumbles.

"No." She laces her hands through his. "Not for lack of trying. But sometimes"—she holds up their joined hands—"all you need is someone to shine a light on your shadows until you're strong enough to face them yourself. She's scared." Lanie nods toward Paisley, who dips in and out of people with a tray held high over her head.

"Shine a light on her shadows," I mumble. "If only it were that simple."

"Cross my heart," Lanie says, pointing toward Paisley. "That woman is so in tune with you she could tell me where you are in the room with her eyes closed."

"That's the kind of connection you fight for," Dexter says. The honesty in his tone has my spine straightening.

"Are you always so…"

"Nosy? Involved? Pushy?" Dillon asks, joining our circle.

I shrug because any of those adjectives could work.

"It's the Westbrook way." Lanie giggles. "We don't know any other way to be."

"They mean well," Dillon says, but his entire body beams with love. He's told me a little about how this family works, and I'm happy he's had them. "But they have no boundaries."

Dillon angles his body toward mine, blocking out the others and he ushers me a few steps to the side. "If there's one thing the Westbrooks know, it's love. But…"

That tingling sensation shoots up my spine again, and I immediately search out Paisley.

She's standing in a corner with an empty tray pressed to her chest while some asshole looms over her. She can't see me from where she's standing, but I feel everything.

The fear.

The anxiety.

The rage.

It's all there, shining in her watery gaze as the man takes a step closer, bringing them toe-to-toe.

"Finally." Dexter chuckles behind me. "Make that woman yours."

I don't have time to contemplate his words because I move on instinct. My arm is reaching for Paisley before I've even come up with a plan.

She flinches, that fear I saw a moment ago flickering back and forth between me and this stranger like she's searching for the lesser evil, but my mind is already made up.

Tucking her behind me, I step forward, forcing the man to give her some space.

"Is there a problem?" I growl.

"No, Matty," she hisses from behind me even as she fists my shirt at my back. That's when I feel her surrender. Her body deflates like a sad balloon animal and every protective instinct I have roars to the surface.

"I know who you are." The man's voice is gravelly, and he's so close that the stench of stale whiskey assaults my senses.

"Go home, Billy." Paisley's voice quivers, and I don't have to turn around to know she's close to breaking.

"Not without you," he bellows, drawing the attention of everyone at the reception.

Dillon, Easton, and Dexter are behind him a moment later, but he's too drunk or high to realize he's surrounded.

Paisley shakes behind me, but I feel her nodding her head.

I spin in place, take her face in mine, and feel my heart shatter when her eyes fill with tears.

"Please," she whispers. "Don't make a scene. I—I have to go."

I crowd her until she's pressed against the wall, far enough that when I lean down to whisper in her ear, everyone else fades away.

"Why? Who is that man?"

Her gaze searches mine, and I know the instant the fight leaves her body. It's like the sun falling behind a never-ending cloud, and it stirs a beast within me.

"He's my brother-in-law. I'm sorry. I don't have a choice." She breaks free from my hold. "Dillon, I'm so sorry. Something's come up and I have to leave early."

She hands me her serving tray, slides along the wall, and walks toward the kitchen.

The asshole behind me laughs. It's a menacing sound that

has me clenching my teeth and fists in time with the blood rushing through my ears.

Dillon elbows him out of the way and places a hand on my shoulder—he probably thinks it'll keep me from doing something stupid, but I'm well past the point of no return where Paisley is concerned.

"Not now," he whispers.

We stand shoulder-to-shoulder as Billy spins, stutter-stepping when he finds more Westbrooks blocking his path.

Billy's gaze snaps to mine. An eerie grin creeps across his face. "Guess we'll be seeing you around."

He steps forward like he's going to push his way through the Westbrook brothers, but those boys are built like brick fucking houses and refuse to budge.

When he puts a shoulder down like he's going to split the two men, Easton puffs up his chest and Billy bounces back a step.

I give Dillon the side-eye and he smirks.

"We've got this—go check on Paisley."

I grunt because I'd love to kick this fucker's ass but follow Paisley to the kitchen.

Something tells me I'll follow this woman to the depths of hell and still smile at the journey.

By the time I make it to the back, she's already gone, but so is my patience.

The cat-and-mouse game we've been playing is about to come to an end—hopefully we'll both survive it.

Matty and Paisley will have an HEA just as soon as they stop bickering and tell it to me.

In the meantime, meet another single dad, Dexter Cross, in Cross My Heart. It's where the Westbrook world all began.

And if you're all in for single dads, you can meet Becker Hayes, the reluctant uncle daddy, in Love Notes & Lifelines.

Both books are available in Kindle Unlimited.

DEAR READER

This story was difficult to write for many reasons, but mostly because it hit very close to home for me. While it is a complete work of fiction, the stories I heard while researching, from single moms to adult children of alcoholics, made a permanent impression on my soul.

And Penny, in particular, is a character I think many of us relate to but very rarely hear about. I hope this lets you know that I hear you. I see you. And I luv you.

Like Penny, I'm guilty of always trying to do everything myself, and I know many of you are too, but it's okay if you can't. It's okay to admit that you don't have everything together. It's okay to say "my life is messy and complicated," because here's the thing, everyone's life is messy.

Everyone's life is messy.

One more time for those in the back.

Everyone's life is messy.

But not everyone shares it. We live in a world where snapshots are portrayed as real life. It skews how we view ourselves, but it's not real.

Real life is often a shit show of epic proportions that sometimes lands on a rainbow.

And that's okay—that is real.

So, the next time you're wondering how someone can have it all together, or how their house is always clean, or their laundry never piles up, I can tell you, that's not always the truth.

Everyone has a closet where they dump stuff when people come over, or a place to hide the laundry, or a special corner of their house where they can take a picture without their dirty dishes in the background.

We all do.

My house is a mess. I have timers on my phone so I don't forget to pick up my kids. I routinely make to-do lists for my to-do lists full of stuff that never gets done.

That is life, and I hope this story will encourage you to embrace your mess more often.

Kindness & Luv,

Avery

ACKNOWLEDGMENTS

I've learned over the last couple of years that a book can't write itself, and that I, the author, can't do it myself either. It takes a team. A team who works together toward a common goal. A team who lifts each other up with every success and comforts every failure.

I'm eternally grateful for the team who has shown up book after book with support and encouragement. These are the people who stick by me, watch my back, and hear me when I speak.

I couldn't do any of this without them.

My family: John, Ellie, Declan, Rory, and Finn—Thank you for being my lighthouse on my darkest nights. Thank you for supporting me, even when you had no idea what that looked like. And thank you for not always tapping out of my hugs.

TWSS: Holy cow, I seriously LUV you all. Thank you for helping, for teaching, for guiding, and for supporting. But mostly, thank you for being the most amazing humans who show the world that you can accomplish greatness while still being kind.

Rhon: I'm sorry for bothering you every single time you're out to dinner. I will work on boundaries ;) Thank you for being my first line of defense even before I know there's a battle brewing. I'd be lost without you. Xo

Beth: Thank you for seeing my mess and luving me anyway. You, my friend, are a badass who conquers every storm that comes your way, and I'm forever grateful for your friendship. And one of these days I'll stop overusing the word cock on my first draft. Maybe.

Team Avery: Thank you for being the backbone for everything I do. You are the best team I could have ever asked for, and I thank my lucky stars every day that you chose me.

Sensitivity Readers: Thank you, from the bottom of my heart, for sharing your stories with me, and then reading my words to make sure I got them right.

Beta Readers: Thank you for your criticisms and kind words. They both make me cry, but they're both necessary for me to improve as an author. Thank you for handling me with kid gloves while also kicking my bum when needed.

ARC & Street Teams: Without you, no one would have ever heard of me. Thank you for spreading the luv, sharing my books, and taking on the difficult task of reading my stories before they go live—then dealing with a nervous nosy author. I appreciate you all.

The Luv Club: I am beside myself every single time I welcome new members. I never in a million years thought people would be interested in hearing what I have to say, but you all prove me wrong again and again. Thank you for helping make The Luv Club what it is: The kindest place on the internet—our safe space to fall. I luv you all so, so much.

Marissa: Thank you for always being up to travel, even at the last minute, when I call you mid-panic attack, to be my emotional support buddy. I luv you lots!

Lucy: Everything goes our way! Thank you for being one of the kindest humans on the planet. And for showing me that being a number one empath is not a weakness, but my biggest asset as a storyteller. I appreciate the heck out of you every single day. Xo

Kathryn, Hannah & Brynne: Thank you for being my people—the ones I turn to when I'm overwhelmed. The ones who drop everything to give me fifteen minutes to help me through panic-inducing edits. Thank you for being the author friends who feel like family. Our mutual respect and support give me hope on my cloudy days and I luv you all dearly.

Joyce & Tammy: Thank you for being you. Thank you for being my sounding board and safe space to fall, even if that means telling me to suck it up, or simmer down sometimes. I don't know what I would do without your friendship and guidance. I am forever grateful to have you both in my life.

Coach Paul R: Coach Remy is a characterization of a very special coach I had from 4th grade through 12th grade. I don't know how many kids coach Paul taught over the years, but I'm sure it's well into the hundreds, and I'm willing to bet he left a lasting impression on every single one of them. I know he did for me. We need more selfless coaches cheering on our youth and our communities, just because they can. Thanks for everything, Coach!

Kari March Designs: Thank you for giving my story a face, even though I never, ever know what that looks like at first. This one was perfect for Penny and Dillon.

And last, but definitely not least, HEA Author Services: Thank you for pushing me to be better, and for polishing my words when my eyes have become immune to them. And thank you to Jess for being so incredibly patient with me and my millions of questions.

Hello, Luvs!
Want to hang out with me? I'm in The Luv Club every day
sharing my chaos, my crazy, my life. Pop in to say hi, meet
the other luvables, and stay a while. It's the happiest, kindest,
messiest group on the internet and I'd LUV to see you there!
https://geni.us/AverysLUVclub

ALSO BY AVERY MAXWELL

Standalone Romance:

Without A Hitch

Your Last First Kiss

Falling Into Forever

Love Notes & Lifelines

The Westbrooks Series:

Book 1 - Cross My Heart

Book 2 - The Beat of My Heart

Book 3 - Saving His Heart

Book 4 - Romancing His Heart

Book 5 - One Little Heartbreak - A Westbrook Novella

Book 6 - One Little Mistake

Book 7 - One Little Lie

Book 8 - One Little Kiss

Book 9 - One Little Secret